Blood Knot

Denise Ryan

PIATKUS

❀❀ *Visit the Piatkus website!*

Piatkus publishes a wide range of best-selling fiction and non-fiction, including books on health, mind, body & spirit, sex, self-help, cookery, biography and the paranormal.

If you want to:

- read descriptions of our popular titles
- buy our books over the Internet
- take advantage of our special offers
- enter our monthly competition
- learn more about your favourite Piatkus authors

VISIT OUR WEBSITE AT: www.piatkus.co.uk

Copyright © 2004 by Denise Ryan

First published in Great Britain in 2004 by
Piatkus Books Ltd of
5 Windmill Street, London W1T 2JA
email: info@piatkus.co.uk

This edition published 2004

The moral right of the author has been asserted

A catalogue record for this book is available from the British Library

ISBN 0 7499 3462 X

Set in Times by
Phoenix Photosetting, Chatham, Kent

Printed and bound in Denmark by
Nørhaven Paperback A/S, Viborg

My thanks to Gillian Green, Senior Editor, and Emma Callagher, Assistant Fiction Editor at Piatkus

To Peter

Prologue

Crash.

A fright to freak the curl out of your hair. It was like waking up in a bad movie; all alone at night in a dark house in the country, with the sound of glass breaking. She sat up in bed clutching the quilt around her. Then she leaned over and groped on the floor for her scattered clothes, not daring to switch on the bedside lamp. Why did she never fold them in a neat pile? Knickers and socks on top, jeans and sweater underneath. A mess, like her life.

'Oh *God*. Oh –'

Another crash. Not glass this time. It sounded like the intruder – perhaps there was more than one – was smashing china. She thought of her cupboards full of Wedgwood – Samurai, her favourite design. Doors banged. Wouldn't a professional burglar make less noise? Or was this some crackhead whose lonely, confused brain cell couldn't warn its owner to be careful, be quiet, don't get caught and arrested? She stared into the darkness, her heart pounding. Terrific, just what she needed. She had so looked forward to her early night, the luxury of sleeping alone and undisturbed.

She scrambled out of bed and ran to the door, locked it and lodged a chair beneath the handle. Unlike the heroine of the bad movie, she had no intention of creeping downstairs to investigate, confront whoever it was and get beaten up or raped. She darted back and grabbed the phone, her fingers trembling as she felt for what she guessed was the number nine button. She pressed three times. Very good, darling, but no point because the line's dead. Had the intruder cut the line? Her fear was icy, paralysing. She clicked on the lamp. It flickered, dimmed and went out. Of all the times for a bulb to go.

1

'Oh *God.*'

A weapon. She glanced around the dark bedroom, eyes straining to pick out something she could use to defend herself. But what did the intruder have? She crept across the room and picked up the didgeridoo propped in a corner to one side of the wardrobe. Aboriginal artefacts from her trip to Australia's red centre were scattered all over the house – carved wooden goannas and crocodiles, smoke-scented music sticks with charred markings, a toy koala that played *Waltzing Matilda,* a Tasmanian devil. The didgeridoo was small and light, not like the one down in the dining room, which was the genuine article made from a specially selected hollowed-out log – tarred, engraved with thin white criss-cross symbols and a coiled snake, sealed at one end with beeswax. But the smaller thing could still give someone a hell of a knock. She shrank back, gasping as she gripped the rough wooden object. She had not hit anybody for seven years, not since that frosty Christmas Eve when her stepdaughter had called her a drunken whore.

Where the hell was her robe? She found it and dragged it on, then attempted to push the dressing table towards the door. It was too heavy, of course, and the carpet was too thick. Down in the kitchen glasses and another shower of china crashed to the stone flags. She sweated and prayed, snatched up the didgeridoo again and held it ready.

'Oh no!' The intruder was pounding upstairs now, running along the landing, kicking at the door. How could he know this was her bedroom? 'Get out!' she screamed. 'Go away! I've phoned the police – they'll be here any second.' You wish.

More kicks and the door burst open. She lashed out blindly with the didgeridoo. Its wood cracked on metal. She staggered backwards and fell across the bed. The landing light snapped on.

Outlined in the doorway was a figure in bulky black clothes, even black gloves and balaclava. She couldn't tell if the person was male or female, but took a wild guess and decided male. Her heart gave another leap of terror as she saw the double-barrelled shotgun he held, and imagined the bloody holes it could blow in her.

The figure gestured with the gun, and she gathered he wanted her to go downstairs. She got to her feet. She was shaking uncontrollably, and thought her legs might give way. The figure stood back and kept the gun trained on her as she stumbled out of the bedroom, along the landing and down the stairs. In the hall he prodded her in the back and buttocks with the gun barrel. That hurt. Humiliated, she started to cry.

'Don't hurt me – *please*.' Was rape on his agenda? Tears slid down her face. 'Look, I've got cash and jewellery. Credit cards, you name it. I'll show you where everything is. Just help yourself, okay? Only please don't hurt me.'

No response. Fight back, she thought. Do something. But what could you do against someone who had a gun? To come out of this alive and unharmed was her priority. She had to do what he wanted. But what did he want? He wasn't telling.

The blow caught the back of her head and she crumpled, her legs buckling.

When she regained consciousness she was blindfolded, her wrists tied to the legs of the dining table, and her ankles roped together. Her forehead felt warm and wet. Dazed, pain pierced her head and neck. Still he did not speak.

'What do you want?' she gasped. 'Who are you? Why blindfold me when I can't see your face anyway?'

If he meant his silence to freak her, it was working. She got the feeling this bastard wasn't interested in cash or jewellery. Maybe not in rape either. Murder? No! Why? She sobbed and struggled, but the tight, scratchy rope bit into her bound wrists and legs. She started to scream. 'Don't hurt me, don't hurt me!' Her screams didn't seem to bother him. Well, why would they? The nearest house was a quarter of a mile away. And this house had no dogs because she didn't like dogs. Don't let him kill me, she prayed. Don't let me die.

'Please, please don't . . . I don't understand! Who *are* you? Why are you . . .?' Her blindfold was dragged off and the intruder removed the balaclava.

When she saw the face, that smile, she understood. And yet she didn't. She was the first to admit she was no angel. But still, how could this devil hate her so much? The gun was laid across a chair. She had no doubt it would be used on her. Not yet though. This was going to take time.

She had prayed not to be killed, but she knew she would soon beg for death.

The devil's face was the last thing she saw.

3

Ten Years Later

Chapter 1

'I met an arms dealer today.' Francesca Sayle – Frankie for short – grinned. 'No, I'm *not* lying.'

'Never a dull moment being Dutch-English translator cum Economic and Political Affairs assistant at that madhouse of a Korean embassy, is it?' Joe, her husband, frowned and glanced around the crowded restaurant.

'She was American. From Texas. She invited me to have a drink with her in her hotel room, and I accepted. Well, it was just before I had to catch the train back from Amsterdam to Den Haag. She had a suitcase on the bed. When she opened it I couldn't believe my eyes. It was full of revolvers and other handguns, a couple of rifles, boxes of bullets, grenades– I didn't even know what some things were for.'

Joe shook his head. 'Shows you the advantages of delivering a visa as opposed to making the applicant turn up and collect it themselves. How come you had to deliver it anyway? Thought you were too important to be spared for such a menial task.'

'The Consul's assistant is off sick. I volunteered because I fancied a stroll along Amsterdam's shopping streets. And I wanted to visit the flower market.'

Their Dutch friend Lida laughed, spluttering smoke in Frankie's face. 'What kind of visa did Miss Texas want?'

'Tourist.' Frankie waved the smoke away. 'She said, "Honey, you ever want anythin', you give me a call." She gave me her business card.'

'So where is it?' Lida asked.

'I haven't got it with me. I put it in a box in my study.'

'For future reference?' Lida smiled at Joe. 'You better watch out.'

'And when I got back to the embassy the ambassador asked me what was the difference between a civilian and a diplomatic passport. I thought he was joking, but no.' Frankie sighed. 'It's been a surreal day – again.'

'What was this arms dealer woman's name?' Joe drummed his fingers on the white tablecloth.

'The name she gave me, the one that's on the card – Robin Seiffert.'

'She must be mad, showing you her collection of hardware just like that. How could she be sure you wouldn't go straight to the police?'

'It's not actually illegal to be an arms dealer.' Frankie picked up her frosted shot glass of Limoncello and took a sip. 'Immoral, yes. Anyway, you don't mess with people like that, do you?'

Lida laughed again. 'How can an ambassador not know the difference between civilian and diplomatic passports?'

'He was an army general,' Frankie replied. 'This cushy diplomatic posting is a reward before he retires in two years' time with Madame Fang and their Canalettos, Italian dressing tables, Canadian barbecues, Californian real estate—'

'And Philippino slaves,' Joe finished, bored. He smiled at Lida. 'I get this every night when she comes home.'

'Not true,' Frankie protested, stung. She didn't like that smile. Was it because Joe never smiled at her lately? 'Once I've got home, unloaded the shopping, cooked dinner and washed up, all I'm fit for is slobbing in front of the telly.'

'Oh here we go, the put-upon wife act again. *Cooked* dinner?' Joe shot her a look. 'Don't you mean microwaved?'

'Hey, what's wrong with you two tonight?' Lida butted her cigarette. 'Tenth wedding anniversary coming up – is that what's giving you the jitters?'

Frankie wondered again what was giving Joe the jitters. She ran over her checklist: in a crummy mood most of the time, bored and restless. He fretted about his weight, although not enough to limit his intake of wine, oven chips and creamy pasta dishes. He went to the hairdresser more often than she did, and moaned about silver threads amongst the dark blond. He had just turned thirty-nine.

Could that be it? It wasn't Big O birthdays that freaked people, but the ones that came just before. Frankie did not think Joe was having an affair, because she trusted him and believed he loved her. Besides, when would he find the time? He was mostly home when not designing software for the IT company, his job which had brought them to the Netherlands a couple of years ago. Frankie was relieved to ditch her boring Civil Service Executive Officer post and go with him. The career she was interested in was one she could only dream about – being a published writer. She wanted to write a spoof chicklit thriller about the Brontës, several genres rolled into one. An altogether new genre, in fact. Best-selling. With translation rights and Hollywood movie deals.

'So what did you tell His Excellency was the difference?' Lida asked.

'Oh, the passports?' Frankie snapped out of her reverie. 'I told him if you had a diplomatic passport the authorities would warn you of a bomb threat on an aircraft, and if you had a civilian passport they'd let you blow up.'

'Right.' Joe nodded. 'A suitably vivid illustration. Frankie tells it like it is. She came home in a right strop yesterday. Temper,' he explained, in answer to Lida's puzzled glance. 'Nothing to do with the dickbrain dippos, for once. She was pissed off because she didn't get time to write. I mean, can you believe that?'

'Frankie, if you're fed up with the embassy, why not try the International Criminal Tribunal for the Former Yugoslavia?' Lida asked, ignoring Joe. 'I heard they need native English speakers for admin posts. And you won't have to pay Dutch taxes there, just a much lower international civil servant's tax.'

'But will she have time to write?' Joe needled.

Lida smiled. 'Shut up, you. How about it, Frankie?'

'Thirty-eight hours a week reading about war crimes? Don't think I fancy that.' Frankie did not want to say she felt depressed enough already.

'The subject matter's no problem. You just distance yourself.'

'I'm not sure I could.'

'Well, hey.' Lida arched her thin, blond eyebrows. 'You watch the news, don't you?'

'No. I switch over to *The Simpsons*.'

'Lida's trying to help.' Joe lifted his glass and poured Armagnac down his throat. 'Why don't you at least consider her suggestion instead of rubbishing it?'

'I'm not—'

'Yes, you are.' He stood up and pushed back his chair. 'Excuse me.'

'I see he's still being a git.' Lida watched as he strode towards the Gents, her eyes narrowed. She stroked her bare, tanned arms.

'I'm not easy to live with either.' Frankie was conscious of not wanting to sound like the put-upon wife. 'He's right, I do come home in a strop most evenings. It's not the work, it's their attitude. I suppose most diplomats think they're a cut above. I've heard worse stories from local staff in other embassies in Den Haag.'

'How long have you worked there?'

'About a year. Oh, I suppose it's not that bad. At least they bugger off for golf or long lunches several times a week and leave me and the others in peace. They don't take the attaché, but he stays in his attic and only comes down to get coffee. He's reading a book of *Fawlty Towers* sketches at the moment – says he wants to improve his English.'

'Well, how about improving his Dutch?' Lida frowned.

'French and English are the official diplomatic languages. Lots of diplomats in The Hague don't care about learning Dutch. Anyway, these guys have got me, the receptionist and the ambassador's secretary to liase with the outside world.'

'I could also try and get you a job at the OPCW. I've got a couple of contacts in the personnel department.' Lida lit a green Sobranie and inhaled, swiping back a long strand of corn-blond hair that swung dangerously close to its glowing tip. 'Same story there though, I'm afraid. Some pretty confused people.'

'Tell me.' Frankie grinned. 'Got a document from the Organisation for the Prevention of Chemical Weapons the other day, about *subsided* meals and *pubic* interest.'

She tensed as Joe reappeared and signalled to a passing waiter, holding up his wallet. She slid her bare feet back into the black satin pumps. The heels were crazily high, fit only for stumbling from door to cab and back again. Or from one side of the bed to the other. Millenium foot binding. *Bed.* Her heart dipped. Another check on the checklist. Joe sat beside her and signed the credit card slip the waiter placed in front of him. Lida took a 50-Euro note from her wallet and slid it across the table.

'Don't be daft.' Joe pushed it back. 'My treat.'

'Oh. Well, thanks very much. That was a gorgeous meal,' Lida

10

smiled. 'I've been dying for Prosecco, prosciutto and pasta since I got back from the south of France.'

Frankie laid one hand on Joe's shoulder and smoothed her fingers over the soft cotton of his cream shirt, feeling the muscles beneath. She leaned across and kissed him. He flinched, but managed an awkward smile. Hurt and humiliated, she drew back. Lida blew out smoke and scrutinised them in that almost offensive way she had, her blue eyes glittering.

Frankie wondered what was funny.

'Nothing's wrong,' Joe snapped as they got into the cab. 'Not work, not you, not anything. Don't ask me again, Frankie, I'm sick of it. Just give me a break!'

She sat silent, blinking away tears. The September night was cool with a touch of autumn. The journey to their apartment in the Statenkwartier near the dunes took about ten minutes. When they got home she opened the French windows on to one of the balconies and stood in the dark looking down at the wide, tree-lined street with the strip of canal running through the centre. She could smell the sea.

Should she ask the consul for a week's leave on Monday, fly to Liverpool and visit her mother? She was owed some leave, although hundreds of invitations would soon have to be written and sent out for the National Day reception on 3 October, a gigantic task for which the ambassador's secretary would beg her help. Other things also had to be organised. But no, not yet. A week's absence might widen and deepen the growing gulf between her and Joe, rather than make his heart grow fonder. She turned back into the long, high-ceilinged living room.

Joe was stretched out on one of the sofas, his eyes closed as he listened to music on the headphones. Frankie grimaced at the sound of the Bach mass – he never listened to anything joyful or uplifting lately, just heavy, gloomy stuff like this, Matthias' Passion, or bloody boring Elgar. Wild, chaotic piano concertos that sounded like the demented carry-on of some geeking meth-head. You're not sophisticated, she chided herself; you don't appreciate art. She walked to the sofa and tapped him on the shoulder. He jumped, opened his eyes and stared up at her.

'Going to bed,' she mouthed over the tinny roar of the choir,

11

pointing at the ceiling. He nodded and lay back, closed his eyes again. 'Yep,' she muttered, turning away. 'That's what marriage is all about, innit? Communication, companionship, that warm cosy feeling that gets you right here.' She held a clenched fist to her heart. She passed through the hall and sighed as she looked in the mirror. 'What a waste.'

Long, dark, wavy chestnut hair, crystal grey eyes, peachy skin. Slim, sexy black dress, the crazy heels. Didn't look thirty-six. Not that that was old, of course, despite what some people would have you believe. She remembered that slimy chat show host the other night telling some pop star she looked great for thirty-four. Imbecile. Sparkly personality, except lately she didn't feel like sparkling. What was that poem about sand being strewn all over ruddy limbs?

Upstairs she took off her clothes and walked into the bathroom to brush her teeth and wash off her make-up. She went into the little study where she kept her printer, laptop and papers. Several pages of her novel lay on the desk, anchored by a large white quartz stone. She pictured the scene, the Brontë sisters grouped in their firelit sitting room at the parsonage, typing on laptops. Emily grumbling that people would think Branwell had written *Wuthering Heights* because he was a guy and she was a girl, Charlotte snarling that fictional heroines did not have to be beautiful, dazzling and have a D-D cup size in order to grip the gentle reader's imagination, and by God she would prove it. Frankie re-read the first line: *There was absolutely no chance of taking a walk that day.*

'Absolutely no chance of you being able to write, more like' she murmured. She ripped up the pages and dropped them in the bin. 'Moron.'

She got into bed and snapped off the lamp, too tired and dispirited to concentrate on the crime novel she was reading. Or trying to. Each chapter was only two or three pages long, so the fictional dream kept breaking up. She lay gazing through the partially open curtains at the moon, so big and bright it made her heart ache more. What could she do to banish this invisible, crackling field of tension between her and Joe? It was like living beneath pylons, waiting for the chopper to chop off her head. What was wrong with him, with their marriage? Why wouldn't he talk about it? Her eyes filled with tears. She turned and twisted, stretched her limbs and tried to relax enough to fall asleep. No use. She had to talk to him. Now. If he didn't feel like it, tough. She got up, put on her dressing gown and went downstairs.

Joe was still sprawled on the sofa, but the music was off. The balcony doors were open, the long silk net curtains stirring in the night air. He looked startled when he saw her, sat up and swung his legs to the floor.

'I can't take this any more,' she said. 'What's wrong? Don't get mad again, just tell me. *Please*.'

Frankie lost courage as she spoke the words. Whatever was wrong, it would blow over. Lots of marriages hit patches of blankout. It wasn't great but it didn't mean there was a major problem. Why make a big deal out of something when maybe there was no need? She knew she was fooling herself.

'Frankie.' Joe was on his feet, moving towards her. 'I've wanted to talk to you for a while now, but I could never find what I thought was the right moment.' He paused. 'This is really difficult for me.'

Her mouth went dry. He looked so serious, had such an unhappy look in his dark eyes. Her heart flipped, started to do big, fast beats. 'What is it?' she whispered. 'What's happened? Have you lost your job? Are you ill, or—'

'No, nothing like that. I . . .' He glanced away. 'Oh, Christ.'

'Never mind him. Just get on with it.' She knew this was bad. The ground was already cracking and splitting beneath her bare feet, opening up the bottomless hole for her to plunge into. Frankie wished she hadn't asked. She wished she was back upstairs in bed, asleep, avoiding confrontation. Hearing Charlotte Brontë snort, 'If those soppy curates turn up for tea again this Sunday, I may do something unfortunate with a fire dog.'

'You've got to remember I love you,' Joe said. 'Whatever happens, a part of me always will.'

'A part? Which part? And what the hell do you mean by *whatever happens*?'

'Please listen, okay? I'm here for you,' he stammered. 'I still want to look after you, Frankie. You lost out by coming here with me – your career, I mean. Okay, I know you didn't like it a lot, but still. You learnt Dutch, got that stupid embassy job, never moaned about being homesick. We've been together ten years, and I don't regret one minute of that. I've got a lot of respect for you.'

'Well, that's great. I'm really touched.' Frankie could not breathe. *'But?'*

'I'm not happy any more. That is, not enough to stay married.' Joe took another step forward. He clenched his fists, his expression agitated. 'I don't know why I feel this way. It just happened, it's not your fault. This is about me, not you. I'm sorry – you're a lovely, sweet, beautiful woman. The last thing I want is to hurt you.'

'But you are bloody hurting me!' Frankie's voice cracked with shock and disbelief. Tears started to roll down her face. 'Have you – have you got someone else?' There was always someone younger, sexier, more captivating. Not that she had ever seriously worried about it before.

'No.' Joe looked shocked. 'There's no other woman, I swear.'

'Then what the hell is this? Joe, I love you! We can sort this out, we have to. I don't believe you can stop loving me, just like that, for no reason. I *can't* believe it!'

'I couldn't either, until it happened.' He twisted his hands together. 'I tried, Frankie, I really did. Tried to ignore my feelings, hoped they'd go away. Hoped I could sort this. But I'm sorry, it's no use. I just don't love you enough any more.' He paused again and stared at her, his eyes shining with tears. 'I can't force myself to feel something. Nobody can. I'm so sorry,' he repeated. 'I hate to do this to you.'

'Then don't! Please, Joe, don't do it. I can't go through something like this. I love you; we've got a life together. I don't want to lose you, I can't bear the thought of that. Please don't hurt me, please!'

She was screaming, sobbing, waking up the neighbours, making dogs bark and cats wail. Fighting not to be dragged to this dark, lonely, terrifying place that she might never escape from. Joe raised his voice.

'I'm sorry, Frankie. I want a divorce.'

14

Chapter 2

Each bullet is unique and can be traced back to the gun from which it was fired. Everyone knows that. Or how when someone fires a gun it can leave hundreds or even thousands of traces, gunshot residues, over their clothes and skin. You can dump the gun and burn the clothes, of course, if you get the gift of time in which to do that. What I didn't realise was that the treacherous traces can remain on your hair and skin and be detected even after a shower. The only thing that can get rid of them immediately is urine.

How would I have collected enough? Phoned around friends and acquaintances and thrown a wild party, got the guests so off their faces that at some point I could have persuaded them it would be a terrific chortle if they all peed in my bath? And then – oh, horrible! I would have done it though. I would have done everything differently. Like most murderers who get caught, however – and like all innocent people who get convicted – I lacked vital information.

I'm au fait now with such things as post-firing residues, the vaporous cloud of heavy metals that gets released along with the bullet. The report said I had been recently exposed to a discharged weapon; the murder weapon. And my fingerprints were on it. Some guns deposit higher concentrations and therefore result in longer-lasting residues. Even with lead-free ammunition, which was developed to protect firers in indoor ranges from toxic emissions. That's thoughtful, isn't it?

Last night I had the dream where I walk along a cinder path between misty fields until I come to the red-brick Georgian house. I stop outside the closed front door, shivering with cold. Wonder

15

where this is, what I'm doing here. This time the door was open, so I went in. I was filled with joy because I knew the evil had gone. And because I knew that my life was mine once more.

The big rooms were empty and silent, with trailing, ivory silk net curtains at every window. I walked into the drawing room and admired the red marble mantelpiece, the glittering cut-glass droplets of the chandelier. A log fire blazed in the grate. I stepped forward and stretched out my frozen hands to its welcoming warmth. Then I stopped, gripped by terror.

In one corner by the window was a cardboard box full of snakes. Poisonous snakes with sharp, bright-coloured markings. They wriggled and writhed out of the box, slithered along the floor towards me. How many, how long had they been there? Were there more in other rooms? The venom from their bites would clot my blood, paralyse me, stop my heart beating. I would die here, alone and helpless, their scaly bodies slithering over my bloated corpse. I turned and ran screaming out of the house.

I woke up sweating, expecting shouts, angry people banging on the door, bursting in, light blinding me. Nothing happened. My screams were just gasps.

This hostel is a kind of halfway house between the vulnerable ex-con and the cold, cruel world that thinks she should rot. I've got a crap little room that would have Pollyanna begging for Prozac. I have to be in by six each evening, and if I prove myself trustworthy and submissive enough they might soon extend the deadline to ten p.m. Wow. Heady stuff.

I don't want to know any of the other sad bitches in here. Calling a woman a bitch can be a compliment these days, so I've discovered. Means *Being-In-Total-Control (of)-Herself.* I read that on some feminist site I came across while surfing the wild, wicked web during an IT intro course. We're supposed to be living in a post or neo-feminist age, whatever that means. Seems to mean that if you think the old playing field still needs a bit of levelling or the media's definitions of masculine and feminine sucks, you're a scarily uncool, whinging feminazi. Not to mention thick. It's *irony,* love. Don'tcha geddit?

A few other inmates – shouldn't use that word, really, but I still feel like an inmate – tried to crack my silence over coffee and cigarettes, but I told them to get stuffed. I don't smoke and don't want to hear about their dead yesterdays. Or worse, be expected to give an account of my own. And I'm not being arrogant – well, okay, I am – but they're not exactly on my wavelength. Forget total control, most of them have never had the remotest control over any aspect of their lives. They look condemned. Fags, booze and blokes are what preoccupy them. Or kids, if they've got any. And the food; they're always having a moan fest about the food. You'd think they'd been used to Gordon Ramsay or Marco Pierre White cooking for them in the nick. Some of them think they might get a job. Well, I know we all have to maintain a positive level of self-delusion, but give me a break.

The only person I sometimes have a laugh with is Carl, my probation officer. Until he checks the notes in my file and recalls why I was banged up ten years ago. The smiles and eye contact stop then, and he shifts about on his chair like he's desperate to go to the loo. I can see him thinking what a shame, and I wouldn't say no in different circumstances. Sharp woman, sense of humour, good looks, had everything going for her. Why did she have to commit that horrific crime?

Carl hates it when I tell him I'm innocent. Why? Is it because he thinks I'm a hard-arsed liar and that if he drank an exotic cock-tail every time some sad con told him that he'd have gone through several liver transplants by now? Or does he suspect I'm telling the truth? Whatever the reason, I don't say it too often these days. I used to tell everybody. It was taken as a sign of callousness, lack of remorse, denial, stubborn refusal to shut up and do the time after committing the crime. I didn't get tariffs, parole, privileges, and could have ended up doing fifteen or twenty years instead of ten. Innocence and truth are terrifying. Guilt is comfortable, like proper knickers. My appeal failed and I wasn't allowed another. And after all these years I'm acutely aware that anything I say to these professional people is likely to be twisted around my neck and used to garotte me. But Carl's got charm, and I'm a sucker for that distressingly scarce commodity. Not a total sucker though.

He asks if I intend to seek contact with my father, where would I like to live, have I thought about what kind of job I might do? Bearing in mind that it's hard enough for 38-year-old, non-murderers to find jobs. Carl doesn't say that last bit. He doesn't need to. Of course I won't tell him what I really want. As I said – not a total sucker.

Much as I hate the crap room, I'm terrified at the thought of leaving it. What's going to happen to me? Like I don't know. Another room somewhere – or maybe a flat. I'll never get a whole house to myself. Ongoing harassment by social workers and police. No friends except the kind you don't want. If I get lucky, a job that an illegal asylum seeker would sniff at. Any prospective employer will have to be informed about my dark past. Other people could find out. So that's a career and social life gone to hell in a handbag. What else is left? Not much. Might as well shoot myself now, except that I've got no gun.

Carl frowns, grimaces and accuses me of being negative when I tell him my fears for the future. Basically, what bloody future? So I've shut up. I'm not stupid enough to expect workable solutions, I'd just like him to acknowledge that it won't be cherries and roses for me out there. But Carl thinks I should be relentlessly upbeat and cheerful, like some *Cosmo* reader who believes she can have the perfect man, body and career if she just grafts hard enough. A regular little post-neo-feminist Pollyanna. Maybe Carl's not so charming after all.

Prison was hell, but I got through. I gave up arguing with the shrinks' shrunken definitions: psychotic, delusional, in denial, unable to deal with the shocking reality of her crime. I didn't start to scream and throw myself against cell walls, although I was tempted. I didn't cut myself, pop tranquillizers, try to numb the fear, bitterness and panic with whatever recreational drugs were doing the rounds. Contrary to advice, I didn't get myself a girl-friend. After a while I tried to fade away, and eventually reached a point where I wanted to die. But I didn't die. I came out with my sanity intact – at least I think so. Don't want to blow it now. All my life I've felt like I'm speeding towards a green light that turns red just before I get there.

No, Carl, I don't intend to contact my father. He didn't want to know before, and he won't now. He didn't show much interest from the day I was born, but once I'd been arrested and charged with murder, that was it. He didn't visit, didn't phone or write. He refused to help me in any way. I can't bear to see him again and experience that cold, critical, heartbreaking indifference that used to shrivel me up and make me desperate, make me feel like I'd never be good enough for anything or anyone. He's sixty-eight now, which is not so old these days. He could live another ten or twenty years. When he dies I'm sure he'll leave his money to charity. Dear Daddy was big on charity. Just not the kind that begins at home.

What I want is to find the mother I never knew. And her family, if she has one. I wonder what she's like, if she ever thinks of me? I might have brothers, sisters, nieces, nephews, cousins. Maybe I look like them. I'm not fooling myself that they'll want to know me. They might not want to know each other. And who would be chuffed to discover a long-lost rellie who's a convicted murderer? There could be things I won't be chuffed about either. Insanity, for example, or some degenerative, terminal disease that strikes once you hit forty and robs you of everything we term human. All my life I couldn't answer doctors' questions about whether this or that condition runs in my family.

I looked up the word *family*; the dictionary defined it as a group of people that consists of parents and their children. Sounds cosy. Nuclear family, extended family. Family car, family man, family business, in the family way. Family tomb. I also looked up *blood*. Blood brother, bloodbath, bloodcurdling, blood group, blood lust. Blood knot.

I don't expect anything, at least that's what I tell myself. I just have to ask that question. After all these years, I've got to know: *why?* Why did my mother abandon me? My other question is, who really deserved to spend the past decade in jail? Suffering my torture. Enduring my hell. I know I should let it go. But I can't.

Who is the killer?

Chapter 3

'I'm frightened.'

'Why, Estella?'

'Because I'm sixty-five, I've been a widow for eighteen months now, and being alone just gets harder. I can go to all the clubs, coffee mornings and watercolour classes I can cram in, and my friends are very good. But the bottom line is, I come home, shut the door and it's just me.' She sniffed, blinking back tears.

'You know what's worse than being alone?' Her friend Val's voice sounded harsh and tired as usual. 'Never being alone. You don't realise how lucky you are. You can go where you want, do what you like, wake up every morning and just please yourself. You're not stuck with some mumbling old git who dozes in front of the telly all day and asks you what soaps he should watch. And if one more person describes my hours of unpaid babysitting as "enjoying the grandchildren", I'll strangle them. D'you know how long I've been married?' she demanded.

Estella sighed. 'Forty-three years.'

'That's right.' Val trotted out her favourite line. 'You don't get that for murder.'

'I see your point.' So why couldn't Val see hers for once? No use quoting that Janis Joplin song about freedom being just another word for nothin' left to lose.

'Anyway, you're not alone,' Val went on. 'You've got Francesca – Frankie. She's a great girl. A lovely daughter to you.'

'Yes, except that she has to be a lovely daughter from The Hague.'

'Well, that's not Australia, is it? She comes over often enough, and she's always inviting you to go there. Oh, I know why you

20

won't – you were so used to going everywhere with Jack. But you've got to get over that, Estella. Count your blessings, especially where Frankie's concerned. There's this woman in my club and her daughter never even bothers to . . .'

Estella switched to auto-pilot. Val meant well, but couldn't she show some sympathy and understanding instead of this relentless chirping about how bloody lucky she was? All right, she could be worse off; she had no money troubles, for instance. That was certainly a blessing, given the large numbers of poverty-stricken senior citizens in the UK. But everything was relative. Her parents with their great expectations, hence her name, had always admonished her to think of others who were worse off. How was that supposed to make anyone feel better?

Estella wished she had not given in and confessed how bad she felt. It was usually others who told her their miserable stories, and she was expected to listen patiently and respond with the appropriate consoling words. Stepping out of one's appointed role often elicited disturbed reactions. She looked down at the polished hall table, at the letter that lay on top of the Yellow Pages. Of course it was all the fault of *that*. The real reason for her panic. Something she could never tell Val or anybody, not even Frankie. Especially not Frankie.

'So we'll have lunch one day next week,' Val said. 'That lovely old pub where they do the boeuf bourguignon. The boeuf comes from a local organic farmer, so you know you're all right with it. Not that I'm worried about mad cows any more at my age. Let's face it, most people would say I am one. Now you cheer up and I'll see you again soon.'

'Yes, okay. 'Night, Val. Thanks.'

Estella put the phone down and stood in the silent hall, raking her fingers through her fine, silky, blunt-cut, grey hair. She picked up the bunch of keys, locked the porch door and front door and slid the chain in place. She walked through to the kitchen and checked that the back door was also locked. She wanted a cup of tea, then decided on something stronger. So what if she had to get up to go to the loo several times during the night? She didn't have to go to some office the next morning, or wear herself out looking after children. She took the bottle of sherry from the larder and poured herself a generous glass of the sweet, sticky stuff. Now that she was an old fool she could drink sweet sherry without anyone laughing at her. And there was no one here to laugh at her for anything. She swallowed and grimaced, patted her stomach. Why couldn't this nervous indigestion disappear and leave her in peace? Well, she knew why.

Estella did not want to look at the letter again, even though she had not read it properly that morning. She had read enough to make her panic. She recalled slitting it open, wondering what on earth anyone from an adoption counselling charity could want with her? A donation, probably. After reading the first sentence her knife had clattered against the flowered plate, butter and apricot preserve smudging the white tablecloth. She was gasping with shock, her heart pounding, pain stabbing her midriff as the menacing, black-printed words flew at her like punches: *daughter, contact, permission, meet*. She heard herself groan 'No, no'. She thrust the letter back into its envelope and got to her feet, desperate to rip it, bin it, burn it. She had to tell these people no, she would never give permission, wanted nothing to do with this madness. No contact.

It was what people did nowadays, of course. The *me* society. They couldn't be content with their lives the way they were, oh no. Be grateful for what they had. They had to dig, pry, demand, shout about their rights – never mind anyone else's. Strip their own and others' lives bare. What did they hope to discover? That their real Mummy was a fairy princess and Daddy a stockbroker or dot com millionaire instead of the sad woodcutter in whose manky cottage they had grown up? All the time encouraged by social workers and other interfering do-gooders who did nothing but harm. Over the years Estella's terrors had died as she gradually allowed herself to believe this wasn't going to happen, not after such a long time. Now the nightmare was real.

Tears filled her eyes and her hands started to shake again. She took a gulp of sherry, felt its warmth run down her throat and into her stomach. For the first time she felt relief that Jack was dead. How could she have explained this disaster, revealed the humiliation and trauma of her long-buried secret? Jack would have been devastated, perhaps even regarded it as a betrayal, realised that their long, happy married life had been built on lies. And Frankie, what would she think? She must never find out. Estella gulped the rest of the sherry. This had to be buried again. For good.

The stabbing pain came back, making it difficult to breathe, and she felt sick. She took the letter and went slowly upstairs to the room where Frankie's old desk and computer were, along with shelves full of thrillers and crime novels. No private detective stories – Frankie hated those. The study at the front of the house overlooked the narrow hill road, trees and a field. Estella switched on the computer and waited while it chirruped into life, stared across the road and through the trees into the dark centre of the field. She thought she heard male laughter, the clink of bottles. Must be that gang of teenage boys again, boozing and ready for trouble. Useless to wonder why their parents didn't keep tabs on them. This area was definitely going down the nick, but she did not want to move. It was where she had lived with Jack, where Frankie had grown up. It was home.

She drew the curtains and sat down, trying to calm herself with slow, deep breaths. The stupid pain wouldn't go away. No wonder, after the day she'd had. The life she led. She felt so alone.

'Don't panic,' she muttered. 'This is stupid. Don't let it get to you.'

How could it not? She unclenched her hands, smoothed out the paper and looked at the letterhead; a charitable organisation that counselled adoptees and parents. The fact that it was a charity somehow made it worse, more personal and invasive. These people were not just bored bureaucrats, they wanted to interfere. Well, they were not going to counsel *her*. She would make this sound businesslike, final. She double-clicked, moved the mouse and started to type. Somewhere in the dark depths of the field, glass smashed against rock. Estella was sweating now and her breath came in little gasps.

I do not therefore want any further contact with your organisation, certainly not with the person who calls herself my daughter. I will pass on this letter to my solicitor, together with instructions to take action if you reveal any personal information about me, or violate my privacy in other ways. I too have rights under the law.

She had to hope that was true. Estella could have launched into a rant but restrained herself. If she did that they would dismiss her as a crazy old woman. Fury mingled with her fear. Who did these

23

bastards think they were? She printed the letter, signed and shoved it into an envelope, realised that the pain around her midriff was crushing now, seriously impairing her ability to breathe.

What was this, a panic attack? Ridiculous. She had to get a grip on herself. She dropped the letter on the desk next to the dusty old cut-glass trifle dish filled with bits of brown, pink, blue and white china, broken clay pipes and tiny, clay Frozen Charlotte pudding dolls that Frankie had picked up on walks in the fields and on the Moss. She never found anything valuable like gold coins, but she liked these bits of things, especially the tiny dolls, named after Queen Charlotte and traditionally put into puddings in north-west England.

Estella felt as if she was choking. Sweat dampened her cream silk shirt and the waistband of her black trousers. Fresh air was what she needed. She went into the dark back bedroom, opened a window and leaned out, staring down over the sloping, moonlit garden and house roofs partially concealed by overgrown conifers and other trees. Rows of orange street lights and beyond those, dark hills. Miles away on the horizon were Winter Hill and Ashurst Beacon. The chill air smelled of grass and wood smoke. September, her favourite month. And somebody wanted to ruin it for her. Not only the month, but the rest of her damn life.

She gulped for air, clinging to the windowsill. The pain was unbelievable – she would suffocate if she didn't get more air into her lungs. Estella no longer thought this was just a panic attack. She was ill and needed help. She closed the window and staggered out, hoping she could get to the phone in the front bedroom. She was making little mewing sounds now, and her body and clothes were drenched with sweat.

The curtains were open in the front bedroom, orange light slanting across one wall. Estella knocked over a pot of geraniums as she got a window open, scattering soil and petals. She grabbed the phone on the bedside table and managed to dial her next-door neighbour, Carole. She wouldn't make it downstairs, she knew that now, and Carole had a key. She remembered she had put the chain on the front door. Damn. Well, they would just have to break it. Was this death? She was not frightened and didn't care if she pegged out, although she felt sorry for her daughter. She just wanted relief from the pain. Estella pressed the phone to her right ear, grimacing at the loudness of the rings.

A movement outside caught her eye; she thought she saw a figure emerge from the darkness of the field and stand on the edge by the clump of trees. The figure was slim and of medium height, but she could not tell if it was male or female. The person stood still, seemed to be staring at the house. Menacing, malevolent. Pain clamped Estella in a vice and another wave of cold sweat broke and washed over her. Carole answered the phone at last.

'Yeah?' She sounded like she was eating. Crisps, probably. Carole loved crisps. The television was on in the background, an audience laughing and applauding.

'It's me,' Estella gasped. 'I . . .'

'That you, Stellie? You don't sound too good. What's up, love?'

'Call – ambulance.' Estella could hardly get the words out. 'Now.'

'Oh, my *God*. What's—'

'Think it's – heart attack. Call para—' She dropped the phone.

She was dizzy and faint, nauseated, could not talk any more. Her pulse rate was too fast to measure, her heart fluttering in her chest, fibrillating rather than beating. Estella did not hear Carole telling her to hold on, hang in there, she would call an ambulance right now and be round in a minute. Hang on, hang on. She collapsed on the bed and slumped to the floor.

The figure disappeared into the darkness.

Chapter 4

'Hello, my little blonde, green-eyed monster. You look sexy tonight.'

'Good enough to eat, my darling young man?' Monique Thorn grinned up at her husband. 'I've missed you all day.'

'I missed you too. But now I'm home. Everything's fine with your cool company, Thorn Communications.'

'Don't keep calling it my company. It's yours as well. We've been married three years now, and you've taken loads of work off my poor little shoulders. Which is why I can laze at home for days at a time if I fancy.'

'Whatever. How about a snog?' Conal wrapped his arms around her and they kissed, Monique enjoying the fresh citrus smell of his aftershave, his taut body against hers and the silky feel of his dark-brown, wavy hair. She hated the skinhead look, or whatever it was called, that so many men had nowadays. Conal let go of her after a minute, moved to the fridge and took out a bottle of toasty Perrier Jouet. He pulled off his tie and threw it on the table. Monique smiled, stretching her arms above her head.

'So, how was your day in the big, bad city of Liverpool?'

'Well, I'm happy to get home to you and the woolly-back Lancashire countryside.' Conal frowned. 'I just nearly crashed into a cop car when I drove around that bend in the lane. Bloody stupid place to park. Still, no one's going to give them a ticket. Wonder what it was doing there?'

'God, did they take this long to turn up? I meant to tell you, the Ecclestons got burgled last night – well, early hours of this morning. Joanna phoned at lunch time – I'm surprised she waited that long – to chew my ear about how they'd nicked her husband's

26

collection of snuff boxes, and other incandescently boring items I can't even begin to remember.'

Conal smiled. 'The Georgian silver dildo, perhaps?'

'She kept whining, "I can't think why they picked our tumble-down cottage instead of your lovely medieval manor." I got the impression she expected me to apologise.'

'Silly old . . .! And there's no way that place is tumbling down.' Conal gripped the cork and twisted the champagne bottle. He laughed. 'She's probably got the raving hump because the burglars didn't bang her and make old Eric watch. Might have taught him a technique or two, although it's a bit bloody late for that now.'

'You're evil. But it's lucky they didn't pick on us.' Monique shuddered. 'God, the thought of burglars breaking into our home. That's one of my worst nightmares.'

'It would have been those bastards worst nightmare if they'd tried it.' Conal's expression was grim now and she knew he was thinking of the rifle he kept locked in a cupboard in their dressing room. 'Of course I wouldn't admit to blowing their heads off and loving it–'

'You might not love it,' she interrupted. 'You might be shocked and traumatised.'

'Yeah, *right*. I'd blow their heads off then say I was in terror for the lives of my wife and stepdaughter. Not to mention my own. I panicked and accidentally pulled the trigger–'

'Several times with deadly effect.'

He laughed again and put one hand over his eyes. 'Oh Christ, officer! All that blood. I tried resuscitation and phoned the para-medics, but it was too late.'

'Got your story all ready then.'

'Better believe it.' Conal launched into his favourite rant. 'Work hard, make a few quid and every idle, useless tosser in exis-tence thinks he deserves a piece. They'll break into your home then sue you for using unreasonable force when you try to defend yourself and your property. The law's an arse. You need to know the legal loopholes, same as those ferals and their scumsucking lawyers.' The cork popped and champagne foamed over his hand.

She was so lucky to have Conal, Monique thought, as she fetched two champagne glasses. Her few friends – few because years of hard graft had not left much time for socialising – had boring, sexless relationships and scarcely communicated with their husbands or partners any more. Made you wonder how they'd got together in the first place. Of course the honeymoon period couldn't last – you had to work at keeping the magic. The magic hadn't run out on her and Conal though, and she didn't believe it would. The age difference did not matter either because Conal looked older than thirty-one and she certainly didn't look forty. Divorced at thirty and cynical about marriage, Monique had concentrated on raising her daughter and making money. She loved her daughter and the money, and life became good, but at times she felt something was missing. Then she met Conal.

'Oh, thanks. Lovely.' She took the foaming glass he handed her. 'Cheers.'

'Here's to you,' he grinned. They drank and she looked into his dark-blue eyes. She jumped and frowned as the thump of bass vibrated through the ceiling.

'What's that girl playing at? She'll have the plaster off the walls in a minute.' Monique walked to the door and looked across the hall, listening. Eminem, chanting 'Bitch! Bitch! Bitch!' She crossed to the foot of the stairs. 'Lauren! Lauren, for God's sake, turn that . . .!'

No use. Lauren couldn't or wouldn't hear. She turned and went back to the kitchen, shaking her head. Conal sat at the table drinking champagne and turning the pages of that day's *Liverpool Echo*.

'How can she listen to such appalling rubbish? That Oasis guy's right, no one under sixteen should be allowed to buy CDs.'

Conal shrugged. 'It's not that loud.'

'Are you kidding? And it's not just the volume, it's the content. Can't she see how misogynist that screwed-up little creep is?'

'She won't get bothered about misogyny until she's trying to combine a couple of brats with a career.' He topped up his glass of champagne, raised the bottle and glanced inquiringly at her. Monique shook her head.

'I don't know what kind of career she imagines she's going to have to combine with anything when she never does any studying.'

'I was the same at that age. So were you, judging by the stories you've told me. But I admit I didn't stress about combining a career with fatherhood. Or step-fatherhood.'

'Lauren thinks she doesn't have to make much effort because she's got my – our –money to fall back on. Well, she has of course. But that's not the point. I want her to have a career she's good at and enjoys; I want her to be able to take care of herself.'

Not end up dependent on the State or some man, Monique thought but did not say. She recalled her first marriage, stuck at home with no money except the few quid housekeeping that Gerry grudgingly gave her, never going out unless it was to her mother's or the bloody shops. Gerry had wanted kids to prove his virility, but thought fatherhood stopped at conception. And he had cheated on her so many times that she'd lost count. If any man did that to her again . . .! Monique wondered what Gerry was doing these days. Rotting in hell, with any luck. He had shown zero interest in Lauren and had relinquished all contact with his daughter after the divorce. So much for fathers' rights; he didn't even want control, let alone responsibility. Conal got up, came over and put his arms around her.

'She'll be fine,' he murmured, kissing her smooth neck. 'Try not to worry. Don't be too hard on her, you know that won't do any good.'

'True.' Monique sighed, closed her eyes and leaned her head back.

'I noticed today that autumn cold's already starting to bite. Why don't we book somewhere soon?' He slipped his fingers beneath her dress strap and eased it down over her shoulder. 'You know what we both like – some deserted beach to stretch out on with a drink and the lappy or a novel. I'm not bothered about communing with bloody wildlife or local yokels – same difference.'

'Don't overdo the political correctness, will you?' But Monique had to smile because she felt the same way; the only contact she wanted with locals was when they served her an exotic cocktail or a plate of something gourmet. 'But what about Lauren? I can't take her out of school during term time.'

'You don't have to. She can stay with that friend of hers and her family. Or my mother could come over.'

'Yes. I suppose.'

'That's sorted then. Think I'll take a bath.' Conal's hands were cupping her breasts now, his breath warm in her ear. 'Going to join me?'

'I certainly am.'

'Hey, listen.' He smiled, glanced at the ceiling.

'What?'

'Exactly.'

The thump and vibration had stopped, Eminem laid to rest until it was time for his next rant. They drew apart, looking ruefully at one another as feet pounded down the stairs. Monique yanked up her dress strap, slipped on a pair of oven gloves and took out the chicken casserole.

'That looks good.' Conal sniffed. 'Smells good too. We won't get better where we're going. Her ladyship's got the best deal.' He looked round as Lauren bounced in. 'Talk of the devil.'

'What devil?' Lauren stopped.

'You.'

'Oh, you're a mean, rotten old stepdaddy.' Lauren gave him a hug then went and stood by her mother, watching as Monique dipped a spoon into the bubbling casserole. She smiled. 'Sure that's enough for one, Mum?'

'You could always invite somebody round to share it,' Conal remarked.

'None of the boys I know, if that's what you mean. They're all double-sad.'

Monique smiled at her daughter, a teenage version of herself with long, blonde hair and green eyes, biscuit-coloured skin. Except Lauren sometimes preferred to dress worryingly similar to Britney Spears or Christina Aguilera. 'Well, I know you won't throw a wild party while we have dinner with a few boring sods from the golf club.'

The usual love and concern welled up in her. She wouldn't nag Lauren about her musical tastes or lack of application to school work, because Conal was right; her parents had done the same to her at that age, with zero effect. And she had done okay for herself. More than okay. So would Lauren. She was intelligent and determined. It was just that Monique could not help feeling something wasn't quite right. She had no idea what. She knew her daughter would not have friends round tonight – certainly not boys – because she hardly ever did. She didn't seem interested in people her own age. Lauren seemed more innocent, more naive than other fourteen-year-olds, and yet in some ways older. It was strange, unsettling. Sometimes Monique felt she did not really know her daughter, had never known her. She supposed all parents

30

felt that way occasionally. Stop stressing, she told herself. Just relax and don't think too much. That shouldn't be a problem for you. She glanced at the *Lancashire Life* calendar on the wall by the fridge – September already. Where had the year gone? Time passed so quickly she would soon start forgetting her age. Well, no worries there.

'Right.' Conal stood up. He glanced at her and raised his eyebrows. 'What time are we supposed to get there?'

'Sonya said seven-thirty for drinks, eat at eight. You've got about an hour to make yourself even more irresistible.'

He smiled and strolled out, taking his glass of champagne. Lauren sat at the table. Her expression was blank, her green eyes fixed on the champagne bottle. Monique dumped the casserole on a cork mat.

'You seem a bit quiet,' she remarked. 'Anything wrong?'

'Absolutely nothing.' Lauren dug the ladle in and served herself a steaming plateful of chicken and vegetables. Monique dabbed at the spot of sauce that flew up and splashed on her dress, making a dark stain on the purple silk. Oh well, she was going to take it off again anyway. The dress felt a bit tight, and she decided not to eat or drink much this evening; she didn't want to end up with a stomach on her like a poisoned pup. She was bloody hungry though.

'Compromise,' she sighed, patting Lauren's hot pink-clad shoulder. 'That's what life's all about.'

'Read that in one of your stupid women's magazines, did you?'

'Well, no.' Monique's voice hardened. 'Actually I didn't.'

'I looked at one the other day.' Lauren chased a piece of chicken around her plate. '*Woman and Home.* Can you imagine a magazine called *Man and Home*?'

'*Man and Garage*, maybe,' Monique joked. '*Man and Shed.*'

'Pages and pages about how the ageing process makes your tits collapse and your lips go out of shape, and ways to keep them plumped up. All of which involve spending huge amounts of money, of course. Articles about stress incontinence . . . it was scary. Oh, and did you know women have caused a crisis in masculinity by getting more legal rights, qualifications and better jobs? Doesn't say much for masculinity, does it?'

'Well, I wouldn't worry about that, darling, because the way you go on you're in no danger of frightening any males with your qualifications.' Shit, Monique thought. Stop it. 'I don't take those magazines seriously,' she protested. 'They're just a bit of fun.'

'Yeah.' Lauren speared a mushroom. 'Must be a real blast reading about stress incontinence and collapsing tits.'

'Or listening to Eminem rant about bitches and gays.'

'He doesn't do that any more. Anyway, it's just–'

'*Ironic*. Yes, I know. Trouble is, lots of people out there don't get the irony.'

Lauren ate her mushroom. 'Mum, what would you do if Conal left you?'

'Left me?' Monique echoed, shocked. She stared at her daughter. 'Conal won't do that – why on earth would he? He loves me and I love him! What makes you ask such a thing?'

'I just wondered, that's all. I mean . . . he's a lot younger than you, isn't he?'

'Not that much younger.' Monique blushed with annoyance. Children and teenagers were so conservative; it was older people who were generally more open and tolerant, contrary to the myths regularly served up.

'You're forty. It must be difficult to find someone else at that age.'

'Not necessarily. You probably think it would be difficult for someone in their twenties! Anyway, if Conal did leave me I'm not sure I'd want to bother. Finding another boyfriend or husband isn't like getting a new pet.'

'No?' Lauren laughed. 'Mum, you've got your company, you're a millionaire and everything. Done really well. Conal works for you.'

'He doesn't work *for* me, he works *with* me.'

'Whatever. What I'm saying is, even if he left you you'd probably have to give him at least half of what you own, maybe pay him alimony. You could end up a lot poorer. The law's equal about things like that now, isn't it?'

'When it suits men. Women are supposed to do everything.' Monique thought of her first marriage again. 'Have a career, bring up kids, do all the housework and shopping, stay looking good. Otherwise they deserve to be dumped. That's the implication.' Her colour deepened. 'No one lectures men on how to combine kids with a wife, career and house.' She made a mental note to stop buying magazines.

'Don't get upset, Mum.'

'I'm not.' But Monique felt infuriated as she remembered another article, some nonsense about an orgasm pill for women. You needed a man who knew what he was doing, not a bloody pill. And thank goodness she had a man who didn't need a map and torch.

Lauren came up with another chilling question. 'Suppose Conal cheated on you?'

'He'd never do that!' Monique got a jolt of shock. And pure fear. 'I told you, we love each other. Come on, Lauren, this is crazy.' She took a deep breath, one hand pressed to her stomach. 'What's got into you?' She laughed nervously. 'Do you know something I don't? Not trying to tell me you've seen him around with some other woman, are you?'

'Oh, no.' Lauren's eyes were shiny like glass. 'No. I'm sure Conal's not interested in other women.'

'Well, thanks for that. I should damn well hope not.' Monique stared at her again. 'Where's this coming from?' she asked, mystified and uneasy.

'Nowhere.' Lauren shrugged and resumed eating. 'Just being a typical teen.'

Monique glanced at the clock. 'I have to get ready. I'll see you later. You'll be okay here while we're out?'

'Just fine and dandy, Mother dear.'

Monique gave her another long, searching look. Then she hurried out of the kitchen shaking her head, crossed the hall and ran upstairs. She went into her and Conal's bedroom. In the dressing room where rows of polythene-sheathed clothes hung on rails like in a dry cleaner's she slipped off her dress and underwear, leaving them in a heap on the floor, and walked naked into the adjoining bathroom. Conal lounged in a big bath of steaming blue, foamy water.

'You took your time.' He looked her up and down, his eyes lingering on her breasts. 'Thought you were playing hard to get.'

'I was talking to Lauren.' Monique stepped carefully into the bath and sat down. 'My darling daughter's in a really strange mood.'

He frowned. 'How d'you mean?'

'Oh, I don't know.' She didn't want to tell him about Lauren's disturbing remarks and questions because she got a superstitious

33

feeling that voicing them might somehow bring bad luck. Monique often felt frightened because she thought she was too happy. Dangerously happy.

'I thought most teenagers were always in a strange mood,' Conal said. 'Something to do with out-of-control hormones, isn't it?'

'So I've heard.'

'You look gorgeous.' He slid forward. 'Come here.'

She felt his erection under the water. 'Wow!'

'That's down to you, tormenting me by making me wait, alone with my wild fantasies.' He ran his wet hands over her breasts and belly, and stroked her hardening nipples. 'Now, my lady, you'll have to take the consequences of your flighty behaviour.'

Monique giggled. 'I hope so.'

He gripped her wet buttocks and pulled her on top of him. She gasped and bit her lip as he slid deep inside her, couldn't stop herself crying out. Blue water heaved and splashed, bubbles floated and burst. Sensation overwhelmed her. Conal was so sexy, his touch so sure. She had never wanted any man so much. She looked into his eyes and knew he wouldn't be satisfied until she gave in to him, lost it completely. And she did, crying out and clinging to him as she came, unconscious of everything but her own pleasure and the urgent need to satisfy it. By the time they got out of the bath the water was lukewarm.

'We're going to be late,' Monique laughed as she wrapped herself in a big, heated bath towel. She felt fantastic now.

'No worries.' Conal kissed her. 'The cool people always arrive late.' He gazed at himself in the mirror, stroking his chin. 'Should I get rid of the facial hair? Think I'm a bit bored with it.'

'No, don't. It's dead sexy. I love it grazing my skin.'

'As long as it doesn't give you a rash. Your skin's pretty sensitive. Easily grazed.' He traced the line of her jaw and laid one finger on her lips. 'Easily bruised.'

She smiled. 'Good job you're not into bondage and S and M then, isn't it?'

Monique picked out a black dress, blew her hair dry and did her make-up. She didn't mind being forty because she looked and felt good. It was other people who made a big deal of it. She was happy with her smooth complexion, pretty hair, slim figure and barely lined features, although she would never admit that to anyone in case they thought she was an arrogant cow. She slipped on the dress, sleeveless with a V-neckline, and sprayed herself with perfume. Conal, still naked, was wielding the hairdryer now. She went out of the bedroom and up the second flight of stairs to Lauren's room.

Lauren loved her big attic bedroom with its view of gardens, fields and distant hills, so much that she hardly ever came down from it. At almost seven-thirty in the evening the clear blue sky had darkened to violet, and a few stars glittered. One was Venus, Monique thought. Planet of love, a mystery beneath its cloud layers.

The room was neat and minimally furnished, no scattered magazines or posters of simpering boy bands. There was a television facing the bed, hi-fi equipment, CDs and a DVD player. One corner was converted to an office space with a desk, computer and book-lined shelves. Monique searched the wardrobe, opened the desk drawers and looked under the bed. She felt like a nasty spy, not sure why she was doing this or what she was looking for. Lauren would be furious, she knew that much. But she was haunted by the indefinable expression in her daughter's eyes. Her disturbing words.

In one desk drawer was a tiny silver key; it looked familiar, but Monique could not remember what it fitted. She searched the room again, moved a pile of clothes off the old wooden chest and lifted the lid. Beneath some crushed cotton tops and several folded pairs of embroidered jeans was Lauren's old music box, cream-coloured and painted with blowsy pink roses. The key fitted. The ballerina with her smooth golden bob and dirty-white wisp of tutu sprang up and twirled to the tinkling notes of the *Sleeping Beauty* waltz, her figure reflected in two tiny mirrors behind her. Monique pulled out a small notebook. The notebook was bound in bitter chocolate-brown suede, had unlined, cream-tinted pages and a cream silk ribbon. Several pages were filled with Lauren's slanted handwriting. She must have started a diary or journal. She liked to use different coloured inks: black, royal blue, purple, red. The latest entry, dated the previous day, was written in blue.

Of course she should put this back right now. How disgusting, how sneaky to spy on your own daughter like this. But if the journal was locked in a box and buried in a chest, Lauren must have something she wanted to hide. Monique flipped through

35

more pages. Something dropped out of the back of the notebook –
a pair of wrapped condoms. Strawberry flavour.

Monique gasped, dry-mouthed. 'What the . . .?'

'Are you ready?' Conal called up the stairs. 'It is tonight we're
supposed to go out?'

'Just coming.' Unable to resist, Monique scanned the latest
entry.

*We did it today. My first time. It hurt a bit, but after that it
was fantastic! He knew it was my first time and he was so
gentle and careful. He told me he felt privileged. I'm so
happy. He says he loves me, that he wanted me for ages.*

'Oh, my God!'

'Monique?'

'Yes, I'm coming.' She put the journal back, re-locked the box
and replaced everything, put the key back in the drawer. She
found it difficult to stand up and move around, because she was
trembling and her legs felt weak.

Monique tried to tell herself she was overreacting, but did not
succeed. Lauren was underage! It was against the law to have sex
with fourteen-year-old girls, however mature they might appear.
Who was *'he'*? Someone at school? Lauren said all the boys she
knew were double-sad, but she might be exaggerating. It could be
an older boy. Or an older man! Another cold flash of shock hit her.
If it was a man, how could he be gentle and sensitive if he was
capable of seducing an underage girl?

'Oh, *God.*'

Where had Lauren met him? Some terrible Internet chat room?
She had to talk to her, find out everything. But how? Confess to
her daughter that she had searched her room and read her journal?
Lauren would be so angry she would refuse to tell her anything.
And she would not trust her mother again, certainly not for a long
time. Monique's mind was a horrified blank.

'Little green-eyed monster, will you get your sexy rear down
here?'

Monique's throat tightened and tears stung her eyes. Her little
girl was gone – for ever. But Lauren was still young – too young
to be having sex. She sniffed, took a breath and steadied herself. It
might not be an older man, it was probably a boy. A sixth-former,

perhaps. Although that was bad enough. She tried to calm herself. She walked out of the room, along the passage and down the stairs. Conal grinned up at her. He was dressed, ready, pointing at his watch.

'What the hell have you been doing?'

She forced a smile. 'Looking at Venus.'

She couldn't confront Lauren, not yet. Or tell Conal. She needed to think first, decide how to tackle the situation. God, Monique thought, I can't stand the thought of her having sex! She might be ready physically, but she isn't emotionally. It's not right. I don't give a toss if she or anyone else thinks I'm an old-fashioned prude. And what if she gets some sexually transmitted disease? Or pregnant? Condoms can't give total protection. What the hell am I going to do?

Monique knew only one thing. She had to stop this.

Chapter 5

'My marriage is over,' Frankie gasped, sobbing into the phone. 'Joe doesn't love me any more. Just like that. I can't believe it!' She wished she could stop repeating that irritating phrase, but it kept slipping out.

'I don't know what the hell you're doing at work,' Lida exclaimed. 'You're crazy. Why don't you tell the Consul you need some leave, and go home right now?'

'Home, where's home?' Frankie burst out crying again and glanced at the closed door of her office, hoping no one would walk in. 'I don't want to go back to that bloody apartment and sit around – I'd be in an even worse state then. Probably stay in my dressing gown all day and have wine or vodka for breakfast, lunch and dinner. I feel so alone, Lida,' she wept. 'So frightened. 'I don't know what to do. What's going to happen to me? It's all such a total, fucking nightmare!'

'Frankie, listen. You've got to take care of yourself. That's the most important thing. Protect your interests. You should see a divorce lawyer, here or in the UK. As soon as possible. Find out your legal position, what you're entitled to. Or not.'

'I can't see any lawyers yet. I'm not ready. It would be like acknowledging Joe and I are really finished.'

There was a silence. 'Well – aren't you?'

'I can't bear to think that. I know I'm pathetic. I want to be strong and take control and everything, but all I can do right now is whinge. I cried all weekend. Joe's being horrible, so *cold*. He won't talk to me. I just can't believe this is—'

'Frankie,' Lida interrupted. 'I'm really sorry, but I'm afraid I have to hang up now. I've got an important meeting.'

'Oh.'

'A nuisance, but there you are. Listen, call me again, okay? Or I'll call you.'

'Yes. All right.' Frankie got that rug-pulled-from-under-the-feet feeling as she realised she might be spilling out her heart and soul to somebody who wasn't that bloody interested. But she was being unfair; Lida really was busy, working as a lawyer at the War Crimes Tribunal. I mustn't get paranoid and obsessed, she thought. Or try to make Lida take sides. She is a friend to both of us, after all.

'I'm sorry,' Lida repeated. 'I know how terrible you're feeling. Well, no, of course I don't. But take care, Frankie. Speak to you soon, okay?'

'Yeah. Thanks, Lida.' Frankie replaced the receiver. She should not have phoned Lida at work, but she was desperate. Life had changed, literally overnight. Knowing you had a few problems was nothing compared to the sudden shocking and terrifying realisation that your marriage, your life, was falling apart. She had no idea how to cope with any of it.

She wiped her eyes and stared out of the window at the spreading, shedding chestnut tree. Leaves and prickly, pale-green conkers were scattered over the front lawn. A black BMW turned into the drive and she recognised the number plate – the Counsellor's Bad Man's Wheels. Why was he back so early from his appointment at the Foreign Office? There was a knock at the door and the ambassador's secretary, Ms Choi, walked in, slim and elegant in her pale-pink Chanel suit and heels, her straight black hair shining.

'Frankie.' She stopped, staring at her. 'You are sick?'

'No. Well, getting a cold, I think.' Some cold. Frankie wiped her eyes again. If only she could stop crying. She hated feeling so out of control, especially in this environment where self-control was very much prized. She had no intention of telling anyone here that her life was falling apart, and she hoped they would not guess.

'Asian flu,' Ms Choi laughed. She came forward and placed a sheet of paper on the desk. 'Ambassador wants translation about this art exhibition. Maybe he and Madame will go. They like art very much.'

'Yes.' Frankie sniffed and blew her nose. She already had a pile of newspaper translations waiting, but this one would have to take priority.

'*Madame*.' Ms Choi rolled her eyes. 'That woman drives me crazy. She phoned to complain that residence windows are so dirty she cannot see out of them. And now she told doctor she wants body scan because she has stomach ache.' She giggled. 'Doctor says that is not necessary – he also thinks she is crazy. And now she is very angry. But she and ambassador are going to Amsterdam this afternoon, so I will be free to read my novel.' She smiled. '*An Artist of the Floating World* by Kazuo Ishiguro. You have read it?'

'Yep, a few years ago.' Frankie nodded, sniffing again. 'Great book.'

'I wish ambassador and Madame would read books. My life would be so much easier.' Ms Choi sighed and trailed out, closing the door behind her.

Frankie buried her head in her hands. Then she picked up the phone again and dialled Joe's work number. He answered, sounding wary.

'It's me. Can we meet for lunch?'

'No,' he muttered. 'Got too much on.'

'You're too busy to talk about our marriage?'

'There's nothing to talk about,' he sighed. 'Except who gets what. Not pleasant, I know, but—'

'I don't think you've told me everything. There has to be more to this.'

'Why? There isn't. Look, Frankie, please don't call me here. There's no point, and you're just upsetting yourself more.'

'I'm not upsetting my*self*!' she hissed. 'I was perfectly happy until you made your big speech.' At least it seemed that way now.

'I'm just going into a meeting. I'll see you tonight.'

'Oh, yes?' Her tears started to flow again. 'Have a nice dinner ready, shall I, to start our cosy evening? What d'you fancy – tortillas, stir-fry, chicken sodding curry?'

'Don't bother about me. I'll be late.'

'How late? Why, where are you going?'

'Out for a drink with some people from my team. We'll prob-ably have dinner too.'

'Yes, probably. You can sit there drinking and having dinner when you know I'm devastated, crying my eyes out because you

40

don't love me any more and want to throw me away like some old T-shirt.'

'I'm not . . . Look,' he muttered. 'It's not easy for me either. D'you think I'm enjoying this? D'you think I like seeing you crying your eyes out all the time, and knowing I'm the cause of your misery?'

'Sorry about that, I'll try and cheer up. You can't be all that bothered, otherwise you wouldn't do this to me.'

'Of course I'm bothered. I hate it – hate myself for making you so unhappy. Frankie, I think we should try and keep things as normal and calm as possible until we—'

'Break up?'

'Well, yeah.' He paused. 'This isn't helping. I'll see you later, okay?'

'Don't go,' she shouted. 'I want you to talk to me!' But Joe hung up and she collapsed in tears again. The misery and pain, the sheer panic and upset of it all were overwhelming, totally shitty, like nothing she had ever experienced. The humiliation was shitty too. She was being dumped, discarded, scrapped. A lot of people laughed at women like her, or pitied them. Blamed them even, for not being young or attractive or interesting enough. Frankie feared pity most. She felt like a loser. She wasn't even being dumped because she was a best-selling author whose jealous husband couldn't stand her success. She froze. How the hell could she ever write again? You needed calm and peace of mind for that. The phone rang and she snatched it up, hoping it might be Joe. Of course it wasn't.

'Frankie, will you do me a favour?' The counsellor. She closed her eyes.

'Depends what it is.'

He laughed. 'You are not entirely obedient. I want you to make me a cup of coffee.'

She was about to remark on how she was translator and Economic and Political Affairs assistant, not a waitress, when it hit her that she might very much need to hang on to this job. She could look for another, of course, but there were not that many jobs open to foreign women in their mid-thirties. If Joe dumped her – *if*! – she had to find a new place and pay for it all by herself. She didn't earn as much as Joe. Together they were well off, but managing on her own would be a struggle. Frankie did not want to end up on income support – or *bijstand* as it was called in the Netherlands – if she could even get it, which she doubted. As a non-Dutch resident, she was liable for taxes and social security contributions, but not entitled to vote in general elections. Taxation without representation. All this meant she literally could not afford the luxury of telling some unreconstructed type to make his own damn coffee.

Should she go back to England? That might be easier. At least she could stay with her mother until she got sorted, even if that wasn't the ideal option. She swallowed, biting her lip, gripped by humiliation and fear. She wondered if she would ever again feel happy and carefree, get back the peace of mind to write.

'Coffee? Five minutes, okay?'

'Four.' He hung up.

She went into the small kitchen and spooned ground coffee into the filter, thinking she could do with a cup herself. She stood there as the machine hissed and bubbled, looking out of the window into the Scheveningen woods opposite. She felt she was also watching her world shrink. Frankie imagined herself alone, deserted, trying to cope, make a new life. Well, lots of people did that. They had to. She wasn't the first wife to get dumped and she wouldn't be the last. It was a very common experience, if also a uniquely horribly personal one.

When the coffee was ready she poured a cup and took it into the counsellor's office, feeling like a no-count servant girl who hadn't yet escaped to build her own empire. Ms Choi grimaced sympathetically from her desk as she crossed the landing. Counsellor Kim looked her over as she placed the coffee on his untidy desk.

'Why do you wear trousers and jacket like the man?'

Frankie ignored him. Even wearing an Armani trouser suit made her feel depressed because she didn't think she would ever be able to afford another. Just as well it was classic enough to stay in fashion. 'I went to Foreign Office.' He leaned back in his chair. 'That woman – head of Protocol Department – she insulted me.'

A familiar case of Asian politeness clashing with Dutch bluntness, no doubt. Frankie turned to go. The young, bespectacled attaché came pounding down the attic staircase carrying several dirty cups and saucers. He dumped them in the kitchen sink and glanced at her as she poured herself a cup of coffee and added a spoonful of sugar.

42

'You look upset. Counsellor is hassling you?' His voice was hushed.

'No.' She sipped the strong coffee.

He pulled out a cigarette and lit it. 'I had car accident on Saturday,' he murmured, blowing out smoke. 'In Amsterdam. It was in the street of the working girls.'

'There's quite a few working girls streets in Amsterdam.'

'I mean *a* street.' He shook his fist at the ceiling. 'Thank you, God, thank you so bloody much! Now I am waiting for a Dutchman. A flying Dutchman, a crawling Dutchman.' He looked at her. 'Why are you upset?'

'I'm not,' she said. 'I'm getting a cold.'

'Sick? You must go home and rest.'

'I'd rather work.'

'Good, very good.' He nodded. 'You are becoming Korean.'

She put down the coffee and rushed into her office as she heard her phone ring again. She knew it wouldn't be Joe.

'Is that you, Frankie?'

'Val!' What on earth did her mother's closest friend want? Oh no, Frankie thought. Something's happened. I don't need more trouble now. 'How are you?'

'I'm fine, love. It's your Mum I'm phoning about.'

'What's happened?' The attaché lounged in the doorway, smoking.

'I'm calling from your mum's house, love. I came here to pick up a nightie and a few toiletries for her. She's in hospital—'

'*What?* Why?'

'I'm sorry, love. Your mum had a heart attack last night. She's in a bad way. I think you'd better get over here as soon as possible.'

The crushing, squeezing pain and breathlessness had gone, thank God, but Estella felt weak and exhausted, more exhausted than she had ever been in her life. She was also terrified. What if the chest pain came back? What if she had another attack? Her body had let her down and she couldn't count on it any longer, take good health for granted. This was horrible and she wasn't having it. She had to get better, get home and take care of herself again, because who else was going to? Estella was determined not to allow herself to be shunted into some home for the helpless and bewildered. That would be the end.

She hated lying there in Intensive Care on the hard, narrow bed, taped and hooked up to the machines. It was quiet except for the occasional groan or call from another patient. She was in a curtained-off cubicle by the window so she got some natural light, even if it was only of the dull, depressing, grey variety. She longed for blue sky and sunshine. A young nurse came in and started pumping air into the dark-blue blood pressure cuff around her right arm.

'How are you feeling, Estella?' She smiled. 'Still weak as a kitten?'

'Kittens aren't weak,' Estella croaked. 'They're always jumping and racing around, bursting with energy.'

'True. Funny how people say that. I suppose because kittens are tiny and delicate.'

Val was due back soon with the things she had promised to fetch. Estella hoped she would not wander into the study and spot the letter, which must be still lying on the desk where she had dropped it. She needed to get home. But there was no way she could even get out of this damn bed yet. Another nurse came in carrying the ward's phone.

'Call for you,' she smiled, handing it over. 'Your daughter from Holland.'

Estella felt a rush of hope and worry. 'Frankie?'

'Mum, I just heard. How are you feeling? Val told me—' Frankie broke off, her voice choked with tears. 'Oh, shit. I was determined not to whinge. Sorry!'

'Listen.' Estella tried to sound firm. 'Don't go upsetting yourself, all right? I'm going to be fine. I'll be out of here in a few days.'

'Really? But Val said you'd had a major heart attack.'

'Never mind what Val said. It looked worse than it was at first. Besides, you know what she's like – Job's comforter with knobs on! She means well, but she does lay it on a bit thick. If I forgot for a second what day of the week it was, she'd say I had Alzheimers.'

'I'll come over,' Frankie said. 'Get a flight for today or tomorrow.'

'You don't have to do that. Don't go putting your job at risk.'

'I'm not. I'm owed some leave. And for God's sake, my mother's ill. I'm coming, so don't argue.'

'Well, I can't deny it'll be wonderful to see you. Please, love, don't sound so upset. You've had a shock – we both have! – but I'll be all right. Really.'

'You better be. I'll call you back to let you know when I've booked my flight. Or ask one of the nurses to give you a message.'

'That's fine. They're very nice,' Estella murmured. She was suddenly overwhelmed with sleepiness. 'Can't do enough for me. I'm being well looked after, despite the horror stories you hear about hospitals.' She closed her eyes and her grip on the phone slackened. 'It's times like this make me wish you had a sister or brother to –'

She stopped and gasped, opened her eyes and stared at the kitschy picture on the wall opposite her bed, a clipper ship dwarfed by huge, dark-blue, white-crested waves. Remembered the letter lying on the desk in the study, the letter she had not dared draw Val's curious attention to by asking her to post, hide or bring it here.

Who was that person, the dark figure she had seen standing on the edge of the field just before she collapsed? The person who seemed to be watching the house? Maybe it was no one in particular. A passer-by, a dog walker. And yet.

'Mum? Mum?'

Frankie did have a sister.

Chapter 6

When you find any of your family members, knock on doors, the intense, grey-haired lady from the adoption counselling charity advised me. I mean, can you believe that? I don't think she realised what she was saying. Not to realise what you're saying is dodgy at any time, of course, but positively dangerous when it's your job to counsel angry, emotionally vulnerable souls like myself.

She smiled at me as she gave her stupid advice, a patronising smile that made me feel like slapping her. I didn't though. I've kept my head for so many years. But it's getting harder now. I keep thinking, worrying, that I might lose it at any time.

I pictured the scene, let myself feel the feelings. Walking up to my mother's front door, ringing the bell, fighting the fear. I'm full of hope too – terrible longing – and that's even more scary. A shadow looms through frosted glass. The door opens, and she's standing there, this woman, my mother. Enquiring what the stranger at the door wants, looking at me without recognition. How can she not recognise me? That's stupid, I know. Of course she wouldn't. My mouth is so dry I can barely speak.

'Hello. I'm your daughter, Alyssa Antonia Ward. You abandoned me when I was three months old. Please tell me why you did that.'

I don't think I'd use quite those words. But how can you know what you'd blurt out at such a moment? I watch her face, see shock, disbelief and denial flicker over it in the space of seconds. She then gets angry, abusive even, slams the door in my face, and that's it.

Or maybe not. Perhaps she invites me in, hugs me, bursts into tears, tells me how sorry she is, how she never wanted to let me go but had no choice. Asks me lots of questions. I've got lots of questions for her too, of course. We talk for hours. The emotion is overwhelming, unbearable. I couldn't picture any more. At that point I realised the feeling of pressure was the grey lady's hand on my arm. Her patronising smile was gone and she was asking was I all right, would I like a glass of water or a nice hot cup of tea? I took the tea. Hot drinks comfort me. While she was out of her sad little office I took a quick look at the file. And guess what? I found Estella's marriage certificate and a copy of the letter the agency had written her – with her address on. I quickly scribbled it down and slipped the bit of paper into my pocket. Then I discovered something else. Estella is widowed and has a daughter – Francesca – who's a couple of years younger than me. I've got a sister!

Well, a half-sister really. I was astonished, delighted, intrigued. I hadn't felt delighted or intrigued in a long time. I wonder what Francesca's like, if she resembles me at all. What kind of life does she have? God, how I'd love to meet her. Get to know her. Will I ever be able to do that?

The prison smell is still all over my hair and skin. Or so I imagine. Like gunshot residues, I can't shower it off yet. And I don't know what's happening to me – I've got all these strange sensations. The only thing I can compare it to is puberty. It feels like my body and mind are burgeoning somehow, out of control, being swept by longings and desires I kept suppressed during all the years of lock up, lock down, mice, roaches, bad food, disgusting coffee, noise, rage, violence, non-freedom. And shrinks, applying their subjective, stereotypical opinions and calling it science. That was the scariest thing of all. At least the judge didn't say I was mad. *Evil*, that was Mister Justice Dread's take on things.

As well as post and neo-feminists, we now have judges who are au fait with modern society, so I read in papers and magazines as I attempt to familiarise myself with this changed world. They no longer think there are buffets on tube trains. They're younger, and some of them are women; not that I'd necessarily expect more sympathy from a woman. They do normal, everyday things like going to the supermarket and taking their kids swimming.

How am I supposed to find the killer? The person for whose

crime I did the time? If this was a movie, one or two bleedingly obvious hints would have thudded on to my path by now and I'd be on the case, moving purposefully towards my aim of sweet revenge served very cold. As it is, I don't have a clue, don't even know where to start. Or what would happen, what I'd do if I achieved my aim. If I could prove who did it, get them a ten- or fifteen-year stretch and myself a good chunk of compo, would that help assuage the anger and bitterness that eats at my dark soul? I don't know. I don't think anything can make up for what I suffered. I should let it go. If I could find my mother and half-sister, be accepted by them, would that help?

I want love. Not so-called romantic love, which is not and never was the metaphor for salvation it's made out to be. Been there, done that, cut up the T-shirt and used it as a dishcloth. I want my life back. I want a past without the bad bits, a future. Most of all, a present. I've waited long enough. I tuned back in to the grey lady.

'Your birth mother—'

'What other kind is there?' I couldn't resist interrupting. Stupid, of course. You've got foster mothers, grandmothers, surrogate mothers, fairy godmothers. Wicked stepmothers. The term *birth* mother annoys me, I'm not sure why. It sounds somehow disre-spectful, as if a *birth* mother merits no more status than a lab rat or other variety of biological specimen. And sometimes she doesn't. Nowadays it's possible for a woman to give birth but not be named on the birth certificate as her baby's mother. How obliterating is that?

'Your mother hasn't replied to our letter. It's early days yet, of course.' Pause for frown and fiddling with pencil. 'You do realise she may not want any contact with you? People move on, remarry, start new families. A woman may never tell her husband that she once had a child by another man. She may be so ashamed and frightened that she tries to put the whole episode out of her mind.'

Well, thanks for that, lady. I cut the conversation short then. I had what I wanted – more than I'd expected. Unfortunately, however, logical thought deserted me at that point. I was desperate to go and see where my mother lived, maybe even get a glimpse of her. Of course I wouldn't approach her yet, I wasn't stupid enough to do that. I couldn't go during the day – I'd only just managed to schedule the visit to the charity by lying about job

48

interview times – so I had to go at night. That meant slipping out of the hostel. If I got caught I would be in big trouble. That evening I pretended I was going to bed early, something I often do anyway. I like to shut myself away in my room, however depressing it is, and read in peace. I ignored the baleful glances of Audrey, the warden who hates me. She's polite enough to my face, but I know Audrey thinks in clichés about leopards and unchanging spots, and would just love to catch me out in some misdemeanour that could send me straight back to the nick. And there I was handing her the opportunity on a gold plate, if only she knew. Audrey's the reason my deadline hasn't been extended to ten p.m.

Much later I crept out of my room along the deserted corridor and went down the back stairs to the small kitchen on the first floor where you can make tea, coffee and pot noodles. I opened the window, climbed out and slithered the few feet down the drainpipe, scuffing my jacket and jeans in the process. I climbed over the wall and walked quickly down the street of terraced houses, whose residents I'm sure just love having us as neighbours. At the end of the road I took a green double-decker bus into the city centre, then went to Central Station and caught a train to the market town near where my mother lives.

Estella. I love that name, although not the bitchy little character in *Great Expectations*. I was shocked at the cost of the return ticket – everything costs a fortune now – and I had to check that I had enough money for the bus back to the hostel. A cab was out of the question, of course. I hate being given pocket money like some soppy kid. I bet the kids get more. On the train I was nervous and sweating, thinking the few other passengers were giving me funny looks. Well, of course people stare at you if you look nervous. They wonder what's wrong. My thoughts jumped around, chattering and shrieking at me, driving me crazy.

The name Estella made me think of Dickens. Okay, I'm sure he was a great writer and everything – although some of his novels are a bit boring and depressing for my superficial tastes – but his behaviour in dangerous middle age wasn't very nice. Dumping his wife after twenty-two years and ten kids and making a prat of himself with some actress half his age because he reckoned he saw a certain innocence in her. Wonder if she would have kept her refreshing innocence after ten kids? And typical that he got his thong in a twist about dire Victorian social problems while

49

treating his wife and family like dirt. The abandoned wife wasn't invited to the great man's funeral in Westminster Abbey. I'd like to think she didn't lose any sleep over that, but I bet she did.

I looked at my A-Z before getting off the train. Estella really lives out in the sticks. Or woolly-back country, as Scousers term anywhere rural. Her house was on some narrow hill road, just your average semi. The houses were built around a big, dark, rocky field, with an orange-lit church spire looming over them. I kept to the edge of the field because I could hear some lads laughing nearby. I think they were drinking too, and I didn't fancy taking any of them on. I was scared, but my curiosity was stronger. I came to Estella's house and stopped.

I thought, I can't knock on her door, not at this time of night. That really would be thick. I'll just stand here for a bit and watch, maybe catch a glimpse of her if she comes to the windows. All the time I was conscious of what a stupid, terrible risk I was taking by coming here, pushing my luck big time; what if anyone at the hostel discovered I was missing? I tried not to think about that. I couldn't stay there much longer. The downstairs front room wasn't lit, but the hall light was on and so was the light in an upstairs room with a small window, probably the spare room.

I shivered with cold and fear, standing on the edge of the field by a clump of trees. Just as I was thinking I *really* have to go now, I caught a movement in the front bedroom; a curtain being pulled aside and a window shoved open.

I stared as a woman leaned out. She looked stricken, like she was gasping for breath. Was that her – my mother? What was wrong, was she ill? I stepped forward, agitated, forgetting to stay in the cover of the trees. She saw me then, I know she did. She looked straight at me. In the light from the street lamp I could see my eyes, my cheekbones, how my face would look in thirty-odd years time. It wasn't a bad face, in fact it was impressive. I was shaking, and felt like crying for the first time in – well, I don't know. Many years.

She disappeared suddenly, as if she had staggered backwards. I wanted to run, scream, get in that house, get to her. Tell her who I was, that I needed her and she needed me. She was ill, something was seriously wrong, and I had to help her right now. Just as I was about to sprint across the road, a man and woman came running out of the neighbouring house and banged on Estella's front door. The woman unlocked the door, but couldn't get it open.

'The chain's on,' she shouted. 'Get something to break it, *quick!*' Next thing I knew, an ambulance was screaming up the road.

I had found my mother at last. But was it too late?

She was still alive, I gathered that after a few minutes. But it was serious – a heart attack I heard one of the paramedics tell the frightened neighbour woman. I was appalled, in shock, on my knees in the damp grass as I stared at the scene, the flashing lights, listened to the raised, urgent voices. Estella was carried out of the house on a stretcher, wrapped in a blanket, an oxygen mask over her face. Her eyes were shut. The woman, fat with short, fair hair, went with her in the ambulance. I wanted to follow, but of course I had no bloody car. The man stared after the ambulance then went slowly back into his house. In a minute he would remember he had forgotten to lock Estella's door. Without thinking, I sprinted across the road and slipped inside. If someone else had been in the house they would have come out.

The porch was full of big, leafy plants, a thick-bodied spider on one wall. The front door was ajar. I pushed it open and walked into the hall, smelled soap and polish and a faint cooking smell mingled with perfume, like gardenias. Then I saw the four gardenias on the kitchen windowsill, their white blooms leaking scent into the air. There was an empty sherry glass on the table.

I walked around looking at pictures, photographs, a splayed paperback on the arm of a sofa. There were photographs of Estella and a man, presumably her husband, at various stages of their lives. And a girl, growing from laughing baby to smiling teen, to confident woman – Francesca, my half-sister. I was stunned by the resemblance between us; she even had the same kind of posture as me. And that smile. I swallowed, blinked away threatening tears. There was a big framed colour photo of Francesca on the sitting room wall, wearing an ivory silk wedding dress and veil, smiling at the camera as she signed the register. A tall, well-built guy stood next to her. Brown-eyed with dark-blond hair, he looked completely soppy about his new bride. Where did they live, how long had they been married? Did they have kids? Did Francesca know about me? Somehow I thought not.

51

I went upstairs to the spare room, which looked like a study. I saw the letter from the adoption charity lying crumpled on the desk. There was another letter addressed to them. Maybe Estella had just finished typing and printing it out when she got ill. Guilt and horror swept over me. Was this all my fault? Had I dealt my mother a fatal blow? I had to sit down.

I picked up the letter and turned it over. It was sealed, but not so dry that I couldn't peel it open.

I thought, how thick am I?? Touching this, touching things all over the house with my ungloved hands. This is unlawful entry, God knows what else. If I get caught I've done more than enough to put myself back inside for another bloody decade. But I'd gone too far now. And I had to read that letter. I pulled it out and unfolded it, tried to hold it steady.

She didn't want contact. With *this person* as Estella referred to me, her flesh and blood. She had her privacy, her rights, and if necessary she would take legal action to protect them. The tone of the letter was cold and furious, frightened. Denying, obliterating. *This person.* Was that how she regarded me, as some bloody nuisance who wanted to barge back into her life after all these years and screw it up again? Well, okay. I had expected this – hadn't I? Estella felt this way when she didn't even know I was a convicted – albeit wrongly convicted – murderer. It was no use, I had no chance. My quest was scuppered before it could even start.

Sitting at that desk in the silent house, the cold truth hit and shattered me. I realised I hadn't expected this, despite warning myself to be careful, not to hope for much. I had spun myself a web of golden, fairytale bullshit about this sweet, gentle mother who mourned for the long-lost baby daughter she had somehow been cruelly forced to abandon to the care of indifferent strangers. She would wonder how that baby was doing, what kind of woman she had become, if she would ever see her again and get the chance to explain everything. Make up for lost time, love her the way she had always wanted to do. Say 'I'm sorry.'

Life didn't work that way. Hadn't I learned anything by now? My mother was not sorry she had abandoned me; she probably regarded it as one of her most sensible life decisions. The disappointment, the hurt, was crushing. I was being obliterated all over again.

52

'No!' I was rocking backwards and forwards, groaning. 'No, *no*.'

I dropped the letter and leaned my head on the desk. I felt my mother's presence, palpable, breathing around me. I thought I could smell her. She was here and yet she wasn't. How was she doing in hospital? Was she still alive? Did she think of me at all? If so, it was only as a threat, as damage that needed to be limited. She didn't want me, did not want to know me. She probably never had. Welcome to your wake-up call, Alyssa! I felt like I couldn't stand it. But what choice did I have?

Something happened then, something broke inside me. I started to cry, great big sobs that shook my body. Ten years' worth of tears. It felt strange, horrible, messy, frightening. Not me. But who was '*me*'? I wasn't the long-lost daughter and sister about to be welcomed back into the thrilling warmth of the family fold. I was alone, I had nothing. No one wanted me. I was a bloody nobody.

The front door opened. I heard footsteps in the hall.

Chapter 7

'Hi Monique. Good to see you.' The young, blonde receptionist in tight trousers and black sweater smiled at her. 'Highlights and a trim, yeah? Sit down; let me take your coat. Gavin won't be long. Would you like a magazine?'

'No, thanks.' God knew what rubbish she might read to upset her, and she was upset enough already. Monique sat on the red leather sofa and inhaled the slightly pooey salon smell, overlaid with strongly perfumed hair products. She had brought a novel, a beautifully written story about a family trying to survive the siege of Leningrad. Just about as far removed from her own life as it was possible to be.

'How are you?' The receptionist reseated herself and glanced at her little blue china tips box. 'You look great.'

'Thanks.' Shame Monique did not feel great. Two days now, and she still could not untangle her wild thoughts or summon up the courage to confront Lauren about her secret sex life. This was crazy, what kind of mother was she? When had Lauren had sex with this mystery male? She must have skived off school. Monique also wondered – hoped! – whether Lauren was just fooling about, putting her fantasies into writing. She did have an overactive imagination. But strawberry flavour condoms were no fantasy. The receptionist's voice broke into her thoughts.

'Sorry, Monique, but Gavin's just told me he'll be about another five minutes. Can I get you some tea or coffee?'

She nodded. 'Coffee, please.' She looked out of the window at the clear blue September sky, at people hurrying past in the city street. The receptionist brought her a thin white porcelain cup of aromatic espresso with a creamy layer. That did not work its usual magic. Monique took out her mobile and called Conal. He answered, sounding sleepy.

'Sorry – did I disturb your Saturday morning lie-in?'

'No. I was just thinking about coffee and breakfast. About to drag myself out of bed and go down to make it. You're in Liverpool? At the hairdressers?'

'Yes. Just waiting for the master coiffeur.' Monique avoided looking at her reflection in the mirrored wall behind the receptionist's desk. The plethora of mirrors in hairdressing salons always made her feel awkward and self-conscious.

'Let me take a wild guess,' Conal said, breaking the silence. 'Lauren, right?'

'I still don't know what to do,' she sighed. 'There's no way I can tell her I rooted through her stuff – she'll go ballistic, she'll never trust me again. I always hoped we had the kind of relationship where she felt she could tell me anything, but obviously I'm wrong on that one. I'm so afraid of what she's got – could get herself – in to. But I don't know what to do. I'm such a crap mother.'

'Come on, of course you're not. Monique, teenagers never talk about that kind of stuff to their parents, no matter how much they love them. If that was you, would you tell your mum and dad?'

'No. But–'

'No, you wouldn't. Don't go beating yourself up. I can understand you're worried. So am I. But I'm pretty sure it's like we said – she's making all this up, fantasising about somebody she's got a crush on. Somebody she can never have.'

'God, I hope so! But what if she *is* having a relationship with an older man?'

'I know it happens, Monique, but I wouldn't freak yourself too much over horror stories you've heard in the media. Where's Lauren going to meet any older men?'

'Come *on*. Anywhere!'

'Okay, but look – most men wouldn't be stupid enough to have sex with an underage girl, even if they wanted to. They know they can end up in jail. And saying she led them on or that they believed she was older doesn't impress the courts any more these days, does it?'

'I wouldn't know.' Monique's voice hardened. 'I dropped her off at a mate's this morning – one of her few mates. She's

55

supposed to spend the day with this girl and stay for dinner; she said the mother would drive her home. I phoned to check. Never mind Lauren not trusting me, I feel like I can't trust her any more.'

'Try not to get angry. That won't help.'

'I've spoiled her, that's the trouble. I always felt I had to try and make up for her father's total bloody lack of interest. I couldn't deny her things, not when I had the money to buy her whatever she wanted. I thought, that's what money's there for.'

'And it is. Stop putting yourself down. You love Lauren and she loves you. You're a terrific mother, Monique.'

She sighed again. 'Thank you.'

'Are you going to talk to Janice about this at lunch?'

'No. It's private, I don't want to discuss it with anyone but you. And I love Janice, but I've got to admit she ain't one for keeping her big gob shut.'

'That's true.'

'I'd better go,' she muttered as Gavin came smiling up to her, shaking out a silky black gown. 'They're ready for me.'

'Okay. I'll see you later. Give Janice my regards. And try not to worry too much about Lauren.'

'I love you,' she whispered. ''Bye.' She hung up and finished her coffee.

Monique could hardly take in anything Gavin said to her because her head was too full of imaginary conversations with Lauren, conversations that did not, unfortunately, include any answers. Kids, she thought. Who the hell would have them, why did I bother? But she knew. Lauren was worth all the hassle. More than worth it. A few minutes later she pulled out her mobile again.

'Janice? Hi, it's Monique. Listen, I'm afraid I'll have to cancel lunch. Yes, I know you were. So was I. But Conal's mum decided to come for a quick weekend visit,' she lied, 'and we've got to pick her up at the airport later, en famille, so I just won't have time.' She couldn't face Janice, not today. Anyway, Janice would only moan about her husband. For Christ's sake, wasn't there anyone apart from Conal that she could have a laugh with, a *real* laugh? What would she do without him? Monique was horrified to find herself blinking back tears.

'You okay?' Gavin glanced at her in the mirror and paused, holding aloft the highlights comb.

'Yes, fine. Just got a hit of that stuff.' She indicated the little blue plastic tray of creamy tint. 'Makes my eyes water.'

'Oh. *Sorry*.' He moved it further away. 'Yes, it is whiffy. You seem a bit upset though, if you don't mind my saying.' He looked concerned, but there was a gleam in his eye. *'Is* anything wrong?' he murmured, eager as always to be the recipient of confidences. Monique knew Gavin regarded himself as an amateur psychologist in addition to re-toucher of dark roots and snipper of split ends.

'I'm fine,' she repeated. She wasn't one to spill out her soul to hairdressers, and never had been. She sat up straight and flashed him a smile. 'I'll have another coffee when you're done.'

'Sure.' Gavin nodded and resumed his deft manipulations with the highlights comb. He never could get Monique Thorn to open up to him. But he wouldn't pry any further and risk pissing her off. There were enough clients who'd tell you their life stories without being asked. Monique was looking great, he thought, if a little bit anxious today. She was forty, but looked a decade younger. Just as well, given that her husband actually was a decade younger. Gavin remembered the electrifying effect on his staff the last time Conal Thorn had come in to pick up his wife.

The salon was busy and the highlights, wash, trim and blow dry seemed to take forever. Why on earth had she picked a Saturday when she'd had the whole week free? Her head buzzing with caffeine, Monique was relieved to escape into the cool, autumn air. Liverpool city centre was crowded and she wasn't in the mood for shopping. She wasn't hungry either. She decided to drive straight home. When Lauren got in tonight she would sit her down and talk to her, just the two of them. She had to stop procrastinating and take control. Lauren might be furious, might hate her for a while, but surely she would come to realise that her mother's only motives were love and concern for her welfare? Monique hoped so.

She was out of the city and suburbs and driving too fast along twisting country lanes with blind corners when the Lotus choked, coughed its guts out and broke down. She felt stupid and furious sitting there in a canary yellow, incandescently expensive car that was knackered. An AA man arrived, inspected the engine and launched into an explanation to which she barely listened. Except for the fact that he couldn't repair it here and now, and it needed to be towed to a garage. Monique realised she wasn't far from home, just a ten- or fifteen-minute walk; if she hadn't been so preoccupied with Lauren it might have occurred to her to walk home first and then phone for help. She took her bag from the boot and headed off down the lane as he was on the phone making arrangements for the car to be collected.

The walk took longer than she expected, and the sunshine was warmer now. Monique ducked as she passed the Ecclestons' cottage, walking in a half crouch by the hedge so that neither Joanna nor Eric would see her. Maybe they were in their sprawling back garden, cutting, pruning and pulling heads off things as they drank tea and enjoyed the autumn sunshine. She should have gone round to commiserate with them about the burglary, but could not be bothered. Worry about Lauren blanked out everything else.

Monique walked on along the lane, hot and sweaty. Her feet were aching in the tight, black, high-heeled boots, and her jeans felt tight as well. Was she putting on weight? She'd been drinking a bit more these past few days. She reached the high brick mossy walls and stone gateposts of Bay House, typed the entry code and pressed the button to open the gates. Each gatepost was topped by a stone pineapple, a traditional sign of welcome. A red Mini was parked a few yards away on the grass verge. Who did that belong to? She didn't know anyone who owned a red Mini.

Monique headed slowly up the curving, tree-lined drive, looking across to the fields on her left and the elaborate garden on her right, with the stone fountain in the centre. Conal's gleaming, dark-green Jag XJ Sovereign was parked by the front door. He must have been out, probably to buy a couple of newspapers. They did not get any delivered. She opened the front door, hobbled in and dropped her keys on the table. She was panting now; being slim did not necessarily equate with being fit. She should make good, long country walks a regular thing.

'Conal?' she called. No answer. In the kitchen the coffee machine was on and there was a lingering odour of toast and grilled bacon. She picked up the coffee pot, sniffed and made a face. Must have been on for hours. Had Conal gone back to bed? She switched off the machine and went upstairs to get changed. What should she cook for dinner tonight? Cottage pie? Spare ribs

58

marinaded in soy sauce, ginger, chilli and garlic? Conal loved spare ribs. Served with rice or noodles.

Monique walked into the bedroom and stopped, her startled eyes drawn to a red splash on the carpet. It was a dress, the same bright red as the Mini in the lane, a dress that definitely did not belong to her. Next to the dress lay clumpy shoes, a denim jacket, and a beaded soft black leather bag. The bed was a wreck. The bathroom door was open, the shower running. She gasped as she heard Conal's voice, raised in anger.

'Just get out now, will you? I've told you, I can't—'

'Please,' a woman begged. 'Conal, please let me stay!'

Monique experienced a flash of shock that drained her body of strength. No, she thought. *No.* She dropped her bag, took a few steps forward and hesitated. Then she forced herself to walk into the bathroom. She stopped, staring. She saw and yet she did not see, because shock prevented her brain from taking in everything that was happening.

Conal stood there wet and naked. Monique thought dispassionately what a gorgeous body he had, the muscled arms, shoulders and torso, his skin texture enhanced by water droplets. She recalled meeting him at the party six years ago, her wonderful surprise, the feeling that miracles did happen after all – and to her. Why didn't she ever learn? If something seemed too good to be true it usually was. She looked at the girl, also naked, shining black hair cascading down her back. She had lethal-looking nails painted crimson. Her body was beautiful too, and she didn't look much more than twenty-three.

'Monique!' Conal caught sight of her and froze. 'Oh, Christ almighty. Look, please believe me – I swear, this *isn't* what you think!'

'What do I think?' Monique glanced at the girl, who had turned and was regarding her coolly, completely unfazed, a contemptuous expression in her hazel eyes. 'Who's this?' It was difficult to speak because her lips felt numb and stiff, like she'd had a local anaesthetic at the dentist. 'The next Mrs Thorn?'

'Well, I wouldn't say no. Who's *this*?' The girl smirked. 'Is it your mum, Conal?'

'This is Monique, my wife,' Conal shouted. 'And I love her. Now get out!'

'Your *wife*? God, you poor guy. No wonder you're desperate.

59

Conal, did no one ever tell you? Money really isn't every-thing.'

'First time I've heard *you* say that. Get dressed and get the fuck out of here! I should never have let you in – Monique, wait!' He lunged forward and tried to grab her arm. 'Please, I wasn't doing anything. For Christ's sake, let me explain!'

Monique dodged out of his reach. 'I don't think so. It's all very clear.'

She stared into his dark-blue eyes for a second. Wished that this was not true, not real, that she could go back in time and make it not happen. She felt old, humiliated, stupid, naive, all used up. And terrified. This was the start of her worst nightmare.

Shattering, searing hurt overwhelmed her. She turned, slammed the bedroom door on the nightmare and ran away screaming.

'Bad news about your mum.' Joe stood in the middle of the sitting room, hands in his coat pockets. 'I'm sorry. Will she be okay?'

'I hope so.' Frankie was exhausted, drained with crying. 'The hospital staff won't tell me much over the phone.' She sipped her white wine and put the glass on the coffee table. 'This is all I need, isn't it? Can't be just one major life trauma at a time.' She looked at him. 'Where have you been all night?'

'At a friend's. Someone from work. I told you yesterday evening I wouldn't be home. And this morning I wanted to walk for a couple of hours. Clear my head.'

Anger surged in her. She hated being swept along on this roller-coaster of emotion.'Your head seems pretty damn clear to me. You know exactly what you want.'

Joe sighed and rubbed his eyes. He looked pale in the sunlight. 'Do you think you should be sitting there in your dressing gown boozing away the afternoon? I bet you haven't eaten anything either. You're not helping yourself, falling apart like this.'

Frankie stood up. 'What am I supposed to do? My husband's told me he doesn't love me any more and wants a divorce, and now my mother's had a heart attack. For some strange reason, I'm a bit bloody distraught!' Heroine's life falls apart, she thought. Correct opening for a novel. You don't want something like Samuel Richardson's *History of Sir Charles Grandison*, in which good people do only good things. Happiness is boring. Stick your heroine up a tree and chuck rocks at her. Joe moved to the French windows and stared down into the street.

'I take it you're going to stay with her for a while?'

'I've got a flight at noon tomorrow. That was the earliest available.'

'This is important. You could have gone Business Class.'

She shrugged. 'I've booked it now.'

Joe turned, his dark eyes sad. 'Maybe this is the best thing for us at the moment.'

'What – my mother having a heart attack?'

'Of course not! I mean, we could do with some time apart.'

'I don't want time apart.' Frankie collapsed on to the sofa and started to cry again. 'I want to stay here and sort this terrible mess.'

'Frankie,' he said, his voice gentle. 'I've made up my mind. I'm very sorry, but that's the way it is. The sooner you accept it, the easier it'll be. I don't want to hurt you—'

'Stop saying that!' she wept. 'You *are* hurting me. All the time. Unbearably.'

'And I hate that. I know you feel terrible now – so do I, believe it or not. But you'll get through this. It'll be horrible for a while, for both of us. I'll miss you too when we split up. But I'm doing the right thing, Frankie. I know I am.'

Frankie wished she could keep herself together, be cool and strong and not give a damn. She had a headache and stomach ache, felt mysteriously ill. Of course that could be down to drinking as opposed to eating. He was right, she was not helping herself. She had to take care of herself, because if she didn't nobody else would.

'*Have* you got someone else?'

'Christ, not again. No!' he shouted. 'How many more times do I have to tell you?'

'You don't *tell* me anything, that's the problem. You just say you don't love me any more and want a divorce – that's it. What am I supposed to think?'

'Well, not that I've got a fucking girlfriend, because I haven't.' He started to walk out of the room. 'I'm going through some sort of crisis and I need to sort myself out. Sort my life out. I won't stay here and listen to any more of this bullshit.'

'Don't go.' She jumped up and ran after him. 'Joe, what's wrong, what the hell happened to us? I love you, you know that.'

She grabbed his arm. 'We didn't have any problems – did we?'

'No.' He was grey faced now. 'This is about me, not you.'

'How can you say that? What am I, a disinterested bystander?'

'I *mean*, none of this is your fault.'

'That makes me feel worse, not better!'

'I'm sorry. Look, Frankie, I'm not proud of myself for what I'm doing, and that's an understatement. But you'll get over it. Loads of people get divorced. They cope.'

'Well, good for them. I don't give a fuck about other people.' She followed him into the hall. 'Joe, don't go off and leave me alone again. I can't sleep, I can't eat. I'm going crazy here.'

He shook his head. 'I can't stand this.'

'*You* can't stand it? You create this situation then just walk away because you can't stand it. Typical bloody man.'

'Yeah. Be glad to get rid of me then, won't you?'

'No! Stay here, please.'

'I will.' He went into kitchen and got a couple of carrier bags. 'I'm just going to pick up some groceries. We've got to eat sometime, even if you don't feel like it now.'

'Okay. Let me come with you.'

'You can't, look at the state of you.' He stood back and surveyed her. 'Take a shower, get dressed, put some make-up on. Have a coffee. You'll feel better. We'll go for a walk to the beach later. I'll be back soon, I promise.'

'What will you do while I'm in England?' Frankie wiped away more tears as she followed him into the hall. 'See a lawyer? Get the locks changed?'

'Don't be daft. I might see a lawyer.' He put out one hand and touched her wild hair which crackled with static, her flushed, tear-stained face. 'Please, Frankie, try and get yourself together. I'm not worth all these tears.' He hugged her and she clung to him. 'I'll be back soon, okay? I promise. And I'll take you to Schiphol tomorrow.' He disentangled himself from her embrace. 'See you off.'

'Oh yes,' Frankie whispered as the front door closed. 'You'll see me off, all right.'

'How could you do this? You've ruined everything!'

Monique was running along the passageway and down the

stairs, screaming and crying, half-blinded by tears. Behind her the girl's voice was raised in angry questions, Conal yelling at her again to grab her clothes and get the fuck out. She was crying for his treachery, this awful betrayal, the humiliating, terrible, cliché tackiness of walking in to find your husband with another woman. Funny to some people – not to her. She couldn't believe how much it *hurt*. Her happiness and peace of mind was destroyed, gone in the space of seconds. She stumbled, recovered her balance and wiped her eyes on her sleeve. Conal dashed down the stairs after her, tying the belt of his bathrobe.

'Monique! *Wait*. For Christ's sake, listen to me. She's an ex-girlfriend who's been trying to find me. She just turned up here. I haven't clapped eyes on her for years. She wanted to get back with me again. Wanted money. I told her to get lost. I thought she'd gone, but she came back in the house and upstairs and—'

'Shut up!' Monique yelled. 'I don't want to hear. And don't you dare tell me it didn't mean anything and you're sorry, or I'll—'

'I'm not! I've got nothing to be sorry *for.*'

Through her tears she caught a flash of red and black as the girl flitted through the hall and out the front door. Red dress, red Mini. Scarlet woman.

Conal was white-faced. He swept back his dripping hair. 'You've got to believe me! Nothing happened, I swear.'

Monique collapsed weeping on to the sofa. 'I trusted you, I loved you so much. Too bloody much.'

'Monique, I haven't *done* anything! She knocked at the door and said hello, told me she'd just got back to the UK after living abroad for a few years. She used to run a bar in Spain.'

'Yeah. She looks that type.'

'She said she'd found me through asking around amongst friends in Liverpool. We had a chat, but when I realised she wanted a lot more than just to say hello to an old mate I told her to piss off.' Conal tried to take her in his arms, but Monique pushed him away. 'Why don't you believe me?' he cried. 'I'm your husband, I love you! Doesn't my word mean anything?'

'It might if I hadn't come home unexpectedly, walked into our bedroom and caught you naked in the shower with some tart who's also got her kit off! Strewn all over my bedroom floor. And you have the nerve to try to tell me nothing happened. It doesn't say

"yesterday" on my birth certificate, you know. I want you to leave,'
Monique sobbed. 'Just get out. Now. The first time I saw you I
thought you were too good to be true, and I was bloody right!'

'I'm not going anywhere. This is my house too, you know. And
I'm not going anywhere because, for the last time, I didn't fucking
do anything!'

'Shut up,' she screamed again, bunching her fists so that her
nails made little red half-moon marks on her palms. 'Don't insult
me with stupid, crazy lies. I won't listen.'

'You're bloody well going to listen. I'm not lying to you!' He
grabbed her and spun her round to face him. 'Nothing –
happened.'

'Get off me!' She struggled in his arms. 'I don't want you to
touch me.'

'Monique, will you for—'

'Get *off.*' She broke free, dashed out of the sitting room and
across the hall, up the stairs and back into their bedroom. She got
the key from Conal's bedside drawer, ran into the dressing room
and unlocked the gun cupboard. Her hands were shaking. She
wrenched the oiled, polished rifle off its mounts. The gun was
loaded of course; it was nearly always loaded in case burglars
came calling, thinking Bay House was another soft rural touch
with rich pickings. Conal appeared in the doorway.

'Oh Christ!' He blanched. 'Put it down. Monique, come on, put
the gun down.' He stepped back, trying to shield himself. 'This is
stupid – it's crazy. You've made a terrible mistake.'

'Yes!' she screamed, tears dripping off her nose and chin.
'You're right, I did make a terrible mistake. Sitting in the hairdressers, cancelling lunch with a friend, worrying about Lauren.
All the time thinking how much you loved me, how you cared,
how bloody lucky I was. You knew Lauren was out for the day,
and you didn't expect me back for hours, did you? How long have
you and that bitch been . . .?'

Sobs choked her and she couldn't go on. She raised the rifle and
settled the stock on her shoulder, curled one trembling finger
around the trigger. 'I thought you loved me,' she wailed.

'I do! Monique, *please* believe me, you've got this all wrong!'
Conal backed away. He looked like he was going to faint. 'Her
name's Lindsay Roberts, you can check her out. An ex-girlfriend,
like I said. I stopped seeing her before I met you.'

'And now you're seeing her again. You dirty, betraying bastard!'

'I'm not! Why won't you listen, why do you want to believe the worst? Do you think so little of me that some woman could just turn up here and I'd. . .! Monique, don't!' Conal shouted as she levelled the gun, his eyes glittering with terror. 'Calm down, for Christ's sake. I'm not Gerry, I'm not like that bastard you were married to before. Come on, think! You could seriously injure me – kill me, if you shoot.'

Monique trembled all over. 'That's the general idea, lover.'

'Put the gun down. *Please*. This is crazy. Let's talk, sort it out.'

'Bit late for talk, I'm afraid.' She shook back her hair. Tears dripped on to the rifle.

'No! Monique, don't!'

She squeezed the trigger. It took more strength than she had anticipated. And more time. Her finger hurt as she squeezed harder. Was she going to get a result, would this thing actually go off? She sobbed and trembled, then screamed in fright as Conal ducked and lunged forward. He meant to rush her and bring her down.

Monique fired.

Chapter 8

'I got such a shock when I found this!'

Frankie unfolded the letter her mother had written to the adoption and counselling charity. She had to speak in a low voice because the cardiac ward was crowded and there was only a flowered curtain for privacy. It seemed busy and chaotic after the quiet efficiency of the intensive care unit. 'You obviously didn't have time to post it before you–' She paused. 'Got taken ill. Mum, what on earth is going on?'

So here it was, another evil moment she had feared and dreaded for almost four decades. Estella had sometimes wondered what she would be doing if and when it occurred. Well, here she was lying in a hospital bed after a heart attack, sipping tea. She felt better now, stronger. Physically, anyway. The clot-busting drugs the doctors had speedily administered in Casualty had done the trick; she would walk out of here with most of her heart muscle still functioning. She looked at her daughter.

'You want to know what's going on? I could ask you the same question.'

Frankie flinched. 'What do you mean?'

'You look terrible. As if you've been crying for days. Something's happened, hasn't it? Not just my little episode.'

'I'd hardly describe your heart attack as a little episode. Look, we're not talking about me. What about this letter, who's–'

'Those diplomats giving you the run around?' Estella was not just trying to put off the evil moment, she really was worried about her daughter. 'I've told you before, you should give up that job and concentrate on writing.'

'*Mum.*'

'Have more faith in your talent. I'm sure Joe wouldn't mind supporting you while you give it a go. What is it, love?' Estella reached out one hand as Frankie bowed her head and started to cry. The letter fell on the bedspread. 'Tell me,' she whispered. 'Don't think you'll worry me. The worst is not knowing.' That was true.

'Joe doesn't love me any more,' Frankie sobbed. 'He wants a divorce.'

'A divorce? Doesn't *love* you . . .?' Estella was silent, shocked. She stroked her daughter's pale, smooth hand. Frankie's gold wedding band shone in the sunlight, and her diamond engagement ring sparkled. 'I don't understand. I thought you two were so happy.'

'So did I until a couple of months ago. He just . . . I don't know . . . changed.'

'I know you were worried about him. But you obviously weren't expecting this. Has he got another woman?'

'He swears not. It's *me* he's leaving me for, not someone else.' Frankie wiped her eyes. 'Real confidence booster that, isn't it?' She looked at her mother. 'You're taking this incredibly calmly.'

'I know.' Estella nodded. 'I'm surprising myself. If you'd told me this time last week I would have panicked.' She paused. 'Spent my whole silly life panicking.'

'Of course my problems are nothing compared to what's happened to you. My husband's leaving me – but you could have died.'

'Well, it's not an importance competition.' Estella squeezed Frankie's hand. 'I'm so sorry, love. I was very fond of Joe, you know that. But if he can hurt you like this, turn your life upside down, then that's it. I don't want to know him any more. You're my priority. And self-preservation should be your priority now.'

'Ten years of marriage,' Frankie muttered. 'All for nothing.'

'Better ten than twenty or thirty. You're still young, you can start again. You're talented, strong, got everything going for you. I know it's hard to believe now,' Estella said, 'but you will be all right. You'll get over this.'

'That's what Joe said. It sounds a lot nicer coming from you.' Frankie shook her head, staring at her mother. 'I can't believe how calm you are about this!'

Estella grimaced. 'I don't think I'd be calm if your husband walked in here right now.'

'I don't want to sound like some pathetic victim. The wronged wife. Joe's unhappy, he's not himself. He says he's going through some kind of crisis.'

'Yes. The one that tends to start around age forty.'

'There's two sides to every story. Maybe there were signals I didn't pick up on because I was too tired and busy, too self-absorbed.'

'Don't you dare blame yourself!' Estella sat up straighter. 'You were never so busy you ignored your marriage. I often thought you bothered too much about him. If you always have to worry about how someone feels, what they're thinking, what you might be doing wrong – is it worth it? You've got no life of your own.' She paused. 'I don't imagine Joe's fretting about your feelings, is he? Not if he can devastate you like this. Have some pride,' she urged. 'Don't fall to pieces because some man doesn't want you any more.'

'Joe isn't *some man*. He's my husband and I love him. I want us to stay married.'

Estella nodded. 'I realise that. But given what you've told me, it may not be possible. I just want you to be strong. To know you'll get through this.'

Frankie was silent, wiping away more tears. 'Can we change the subject for now?' She picked up the letter and smoothed it out. 'Tell me about this. What's going on?'

Estella felt panicked. 'I'm so frightened. I don't want to lose you,' she blurted, calm sensibility suddenly deserting her.

'Mum, what the hell are you talking about? Lose me? There's no way that could happen. Don't get so upset. Okay, I'm one to talk! You'll never lose me. I promise you.' Frankie held out the letter. 'It says here that this woman, Alyssa Ward, is your daughter.' She looked at Estella. 'That's not a mistake, is it?'

'No. Unfortunately.' It was Estella's turn to grope for tissues. 'I've dreaded this,' she muttered. 'For years. I was just starting to think it would be all right, that nothing would happen.' She shook her head. 'Stupid of me to think I was due for a bit of peace, wasn't it?'

'Tell me what happened.'

Estella leaned back against her pillows. 'Before I met your

father I had a relationship with another man. After a few months I got pregnant. I was terrified, didn't know what to do. I didn't want it, but I was also frightened of having a termination. I didn't dare go to our family GP, and there weren't those clinics they've got now. Not where I lived anyway. I read a novel in which some female character drank a bottle of gin and sat in a bath of hot water to bring on a miscarriage. I tried that, but it didn't work. He—'

'Hang on . . . he? Who? What was his name?'

'Oh. His name was Philip. Philip Ward. He was an accountant with a city firm, doing very well. I thought he was a cut above and I was flattered when he took up with me. I dreaded telling him about my pregnancy – I thought that would be the end of us. But when I finally got the courage to tell him he was pleased, proud. Seemed to think he'd proved himself a real man. At least that was the impression I got. He wanted me to have it, and eventually I agreed. He said we could live together, get married if I wanted. My parents were ashamed. And furious. They tried to keep it a secret from everyone they knew. Talk about Victorian values! I hated them for that. It was their grandchild, after all.' Estella clenched her fists. 'They could take that attitude and still go to Mass every Sunday. My mother often went a couple of times during the week too.'

Pity welled up in Frankie. 'So what happened then?'

'Philip and I moved in together. I know I should have been grateful not to be abandoned and all that. People kept telling me how lucky I was. I was secretary to the headmaster at a local school, but I had to give that up. It was a Catholic school, and they weren't too keen on the idea of an unmarried woman waltzing around with a pregnancy bump. It was terrible when the baby was born – I didn't feel any of those feelings you're meant to feel. And I'd hated being pregnant. It all just felt like the most awful burden. Endless crying, feeding, nappy changing – they didn't even have disposable nappies then. Sleep deprivation. As if that wasn't bad enough, people thought I should be bursting with happiness because I'd got what all women were supposed to want.' Estella paused. 'And then . . . Philip changed.'

'How?'

'Oh, it started off as the old story. Being proud and pleased at fathering a child didn't translate into the idea that he might actually help to look after it. He wouldn't lift a finger. I was depressed and exhausted. Things just deteriorated between us. He got aggressive, we had terrible rows – that's when he was home to have them. One row we had, he punched me in the stomach and kicked me a few times. I thought it was all my fault because I couldn't love him or the baby. He named her Alyssa Antonia. It's all about love, isn't it?' she sighed. 'If it's there, you'll do anything. But if not . . .' She shrugged. 'Next thing I found out he was having an affair.'

'Oh God.' Frankie groaned. 'Look,' she said, anxious at the strain on her mother's face, 'you don't have to tell me everything now. You're upset enough.'

'I'm all right. Don't worry. The affair with this woman – Vivienne, her name was – had been going on for a couple of years. They broke up then got together again.' Estella grimaced. 'After I gave birth. It could have been before that, for all I knew.

'How did you find out? Did he tell you about her?'

'A neighbour told me, someone I used to have coffee with occasionally. She came round one afternoon looking shocked. Enjoying herself too, though. She said she'd seen Philip in town, holding hands with some skinny blonde in a black PVC mac. He wasn't acting like she was his sister. When Philip got home that night I confronted him. He was late and drunk because he'd been to the pub – or been with her. He denied it at first, I don't know why he bothered to do that. But then he admitted he was seeing someone. He said she was a lovely girl who'd make a much better mother than a cold, heartless bitch like me. I said maybe this lovely girl would like to try out her mothering skills on the screaming brat upstairs, because I'd had enough. He started knocking me about, beating me up.' Estella shuddered. 'From then on things got even worse. Sometimes he was so angry and full of hate that I thought he'd kill me. I don't want to tell you everything,' she muttered. 'I can't. One night he was . . . hurting me. When he finally let me go, I decided that was it and I was leaving him. But he caught me and started attacking me again. I managed to grab a half full bottle of Scotch off the sideboard and brain him with it. He went down like a sack of rice. I was terrified I'd killed him.'

'My God!' Frankie stared at her. 'What happened then?'

'He started swearing and groaning after a minute, so I knew he'd live. But I had to get out before he recovered. I crawled upstairs and threw some things in a bag. I didn't have much. The baby had stopped crying for once. I went into her room and looked down at her, asleep in her cot. She looked so peaceful. That was the first time I felt something, got some idea of how it could be, how it should feel. But I couldn't take her with me – I didn't know how I'd look after myself, never mind a baby.' Tears filled her eyes. 'I said goodbye . Told her I was sorry.'

'Oh, *Mum*.' Frankie got up and put her arms around her. 'I'm sorry too. You went through hell.'

'I never went back. Never saw her again. Or him. I stayed with my parents for a couple of weeks. I had nowhere else to go and they couldn't quite bring themselves to slam their door in my face. Besides, I didn't have my little bastard with me, did I?' Estella's voice was bitter. 'I found an administrative job in an engineering company, and got myself a flat. I thought the best thing to do was try to put Alyssa out of my head. Like she'd never happened. So I just let her go. I despised myself for that, thought I was a terrible person. Sometimes I still do.'

Frankie grabbed her hand. '*No*. That's—'

'Let me finish. After a while I met your father. I kept meaning to tell him what had happened, but I could never do it. He was a lovely man, and I felt guilty for not being honest with him. Sometimes it was on the tip of my tongue to just blurt out everything. Then I'd think, what's the point? I might hurt him terribly; he'll think I've deceived and betrayed him. He'll be right. It will look even worse because I waited so long. He might leave me. Or he might not. But even if he didn't we'd never be the same again. I couldn't take the risk. The more time passed, the more impossible it became. So in the end I never told him. Or you.'

Frankie took a deep breath. Her mother had worked so hard all these years to bury that horror and deny her feelings. No wonder she was terrified now. 'You won't lose me,' she repeated, her voice gentle. 'I promise. There's no way that will happen. You're my mother and I love you. That will never change. You do believe me?'

Estella nodded, gripping her hand. 'I don't want to see *her*.'

'You mean Alyssa Ward?'

'Yes. I can't. Why now, anyway? What does she want after all these years?'

71

'Obviously, to meet you and talk. Ask you some questions.'

'I don't want to meet her. Or answer any questions.'

'Well, you don't have to. It's your decision.' Frankie hesitated. 'How old would she be now?'

'Thirty-eight. Two years older than you. Why?'

'I once read somewhere that adopted people often don't seek contact with their real parents – or parent – until they're in their thirties or forties. Or if they have children of their own that sometimes makes them want to find out more about their families. As she's been to this charity, I'm sure they will have advised her not to expect too much. She won't be hoping for some fairy-tale reunion.'

'How can you be sure? We don't know anything about her. And I don't want to know anything. I mean that. I won't change my mind.'

'Okay. All right.' Frankie looked away, fell silent. She dared not upset her mother more by revealing the treacherous thought that occurred: Estella might not want to meet Alyssa Ward, but she herself did. I've got a half-sister, she thought, taking it in at last. A thrill and painful longing ran through her. For a second she even forgot Joe. A sister! *'There is no friend like a sister, in calm or stormy weather.'* Somebody to talk to, share burdens with. How wonderful. Of course not all sisters had that ideal relationship with one another. Still.

Panic gripped her. Her mother could have died from this heart attack. Suppose she had another, fatal this time? Joe was going to divorce her. She could end up with nothing, nobody. Be all alone in a cruel world. She gave a little gasp of terror. She wanted to know this sister. She had to meet her.

'Are you all right?' Estella asked. 'You've gone pale.' She forced a smile. 'Don't want you joining me in the next bed, do I?'

'I'm fine.' But Frankie felt cold. She got up and looked out of the window, blinking in the sunlight. Down below she could see parked cars, an ambulance stopping. She had to be very careful, of course, not allow her vulnerability to get the better of her. She knew nothing about Alyssa Ward.

'You be careful,' Estella warned.

Frankie turned, flushing. 'What do you mean?' Did her mother guess her thoughts?

'She might be a criminal. Or mad. Suppose she wants revenge?'

72

'Oh, come on.'

'It's possible. I think she knows where I live. That night I was taken ill, I was in the front bedroom phoning Carole for help when I saw someone outside, standing at the edge of the field. It looked like they were watching the house. It was too dark, I couldn't see if it was a man or woman. But it might have been her. And I'd got the letter that same day. Bit of a coincidence.'

Frankie stiffened. 'It probably was just coincidence. That could have been anybody. A passer-by, a dog walker.' An opportunist burglar, she thought but did not say.

'Whoever it was didn't pass by. He or she stood and watched the house. And I didn't see any dog.'

'Alyssa Ward can't possibly know your address.' Frankie felt a prickle of alarm. 'They – the social services or this charity or whoever – surely wouldn't give it to her without your permission?' She walked back to the bed and sat down.

'I don't think it works like that. Somebody's address isn't confidential information.'

'It should be in this case.'

'Even if it was, she could easily have got copies of my birth and marriage certificates, and got help from this adoption charity. They have people who investigate and locate missing family members for you, if you want. And there's the Electoral Register. There's all kinds of easy ways to find out where some-body lives. Maybe those interfering social workers did give it to her. They think they're God, those people. You post that letter I wrote them,' Estella said, clenching her hands again. '*Please*. Today!'

'I will. I promise.'

'And phone. Complain. Making a fuss is the only way you get anywhere these days. Tell them not to pester me, that they've got no right. Threaten legal action, that'll put the wind up them.'

'I'm sure there's no need to resort to threats. But I'll make sure they leave you alone. Mum, please try not to worry, you won't do yourself any good. You must try and rest, relax. I'm here, you've got me. You've got Val and other friends. Everything's going to be okay.'

Frankie wished she could believe that. Misery and apprehen-sion swept over her again. If only Joe still loved her, if only he was here to give her support. It would mean so much. But she had to get used to doing without that. And she'd had plenty of practice lately.

'I don't want to see her. I won't – no one can make me!' Estella started to cry. 'What am I going to do? Oh God, why did this have to happen?'

Chapter 9

'Don't shoot again! Don't kill me!'

Conal staggered back, ashen-faced and terrified, clutching at his upper arm. Blood flowed between his clenched fingers and trickled over the back of his hand. 'Monique, no! Think what you're doing.'

Ancient plaster dust floated down and gave his dark hair a white dusting, like icing sugar. Monique dropped the rifle and sank dizzy and trembling to her knees, the gun's roar reverberating in her ears. The barrel really did smoke. The smell was horrible, metallic like blood. And there was enough of that.

'Oh God!' she sobbed. She could not believe what she had just done.

Go on, she urged herself. Finish the job, you pathetic, sad, cowardly wimp. But she was too drained to move. All she could do was stare at his blood on the pale blue-carpet. It was probably less than it looked. How much blood did the human body contain – seven, eight pints? She remembered visiting her GP when she'd suffered heavy periods for a few months; he had given her a patronising little lecture about how a 10 ml test tube of blood looked like nothing, but if you smashed it on the floor you could be forgiven for thinking there had been a massacre. In other words, don't be a hypochondriac, Missis.

'Think what you're doing,' Conal repeated. 'You could get fifteen or twenty years if you murder me – more! You'll lose this house, all your money. You'll lose Lauren. Is that what you want? What will she do without you? Your parents are dead, there's no one else who'd have her. If you don't care what happens to me or yourself, think of her.' His legs gave way and he slid to the floor, leaning against the door post. 'Monique, please. Drive me to A & E. I could be bleeding to death here.'

'No you're not.' Her voice was flat, small, numb. 'The blood's bright-coloured, oxygenated. Arterial blood would be darker. I only winged you.'

'What do you know? You're not a doctor. I need urgent medical help. Come *on*.'

She got to her feet, staring at him. Her handsome husband didn't look so cool and sexy now, bleeding and terrified for his life. He looked colourless, shrunken, diminished. 'I could lose Lauren anyway if I help you now.' She paused. 'What's to stop you telling the doctors and the police that I tried to murder you?'

'I won't. I promise. I'll say it was an accident.'

'I don't think the law allows me to plead provocation. That's only for men who murder their wives and girlfriends. You and your girlfriend –' Monique choked back more tears. 'You could get me out of the way, locked up with the drug addicts and nut jobs. Have this house and my money all to yourselves.'

Conal shook his head, his eyes desperate. 'She's *not* my girl-friend! I told you what happened, and it's the truth. I know how it must have looked, but I swear I'm innocent. I'd never cheat on you. I love you.' He shifted and gasped, his face creased in pain. 'Please help me, I'm in agony here.'

Monique's voice cracked. 'And that's my problem because *what?*'

'Because you don't want to kill me for something I didn't do and get banged up for the next decade,' he shouted, his eyes full of tears.

Monique stooped and picked up the gun again. She chewed her bottom lip.

'I'll say I lost control and did it in the heat of the moment. That's what all those guys who murder women say. And I'd be telling the truth.'

'The truth is, I didn't *do* anything.'

'I'm warning you. I'll kill you if you tell any more lies.'

'I'm not lying!' Conal shouted, panicked again. He cringed, tried to wriggle backwards. 'Calm down for fuck's sake, get your head together. I love you, how many more times do I have to tell you that? This is really about your first marriage, isn't it? You couldn't trust that bastard Gerry and now you think you can't trust me.'

'Gosh, wonder how I got that impression?'

'I'm not like him.' Conal's voice dropped to a whisper, his lips pale and stiff. 'I never was, never will be. I haven't cheated on you, Monique. I'd never hurt you like that. For God's sake, believe me, *please*.'

His insistence that he was innocent, even at loaded gun point, made Monique waver. Suppose, just suppose, he was telling the truth? That was a low blow, to mention Gerry. But he was right, this was partly about her first marriage. Monique had sworn to herself that she would never again allow any man to cheat on her, humiliate her, tolerate him making her life an ongoing hell of misery. She couldn't bear the thought that it had happened again. But maybe she was wrong. She hadn't stopped to think, had she? Just reached for a gun, like some psycho. Shoot first, think later. If at all.

Conal was shivering now, in shock. Yes, he did need urgent medical help. Monique loosened her grip on the gun, knelt and laid it back on the carpet. The white-hot heat of anger was gone. She couldn't kill him now, could not even contemplate it any more. He was right, there was no way she wanted to get sent to prison and leave Lauren alone. And Conal did love her, of course he did. Monique knew it, felt it, basked in it every day.

Why would he suddenly stop loving her, cheat on her like she was nothing to him? And why be so stupid and careless as to let that girl come here when she or Lauren might walk in unexpectedly at any moment? He could not be sure that wouldn't happen. It would be a lot more sensible to meet her somewhere else. And the girl did seem a hard-faced character, standing there naked and smirking, unfazed by the sudden appearance of The Wife. Maybe she made a habit of stripping off her kit in front of men she fancied.

Tears flowed down Monique's reddened, ravaged face as one doubt after another crowded in and overwhelmed her. None of this was Conal's style. He could be telling the truth. She had got it wrong, overreacted big time. The enormity of what she had done started to sink in.

'Oh God!' she whispered. 'Oh God, Conal, I'm sorry!'

She was naive, an imbecile, a fuck-up from start to finish. She should shoot herself instead of Conal. What had she done? She could have killed him! And what had she done to their marriage? Could he ever forgive her?

'Monique,' Conal groaned. '*Please* . . . help me put some clothes on . . . drive me to A & E. Or phone an ambulance if you're not up to driving. I need treatment. I can't stay stuck here like this any longer.' He pressed three fingers to his wrist. 'I think my pulse is getting weaker.'

'I will,' she gasped. 'I'll help you, I'll help you. Oh God, I'm so sorry!'

'Monique!' a nervous female voice called from downstairs. 'Conal? Hello?'

They stared at one another in fright. 'It's Joanna.'

'Christ,' Conal whispered. 'That dozy slapper must have left the front door open when she ran out.'

'Hello? Where are you?'

Monique clapped one hand to her mouth. 'She's coming upstairs.'

Joanna bloody interfering Eccleston, barging in here to bore them with something else they didn't give a toss about. Monique started forward, tripped over the rifle and fell on her hands and knees. The rifle swung round and skittered a few inches towards Conal, the barrel pointing straight at him. He cringed, and gave a cry of fright.

'Watch what you're–'

Joanna reached the top of the stairs and Monique realised the panting meant she had brought her senile, slobbering black labrador with her. She had thought there was something seriously amiss with Joanna's fitness level. The dog stopped and barked, then began to growl low in its throat.

'Stop that, Minty, behave yourself. Where are your manners? Oh, there you are,' Joanna called, spotting Monique. 'I just thought I'd pop round and update you about our burglary.' She looked like the Queen in her country outfit of head scarf, green quilted anorak and wellies. 'We had another phone call from the police earlier, some detective actually. The stupid young man said–'

They were never to find out what the stupid young man said. Joanna's eyes widened in shock as she took in the scene, the rifle lying on the bloodstained carpet and Conal sprawled against the door post, grey-faced and bleeding, his hair sprinkled with plaster dust.

'Oh, my God!' She took a step back, one hand to her mouth. The labrador barked again. 'What's *happened*?'

Monique got to her feet. She was unable to answer immediately. She could only think of police and prison, of losing Lauren. Losing Conal. Crimes of passion might make absorbing films or novels, but in reality they were just stupid, cruel, futile, tragic acts. Stupid most of all. She stared at the gun. Suppose she had killed Conal; suppose he was lying here dead now because of her crazy jealousy? She needed to sort herself out. Big time.

Monique found her voice and faced the round-eyed, quivering Joanna who looked as if she feared somebody was about to gun down her and stinky old slobber-chops Minty.

'Help!' she screamed. 'Call an ambulance, *quick*. Conal's had a terrible accident!'

Back in her mother's chilly, silent house Frankie poured herself a vodka and tonic and nibbled a few macadamia nuts. Then she remembered she had to eat properly, so she made herself toast and a cheese omelette, and ate an orange afterwards. The sun faded and the afternoon darkened as the sky clouded over. When she had finished eating she picked up her drink and trailed around the house looking at pictures and photographs, missing her father, missing Joe, feeling isolated and heartbroken by the events that had blown up out of nowhere. The phone rang and she answered it fearfully, hoping it wouldn't be the hospital with bad news about her mother. She had had her fill of bad news.

'It's Val. How's your Mum, love?'

Frankie closed her eyes in relief. 'Better than she was. I left her sleeping. The nurses say she needs a lot of rest.'

This Alyssa Ward business wasn't helping her mother get that rest. Frankie had posted the letter. She longed to meet Alyssa, but was afraid of what it might lead to, and did not want to risk landing herself in some situation she couldn't control. Another one! Most of all she hated the idea of deceiving her mother. If Estella found out she would regard it as a betrayal, and it would confirm her deepest fears about losing her daughter's love and being abandoned.

'I won't pop in this evening then, it might be too tiring for her. Are you going back?'

'Yes, around six-thirty.' It was a long, cold walk to and from the hospital; Frankie had no car and public transport was not really an option around here. But she didn't mind walking, as the exercise helped rid her system of adrenalin. She said goodbye to Val and hung up. Her mobile rang and she dashed into the living room and pulled it out of her bag, her hand shaking. She could not stop hoping that Joe would call to tell her he'd had a change of heart. But even if he did and they stayed married, how could she live with the fear that he might some day have another 'crisis', perhaps in three, five, ten years' time? The older she got, the more difficult it would be to start again.

'Hello?'

'Where's my money, bitch?'

She gasped. *'What?'* The man's voice was soft, with a foreign accent she could not place. It wasn't Dutch. Could it be eastern European? Whatever. This was nasty, but obviously a mistake.

'You've got the wrong number.' She wanted to add *'you moron'*, but did not dare. Frankie had not expected to get wrong numbers on a mobile but it happened frequently, especially when she was abroad. Shaken, she hung up and dropped the phone on the sofa. The door bell startled her further, three long sharp rings. The mobile jangled again, joining in the racket. She grabbed it, her heart racing.

'Don't you hang up on *me*, Francesca Sayle!' The man's voice was louder now, angry. 'What are you doing, you and your fucking useless man, to get my money? One hundred and fifty thousand Euros. I don't let anyone get away with owing me. *Ever.* Not money, not anything. Your man stole something else from me too.'

Frankie had to sit down. 'I don't . . . what *is* this? Who are you?'

'You know. You better be working on it. Not much time left.'

One hundred and fifty thousand Euros was about a hundred grand. *One hundred thousand pounds*! 'I don't owe anybody money,' she protested, horrified. 'Neither does my husband.' Although how would she know? Joe never told her a damn thing lately. What the hell was going on? What had he got himself into?

Her voice trembled. 'You've made a mistake.'

'No mistake, bitch. Don't fuck with me. You don't get my

money soon, I kill you. You and your thief husband. I blow your heads apart. Not pretty, eh? Someone steals from me, I steal back. Always. I take everything – including their life. He's a nobody, so are you. Two dead nobodies, if you don't get my money.'

He hung up. Frankie had only ever heard people talk that way in very bad films, and the language would normally have made her laugh. Or groan. But this was real, this man knew her name and it sounded as if he meant every word. She dropped the mobile again and sat staring at the photograph on the wall of herself and Joe on their wedding day. She looked so naively happy, stupidly confident. Would she have put on that big cream silk frock and floaty veil, made all those mind-blowing promises, if she'd known what lay ahead? Not bloody likely. She dialled Joe's work number, his mobile, and finally their home. No answer. *What* money? She had to talk to him, but where was he?

She jumped up as the door bell rang again. She crept into the hall and saw a shadow behind the frosted glass of the porch. She did not want to answer the door, not after that phone call. The shadow disappeared. She stumbled into the kitchen and wrenched the handle of the back door. Of course, it was locked. It had been locked when she arrived and she couldn't find the key, which normally hung on a hook inside one of the kitchen cupboards along with the shed and garage keys. Carole the neighbour didn't have it either. Frankie leaned on the draining board, her head in her hands.

How could this happen? She wasn't in danger now, surely, on top of everything else? Why didn't Joe answer? She ran back into the living room, got her mobile and dialled his numbers again, left a message on the voice mail.

'It's Frankie. I had this weird, horrible phone call. Some thug says you – we! – owe him a hundred grand.' Her voice shook. 'He says he'll kill us both if we don't get the money soon. You've got to tell me what's going on. Call me back. *Now*.'

She put the phone on the coffee table and wiped her sweating palms on her jeans and jumper. The jumper rode up, revealing several centimetres of smooth, flat stomach. Frankie shivered. It wasn't yet time for the heating to switch itself on and she wasn't warm enough – she needed a cardigan. The comforting, long, thick, black one with the pockets stuffed with perfumed cotton handkerchiefs and cellophane-wrapped lemon sherbets. She walked out of the living room and turned to go upstairs. A sudden scrabbling sound came from the kitchen.

She stopped and froze. It was gloomy twilight outside now, the wind rising, raindrops tapping the windows like ghostly fingernails. She heard a click. Someone was fiddling with the back door lock, trying to get in. There was no time to phone the police.

She dashed down the hall to the kitchen and grabbed the yellow-handled hammer from the wooden clothes pegs box her father had made years ago. She held it poised, her arm trembling and her heart pounding with terror. Another click and the door opened. Rain and cold air rushed in.

Frankie found herself staring into clear grey eyes like her own, which widened with shock at the sight of her. A pale, oval face framed by damp, dark-chestnut hair. The face was beautiful, slightly older. More lived in, more lines around the eyes. It was the face of someone who had known torment.

'Who the hell are you?' Frankie croaked, dry-mouthed. But she knew. She lowered the torch. They stared at one another.

'Francesca!' the intruder whispered.

Chapter 10

God almighty, what's she doing here? I thought the house was empty!

A hell of a way to meet my new sister. First and last time, judging by the look on Francesca's face. Don't tell me I've blown it already. If I have, it's my own fault.

I can't believe how we resemble one another. Never mind sisters, we could be twins. Although Francesca looks like she's led a more comfortable, sheltered life. I don't imagine she ever got sent down for murder. Or anything else. Her skin, hair and clothes look a lot better too.

'I'm sorry! Look – this is all wrong.' Tell me. I'm stammering like an imbecile while I fumble for an excuse, an explanation. 'I didn't mean it to happen like—'

'Would you care to explain how you come to have my mother's back-door key?' Francesca's voice is icy, furious, and I can't blame her. But I can tell she's more frightened than angry. Terrified, in fact. 'Before I phone the police.'

'No. Please don't do that.' Oh God no. End of new beginning. 'There's no need to call them, honestly. I promise. Please, just let me explain, okay?'

I don't move or step forward, because she's panicked enough. She could do me some serious damage with that hammer. I lay down the key, slowly and gently, on top of the small freezer by the door. Next to a gardenia and a white, gold-rimmed china saucer full of rubber bands. There's a fridge next to the freezer, its door covered with cute magnets of old Dutch masters: Johannes Vermeer's *The Kitchen Maid* and his *Girl With Pearl Earring*, Hans Bollongier's *Still Life* of flowers. Avercamp's *Winter*

Landscape with Iceskaters, Vermeer's view of Delft, and another still life with cheese, grapes and walnuts. I know those pictures because I used to take art books out of the prison library to satisfy my constant craving for something beautiful to look at. Something to keep my soul alive.

'I'm Alyssa Ward,' I say, trembling. 'Your sister. Well, half-sister.' I don't like the term 'half-sister', it sounds lame. The perfume from the gardenias makes me want to cry. I already associate their smell with my mother. 'I know my – your – our mother was taken ill, that she's in hospital. I was outside that night, I saw the ambulance.'

A flash of alarm in Francesca's eyes. 'What were you doing here?'

'I wanted a look at her house. I wasn't going to knock at the door or try to speak to her. I knew it wasn't the right time for that. I just hoped I could catch a glimpse of her. When the ambulance drove off, your neighbour forgot to lock the door. I ran across the road and came in. I know it was wrong, but I couldn't resist it.' I rush on, the words tumbling out. 'Don't worry, I swear I didn't disturb anything. And I wouldn't dream of stealing. I just wanted – I don't know really. I was only going to stay a minute. But the neighbour suddenly came back and I got a fright. I didn't want him to find me. I hid upstairs until he'd switched off the lights, locked the front door and gone. The only way I could get out was through the back door, and I didn't want to leave that unlocked. So I took the key.'

'Why come back now? Or rather, gain unlawful entry a second time?'

I don't like the way she puts it in legal terms. 'I wanted to return the key.'

'How thoughtful.'

'I assumed your neighbours would come in to check the house, and that they'd re-lock the door before nightfall. I wasn't going to pry, I swear.'

'No,' Francesca says. 'Of course you weren't.'

'I wasn't! Look, I know I shouldn't have done this. It's wrong, incredibly stupid, the worst thing I could do. I realise you and your – my – mother may not want any contact with me. Especially now. But please don't call the police. There's the key. I'll go away, I'll never bother you again if that's what you want. I don't mean any harm.'

'How do I know that?' Francesca takes a step back, still gripping the hammer. 'You could be anybody, anything. How did you get my mother's address? How do you know about me?'

'I got copies of her birth and marriage certificates. Found out her late husband's name, and that she'd had one child – one other child apart from me, that is. Everything I did was entirely legal.' I can't keep a touch of resentful sarcasm out of my voice; Francesca is assuming the worst before she knows it. 'The adoption charity helped me investigate further. The rest was easy.' Of course I wasn't going to mention my unauthorised research in confidential files.

'I don't believe this!' Francesca flushed with anger. 'No wonder my mother's in a state. You know she's ill – she doesn't need this. What about her privacy – my privacy? You can find out all this personal information about us, but we don't know a damn thing about you. Can you prove who you are? Have you got ID?'

'Not on me.'

'No. I didn't think so. Even if you are who you claim to be–'

'I am! Of course I am.' I tell myself to calm down. Francesca's bound to be upset initially. And suspicious. But I'm upset too. 'Why would I lie? Look at us, for God's sake, you can see the resemblance. I'm not after money, if that's what you're worried about. Surely that's obvious.' I fling out one arm, startling her. 'I mean, this is nice but it's not exactly Buckingham Palace, is it? No, no, I'm sorry!' Nice one, Alyssa. 'Please. I'm sorry, I didn't mean that.'

'You've got one thing right.' Francesca hit back. Hard. 'My mother doesn't want contact with you. She's definite about that.'

So nothing's changed. I didn't expect it would have, but still. I swallow another stone of disappointment. 'Why is she in hospital? What's wrong with her, if you don't mind my asking?'

Francesca obviously does, but she answers anyway. 'Heart attack.'

'Oh. I'm sorry. Is she going to be all right?'

'I hope so. The doctors tell me she's making good progress.' Francesca lays the hammer on the draining board. 'She was writing a letter to your interfering charity when she was taken ill. I'm not saying her heart attack wouldn't have happened anyway, but I'm certain the shock and trauma of having this business resurrected didn't exactly help. Her life's difficult enough without –'

Francesca stops, shakes back her hair and chews her lip in a cute, girlish way. She looks young for her age. I guess she's reminding herself to be circumspect, not give out too much information to this disturbing alien who's invaded her and her mother's lives. Maybe she regards me as a jealous, bitter, eye-to-the-main-chance character who hates her for having had two biological parents all to herself.

'I'll have to get the locks changed.' She glares at me. 'You could have had a duplicate of that key made.'

'No, I didn't!' I'm angry again. Although what do I expect? This couldn't get any worse – I've got it just about as wrong as it's possible to get anything. 'There's no way I'd do that. I wanted to return it – I'm telling you the truth.' I pause, can't resist asking another question. 'Do you live near here?'

'That's none of your business. Nothing about me or my mother is any of your business. Despite what you want to think. Now leave that key and get out, or I will phone the police.'

'But Francesca, please, can't we just—'

'Why come here now?' she bursts out, suddenly terrified again, like she's just thought of something else that freaks her. 'What do you really want?'

'To see my mother. To see you! That's all. I just wanted to see you both. I don't have any other family.' Except my father, and he doesn't count. 'I was so excited to discover I had a sister.'

I'm choking up, my eyes filling. It's a weird sensation. I started crying that night I read Estella's letter saying she didn't want contact with me. Now it seems all those dammed-up tears are determined to flood out. 'You know I'm Alyssa Ward; you know I'm your sister. I just want you to give me a chance. I don't expect some fairy-tale reunion.' No? 'But give me a chance, please, please!' The tears are rolling, dripping off my chin and landing on the glossy gardenia leaves.

I bow my head, sobbing. I can't go on. I feel Francesca's stare. Her anger and doubt, her fear. And another feeling – what could that be? Curiosity, hunger? I grab a tissue and wipe my eyes, blow my nose. The phone down the hall rings. I look up and meet Francesca's grey eyes. It's like looking into a mirror. She turns pale at the sound of the phone, and her lips look thinner.

'Don't you want to answer that?' I whisper. 'Could it be the hospital?' Perhaps she's afraid it might be bad news about Estella.

Francesca shakes her head, twists her hands together, and I

wonder again if something else besides Estella's heart attack and the appearance of the alien sister is upsetting her. She looks so frightened. I ache to find out more. To help.

'Wait here.' She turns, walks out and shuts the kitchen door behind her. It was a thick, wooden door which stuck when closed, so there was no way I could get to hear anything she was saying on the hall phone without being very obvious and unclever. Even if I could eavesdrop, being able to earwig only one side of the conversation wouldn't necessarily give me an accurate picture.

I sniff and blow my nose again, trying to get myself together. I'm not used to all this unleashing of emotion. It's very wearing. Feels like training for the SAS, jogging miles over remote, mountainous countryside with a rucksack full of bricks strapped to you. What do they call that? Beasting?

Francesca stays on the phone. I open the fridge and see two bottles of Gewurztztraminer, bottles of soy sauce and sweet pepper sauce. Packs of unsalted butter. Free-range eggs, mature Cheddar. Spring onions and flat field mushrooms in the veg compartment. There was a tin of coffee beans, finest Arabica. How I'd love a cup of fresh ground coffee to restore my energy. I shut the fridge before I get too carried away. Francesca's voice rises in what sounds like panic, then drops low again. I can't make out what she's saying. Who is she talking to, what's going on?

I retreat to my stand by the door and freezer, my mouth watering and stomach growling. I haven't eaten since twelve, a stale Danish pastry with not enough icing or sultanas. It's getting dark and I'm due back at the hostel soon – a long journey, train and then bus. Can I make it in time? Audrey will be on the prowl, hugging a mug of instant coffee, glancing at that thin little jewelly watch on her thick wrist. Ward's late. Seriously late. *Result*. Come on, bitch, make my evening. I can imagine the gleam in her red rodent eye. Why does she hate me? Maybe I don't look cowed and ugly enough. Punished enough. Well, tough titty said the cute little kitty. Francesca reappears, shoving open the sticky door.

'Are you okay?' She looks worse now, like she might faint. I forget Audrey and deadlines and punishment. 'Francesca, is it bad news? Your – our –'

'It's not Mum.' She brushes one hand over her eyes, as if removing cobwebs or a veil. 'And most people call me Frankie.'

87

'Frankie.' I like that. By 'most people', does she mean family and friends? I'm flattered, and experience a rush of dangerous hope. But I'm shifting from one foot to the other, like I'm desperate to go to the loo. If I don't leave in about one minute I'll be in huge trouble.

'I'll go.' I try to smile. 'Leave you in peace. But can I come back once you've had some time to think? Say, tomorrow or the day after? Please can we talk more?'

She doesn't answer, just bursts out crying. It's the long-drawn-out groaning of someone in deep distress. 'Frankie?' I step forward, startled. 'What's wrong?'

'Everything!' Suddenly she no longer cares; she abandons caution, drops all her defences. 'My husband's dumping me,' she wails. 'Our marriage is over.'

'I'm sorry.' If there's anything better to say, I can't think of it at this moment. Given how soppy her husband looks about her in that wedding photo, I had the impression she was happily married. The happiness obviously hadn't lasted. I thought of something else. 'Have you got kids?'

'No, thank goodness. Someone just threatened to kill me – me and Joe – if we don't pay a hundred grand. I don't get it, I just don't–'

'A hundred grand?'

'I haven't got that sort of money except in my dreams, and neither has Joe. I just talked to him. He says it's his fault and he'll sort it, that I'm not to worry. Not to worry! Turns out he's been gambling for the past few months. That's how he ran up this terrible debt. He never did anything like that before! I can't believe he's been this stupid. He won't tell me everything, including how he imagines he's going to sort it, but he obviously didn't get credit from the bank! He must owe the money to a criminal. I don't know what the hell to do.'

I don't ask why the criminal threatens the wife when it's the husband's debt. That's how those scum operate. They're ruthless; they don't give a toss how they get their money as long as they get it. Shocked, I go to Frankie, put one arm around her and draw her close. She goes rigid for a second, then relaxes against me. Simple human warmth, contact. Giving succour. My sister, my sister. It's too much.

'It's all right,' I whisper, hugging her. 'I'm here.' A tidal wave of love for her crashes over me, leaving me weak. I want to protect her. 'I'll help you.'

'What?' Frankie breaks away and grimaces at me through her streaming tears, ashamed of her lapse of control. 'Got a hundred thousand pounds going spare then, have you? I'm really glad you turned up. This must be my lucky day.'

'No, I haven't got that kind of money either. But maybe we can think of something.'

'Yeah. Right.' She stares at me. 'Well, seeing as it's confession time, what are your closet skeletons? I know you're a couple of years off forty, so don't tell me you haven't got any.'

I hesitate. I intended to tell so many lies, spin up a giant, sticky, silken web of concealment and deceit. Invent a new past, present and, hopefully, a future. But that's going to require a nightmare amount of maintenance, exhausting, continual high-level awareness that even the best-trained and most experienced secret agent couldn't manage. And secret agents go undercover for days, weeks, months or perhaps a couple of years, not the rest of their lives. Sooner or later I would make slip-ups. Fatal ones. I realise I want honesty … Whatever it takes … Can I trust Frankie? It's a risk. But I have to take it.

I feel like I felt when the judge pronounced sentence, the full whack, calling me an evil woman. I remember I was dizzy and there was a heavy sensation in my guts, cramping like when my period starts, only worse. I didn't have periods for ages after I went to prison. My body shut down.

It was one of those old-fashioned court rooms with dark panelling and polished brass rails. I bet Judgey wished he could don the old black cap and express his lying hope that God would have mercy on my eternally stained soul.

'Well?'

I've been silent too long. Frankie knows there's something big coming. Her voice sounds similar. I had no idea things like voice and posture could run in families.

I take a breath. My mouth's gone dry. I don't know if I can speak. But I croak out the words. Confession time.

'I've been in prison for the past ten years. I was accused – convicted – of murdering my stepmother. But I didn't kill her. I'm innocent.'

Yeah. *Right.*

*

'Monique, would you please leave now?' Conal lay back, his face almost as pale as the hospital pillows. His trembling fingers brushed the sling of his heavily bandaged right arm. 'The doctor told me to get some sleep and that's what I'd like to do.'

'Please let me stay.' She put up one hand to stroke his hair and withdrew it when he flinched. 'I'll just sit here. I won't disturb you.'

'You think I can sleep with you watching over me? I don't want you to stay. The truth is, I'll feel a damn sight happier and more relaxed, not to mention safe, if you're not around. '

'Conal, please.' Monique was hurt, although she knew she had no right to feel that way. 'I know you're angry and frightened, and I don't blame you.'

'Nice one. Thanks for that.'

'I overreacted, I did a terrible thing. I've said I'm sorry.'

'Yeah, I know what you've *said*. Problem is, it's thinking that doesn't seem to be your beanfeast. Especially where I'm concerned. Shoot first and ask afterwards, like some psycho gangster. At least I know what you really think of me now. How little faith and trust you've got in me, in our marriage.' He shifted in the bed and gasped with pain. 'Suppose the nurse comes in to check my blood pressure? You might think I'm screwing her and shoot me again.'

Tears stung Monique's eyes. 'Don't be ridiculous!'

'Well, sorry about that. Sorry for being ridiculous. My crazed wife shot me, you see, she tried to kill me, and it's just pure good luck that I'm not lying tootsie-tagged in the morgue now instead of in this nice private room with rose-pink walls, matching bedspread and panoramic view of the consultants car park.'

'D'you think I don't know that? I feel terrible, I can't believe I–'

'Spare me about how *you* feel, okay?' Conal interrupted. 'Anyone would think you were the victim here. I'm in shock, in pain and exhausted as well as frightened. I'll stay in pain until this wound heals, and then I'll need physiotherapy for the arm and shoulder. When I'm done with all that I'll have a scar for the rest of my life to remind me of how I married a loony.'

Monique turned away and covered her face with her hands.

'And as if all that wasn't enough, I've taken the blame for what you did,' he went on. 'Told the police I shot myself accidentally, let them think I'm some total, freaking monkey chunk who's no more fit to handle a gun than a toddler would be to pilot a space shuttle. They're bound to confiscate my licence.'

'I know. I really appreciate you covering for me.'

'I don't know why I'm doing it. I must be crazy.'

'You're doing it because you love me. As I love you.' Monique turned. 'You know I didn't mean it. And because Lauren would be left alone if I got sent to jail.' She hesitated. 'You won't leave me, will you, Conal?'

'You always did push your luck.' He laughed weakly. 'You think it's a good time to ask me that question?'

'No. But I'm desperate. Conal, you know you don't have to be afraid of me. I feel terrible, I'll never forgive myself . . . I can't tell you how sorry I am. I could shoot myself right now!'

'Oh, for–' He shook his head. 'Ditch the melodrama, for Christ's sake. Don't you think there's been enough of that for one day?' He shivered. 'Just *go*.'

'All right. If that's what you want.' Monique picked up her bag then hesitated again. 'Please, Conal. I'm sorry to keep asking, but I'm so scared and I really need to know. Tell me you won't leave me. Tell me our marriage will be okay, that I haven't destroyed everything.' She started to cry again.

'Monique.' Conal looked at her, his tired eyes glittering with anger. 'You're going to escape a stretch for attempted murder or manslaughter. Lauren won't have to visit you in jail every week. The company won't lose business because clients think there's a mad woman at the helm. So stop whinging and be grateful – *very* grateful for all of that, because anything else is a bonus.' He paused. 'Now get the fuck out and leave me in peace.'

A nurse knocked and hurried in. She stopped when she saw Monique. 'Oh come on now, Mrs Thorn, you're not still crying? You musn't be so upset.' She smiled. 'Your husband's going to be fine, honestly. But he really does need to rest now.'

'My wife is just leaving,' Conal announced.

Monique stared at him, desperate to find some spark of warmth in his dark-blue eyes. There was only shock, pain, anger. Worst of all, contempt. She could do nothing now except wait. And hope.

She turned and walked out.

Chapter 11

'Of course Agron Xhani won't kill Frankie! He won't even hurt her. Or you.' Lida finished snorting the line of coke and picked up her glass of rosé champagne. 'He wants his money, doesn't he? So why would he kill – what do you call it in English? – the goose that lays the golden egg? He knows you need time to find that money.'

'Yeah. Like the rest of my life!' Joe lay back in bed, his eyes on Lida's round, firm breasts and tanned, slender thighs. The sight didn't turn him on the way it usually did. 'I tried the bank,' he sighed. 'When the manager stopped laughing over my loan application she told me I could only have about a quarter of what I need.'

'Well, that's something.' Lida swigged the champagne. Joe noticed she was drinking from one of the Waterford crystal toasting flutes he and Frankie had bought during a holiday in Ireland. 'Now you only need to find the other three quarters.'

'Simple, isn't it, when you put it like that.'

'Can't you sell this apartment very quickly?'

'It's rented.'

'Oh.' Lida giggled suddenly. 'Is Frankie insured?'

He looked at her. 'What?'

'I mean, don't you have a life insurance policy on her? Which means she's worth a lot more dead than alive. Fix it so she has a fatal accident.'

Joe flinched and turned red. 'That's not even remotely funny.'

'Come on.' Lida crawled towards him. 'I didn't mean it.'

'You fucking did.' He shivered. 'Don't you ever mention

anything like that again. And have more respect when you talk about Frankie. She is supposed to be one of your best friends, after all.'

'My friend and your wife, Mister Double-Standards.' Lida's eyes glittered with coke and impatience. She slid her arms around his neck. 'Chill out, *schatje*, darling. Frankie's not in danger and neither are you. Well, not for now. You have to come up with that money though, and you will. Don't you think it's time you told her the truth?'

'About me owing a massive gambling debt to an Albanian gangster? Frankie's not thick – she might not know the details, but she'll guess it wasn't our bank manager who threatened to kill her! And there's no way I'm telling her I caught your coke habit as well as the gambling, which is the other reason I owe that bastard. She'll freak.' He paused. 'Freak more.'

'I meant the truth about *us,* about why you're dumping her. Our beautiful relationship, remember?'

'If I'd got that ultimatum from Xhani a day earlier I would have postponed telling her we were through.' He frowned. ' I'm not dumping her exactly.'

Lida laughed, pushing her breasts against him. 'What would you call it then?'

'Frankie and I are splitting because things are no longer good between us. If I'd been happy with her I'd never have looked at you, would I? Well, I'd have *looked*. Put those away.' He frowned, glancing at her breasts. 'I'm not in the mood. A huge gambling and coke debt doesn't exactly–'

'Give you a huge erection.' Lida let go of him, her expression sulky. 'I've noticed.'

'There's no way I'm telling Frankie about us. Not yet, anyway. She couldn't take it. I've hurt her enough. And her mother's had a heart attack – she's got that to cope with on top of everything else.'

'Welcome to the real world, Frankie.' Lida poured herself more champagne and raised her glass in a mocking salute. 'It will give her something to write about. Nothing is wasted on writers, isn't that what they say? You'll find yourself the main character in her novel – that's if any publisher is stupid enough to buy it.'

'Never mind her bloody novel. Look, you don't understand. Frankie's in a right state. And terrified now that Xhani's

93

threatened to kill her. God knows how he got hold of her mobile number.'

'Ways and means. I told you, he won't do anything. Certainly not yet.'

'I know what you told me. But I've read about Albanian gangsters in the papers–'

'Oh.' Lida smirked. 'The *papers*.'

'They don't mess about. They've murdered people for a lot less than what I owe. They're your worst nightmare.' Joe broke out in a sweat. 'Christ, what the fuck have I got myself into? Even if I can get my hands on all that money and pay him and he doesn't decide to kill me just for the hell of it, I could be financially crippled for the rest of my life.'

'Better than being dead.'

'Thanks. You're such a comfort.'

Joe caught sight of himself in the dressing table mirror and experienced the slight shock he usually got these days on seeing his reflection. He looked pale and ill, stressed, his face thinner, his eyes brooding and hollowed. His heart was pounding and he had a headache. A right wreck. He didn't think he'd go on with the coke, even if he could have afforded to. The truth was, he preferred booze. But Lida loved coke. She had never told Frankie about her habit, mocking that Frankie was too uptight. Joe had believed she and his wife were good friends, but now Lida didn't seem to give a damn about Frankie. He realised it was hypocritical of him to think she should. He looked down at her sprawled in the nest of crumpled pillows.

'You think this is all one bloody great joke, don't you?'

'No.' Lida sat up and kissed him. 'I love you, don't forget. I don't want anyone hurting or killing you.'

Joe looked into her eyes. He had taken stock of his life several months ago, and decided he deserved better. Before it was too late. Lida was one of those better things. She was beautiful, easygoing and never fed up the way Frankie could be at times. Although Joe had to admit Frankie had good reason to be fed up, especially lately. He felt sorry for her, but that was just the way it was.

'You're too soft on her,' Lida was saying. 'She can take care of herself. She has to accept that her marriage is over and move on. I don't see why I should be painted as the champagne and lingerie, husband-stealing bitch. It takes two to tangle.'

Joe smiled. 'Tango.'

'Whatever. Frankie's got a job, she'll have to hang on to that.'

He frowned. 'She had a better job before she gave it up to come here with me.'

'So what? She'll have to work hard. Look at me – I spent years doing law studies and passing exams before I became a prosecutor at just thirty.'

'Yeah, a right little girly swot. Having a judge for a dad didn't hurt either.'

'I still had to work hard. Frankie will have to forget her stupid little dreams and face reality. I hate whinging women.'

'Feminist of the millenium, that's you.'

'Feminism!' Lida grimaced. 'Another excuse to whinge and justify being a loser.'

'A lot of people wouldn't agree with you there. If it hadn't been for all those whinging feminists you'd never have got to go to law school, never mind become a prosecutor.' Joe didn't care; he only said that to wind her up. He turned over in bed and looked out of the window at the darkening, violet sky. The street lamps flickered on. He groaned. 'How the *fuck* am I going to get that money? Can't you help me?' he asked as Lida stroked his face. 'It was you got me mixed up with all this crap.'

'Got a mind of your own, haven't you? You didn't have to get carried away and end up owing all that money. And how was I to know that my supplier of Columbia's finest would turn out to be an Albanian gangster?'

'You wouldn't have had to be a hot-shot lawyer to make an educated guess.'

'Listen.' Lida sat up and drank more champagne. 'Actually, I *was* thinking about how I could help you. I had an idea. I can ask my parents for help.'

'Your parents? What the hell will you tell them?'

'The truth, of course – that my lover needs the money to pay off his drug and gambling debt to a gangster.' She started to laugh.

'For Christ's sake, Lida!' he exclaimed, dismayed. 'This isn't funny.'

'No. You're right.' She coughed. 'I'll tell them I want to buy a house. That's not a lie, actually. We should get a place together.'

Joe was amazed to feel depressed as he contemplated a new life with Lida. He had met her parents a couple of times and didn't like them; the feeling was mutual. They didn't think some married Brit guy from the north-west of England who worked for an IT company and barely spoke Dutch was good enough for their precious only daughter. Lida's mother was pally with a couple of the Queen's ladies-in-waiting, and her father hobnobbed with cabinet ministers. They probably imagined Lida marrying minor European royalty or some top businessman, judge or politician. Or a best-selling author. Her mother loved authors and saw herself as running her own literary salon from their villa in snob Wassenaar. They thought they were being clever by not openly voicing their disapproval of him, but their hope that Lida's unfortunate fling with her bit of rough would blow over soon was rather too obvious.

Joe still liked and respected Frankie, and he would miss her. Her laugh, her kindness, her sense of humour. Her cooking! And she was beautiful, even if he didn't fancy her any more. But you couldn't stay with someone out of pity. This was difficult, more difficult than he had imagined. But he was doing the right thing.

'Your parents will buy you a house? Just like that?'

'No problem.' Lida snuggled up to him again. He smelled her sweat and perfume. 'And I've got some savings. I can use those too.'

Joe was delighted, filled with new hope. Lida could have had any man, even the minor European prince, her parents dream son-in-law. But she wanted him. Enough to be willing to help him pay off a hundred grand debt. Or pay off the lot. He couldn't believe it.

'Don't worry,' she whispered, kissing him. 'We'll get that money. It will be all right, I promise you. My parents won't say no.'

'Are you sure about that?'

'I'm sure.'

'They might make the condition that if they give you the money you give up me.'

'That's not a condition they can enforce, is it? I'll promise anything, tell them whatever they want to hear. Once the money's in my account you pay off Agron Xhani, and you're safe. That's the most important thing.'

'You'd do that for me?'

'Of course. As I said, I love you.'

'I can't believe it, it's . . . this is fantastic! How long d'you think it'll take?'

'Oh, a few days. Maybe a week. I'll call my dad later. Or go round and see him and my mother. Yes, that would be best.'

Joe smiled, relief and new energy surging through his stressed-out, coked-up system. He grabbed her. 'Come here.'

'I thought that would make you feel better.' She laughed. 'More in the mood.'

He certainly was now. He swore as the doorbell rang twice. 'Who the hell's that?'

'Who cares? Ignore it.' Lida took his hand and guided it downwards. The bell rang again, like somebody was leaning on it.

'I hope it's not the police.' Joe was only half-joking. 'Come for you and your little bag of white powder.'

'Shut up.' She pushed herself against him. The bell didn't stop ringing.

'Christ!' He glanced up. 'Maybe it's Frankie. She can't find you here, she'll freak!'

'*Joe*. Think, will you?' Lida looked pained. 'Why would she ring the bell? She's got her own key, hasn't she? And Ms Economy Class can't have flown from Liverpool to Schiphol airport and taken a train to Den Haag when you only spoke to her a couple of hours ago. She's in England and she'll be there for another week at least. Relax!'

'I would if whoever's ringing that damn bell would piss off. But yeah, you're right.'What was the matter with him? Joe's erection subsided, and he leaned on his elbows looking down at Lida. 'I'd better go and see who it is,' he muttered. 'Tell them to fuck off. Might be kids. Filthy little sods left dogshit on the doorstep a few weeks ago.'

'This is crazy.' But Lida was smiling, her eyes shining. 'You better hurry and get back here. I'm feeling very frustrated and you'll have to make it up to me.'

'I will.' He stroked her breasts and gave each nipple a playful pinch. 'Back in a minute, okay?'

Joe pulled on his dressing gown and went down the two flights of narrow stairs. The tiles on the hall floor chilled his bare feet. Anger rose in him. If it was those little bastards from around the corner again he would punch their lights out and plead provocation if he got done for child cruelty. He knotted the belt and wrenched open the heavy front door.

'What the–'

It wasn't dirty, undisciplined brats. Or dogshit. He wasn't to be that lucky. A punch in the face knocked him backwards as a bunch of men burst in, crowding the small space. He couldn't tell how many. Joe felt warm blood gush from his nose on to his shaking fingers. They grabbed him and hauled him upstairs. They had guns and wore black balaclavas. He wondered if any of the neighbours had seen them, if somebody would phone the police. Probably not – they wouldn't want to get involved. Shocked and dazed, he was unable to cry out or struggle, warn Lida. But it was him they wanted. He hadn't expected this, hadn't dreamed they would come for him, or not this soon. Agron Xhani knew he needed time.

'I'll get the money,' he gasped as they dragged him over the smooth parquet of the living-room floor and threw him against the wall by the sideboard. 'Just give me a couple of days, please, that's all I–'

A kick in the stomach cut him short and he coughed and retched as they tied his hands behind his back. There were four of them. Through his tears he looked at their cold eyes, their pale, set lips. Felt pure fear. A greasy cloth was stuffed into his mouth, making him gag. Two of them ran out and up the second flight of stairs, presumably to check if there was anyone else in the house. If they were looking for money they'd be on a hiding to nothing. He heard Lida scream. Once. Bumps and thuds sounded on the stairs and a minute later she was dragged, still naked, into the living room. Her hands were tied behind her back and she was gagged too. They stared at one another. Joe hoped, stupidly, that somehow Lida could help him. He could tell from the look in her eyes that she had the same futile hope about him.

One of the men grabbed her breasts and fondled them. Lida struggled, moaning behind the gag. Another man, who seemed to be the leader, laughed. They pushed her to her knees and started beating her. Joe flinched at the sound of the slaps and punches against her bare flesh. He shut his eyes and turned his head away, but they forced him to watch. Lida's beautiful face was a mess now, red and swollen, blood trickling from her mouth and nose.

Joe could hardly take in the horror of it all. Were they going to

98

beat him up too? When they laid Lida on her back and kicked her legs apart, he knew what was coming next. The leader turned to him and smiled. Why? he thought. What's the bloody point of this? But he knew, of course he knew. They wanted to demonstrate their power. Lida's eyes were frantic, her bare, spread legs scrabbling on the shiny floor. Judge Daddy couldn't help her now. No one could.

The men took turns to rape her, in between continual slaps and punches. None of them spoke. There were only grunts, low laughs and Lida's frantic, agonised mewings. The horror seemed to go on and on. Joe was crying behind the gag, tears rolling down his face, his chest heaving with the effort to breathe. He had never felt so terrified, so powerless. By the time they pulled out her gag Lida could no longer scream or even speak. Joe thought they were finished. At last, at last. Get out and leave us alone. But they were not finished. One of them grabbed Lida by the hair and knelt over her bruised, bleeding, tear stained face.

Let it end, he prayed. Let it be over. He couldn't believe he and Lida were not still upstairs in bed, drinking champagne, ready for sex. Joe felt like he never wanted to have sex again after witnessing this. The men finished with Lida at last, got to their feet and did up their trousers. She lay shivering, gasping and sobbing. Their leader turned to Joe and picked up his gun.

'You think you can fuck with Agron Xhani,' he whispered. 'So he told us to fuck with your wife.'

They came over and started to beat him. Joe tried to struggle, roll over, protect himself from the kicks and blows, scream for help. But he could only scream inside his head. The beating didn't last long, and they pulled out his gag. Maybe they were tired after raping Lida.

'I'm not his–' Lida tried to roll over on one side and draw up her legs. 'Joe, tell them,' she gasped. 'I'm not his wife!'

But they weren't listening and Joe couldn't tell them anything. He vomited and lay gasping. He imagined Frankie lying there in place of Lida, naked, humiliated, beaten, raped. What the fuck have I done? he thought.

He had been restless, dissatisfied, wanted a laugh and some excitement. Now he'd had all the excitement he could handle. He looked into Lida's eyes again and saw the expression in them as she realised he had no intention of telling these thugs that she wasn't his wife. He might be a total shit, but no way would he tell them they had beaten and raped the wrong woman.

He tasted blood in his mouth. His body was on fire. He lay there unable to move, wondering if any bones were fractured or broken. It hurt him to breathe. The leader gestured to the others to get out. When they were gone he knelt beside Joe.

'This is a warning,' he whispered. 'Agron Xhani wants his money. You have ten more days. Police cannot help you. Don't call them or we kill you. You get the money, then you're safe. Now I give your wife a souvenir of our visit.'

'No!' Joe whispered as he saw the knife. 'No, don't –' The man got up and went back to Lida, grabbed her by the hair again. Lida uttered a quavering wail of pain and terror as the blade sliced one side of her face from eye to chin. Blood flowed down. The man came back and stood over Joe. Joe turned his head away, sick with horror as Lida's blood dripped from the knife blade on to his face.

'Next time she dies.' The man's voice was calm. 'You too. Unless you get the money. Goodbye for now.' A second later he was gone.

Joe passed out.

Chapter 12

Last night I dreamed about the murder.

Blonde, blue-eyed, tarty Vivienne Ward, my wicked step-mother. The Snow Queen who lodged the sliver of ice in my heart. It was the first time I'd dreamed about it. Why now after a decade of nights in moonlit cells, surrounded by unearthly shouts, cries and groans? Wouldn't that be the classic setting for sweat-drenching screamers? Must be a self-protection mechanism, a section of the brain shutting down until the subconscious reckons you're ready to deal with the hidden horrors that lurk. Well, my subconscious has got it dead wrong. I'm not ready for anything.

If I must have bad dreams give me the silent, mysterious, Georgian house with its firelight and drifting silk curtains. At least that's beautiful – until I see the snakes and imagine their fangs squirting venom into me. Still don't know what the hell that's about. But I'm not planning to ask any shrink. I'll just have to wonder. Maybe I'll find out some day; a flash of light that illumi-nates all my dark, cobwebby places!

Francesca – Frankie – gave me fifty quid cash and phoned a minicab to take me back to my hostel home from home. I thought she'd given me too much money, but the half hour journey was expensive; back to Liverpool, across the city during rush hour, up that long hill past the two cathedrals. I told the driver to stop for a minute while I ran into a barricaded off-licence to buy sweets, crisps and a bottle of Aussie Cabernet Sauvignon. I stuffed the yellow carrier bag into my rucksack – didn't want Audrey or any other busybody seeing it – and got the driver to drop me down the road from the hostel. I didn't want him knowing my real destina-tion. I walked in with minutes to spare before curfew.

Audrey the android was out of her office and pacing, glancing at her little jewelly wristwatch, the beginnings of a triumphant smile tweaking the corners of that grim, meat-cleaver mouth. It's funny – if you're in the mood to appreciate humour – with those powerful arms and shoulders, great big arse, flat, greasy hair and little red bog-rat eyes, Audrey looks much more murderous than any of her charges, me included, ever could. Another of life's fine ironies. When she saw me her smile died the death, and the piggy bristles around her nose and mouth twitched with rage. I pretended not to notice her and headed down the hall. I had more important things to worry about. Such as, would Frankie my sister speak to me again?

Was our relationship dead in the water before it had had a chance to get started? What the hell did I think I was doing telling her the truth? When did that ever help? Truth should be hidden; people can't take it. Even when they think they can.

Audrey shouted something after me, like how come a bus ride across town for a job interview in a dry-cleaning factory could take so bloody long? I replied that there were a lot of other job applicants and the bus had got stuck in traffic on the way back. I knew I wouldn't get that job; I'd made damn sure of it. I sat flexing my hands like I wanted to strangle someone, and gave the nervous personnel boy and departmental supervising lady a creepy stare while I answered their stupid questions in psychotic monosyllables. Whatever I end up doing, it won't be dry cleaning. Nothing wrong with it, it's an essential service. But the only time I intend to come in contact with it is when I pick up my newly cleaned Armani trouser suit, dahling.

I shut myself in my room for the night and sat on the bed eating smoky bacon crisps, fruit pastilles and a king-size Mars bar. That big, berry and vanilla-perfumed Aussie beast of a wine almost knocked me out after a couple of glasses. Alcohol could not dispel the image of Frankie's shocked expression though, the terrified look in her eyes. Did she give me the cash just to get rid of me rather than help me avoid trouble? I told her everything – well, almost. She didn't have a clue what to say. Or do. Maybe it was too much for her on top of the other stuff. Does she even care? I mean, her life's in danger. Why would she give a toss about me?

She said she wouldn't tell Estella about our meeting. I gather our mother couldn't take it. I asked Frankie if I could go back the next day and talk more, ask her more questions, make her understand about me. She just told me to go, please go. She'd got enough problems of her own. I want to help her, but will she let me? How could I help anyway? I think I've blown it.

Another of the wardens, Bren, knocked at my door and came in. I hid the wine, but I'm sure she smelled it. She just grinned though and told me to have fun. Said I should stick out for a better job than the rubbish I'd had interviews for so far. She reckoned I could get something clerical or admin. As long as it's not in a law firm, of course. Ha-ha. Bren is nice. She means well.

The dream. Oh God. I was creeping up the path to the house. Shivering. Not with cold, but with hate. A lifetime of it. Why did I hate Vivienne? Okay, she was a sadist. But it was all my father's fault really. He married Ms Whiplash, let her rule over me because he couldn't be bothered. But he didn't have Vivienne's slyness and cruelty. Some people do bad things because they're stupid, careless, ignorant or insensitive. Others just like to cause suffering, because they can get away with it and it makes them feel good. My father didn't know the half of what Vivienne got up to while he was working all those hours at his office, or flying around Europe on his bloody business trips. He didn't know about her affairs. At least I don't think so. But he wouldn't have wanted to know, because he loved Vivienne. More than me, more than anyone. He was also lazy, one of those people who go into irritated and anxious denial over anything that might threaten their quiet little life. That's why he allowed his daughter to believe her wicked stepmother was her real mother. Until one fine day wicked stepmother told daughter the truth.

I didn't believe it at first. I thought, no, she's just being vicious.

'I need to get out of here before I catch that killer flu. Or one of those fatal, flesh-eating superbugs.'

'You won't catch anything. Don't go looking for worse things to happen.'

'The nurses don't always wash their hands or change gloves between patients. I've watched them. And I wish somebody would switch off that damn television.' Estella leaned back in bed. 'Not that I could watch anything in peace if I wanted to, with all the coming and going. Can't concentrate on reading either,' she fretted.

'You'll be out of here soon.' Frankie glanced at her mother's barely touched evening meal – limp green salad and a lump of Cheddar. Of course you couldn't expect lemon and olive oil-dressed wild rocket leaves on the NHS.

'Ridiculous, isn't it?' Estella followed her glance. 'Why on earth don't they grate the cheese and make it go further instead of giving everyone a great lump they can't possibly eat at one meal? There must be nearly two hundred grams there. If you had a piece that size at home in the fridge it'd take you several days to get through it.'

'Yes.'

'You're quiet,' Estella remarked. 'Or am I moaning too much? Still, you've got a lot to think about. We both have. Heard from Joe?'

'He phoned earlier. We had a brief talk.' Frankie shrugged. 'Nothing's changed.' She had no intention of telling Estella about the threatening phone call.

'Hm. Did you post my letter?'

'Yes.'

'Thank goodness for that.'

Frankie watched her mother's expression clear, her strained features relax slightly. Just as well she didn't know her long-lost daughter Alyssa Ward was a convicted murderer. Frankie still could not believe it herself. Another cold flash hit her as she recalled Alyssa's shocking confession. Convicted of shooting her stepmother! Alyssa swore she was innocent. As did a lot of convicted criminals. Frankie should check out her story, and normally she would have done that immediately. But she had more urgent priorities now. A chill swept over her as she thought of Joe's gambling debt, and the threat to her life. Another thing she couldn't believe. Shock and disbelief were stupid, dangerous. She needed to wake up. Fast.

'You haven't seen *her*?' Estella pulled up the sheet and glanced at a passing nurse and doctor, who were followed by a grey-haired woman carrying a cut-glass vase full of pink tulips.

'You mean Alyssa Ward? No. Of course not. Why would I have?'

Frankie decided the only sensible thing was to tell her brand-new half-sister to go to hell. So why hadn't she done that? 'Look – the letter's posted now. Those social workers or whatever they are will tell her you don't want contact. She won't bother you again.'

'She'd better not. I just want to live out whatever years I've got left in peace.' Estella's eyes filled with the tears that came so easily now. 'I don't even want to think about her.'

'Well, don't.' It had to be guilt that made her mother feel this way. Frankie took her hand and squeezed it. 'Just concentrate on getting better, okay?'

'That – and *you*. Be careful, Frankie.'

She flinched. 'What do you mean?'

'You're going through a horrible time. That makes you vulnerable. This woman might try to get to you somehow. If she knows about me she could easily know about you. Maybe you imagine it would be lovely to have a sister around, someone who'd love and support you, make you feel less alone. But it won't work like that. She's probably full of anger, jealousy, resentment. You don't know what you might get yourself into.'

'Don't worry about me, please. Don't think about it any more, just get better!' Frankie decided she would see Alyssa one more time – to tell her she did not want contact with her any more than her mother did. Her mother was right; it wasn't going to work, and she didn't want to get into this. Especially not now.

'Have you thought about what you'll do when you and Joe get divorced?' Estella asked, raising another subject Frankie did not want to get into. 'I mean, will you stay in the Netherlands or come back here and get another job?'

Would she still be alive to make that decision? Frankie shivered. 'I don't know.'

She could not mention Joe's gambling and the terrible debt he had run up. She found it incredible, would never have suspected that he was even interested in gambling. And certainly not to the extent that he'd borrow from some criminal and put himself and her in danger. There might be other things she didn't know. Frankie was too stunned to be angry. Right now she could feel only bewilderment and fear. Could Joe get a loan, she wondered? He earns a lot more than I do.

'You make sure you get everything you're entitled to.' Estella's voice broke into her thoughts. 'You've been married for ten years, and you gave up a good job to go with him to the Netherlands. He might dump you, but he can't leave you with nothing. You're not alone,' she said. 'You know you've always got a home with me.'

Frankie nodded. She knew she should be grateful for that. Imagine if she had nowhere to go. But the thought of taking up residence in her old bedroom again, the place where she had dreamed her teenage dreams, to be back where she started and having to try to make a new life, made her feel paralysed with depression and hopelessness. Who exactly was this man threatening to kill her and Joe? No good saying it was Joe's problem, the thug wouldn't listen. What the hell was she going to do? Could he find her in England? She got up, unable to sit still any longer.

'I'll be off now.'

'All right, love.' Estella smiled up at her. 'Don't walk home, it's dark and getting late. Take a cab. The consultant's supposed to be coming round in the morning,' she said. 'I'll ask him when I can get out of here.'

Frankie's mobile rang as she stepped out of the lift. A passing doctor glanced sharply at her and she realised what a state she must look – scruffy clothes, no make-up, wild, unwashed hair. Frightened eyes. He probably thought she had escaped from the psychiatric unit.

'Frankie!' Joe's voice was high and tearful. 'You've got to get back here. I'm in hospital – the Westeinde hospital in The Hague. You've got to–'

'Hospital?' She stopped, shocked. 'What's happened?'

'Those bastards kicked the crap out of me!' Joe choked up, started to cry. 'They–'

'*Who?* What bastards?'

'Thugs who work for Agron Xhani. The gangster I owe the money to.'

'The man who threatened me?'

'Yes.'

'Oh God, Joe!' Heart thudding, Frankie walked on down the corridor past the flower and sweets stall. The beating must be a punishment, a warning. She had no hope that Xhani would forget the debt, not after what he had said to her. And not after this.

'It was a warning,' Joe said as if he guessed her thoughts. 'They nearly killed me.'

Frankie remembered something. 'He – Xhani – told me you'd

stolen something from him. In addition to owing that money. What does he mean?'

'I don't know, I haven't a fucking clue!'

Frankie was surprised not to feel great shock and concern for Joe. Only for herself.

'And Lida . . . they . . . oh, Christ!'

She stopped again and frowned. 'What the hell's Lida got to do with this?'

'They raped her – all four of them – beat the crap out of her!'

'*What?*'

'She was there when they broke in. We can't tell the police the real reason for the attack,' Joe sobbed. 'Otherwise we're dead, all of us. You and me are dead anyway if we can't get the hundred grand. Xhani owns the casino where I played. Another reason Lida can't tell the police is because Xhani was her supplier.'

'Supplier? Of what?'

'Coke. Cocaine.'

'She knows this bastard? That's how you met him, through her?'

'Right. She's letting the police think the rape might be because she's a prosecutor at the War Crimes Tribunal – some revenge attack. If she confesses to taking coke, that's her career down the toilet.'

'What, even in the drug-tolerant Netherlands?'

'Of course. Oh and by the way, thanks for asking how I am. I'm really touched by your concern!'

'What happened to your concern for me?' For the first time anger gripped Frankie. 'So the lovely Lida's a cokehead. What was she doing in our home? I can't believe she wanted to know how I was. She's proved a major let-down as a friend. Just as you've proved a major let-down as a husband.'

Joe sniffed, gulped a breath. 'I'm sorry. I didn't want you to find out like this.'

'Find out what like what?' Frankie tensed, trying to steel herself for whatever horrible revelation might be coming next.

'Lida and I were–' He paused. 'You know. Together.'

Frankie reached the lobby with its reception desk and small café and sank on to a plastic, pea-green chair. Cups, saucers and spoons clinked in the background. A couple of paramedics stood talking to the receptionist. She closed her eyes. 'How long?' Huge shock and bitter hurt struck again. Tears welled behind her eyelids.

'A few months – I don't know! What does it matter?' Joe's voice rose in panic again. 'They made me watch. Everything. When it was over one of them slashed her face. Lida's not lovely any more,' he sobbed. 'She's a mess, Frankie, a terrible mess. They did it because they thought she was you – my wife.'

Frankie gasped again and opened her eyes, the tears dripping down. She shook her head, unable to speak.

'Jesus Christ, I can't stop shaking. They said we have to come up with the money,' Joe went on. 'Or Xhani will kill us. Lida promised to help me get it, but now . . . I don't know. Can't you help? Borrow it from your mother or–'

'Are you crazy? You stupid, selfish, bastard.' Frankie wiped her eyes. '*You* borrow it – you've got more chance than I have. Do you seriously think I'm going to even mention this to my mother? She's in the cardiac ward, in case you've forgotten. There's no way she could get that kind of money, even if I was prepared to ask her. You got yourself – and me – into this mess. It's your problem. *You* sort it.'

'It's your problem too, Frankie. Sorry, but it is. Xhani's going after you as well; he doesn't care how he gets his money. This is a shit world and that's the way it is. And it won't be long before he finds out his hired help raped and kicked the crap out of the wrong woman.'

'The *wrong* . . .? How dare you talk like that.'

'I'm sorry. I didn't mean it – that didn't come out right.'

'Nothing you say comes out right.' Frankie got to her feet again and hurried towards the exit. Outside there was a gusting wind and dark, cloudy sky. Panic overwhelmed her. 'How the hell do you even imagine I'm going to get my hands on one hundred thousand pounds?'

As she spoke the words a woman in front of her stopped, turned and looked into her eyes. Frankie bumped into her and dropped the mobile, cutting off Joe's frightened shouts. She reached down to grab the phone and saw polished, black, high-heeled leather boots, long legs encased in dark-grey trousers, a small waist and tight black top, and a black suede jacket flung over slim shoulders. Long blonde hair, silky as ever, watchful green eyes with curling, mascara-ed lashes. The green eyes were red-rimmed. A lot of people cried in hospitals.

'Monique Miller!' she stammered, astonished and dismayed. Had Monique heard that bit about the hundred grand? Frankie wanted to run away. The two women stared at one another.

'It's Monique *Thorn* now, if you don't mind. Well, well. Frankie Sayle, my childhood friend, bridesmaid and partner in crime! This is a surprise.' Monique did not smile. 'Don't tell me you still live around here?'

'No. I'm staying for a while. At my mum's. She's in hospital.'

'Oh. Sorry to hear that.' Monique continued to stare at her. 'I'm remembering all those good old times already.' She hitched her bag over one shoulder. 'Drowned any butterflies lately?'

Chapter 13

Why did Vivienne wait so long?

How could she zip her contemptuous, pink, gloss-slicked lips and sit on such a bombshell all those years? I was twenty-seven when she told me. Looking back, I think she regarded her sad, savoured secret as the big gun in her armoury. Her battle plan was to hold back the most deadly weapon until she could unleash it with maximum effect. She knew my father would never have the guts to tell me she wasn't my mother, or not unless he was forced to. He preferred to let people discover things for themselves: the hard way.

Vivienne's timing was right on the money. I'd survived, got an education and a place of my own, escaped her sadistic clutches without becoming too bitter and twisted. Or so I imagined. I'd qualified as a fledgling barrister. Criminal law. Not making a fortune, like a lot of people think barristers do, but I'd had a few good cases and was doing okay. I was also about to marry the kind of man I had come to believe existed only in fantasies – Tomás was kind, generous, a laugh, sexy, knew how to delight in every way. Yep, should have known better. When things seem too perfect it's because they are. Viv knew exactly how to shunt my life off its tracks. She got just one thing wrong – she thought she would be around to take pleasure in my pain.

When you get married you need a copy of your birth certificate. I had never seen mine up to then. The time I was eighteen and needed a passport to travel around Europe with a couple of mates, then South America, Australia and the US, Dad took care of it for me, telling me to just sign the boring old form at the bottom because he'd fill out the rest, and hand him one of my unflattering black-and-white mugshots taken in a booth at Lime Street station. I remember feeling surprised, touched and flattered, the way you are when someone you think doesn't give a damn suddenly takes an interest. Years later he reacted with anxiety when I told him Tomás and I were going to get married. I thought it was because he didn't like Tomás, although I couldn't imagine why not. Vivienne went around sporting a big smirk. How do you make God laugh, she asked? Tell him your plans. I didn't know what she was on about, and cared less.

Dad offered to get me a copy of my birth certificate too. I was touched and grateful again, especially as I was so busy with work and wedding arrangements. He said before he gave it to me we should have a talk. The spark of paternal interest made me warm towards him further, and think this might be a new beginning. I laughed and said fine, thinking if this talk was about the birds and bees it was *way* too late. Maybe he was going to apologise for not being the best of fathers; if so, I would reassure him. I was happy, stupidly happy. I got really carried away and even imagined him seeing a grandchild of his for the first time.

Vivienne phoned the chambers one afternoon to say the certificate had arrived and I could drive out to the house and collect it. When I got there she told me Dad had had to go away at short notice, to Madrid, and would be gone a couple of days. I was disappointed, but not surprised. Vivienne wore a white suit with big shoulder pads, like Joan Collins in her *Dynasty* days, and her hair was cut short and retouched with blonde highlights and a rinse to hide the remaining grey. She stank of booze. One of her long, sexy lunches, no doubt, trying to prove to herself that she hadn't lost her crackle at fifty-whatever. How sad is that, to define yourself by whether or not you can get someone to fuck you? Had the poor guy left, or was he upstairs, naked and handcuffed to the bedpost? I didn't care; I just wanted to get out.

Vivienne was sniggering as she whipped the birth certificate from the envelope and handed it to me. I unfolded it, stared at the registrar's slanted handwriting and gasped – was this some kind of joke? No joke, she laughed. I'm your wicked stepmother, my dear. She actually used those Grimm words.

Stunned, shaking my head, I thought, No, it's not true. Dad would have told me before now – he wouldn't have let me grow up, reach the age of twenty-seven, without knowing this. And how could Vivienne have kept her mouth shut? It's not possible. Who is this Estella whatsername? It says here she's my mother, but that can't be right! This is a mistake.

I was breathing hard, still shaking my head, trying desperately to think straight. Vivienne knew a lot of dodgy men; one of them could be a forger. She'd done this to freak me. Like the time she brought me breakfast in bed and stuck my dead kitten instead of hot, buttered toast on the plate beneath the white, embroidered tray cloth. She never had an original idea in her thick head, and I knew she'd watched Bette Davis in *Whatever Happened To Baby Jane?* on telly the previous night, substituting my kitten for the rat naughty Baby Jane had put on her crippled sister's plate. Now I was wondering whatever had happened to Baby Alyssa?

I started to cry, get hysterical. I screamed that it wasn't true, that this was her sick idea of humour. Hurting people, cheating and lying, being a fuck-up, that was all she was good for. Vivienne got furious then. It's real all right, she snarled. Check it out if you don't believe me. What will your sexy Tomás think? Won't know what he's marrying now, will he? Might have second thoughts; he won't want to mix his gene pool with yours. I don't blame him. You were abandoned, she shouted. Your mummy didn't love you. She was a stupid, dirty slag, she never wanted you, so she walked out and left you lying in your own baby shit. She didn't care whether you lived or died. How does that feel?

It felt like everything was crumbling, collapsing. It was like waking up from a bad dream to find myself in a nightmare. My life was a lie, a delusion. I wasn't this person, I was someone else. I couldn't take in the enormity of it. I managed to say that if Vivienne wasn't my real mother I could at least be glad about that. She threw an empty champagne bottle at me.

I ran out of the house sobbing and shaking, my face streaming with tears, got into my car and drove off. My next thought was to phone Dad, but I didn't have a number for him in Madrid, and there was no way I was going to go back in there and face *her*. Deep down, I knew it was all true. I recalled my father's anxious, irritated, evasive behaviour both times I'd needed a copy of my birth certificate. How he'd said he wanted to talk to me. The fact that I didn't resemble Vivienne in any way, never had. Yes, I could be very glad about that. But not yet. Not unless and until I could piece together every bit of my shattered life. Abandoned as a

112

baby! Why didn't my mother want me? Why couldn't she love me? Even Vivienne's mother had wanted her. My father's deceased mother had adored her cold git of a son. Hitler's mother had loved him. What was wrong with me?

I sped off down the lane, sobbing loudly, my mind a panicked blank, and almost crashed into three people on horseback, scaring the hell out of them and their four-legged friends. I saw the riders startled expressions turn to fury, their lips form swear words to shout at the bitch motorist. I wound the window down and swore back, yelled my head off. Why couldn't the imbeciles canter across the fields and bridle paths that were all around, instead of choosing to trot three abreast down the middle of the lane? Sheer bloody-mindedness.

I drove back to Liverpool, taking about fifteen minutes instead of the usual thirty. It was a cold, sunny day. I drove along the Dock Road past the Irish boats and the old tobacco warehouse. I could smell coffee, chips, traffic fumes. Scavenging seagulls swooped over the sparkling river. I passed the Queen Elizabeth II law courts and the statue of Queen Victoria on her throne, not looking amused. I didn't go back to the office. I couldn't. Tomás was expecting me to phone him, but I couldn't do that either. We were supposed to go out to dinner that evening. Some story I'd have to tell over the wine and candlelight. Hey darling, guess what? I found out this afternoon that my life to date is one great, stupid, pathetic lie. A big piece of me is missing – just *gone* – and I haven't a clue what to do. How about that?

I went to a bar. Several bars, and then a pub. When in terror and turmoil, drink. I couldn't stand to go back to my empty flat in Sefton Park. My wedding dress was there, yards of ivory Duchess satin packed in layers of tissue in a big white box. A white carrier bag contained my long, silk veil, embroidered with seed pearls. I drank shots of vodka, one after the other. My fellow drinkers didn't bother me; they could see I was upset, unstable, and you never know what people like that might do. I must have looked strange sitting in that tiled, mirrored, brass-railed Edwardian pub in my black suit, tights and black high-heeled pumps, my hair unravelling – along with its owner – from the inexpert knot I'd hurriedly twisted it into that morning. The bundle of tied briefs on the table. Why on earth hadn't I left them in the car? Habit, I suppose. Looking at them gave me an idea – a really stupid one. Of course it didn't seem stupid at the time.

I took a cab to another bar down an alley off the Dock Road by beautiful St Nick's Church, where I knew a loyal client of our firm spent much of his time. Danny Paglino was delighted to see me because I'd just got him off a firearms charge. It wasn't any cleverness on my part; the officers of the law involved couldn't get their shrunken heads around the fact that if you wanted to make charges stick it was best to do things by the rules of evidence. They ended up being reprimanded by the judge, and left court muttering about fucking lawyers and giving me murderous looks. Danny wanted to know what he could do for me, apart from insisting on ordering a bottle of the establishment's finest sparkling wine. I told him. He was gobsmacked initially, but then burst out laughing and said, well, in the immortal words of Dirty Harry, there was nothing wrong with shooting as long as the right people got shot.

Next thing I remember is that it was dark and cold and I was back at Vivienne and my father's house, sitting outside in the car. The gun in my hands. I was going to teach Vivienne a lesson at last, make her pay for all those years of torment which had culminated in this enormous, shattering betrayal. I wanted to get my father too, but of course he wasn't bloody there. I understood how misery, rage and hatred can literally shrivel you from inside, suck up your energy and spirit. I felt as if I'd aged decades in the past hours.

Sitting there in the dark, however, wrestling with rage and hate, I eventually started to sober up and recover some capacity for rational thought. What was I doing with a gun in my hands? Was I insane? Okay, yes, temporarily. But no way was I going to go in there and blow her face off. Ruin my life for Vivienne? For my father? They really would have won then. And I refused to let them. I would, however, vent my feelings, tell Vivienne what I thought of her and my father, how much I despised them. I would tell her she could go to hell because I was damn well going to be happy. That would be my revenge.

I would marry Tomás. I might even look for my real mother and her family, if she had any. Maybe she did love and want me, but had to give me up for some reason. That happened a lot. When my father got back I would confront him too, tell him how weak and

114

pathetic he was, and that I never wanted to see or speak to either him or Vivienne again. My new life would begin with my wedding to the man I loved. And they were not invited. They were out of my life. Forever.

I put the gun in the glove compartment, thinking I'd dump it somewhere later. I got out of the car and ran up the drive to the house, the keys in my hand. It was nearly midnight. The front door was open, but that didn't surprise me. Vivienne was never very security conscious; she had probably come home drunk. I hoped she would be in a fit state to take in what I had to say to her.

'Vivienne?' I walked into the hall. 'Where are you?'

No answer. A weird smell hung in the air; chemical, rot, metallic, acrid. Something burnt? I didn't know, but it gave me the creeps. I clicked on lights and saw broken glass, smashed china scattered. My mouth went dry and my heart started to pound with fright and the after-effects of all that vodka. Had she been burgled? When I saw Vivienne's bathrobe lying crumpled on the threshold of the dining room, instinct warned me to get out, go *now,* run as fast as you can.

Why didn't I obey? I suppose because we're conditioned from childhood not to, taught that instinct is illogical and capricious, an evolutionary tool superfluous to requirements. And much of the time it is. But not always. I found her in the dining room.

My immediate impression was that Vivienne's face had melted.

I later found out it was sulphuric acid. H_2SO_4, if I remember the Periodic Table correctly. I could smell blood and gunpowder, charred flesh. She was dead, but the acid was still burning into her skin. I stood there paralysed, unable to comprehend the horror. I heard myself gasp with panic and revulsion. Saliva rushed into my mouth and I bent and threw up. After that I straightened up, tried to get myself together and turned to go. I had to get out of that terrible house of death.

Who switched off the dining room light and shoved me so hard that I staggered backwards and fell on top of Vivienne's corpse, getting her blood and gunshot residues on my clothes, skin and hair? I also got two small spots of acid burn on my left wrist, was lucky not to get worse. Lucky, yeah, that's me. Who did I thrash around in the dark wrestling with, screaming for help that I knew wouldn't come, thinking this masked figure must be her murderer and that now he wanted to kill me? My hands gripped cool metal, a gun barrel – the murder weapon? – and I tried to shove it away. But he didn't kill me. He ran off, leaving me half stunned and groping in the darkness, in a state of total freaked-out shock and panic.

I staggered back to my car, got in and drove off, tried to concentrate on not crashing and killing myself or someone else. Who was that mystery figure, why had he – I presumed it was a 'he' – killed Vivienne? By the looks of things, he had hated her even more than I did.

I knew I should go straight to the police. Trouble was, I had Vivienne's blood, other body fluids and hairs on me, and I thought that gun barrel the killer had tried to ram against my throat was the murder weapon. I had another gun in the glove compartment of my car, for God's sake, bought from a known criminal, my client. Even though that gun hadn't killed Vivienne, it was obvious I had both method and opportunity. And a motive, once I was forced to reveal my terrible relationship with my wicked stepmother. You didn't need to be Director-General of the National Crime Squad to work out that I would be suspect Numero Uno. Maybe I was worrying about nothing, and the police would believe me. Or they might not. Apart from that, I was a barrister; they hated fucking lawyers. And this particular fucking lawyer had just earned several of their number a stinger of a reprimand from a very pissed off judge. Enough already.

I drove into the city along Scotland Road and Byrom Street, up William Brown Street past the big library, museum and Walker Art Gallery, and past St George's Hall. A beautiful, historic part of Liverpool, but I couldn't appreciate it just then. I headed up Renshaw Street and Upper Duke Street and turned down faded but elegant Georgian Gambier Terrace, where John Lennon was once supposed to have shared a flat. I never liked the Beatles' music or John Lennon, and thought 'Imagine' one of the most incandescently crap songs ever penned. But you don't go around Liverpool broadcasting those opinions if you care about the state of your health.

I wanted to go to the police. It was the right thing to do. I was innocent; I had nothing to fear. At least that was the theory. But knowing the legal system from the inside, I realised I had plenty to fear – mistakes, muddles, leads not followed up, other stuff left undone. Indifference, stupidity, limited minds, cynicism. If you're innocent you've got *everything* to fear. I was terrified the police wouldn't believe me, wouldn't even bother to launch a murder inquiry once they had what seemed like a bleedingly obvious suspect. I'd go down for a crime I had contemplated but not committed. Lose my career, my new start, my freedom. Lose Tomás. I was terrified. I couldn't risk it.

If I kept quiet everything would be fine. Of course they would interview me, talk to everyone who had known Vivienne, especially the nearest and so-called dearest. But nobody knew what had happened between us the day she was murdered. The police might do some real detective work and find the murderer, get a confession. I'd be in the clear. My prints might be on the murder weapon, but they had no reason to request a set from me. I just had to stay cool and keep my head down. Right now I had to get myself together and dump the gun I'd bought from Danny somewhere it could never be found. He wouldn't want to buy it back, as the piece almost certainly had a history. It gave me the chills to think how insanely stupid I'd been. I worried briefly about who Danny might tell, or what I'd do if he tried to blackmail me. But what use was it to worry? I had no time, it might not happen, and if it did I would have to deal with it.

I parked in a quiet street and used tissues and the remains of a bottle of sparkling mineral water to rub the blood smears off my face and hands. Thank goodness for black clothes. I dabbed at the stinging spots on my wrist. I couldn't stop crying and shivering. What I needed to help me calm down was another drink, but going to a bar or pub wasn't a brilliant idea in the circumstances. I had to dump the gun now. But where?

I decided on St James' Cemetery, the old graveyard below Gambier Terrace next to the Anglican cathedral. Catacombs were set into the walls, a series of gradations that sloped down from the terrace. Dad used to take me there sometimes when I was little; he liked to wander around gloomy historical places. The cemetery spread over 10 acres and contained about 58,000 corpses. The last burials took place during the 1930s. St James' contained the grave of the first railway casualty, William Huskisson MP, run over and killed by Stevenson's *Rocket* at the Rainhill trials. There was Catherine 'Kitty' Wilkinson, friend of widows and orphans and instigator of washhouses and baths for the poor during the cholera epidemic of 1832. Captain Elisha Lindsay Halsay of South Carolina had met '*an untimely death in the Bay of Biscay, 1844*' when the ship's cook, John Kent of Liverpool, stabbed him to death. On his return to port, Kent managed to convince a jury that he had acted in self-defence.

I grabbed the plastic-wrapped gun and a torch, got out of the car and climbed over a fence. I went down a steep, dark, walkway; the graveyard had been a quarry before it was landscaped in 1829. I came to the tunnel under which Victorian and Edwardian funeral carriages had rolled. The tunnel sides were lined with ancient gravestones set in the walls. I switched on the torch and went cautiously down it, hoping not to encounter any dossers, crackheads or marauding rapists. Although none of them could be anything like as terrifying as the horror I had just experienced.

Water dripped from the slimy stone ceiling. I came out into the cemetery and stopped, listening for sounds. All I could hear was long grass rustling between the gravestones and tree branches creaking in the breeze. Deeply creepy, not the best place to come after walking in on a murder scene. I flashed the torch, looking for somewhere suitable to hide the gun.

Family graves were common. Fathers and sons lost at sea, sisters and brothers dead from childhood illnesses. I chose a spot by the grave of Margaret, Thomas, Savinah and Alice Ellis, none of whom had lived to celebrate their first birthdays. Poor little things. So cruel, so unfair! How can anyone say we're put in this world to learn lessons? What lessons did those babies have to learn? I started to cry again. Shouts and laughter came from the street above. Dark clouds hid the moon and a few drops of rain fell. I pulled some heavy stones from the crumbling wall behind the trees and stuck the gun in a small space. Put the stones back. It was hard work and I was sweating by the time I finished. I ran out of the cemetery, climbed back to street level and collapsed into my car. I drove slowly back to Sefton Park.

Tomás was pacing the big sitting room, his dark eyes distraught, overcoat and tie flung on the sofa. He took one look at me and realised something bad had happened. Where had I been, why hadn't I called him? Had someone attacked me, was I hurt? I fell sobbing into his arms and spilled out my gruesome story, all

118

my fears, told him how I didn't dare go to the police. I'd thought of lying to him, concealing what had happened, but I was too freaked and in the end I had to tell him the truth. I didn't want any secrets between us, especially not one like this.

I was hysterical. Tomás made me lie on the bed while he gave me a drink and then made me tea. He wrapped his arms around me and rocked me while I cried. He said what a shock, how terrible for me. But that Vivienne had caused me nothing but misery, and to be honest he wasn't sorry she was dead. Of course no one deserved to be tortured and murdered like that. He said after we were married and I'd had time to get over the shock of what happened, I could look for my real mother if that was what I wanted. If it didn't work out with her for whatever reason, so be it. The main thing was he loved me, we had each other, he would look after me. We had a lifetime of happiness ahead. That was what mattered.

He was wonderful, so calm and comforting, so understanding. There was only one thing Tomás did not agree with me about. I had to report Vivienne's murder, he said, because not to do so was taking too big a risk. The police would interview me, my father, other people; it was bound to come out that my relationship with Vivienne was like something out of a Brothers Grimm tale. I had no alibi for the night of her murder and unfortunately Tomás couldn't provide one, not after having spent the evening phoning around colleagues and friends to ask if any of them had seen me or knew where I was. I need not tell the police about buying the gun from Danny Paglino – better not. I should just say I'd gone to the house to confront Vivienne, and tell the police what had happened after I got there. If I didn't go and make a statement soon it would look suspicious.

I was telling the truth, he said; it all fitted. I didn't have to be so frightened. He would go with me to the police station, stay with me, make sure they did everything right. It would be another traumatic experience on top of what I'd already suffered, but I had to go through with it. The police could arrest the murderer, maybe get a confession, and I could carry on with my life. There had to be plenty of suspects, given the life Vivienne had led. Maybe one of her boyfriends had murdered her. Or my father could have hired a hit man to kill her while he was in Madrid.

I had to laugh at that one, despite my shock and trauma. Fussy,

119

critical, irritable, head-in-the-sand Daddy hiring a hit man? He wouldn't even know how to go about doing that. Besides, he loved Vivienne, he was crazy about her. Totally unlike him to be crazy about anyone, but there you go. We don't generally kill the things we love. We just go on loving them no matter how much they hurt us or fuck up our lives. Another argument against a hit man was that this murder was a work of pure hate. It was horrible, messy and very personal. Nothing clean or professional about it.

I knew Tomás was right when he said I should go to the police. But I was hysterical, terrified, in too much of a state to go anywhere or do anything. I couldn't face it. In the end he could see it was no use. I pulled off my clothes, dumped them in the washing machine and switched it on, took a long shower and then we went to bed. Tomás held me all night long, kept telling me how much he loved me and that everything would be all right. I fell asleep in his arms and didn't wake up screaming.

Next morning I was back in court prosecuting a girl who had stabbed one of her mates in a club during a fight over some guy. I promised Tomás I'd go to the police station at lunchtime. He insisted on coming with me.

My father discovered Vivienne's body that morning when he walked in with his airport carrier bag full of Scotch and cognac. I got back to the office at lunchtime. Tomás was waiting. He made me eat a sandwich and drink a cup of coffee. After that we went to the police.

So began a very long afternoon. It was draining and terrifying, but there was a lot worse to come. The horse riders I'd nearly crashed into in the lane the day before had memorised my licence plate number and reported me for dangerous driving, so I had to try and explain away that one first. And I might have succeeded, had not my devastated, grief-stricken father revealed that Vivienne had phoned him in Madrid the previous evening and told him I'd gone to the house, aggressively demanded my birth certificate and thereby forced her to confess she wasn't my mother. Something that yes, of course, he should have told me a long time ago. Vivienne had expressed herself as terrified because I had run off in an enraged and hysterical state. Shouting abuse and threatening her, swearing revenge.

Screaming that I would kill her.

Chapter 14

'This is bizarre! Monique, how on earth did Conal manage to *shoot* himself?'

'It was an accident, Glynis.' Monique tried to keep the irritation and fear out of her voice; it was hard to stop herself losing it big time. She jumped as tree branches brushed the windows. It was raining outside and blowing a gale, dark now, and Lauren still wasn't home. Normally she would have been frantic about that. 'Conal says it was sheer carelessness on his part.'

Thank goodness his sixty-something, divorced mother lived on Guernsey and had broken her ankle, so she couldn't land on their mediaeval stone doorstep tomorrow...Was it some psychic moment that had made Glynis pick up the phone and call at this inconvenient time, or did she have nothing better to do?

'But Conal's not the careless type. Oh, this is awful! What happened, exactly?'

'He was cleaning the gun, reached for something – a cloth, I think – and stumbled. That's when it went off.' Monique thought how lame that sounded.

'You're telling me he was cleaning a *loaded* gun?' Glynis' voice was a squeak of incredulity. 'I can't believe it! It's totally unlike my son to do anything that stupid.'

'Yes, I know. It's just . . . Conal forgot it was loaded. He'd only recently got up, apparently, and he was still a bit tired. Hungover.'

Monique cringed as the two uniformed police officers seated on the opposite sofa exchanged glances. She was making it worse. A tired, hungover man attempting to clean a loaded rifle went beyond black comedy, beyond farce. Conal was right, he did look like a freaking monkey chunk. Well, better that than a murder victim. Oh, my God, she prayed. Please don't let him leave me! The wind moaned around the house like some restless, prowling spirit. Sodden leaves whirled against the windows and stuck.

'Good grief!' Glynis exclaimed. 'He could have blown his head off. How was he holding the gun when it went off? What angle?'

'I don't know. I didn't see what happened.'

I didn't see what happened was starting to sound like a mantra. Monique shifted on the sofa and glanced at the cup of cooling coffee that the solicitous Joanna had brewed for her. She wanted a big Southern Comfort with coke and she would have one the minute this lot pissed off and left her in peace. She sniffed hard and wiped away the tears that kept flowing, conscious of Joanna's sympathetic gaze. She wasn't sure what the police officers were thinking, but they appeared disturbingly unsympathetic. Suspicious, even. And no wonder. But if she and Conal stuck to their story about how the shooting was an accident, the police couldn't do anything – could they? Of course these two might be just annoyed that the law apparently permitted hungover imbeciles to keep loaded guns in their homes.

'I'd just got back from Liverpool.' She blew her nose. 'I'd been to get my hair done. The car broke down in the lane, so I had to walk the rest of the way. I was in the hall taking off my boots when I heard a shot. I dashed upstairs and found him lying there.' It struck Monique that she was talking too slowly and carefully, as if she was giving evidence in court, trying to defend herself from the sarcastic questions and whiplash glare of the prosecuting counsel.

'Oh, my *God*.'

'It's all right, Glynis, really.' Was it? 'Try not to worry too much, please.' Monique nodded her thanks as Joanna pushed the cup of coffee into her free hand. 'He'll be out of hospital in the morning. They want to keep him in overnight for observation, because he lost some blood and is suffering from shock. His blood pressure was a bit low, but he's stabilised now. He'll be fine, I promise you.' She wished she could be sure her and Conal's marriage would be fine. 'He has to rest the arm and shoulder, give it time to heal. Have some psycho ...' God's sake! she screamed silently at herself. '*Physio*therapy sessions.'

'This is terrible, he could have been killed. I always told him he shouldn't keep a gun in the house.'

'Yes, Glynis. I know you did.'

'So did you. You once warned him he was more likely to get shot with it himself rather than wing any intruder. I remember your words distinctly.'

'Do you?' Thanks for that, M-in-L.

'What about Lauren? Was she there when it happened?'

'No, thank goodness. She's been out all day. I'm expecting her back any minute.'

Another thing she had to face but which would now have to stay on hold a bit longer – her daughter's secret sex life. Monique wasn't sure whether or not to tell Lauren the truth about the shooting. She had to tell her something, of course. Maybe it was best to stick to the accident story. The poor girl didn't have to know she had a jealous, crazed sicko for a mother. But if Conal decided to leave, divorce her, Lauren would have to know the truth. She adored Conal, so she would be shocked and devastated. Monique could not, did not even want to imagine her own heartbreak if Conal divorced her.

'I'm sorry to question you like this, love,' Glynis said, hearing her sob. 'I know you're upset; this must be an awful shock for you. And I know Conal's going to be all right. I'm so worried because apart from everything else, I simply can't imagine how he could possibly be that careless.'

'Neither can I.' Or the police, judging by their attitude.

'Is he stressed, has he got something on his mind?'

'No, nothing like that. I'd know if he had. Glynis, I'm sorry, but I have to hang up now. There are two police officers here.'

'Police?'

'Yes, they're interviewing me. And my neighbour. Going over what happened.'

Monique felt frightened again. Would the police believe her and Conal's story? She jumped as Joanna's hand settled on her shoulder. If only the woman would bugger off. She was loving this. At least her bloody husband hadn't turned up.

She said goodbye to Glynis and faced the police officers again, smoothing her sweaty hands over denim-clad thighs. Maybe she should have changed into a skirt or dress after she got back from the hospital, put up her hair, cast herself in the role of ditsy wife. Monique had a nasty feeling she didn't look right – the tight jeans and clingy, sky-blue, cashmere sweater revealed the curves of her

123

breasts, buttocks and small waist, her newly cut blonde hair hung loose and shining, and she'd put on more make-up, painting her lips a defiant, glossy red. Her long nails were perfectly manicured. Despite the tears she thought she seemed too polished, too hard. Then again, certainly not too clever after some of the things she'd said. Monique's fear increased as she recalled bumping into Frankie Sayle at the hospital. What must the odds be against meeting up with *her* again after all these years, and in such circumstances? She took it as a bad omen.

'Right, Mrs Eccleston.' One of the officers glanced at Joanna. 'We've gone over your statement. You're happy with it, are you? Convinced that this shooting was an accident, even though you didn't actually witness it yourself?'

'What are you talking about?' Joanna whipped her hand off Monique's shoulder. 'Of course it was an accident.' She glared at him. 'I don't know how you can dare to insinuate otherwise.'

'We're not insinuating–'

'Haven't Mr and Mrs Thorn suffered enough without you making things worse? Asking if they're happily married, indeed! What exactly is that supposed to mean? And why aren't you out catching criminals?' Joanna demanded, easing into her rant. 'Too frightened of them, I suppose.'

The other officer nodded. 'Criminals might have guns.'

'Don't get sarcastic with me, young woman.'

Monique threw Joanna a pleading glance. The last thing she wanted was for her to make things worse by antagonising the police.

'We're not making insinuations,' the male officer resumed. 'Or blaming anyone. This is purely about trying to establish the facts.'

'Well, now that you've established them why don't you go away and leave Mrs Thorn in peace? I understand you even harassed Mr Thorn in his sick bed.'

'We asked him a few questions once the doctors had treated him and assured us he was stable. Mrs Thorn–' The policeman turned back to Monique. 'We may decide to confiscate your husband's gun licence – temporarily, anyway – in view of his admission that he handled the weapon in an extremely negligent way. This incident could have proved fatal.'

'So tell him that, not me!' Monique snapped, her nerves on

edge, forgetting to act the ditsy wife. 'He's the one who insisted on buying the bloody thing.'

'We will tell him. Again.' The officer slipped Joanna's statement into a file. 'If an intruder gained entry to these premises and Mr Thorn fired the weapon and caused injury, that could have very serious consequences for him.'

'Oh, yes.' Joanna turned red. 'We know that, don't we? God forbid that anyone be allowed to defend themselves and their property. We might injure a burglar, oh dear!' She stood up, nervous fingers plucking at the pleats of her tweed skirt. 'My husband and I just got burgled. And let me tell you, that's no joke. If some criminal decides to break into your home and ends up getting more than he bargained for, it's a bit late for him to start whinging about his human rights.' She tapped her chest. 'What about *my* rights?'

'Have you considered counselling, Mrs Eccleston? Victim Support?'

'Don't you talk to me about counselling!' Joanna clenched her fists. 'If you people did your job properly there wouldn't be all these victims who need support. I never heard of such impudence.'

'Right. Well.' The officers glanced at one another again and got up. 'I think we'll leave it there. For now.'

For *now.* Did that mean they'd be back? Monique wasn't going to ask. She stood up too, desperate to get them out of her house. She remembered she hadn't offered them tea or coffee. Maybe they were pissed off about that in addition to drunken, gun-toting imbeciles and ranting seniors. They probably thought they had better things to do. They left, heads bowed against the onslaught of wind and rain. Monique shut the door and sighed. She felt exhausted.

'What a waste of taxpayers money.' Joanna rubbed her hands together. 'I don't know about you, but I could do with something strong and colourless to drink. Shall I pour us both a large gin-and-tonic?'

'Not for me, thanks, Joanna. Lauren will be back any minute and I'll have to tell her about the . . . the accident.'

'Oh. Yes, of course. Well, you don't mind if I help myself.' She turned and strode towards the kitchen.

'Joanna, wait a minute, please.' Monique was having

murderous thoughts about people who outstayed their welcomes and couldn't take hints. 'You've been terrific and I'm very grateful. But I'd rather be alone now, if you don't mind.'

It was obvious Joanna did. She stood there disappointed and slightly offended. 'It's no trouble for me to stay.'

Only to piss off. 'No, really.' Monique folded her arms. 'Thanks very much for everything. Give my regards to Eric, won't you?'

'Well, we're neighbours and we have to stick together out here. If you need me again, just pick up the phone. Any time.'

'I will. And thanks again. Goodnight, Joanna.'

Monique poured herself the Southern Comfort with delicious, full sugar Cola and sat at the kitchen table to gulp it while she contemplated the possibility of a shattered marriage, shattered by her own stupidity and craziness. Please God, let Conal forgive me! She longed to phone him, but he would be asleep now. Even if he wasn't, he would not want to talk to her. There was nothing she could do but wait and hope. It was terrible to have a problem you couldn't just chuck money at. Monique felt powerless and filled with panic. If Conal left her after this shooting 'accident', wouldn't that look very suspicious? What would the police do then?

She finished her drink and flung the empty glass against the far wall. Screamed and cried until the tension drained from her and she was spent. She poured herself another drink, gulped most of it and leaned her head on the table. She felt alone, devastated at the thought of a future without Conal. Terrified to think she could have killed him. She wished he would phone and comfort her, tell her everything would be all right. But there was no comfort. She didn't deserve any after what she'd done. She was lucky not to be locked in a cell facing a manslaughter or murder charge. This might be as good as it was going to get.

Monique remembered her strange meeting with Frankie Sayle. Who had Frankie been talking to, and why was she so desperate for a hundred grand? Sounded like she was in a lot more trouble than that summer day in junior school when the pair of them had drowned the poor, beautiful, Red Admiral butterfly in the caretaker's watering can, been caught by him and hauled in front of the class to face shame, disgrace and opprobrium. Today they would have been regarded as fledgling psychos and sent to psychiatrists. She and Frankie had done other wicked things: gone into

126

the churchyard at lunchtime to climb up and strike mocking poses on the statue of patient, long-suffering Jesus, sneaked into the church and frolicked on the altar where females were only permitted at their weddings and funerals, joked about mortal sin as they teetered along the altar rails overcome by giggles. One day the priest had caught them and reported them to the headmaster. At the comprehensive they had stolen sweets, crisps, pop, exam papers and later on, each other's boyfriends. It wasn't so much a friendship as an evil association, a fatal attraction.

She and Frankie had gradually lost touch with one another after Monique got married and had Lauren. Monique had suspected that Gerry fancied Frankie, mainly because that was the only one of her friendships he approved of and encouraged. Frankie did not return the compliment – she thought Gerry was a creep and had warned Monique not to marry him. That had resulted in a row and several months of not speaking to one another. Monique had almost had to look for another bridesmaid. The fact that she should have listened to Frankie only made her dislike her more.

In the end she and Frankie had drifted apart. It had to be almost a decade since they had last met. Where did Frankie live now, Monique wondered? Was she married, did she have kids? Monique would not have expected Frankie to stay in Merseyside or the north-west; she imagined her travelling the world and settling in a foreign country, maybe marrying some rich criminal. But she obviously hadn't married anyone rich if she was wondering how to get her hands on a hundred grand. Why did Frankie sound so scared, why did she need that money so badly? A hundred grand was nothing to her. That thought would once have cheered up Monique big time. But it was going to take more than counting the coins in her pot of gold to make her feel better now.

A car drove up to the house and a few seconds later the front door slammed. She got to her feet, wiped her eyes and stumbled into the hall. Lauren was taking off her denim jacket, smoothing her windswept, bright gold hair in front of the mirror. Her unzipped bag lay on the floor, trainers and the handle of a tennis racquet sticking out.

'Sorry I'm late, Mum. I stayed for dinner and then we watched a DVD of that Eminem movie. I know I should have phoned, but …' She turned, startled as she caught sight of her mother's ravaged face in the mirror. 'What's wrong? You're not this pissed off with me because I'm a bit late, are you?'

Three hours late, to be precise. But Monique let that go because it didn't matter. She burst into tears again. Christ's sake, she thought, get yourself together. This isn't just about you and your pathetic, stupid misery. You nearly killed your husband!

'Mum!' Lauren's voice was filled with alarm. 'What's wrong?' Monique felt her daughter's arm slide around her shoulders. 'Has something happened?' She paused, glancing around. 'Where's Conal?'

'Let's go and sit down.' Monique wiped her eyes on her sleeve. 'We have to talk.'

'About what?' They went into the sitting room and settled on a sofa. Monique thought her heart would break. She raised her head and looked at Lauren through her falling tears.

'Mum, you're scaring me.' Her daughter's beautiful face was a mask of alarm. 'For God's sake, what's happened?'

'It's Conal,' Monique gulped. 'He's in hospital. He – I–'

'In *hospital*?' Lauren let go of her and jumped up. 'Why?'

'There was an accident. He was cleaning the rifle and he – he shot himself.'

'Oh, my God. Oh, my *God!*' Lauren turned white. 'Is he badly hurt?' She gave a little sob. 'Is he going to die?'

'No! Nothing like that, I promise. Look, you mustn't worry, there's really no need. It's not serious. He's fine, he'll be out in the morning. The bullet hit his upper arm and caused some blood loss. He'll have a stiff, painful arm and shoulder for a while, but that'll soon–'

'How could Conal shoot himself in the upper arm? That's impossible! Where were you when it happened?'

'Well, luckily I came home early because I decided not to have lunch with Jan. I was in the hall and I heard a shot. I dashed upstairs and found him.'

'Conal wouldn't clean a loaded gun, he's not that stupid! And why would he clean it again so soon anyway? He only did that the other afternoon – he was doing it when I got in from school.' Lauren started to wail. 'You're lying!'

'Lauren, what–' Monique was shocked and unnerved. If she couldn't persuade her teenage daughter it was an accident, how

128

could she expect to persuade anyone else? Most importantly, the police. 'How can you say that?'

'You did it, didn't you? You hurt him!'

'Me? No! Never. It was an accident.' Monique stared at her, horrified. 'What are you talking about?' she whispered. 'Why would I want to hurt Conal?'

'Because you found out. Look, I can understand you lost it; I realise you must be feeling terrible. But you shouldn't have done it. You're crazy, Mum. For God's sake, you could have killed him!'

'Found out what?' Monique's legs felt weak and she had to sit down again. What the hell was this about – why did Lauren imagine she would have a reason to shoot Conal? Was Conal lying after all? Maybe he really was having an affair with that girl in the red dress; maybe Lauren had found out and Conal had somehow persuaded her to keep quiet, involved her in a conspiracy of silence against her own mother.

A wave of anger, hurt and sick jealousy crashed over Monique. There she was, a pathetic sad act pleading with her husband to forgive her, not to leave her, when all the time he was the guilty one! 'Found out *what*?'

'You know what!' Lauren screamed, tears pouring down her face. 'I'm sorry, okay? I love you, Mum. I never wanted to hurt you. I can't believe Conal told you. He promised me he wouldn't say anything.'

'Told me?'

'About us. Him and me. I'm sorry, Mum, but I couldn't – I *can't* help it.' Lauren's green eyes were dilated with shock and misery. 'I love Conal!' she cried. 'He loves me. We want to be together.'

Chapter 15

'That's quite a story.' Alyssa got up and walked to the window.

'I don't know why I told you. Or why I came here. I must be mad.'

Or desperate. Sitting around her mother's silent house, tormenting herself by thinking about Joe's affair with Lida, wondering if someone might be going to come after her and kill her, not to mention how she was going to get a hundred thousand pounds, was driving Frankie crazy. She kept imagining Lida lying injured and traumatised in a hospital bed, with panda eyes and a slashed face. That could have been her.

She laid her bag on the stained, cigarette-burned sofa and glanced around the living room of Alyssa's flat at the top of the Victorian house in Bold Place which overlooked the ruins of St Luke's Church and gardens, kept as a memorial to the May Blitz of 1941. Incendiary bombs had destroyed the nave and chancel, but the tower and outer walls remained largely intact. St Luke's bells had first rung out over the city in 1829 and it had been known as the 'Doctors Church'. The church and gardens, surrounded by tall, black, wrought-iron railings and chained, padlocked gates, were now closed to the public due to danger from falling masonry.

'Well, I'm really glad you came. And that you confided in me. Thank you for giving me another chance.' Alyssa lifted the dirty lace curtain and fiddled with the catch of the paint-peeled, sash window. 'Look at that.' She pointed at the church, at the trees and bushes that grew all down the rubble-strewn nave. 'It's a wonder this building survived the blitz, being so close.' She turned. 'I think I can sense something, an atmosphere. Terror. It's probably my imagination playing tricks.'

Frankie grimaced. 'Think I can sense cockroaches. It's got that smell I remember from flats I shared during my student days.'

'Yes. But I haven't seen any cockroaches. If the beastly beasties only crawl out at night it means you haven't got too much of a problem.'

'Yeah, well. Fingers crossed.' Frankie looked at her. 'This is all a bit sudden, isn't it? I didn't know you were moving out of that hostel.'

'Neither did I.' Alyssa let the curtain fall. 'The arbiters of my destiny do things in a disjointed kind of way. I think they were pushed for space at the hostel and it wasn't long before I was supposed to leave anyway, so they dumped me here. It's not much, but at least it's nice and central. With period features.' She pointed to the ancient gas fire with its hearth of cracked blue tiles. 'And I'll get dole . . . what do people call that nowadays?'

'Income support. Or job seekers allowance.'

'Sounds suitably positive and upbeat. Well, it'll pay my rent and food and stuff while I'm seeking some shit job.' Alyssa paused. 'That's if I can find even a shit job.'

Frankie did not try to come up with any comforting platitudes, which she had a feeling Alyssa would not appreciate anyway. She wondered if income support and an isolated existence in some cockroach-ridden Victorian inner-city dump was to be her fate as well, if she managed to avoid being murdered because of her husband's debts. Could this Agron Xhani get to her in England if he wanted?

She looked out of the window again, down into the nave of the church. The trees and bushes were starting to turn autumnal colours. One of the sandstone tomb slabs was slightly skewed, as if a vampire had climbed out for a night of blood-boozing and never returned.

'Would you like a coffee?' Alyssa asked. 'Only instant, I'm afraid.'

'Thanks. I take sugar, so that'll mask the taste.' Frankie followed her into the small kitchen. 'Period features in here as well,' she commented, noting the ancient gas cooker, wooden cupboard and scuffed brown lino curling up at the edges.

'Yeah. It's great, isn't it?'

'So, what will you do now? Apart from looking for jobs.'

'Well, I'd love to get to know my new sister.' Alyssa filled the

131

kettle and spooned coffee into two mugs. 'And I hope she'll want to know me.'

'I'm still not sure about that.' Frankie frowned. 'And I feel horrible about going behind my mother's back. She mustn't find out we've met, and that I'm seeing you. She couldn't take it, especially not at the moment.'

'So you've said. Don't worry, she won't find out. Who's going to tell her? Not me. I know she won't change her mind about meeting me. Not yet, anyway.'

'She may never change her mind.' Frankie's voice was sharp. She felt annoyed with herself as well as Alyssa. She was getting the woman's hopes up by coming here. Should she even be alone with a convicted murderer? How did she know Alyssa was telling the truth when she said she was innocent?

'How's Estella doing?' Alyssa poured just-boiled water into the cups.

'The consultant said she can go home in a couple of days. She'll have to be on some kind of heart medication, at least for a while, and then they'll review it. But yes.' Frankie nodded. 'She does seem a lot better.'

'I'm glad.' Alyssa reached for the sugar. 'Look . . . I realise she's terribly upset because I've suddenly turned up after all these years and want to meet her. But doesn't she think about how you must feel? You've got a sister you never knew about until now. Surely she can accept that you'd at least want to meet me? If not yet, at some point in the future.'

'She's thought of that. She said it wouldn't work out. That I was too vulnerable right now and you might try to use that. And –' Frankie hesitated '– she's afraid you might want revenge.'

'Because she abandoned me?' Alyssa paused and looked at her. 'Is that what you think?'

'I did wonder. But now that I've met you and had some time to mull over what you've told me – I don't really think so. Anyway, what revenge? We're not rich, there's nothing valuable you can steal from us. My mother's a lonely widow who's just had a heart attack and is freaked because her long-lost daughter wants to meet her. My husband's dumping me, my life's falling apart. I could get murdered.' Frankie's voice trembled. 'What more could anyone do to either of us?'

Alyssa sighed and shook her head. She opened the fridge.

'D'you take milk?'

'Just sugar.'

'Same as me. How much?'

'One spoonful and a bit.'

Alyssa smiled. 'Same!'

She looked better when she smiled, Frankie thought, studying her. Well, who didn't? But it made her look different somehow. Pre-jail different? Alyssa wore faded blue jeans and a red jumper with a dark-blue band across the middle. Had she been wearing those clothes when she was brought to prison a decade ago?

'You can ask me anything you like –' Alyssa stirred the coffee '– about my dark past.'

Frankie blushed. 'I was just wondering if you were wearing those clothes when they took you to prison.'

'They're old, aren't they? But no, I wasn't. Female prisoners can wear their own clothes.' Alyssa's smile broadened. 'I didn't have to wear pyjamas with black arrows all over them, like in a chain gang.'

'I didn't imagine so. What was it like . . . being in there?'

'If I tell you that most of the women are mentally ill and – or – drug addicts, hurt themselves, and that the few sane ones may not come out with their sanity intact, I think you can paint a picture.'

'My God.' Frankie shuddered.

'A lot are on medication when they're admitted. Even if you're not, you can end up on it. Tranquillisers, anti-depressants. Most people tell you to "get yourself a girlfriend". Which usually means getting coerced into abusive relationships. More women than men get sent to jail but most of them aren't there for violent offences, like the guys. But hey, *I'm* still sane.' Alyssa smiled again, but her smile was strained this time. 'At least that's what I like to tell myself.'

'Did you serve your whole sentence in the same prison?'

'No. I started off *dahn saff*. Then the less time I had left, the further north they moved me. Until I ended up back on good old Merseyside. And now here I am. Ten years older, but not much wiser – wise about things I need to know, that is.'

'If you didn't kill your stepmother, who did? Or who do you think did?'

'That's one of the things I'm not wise about. If I get any ideas I'll let you know.'

'Suppose you find out, what will you do?' Frankie was still not sure she believed Alyssa's story.

'Wreak violent and bloody revenge, of course. No, I'm joking. I'll go to the police, get a lawyer. That's if I've got proof, of course.' Alyssa picked up her mug and gestured towards the living room. 'Shall we? The other thing I want,' she said as they sat down again on the horrible sofa, 'apart from getting to know you and trying to build myself a life, is to look up my ex-fiancé.'

Frankie started. 'D'you think that's a good idea? I mean, not to sound nasty, but–'

'Oh, I know. Tomás could be married, have kids, not want his dark lady from the past intruding on his cosy life. But he loved me, Frankie, he knew I was innocent. He's such a good man. All I want is to let him know I'm out, maybe see if he can help me find a slightly less shit job. It was thanks to Tomás that I was allowed to appeal. He tried so hard to prove my innocence. I'd like to talk to him again about my case, or ask him to talk to someone for me. You never know, there might be just one tiny bit of evidence that was overlooked or some information that could point to some-thing, give me a clue as to who the murderer is.'

Frankie nodded. 'I suppose that's possible.' She wondered if this Tomás Slaney was real or some fantasy figure who had helped Alyssa survive her years in jail. He certainly sounded too good to be true. 'If you could prove your innocence you'd be entitled to compensation,' she said. 'One hell of a lot, I'd imagine. Not that that would make up for–'

'No, it wouldn't. Nothing would. Tomás was so loyal to me when I got accused and arrested.' Alyssa blinked hard and glanced away. 'He stuck by me, visited me in prison, said he'd wait for me and he didn't care how long it took. I told him to go away and get a new life, but he wouldn't listen. When my appeal failed and I knew I wouldn't get another, that I'd have to do the full whack – that was it. I couldn't stand it any more, couldn't stand the thought of him putting his life on hold for me. I was a mess; I just wanted to fade away and die. I refused to see him, stopped answering his letters. In the end he got the message. He wrote me one last letter saying he'd always be there for me, would never forget me, and that I was to contact him for help as soon as I was released. Whenever that was.'

'He must have loved you very much.' Even if this Tomás did

exist, what he had written then and what he might think now could be very different. Frankie was silent. 'How will you find him?' she asked eventually. 'It's been years. He might have moved. For all you know, he could be living in the US or New Zealand.'

'No. Tomás Slaney was – is – a barrister specialising in fraud cases. I looked him up on the Electoral Roll. He has moved, but only out of town to some posh place on the Wirral. He's not in the phone book, so he must have an unlisted number. I don't know if he still works for the same firm, but I can find out. I might write to him. Or go to the Crown Court one day and hang around until he comes out. I've got time.' Alyssa looked moody. 'Plenty of *time*.' She took a sip of coffee. 'That's one thing you don't have, of course. Is there any chance you and your husband can get that money?'

'Not unless we rob a bank or nick an old master from some gallery.' Frankie shook her head, her eyes filling with tears. 'I don't know what to do. I don't want to go back to the Netherlands, but I can't stay in England much longer either. Or not at my mother's house – I could put her at risk. I can't tell her anything about this. If she knew my *life* was in danger –'

'You can stay with me.' Alyssa glanced around the living room. 'This place isn't exactly the Ritz. But nobody knows about you and me. You'd be safe here.'

'But what would I tell my mother? And what about Joe?'

'What about him?' Alyssa's clear grey eyes narrowed. 'It's his fault you're in this mess. As if it wasn't enough to dump you for that Dutch tart after ten years of marriage!' She paused. 'You said she's rich, a lawyer, got a judge for a dad. Surely she could lay her hands on a few euros?'

'Lida appears to have gone back on her promise to help him. Of course she may not be in a state to help anyone right now, including herself. Joe says he can't get in touch with her. He doesn't know where she is. They were both taken to the same hospital, but Lida's parents turned up and whisked her away. He only found that out when he tried to see her and one of the nurses told him she'd gone. Joe said Lida got him into gambling when he – when they –'

'When he started shagging his wife's friend. Sorry,' Alyssa said as Frankie flinched. 'But that's what happened, isn't it? Blames everyone but himself, your Joe. *She* got me into this, *they* did that. Not good enough, is it?'

'I know he's been a bastard. I know we're finished, whatever happens. I have to accept that, and in time – if I get the time – I will. But for God's sake, I don't want him to be murdered!'

'And I don't want you to be murdered. Think of yourself, Frankie.'

'I considered going to the police and asking for protection. But what will that do except get me or Joe killed quicker? So I thought of something else.'

'What?'

Frankie paused. 'Why am I *telling* you all this? I don't even know if I can trust you.' Tears filled her eyes. 'I'm pathetic, I'm desperate.' She put her mug on the floor because there was no coffee table, grabbed her coat and stood up. 'I should go.'

'No. Please, not yet.' Alyssa stood up too and gripped her arm, her eyes shining. 'I'm your sister. You can trust me, Frankie, you *know* you can. Even while you tell yourself you can't.'

'Is that right?'

'I'd do anything for you. It's hardly any time since we met, and I don't blame you for being suspicious in the circumstances. I didn't exactly handle things well. And I realise my mother may never want to know me. But you're my family. Please give me a chance.' Alyssa let go of her arm and stood back. 'Sorry.'

What do I have to go back to, Frankie thought? An empty house where I get the chills every time the phone rings. Another visit to that bloody awful, depressing hospital this evening. She might even run into Monique Thorn again. That had been an unpleasant shock. She felt helpless again, frightened, vulnerable and alone. She missed Joe, despite everything. You couldn't be married to someone for ten years and not miss them, no matter what they had done. A big hole had been punched in her life. She felt drawn to Alyssa, more than she wanted to admit. She couldn't get over how they resembled one another, seemed to have the same tastes and sense of humour. It was as if they knew each other already. Guilty of murder or not, whatever lies Alyssa might have told, Frankie could not help liking her new sister. Very much.

'Okay. I'll stay another hour or so.' She slipped on her coat and hitched her bag over her shoulder. 'It's a nice day, why don't we go for a walk?'

Alyssa took a long breath. 'I know,' she smiled. 'You want some proper coffee."

'You read my mind.' They went out and down the stairs. Alyssa was right, Frankie thought, this house did have a funny atmosphere. From behind a door she heard a baby crying and a dog barking, but no adult voice soothed or admonished. 'So you don't have any other family?' she asked.

'Just my father. But I haven't heard from him since before my trial. He never wanted to know, and he certainly won't now. He was an accountant and worked for some big firm, always going off on trips abroad. He'll have retired a couple of years ago, I imagine. He was so uninterested that I wondered why he'd bothered to keep me.' She laughed. 'I think it was touch and go as to which parent abandoned me first.'

Frankie winced. 'Do you blame my – our – mother for what happened? You must do to some extent, surely?' She felt nervous again as she remembered her mother's fears that Alyssa might want revenge. She dismissed the thought ... What revenge could make up for the enormous hurt of being abandoned by your mother? Alyssa did not seem angry or bitter towards Estella. Frankie's instinct told her neither she nor Estella needed to fear Alyssa. She was nevertheless relieved to be out of that flat, walking down narrow Bold Street surrounded by happy shoppers and people stuffing chips in their faces.

Alyssa took a few seconds to answer. 'I don't blame her, no. I mean, from what you've told me, life wasn't exactly easy for her when I was born ... She obviously still feels awful about what happened ... Guilty. That's why she won't meet me. I do understand. But I would still love her to talk to me some day. Answer my questions. I feel she owes me that. Never mind me, it could do her some good too.' Alyssa's voice turned shaky. 'The fact is, the bottom line is, she abandoned me. To know my mother didn't want me, or not enough to keep me with her, that feels . . . well, it feels like all I've ever been is her dirty little secret. Oh God.' She stopped and put one hand over her eyes. 'I'm sorry!'

'You're not anyone's dirty secret. Don't ever think of yourself like that. Don't even say it.' Frankie hesitated then gave her a hug. Alyssa leaned against her, her body trembling. Then she pulled away and tried to smile.

'I'm okay, honestly. And I don't want to whinge all over your cool coat. Looks bloody expensive.'

'Sod my coat.' Frankie had bought it with her first month's salary from the embassy.

'I don't get it.' Alyssa wiped her eyes with the tissue Frankie handed her. 'I didn't whinge the whole time I was inside. Now it's all raw, bleeding emotion. How sad am I?'

'It's called post-traumatic stress, isn't it? All the time you were in prison you were trying to cope with that ordeal, just get through each day. Each week, month, year. It must have been terrible. Even worse if you –' Frankie paused. 'Because you were innocent.'

'Thanks for that, sis. Even if you're not sure you mean it.'

Frankie let it go. 'You're out, but of course that doesn't mean it'll be easy from now on. You have to build a new life. And you've got time to reflect, experience all the emotions you didn't allow yourself to feel during those years. It might be too difficult for you to cope with alone. Maybe you should talk to somebody.'

'A psychotherapist? Forget it. I'd rather talk to you. And Tomás, if he wants anything to do with me again. Whatever happens, I will cope. I have to.'

They walked down to the Pier Head and found a café that looked out on to the river. They sat at a table outside. When their coffee was served Alyssa leaned back and lifted her face to the sun.

'This is a normal, cosy, everyday thing, isn't it?' she murmured. 'Taking a walk and having coffee with your sister. It's what billions of people all over the planet do, and they think nothing of it. Except maybe how enjoyable. But to me it feels completely weird. Mind-blowing, in fact.'

'Are you okay?' Frankie looked at her. 'Would you like a drink as well as coffee?'

'You're joking. I'm intoxicated enough as it is.' Alyssa opened her eyes and sat up. 'I'm fine.' She smiled. 'Really.' She picked up her cup and took a sip of coffee. 'That tastes a lot better than the crap I've got. So –' she glanced around and lowered her voice '–what we talked about earlier. You said you'd thought of something. What is it?'

Frankie wondered again if she should confide in Alyssa. But who would Alyssa tell? And who would believe her if she did tell anyone? She leaned forward. 'I know the name of the guy Joe owes that money to.'

'The gangster?'

'Yes. I thought I could go and talk to him. Tell him Joe dumped me, that he doesn't care and I'm nothing to him any more. That this is really not my problem. Lida's the one who matters to Joe now.'

'Okay.' Alyssa nodded slowly. 'Let me get this straight. You want to talk to the guy who had your husband beaten up and his girlfriend raped and cut – and that could have been *you* – and tell him you haven't got the money and it's not your problem?' Her cup clattered on to the saucer. 'Please tell me you're joking.'

'I know it's a long shot. I'm taking a big risk. But what else can I do, sit back and wait for him to murder me? Which he will if I don't do something quick. I won't go empty-handed – that *would* be stupid. I can get together a few grand, so can Joe. I'll tell this guy it's all I've got.' Frankie's eyes sparked with malice. 'Tell him to ask Lida for the rest.'

'And you think that'll work? That he'll believe you? You think he'll say, "Oh yeah, okay love, no problem"? Forget it. He'll put a bullet in your head. After he's set up another gang bang.'

Frankie flinched. 'It might work. It's in his interests to at least listen to me. And I know organised crime is spiralling out of control all across Europe, but these people still can't just go round killing anyone they want. I mean, even the police are bound to notice sooner or later!'

Alyssa leaned forward, strands of lank hair falling over her face. 'Frankie, let me give you the benefit of my highly unpleasant experience. People who use violence, who commit rape, murder, you name it – they're all the same. They've got dead eyes, dead voices, dead minds; you can't make a connection. They go through the motions, but it's like something's missing. Something *is* missing. They're totally paranoid. Most people avoid them. You can't *talk* to the likes of that. It just doesn't fucking work.'

Frankie was silent. She felt the warm sun on her face, smelled the salty breeze blowing down river from Liverpool Bay. Alyssa did not have dead eyes or a dead voice. Both were full of intelligence, passion, longing, urgency. If she was putting on an act, she was very, very good. 'Did people avoid you in prison?'

'No.' Alyssa laughed, but she looked hurt. 'I avoided them. A lot of them wanted to be best mates with me. Wanted to tell me all about their snotty kids, their dear old mums, their useless boyfriends or husbands who'd dumped them the minute they got arrested. Some of them wanted sex. And of course they all wanted free legal advice. I was very much in demand.' She picked up the cup. Her hand shook and she put it down again. 'Maybe I can help you get some of that money.'

'*You?*' Frankie stared at her. 'Who's joking now! How the hell?'

'Not by committing a crime, if that's what you're worried about. Which you are.'

'Well, how would most people get that kind of money without committing a crime? Even if you obtained it by legitimate means and I paid the debt and everything was hunky-bloody-dory, I'd be under a horrendous obligation to you. What would you want in exchange?'

'Nothing but your love and trust, dear sister.'

Frankie's unease mounted. She was getting in too deep and she had to pull back. This sibling thing was too intense, more intense than the start of a love affair.

'Money can't buy love and trust,' she said. 'Didn't anyone ever tell you that?'

'No.' Alyssa turned pale. 'I imagine it's normally the sort of thing your mother tells you … Problem is, I didn't have a mother around to give me all those handy hints on how to get through life. Only some sadistic bitch who starred in all those famous fairy tales – *Snow White, Sleeping Beauty, The Snow Queen*. Handing out poisoned apples, abducting little children and taking them to her palace in the far north, turning them into statues of blue ice.'

'I'm sorry.' Frankie felt guilty. 'You don't look like someone who ate a poisoned apple. Or got frozen into an ice statue.'

'No. I just feel like one.'

Frankie stood up. 'I have to go now. Got to get back and visit –'

'Your mother. Yes. I know.'

'I'm sorry,' she repeated.

'Shall I give you a call in a few days?' Alyssa stared at the river. 'Or not?'

'A few days? Yes. Sure.' If she was still alive, Frankie thought but did not say. She decided she would confront Agron Xhani.

Chapter 16

'You lied to me,' Monique wailed. 'You lied about everything. You *bastard*.'

'Calm down, will you? I didn't –'

'Don't tell me any more lies, I don't want to hear. You couldn't be content with screwing some tart and letting me think I'd over-reacted and got it all wrong, could you? You had to seduce my daughter as well! Lauren's fourteen, for Christ's sake, she's under age. How *dare* you touch her! You make me *sick*.'

'Monique, I did not seduce Lauren. She's lying.'

'Lauren's lying, that tart the other day was lying. You're surrounded by malicious people who want to get you into trouble, aren't you?'

'It certainly seems that way.' Conal lay on the double bed in the guest suite, white-faced, his arm and shoulder wrapped in a sling. He looked exhausted. 'It's like I said – Lauren made a pass at me and I told her not to be so stupid. I told her I wasn't having it and you'd be terribly hurt if you found out. She got upset then. I promised I wouldn't tell you as long as she promised never to try it again. She swore she wouldn't, and I thought that was the end of it. Now I wish I had told you. She wants to get back at me for hurting her pride.'

'I told you to stop lying! Don't you dare blame Lauren. God, to think I was feeling so terrible about what I'd done. Pleading with you to forgive me, hoping I could save our marriage.' Monique paused, gasping for breath. 'How could you *do* this?' she screamed. 'I loved you so much; I trusted you.' She grabbed a flowered Wedgwood plate from the dressing table and flung it, smashing it against the eggshell-blue wall, just below the window. 'I'll make sure you do time for this, I swear.'

'You won't, Mum.'

Monique whirled round. Lauren stood in the bedroom doorway, pale and tense. 'Been eavesdropping, have you?' she hissed. 'Why are you still here? I thought you'd gone to school. Although I'm glad you haven't because you'll be able to adjust your skirt and change out of those shoes.' She glared at the dark-blue pleated school skirt pulled up to reveal an expanse of bare tanned thigh, and Lauren's scrunch-dried mass of blonde, glitter-gelled hair. 'What do you look like?' Jailbait? *No.* 'You're a mess.'

'Mum, I know you're upset, but don't talk to me like that. You've got no right. You had no right to go into my room and read my diary either. I won't forgive you for that. And Conal's not going to prison. That can only happen if I give evidence against him, and I'll never do that. I'll deny everything to the police.'

'Yeah.' Conal shifted into a sitting position, wincing with pain. 'Deny it because nothing bloody happened. You vicious, lying little bitch.'

'Lauren flinched. 'Conal, don't call me that. Please.'

'This is a nightmare – another one.' Conal stared at Monique, his eyes full of tears. 'You're crazy, the pair of you! You feed off each other's craziness.'

Monique tried to quell her hysteria. 'Lauren, go to your room and get changed. Hurry up or you'll miss the bus. Leave us alone, we need to talk.'

'Tell her you're lying,' Conal shouted. 'Tell her!'

'I love you.' Lauren had tears in her eyes. 'I love Mum too.'

'Nice way you've got of showing it.' Monique flung out one arm, pointing at the door. 'I *said,* go and get changed.'

Lauren lingered, looking as if she was about to argue, but suddenly stepped back and slammed the door. She clumped up the attic stairs.

'I didn't touch her,' Conal repeated. 'I'm not having an affair with her or anyone. I don't believe this! It feels like I'm the only sane person in a loony bin.'

'Be glad to move out then, won't you?' Monique sobbed. ' I want you out of my house. Today. I contacted my solicitor and I've got an appointment this morning to get the divorce started.

You leave me no choice.'

'What about my choices? This is my house too. You can't just throw me out. Monique, *please*.' Conal wiped his eyes. 'For Christ's sake, be reasonable. Haven't you done enough damage?' He pointed to his bandaged arm and shoulder. 'And Lauren – I can't believe she'd lie like this. I should have told you she'd made a move on me. Not doing that was a huge mistake. I didn't want to upset you.'

'You've made a lot of mistakes. Too many.' Monique pulled the belt of her grubby blue bathrobe tighter and caught sight of herself in the dressing-table mirror. She had aged in the past few days ... Her hair was limp, her face had gone thinner and her complexion was reddened with crying. She had bags under her eyes. She looked mad, traumatised. 'I'm going to tell the police and my solicitor what you did to Lauren. I meant what I said – there's no way you'll get away with *that*. Whether she cooperates or not.'

'Now just hang on one bloody minute here!' Conal struggled off the bed and got to his feet. He looked like he was going to faint. 'You need a shrink, Monique, not a lawyer. This is all in your fucked-up head. I'm innocent and I'm entitled to protect myself. If you tell the police I seduced Lauren, I'll tell them you tried to murder me.'

'You can't,' she gasped. 'It's too late; you've made a statement. You'd have to admit it was all lies. That's perjury. You'd be in big trouble even if they believed you.'

'Oh, they'll believe me all right. I might get charged with perjury, but you'll be in a lot more trouble ... The police are suspicious enough about the circumstances of the shooting. They can't get their heads around it and no wonder, because it wasn't an accident, was it? Those detectives as good as implied they believe I'm protecting someone. They think that someone's you.'

'Okay, fine.' Monique felt terrified, but she brazened it out. 'I'll admit I shot you.' Although she wasn't too sure about that. 'I'll say I did it in the heat of the moment when I found out you'd seduced my daughter. If ever there was a defence of provocation, that has to be it!'

'Oh, you're a lawyer now, are you? Say what you bloody like. You'll still face a stretch. Attempted murder is attempted murder. Look at all the publicity there's been about guns. The law says you can't go around shooting people, no matter what good reason you think you've got, and the courts are hell bent on making an example of anyone who does. And you can't prove I seduced Lauren because it didn't bloody happen and there's no evidence. Even if she cooperated, as you call it, and let doctors and shrinks swarm all over her, there still wouldn't be any. It's your – and her – word against mine. And I'm damn sure mine will prevail, given the fact that I've got a gunshot wound to back it up.'

'Your precious gunshot wound could be seen as proof of your guilt.'

'You reckon? Okay – if you were so furious at what I was supposed to have done to your daughter, why didn't you admit trying to kill me? Why tell Joanna and the police it was an accident? Why back up my statement?' Conal shook his head. 'No, Monique. That won't work, and you know it. You'll just look like the malicious, hysterical bitch that I never dreamed you were and can't believe I married. If you go to the police and try to get me charged with molesting your daughter, I'll tell them the truth about the shooting. And they will believe me.'

She was silent, trying to think of another argument. Even if she could prove Conal had seduced Lauren, that would mean putting her daughter through hell before the case even got to court. *If* it got to court. And he was right, the police were suspicious of her.

She turned away and looked out of the window across the fields, blinking back tears. She loved this house; she had been so happy here. Now, suddenly, all happiness was gone and she was in the midst of her darkest nightmare. She did not see how she would ever come out of it.

'Well?' Conal's voice was harsh, ragged. 'If you go through with this bullshit I'll fight you all the way. I won't take the rap for things I haven't done, things I would never even have thought about bloody doing!'

If she went to prison for attempted murder, what would happen to Lauren? Monique didn't know much about the law, but she did know you could get almost as heavy a sentence for attempted murder as for actual murder. Even if you didn't succeed, you had the intention. She could not risk losing her freedom, leaving Lauren alone. They needed each other more than ever now, even if their relationship had hit an all-time toxic high. She had to try and repair the damage, but right now did not see how the hell she could do that.

'I can't stop you divorcing me.' Conal sat on the edge of the bed, clumsily poured himself a glass of water and popped a painkiller from the foil pack in the drawer. 'And I'm not sure I want to after what you've done.'

She turned. 'What *I've* done?'

'Yes, Monique. Look at the state of me, for Christ's sake! I'm in agony. Not just physical agony. You've got no trust in me or in our marriage – how do you think that makes me feel? You're not the person I thought you were. That goes for Lauren too. I don't see any way back from this.' He took the tablet, drank the glass of water and slowly stretched out on the bed again.

'You're so full of it.' Once Monique would have felt heart-broken by his pain and his clumsy attempts to help himself. 'Well.' She sniffed, forced back another sob. 'All that remains is to see my solicitor about the divorce.'

'You go right ahead, darling. And don't think you can just pay me off and send me on my way like the hired help who didn't prove satisfactory. I'm your husband – God preserve me! – and business partner. I'm entitled to half of everything.'

'Half of–' Monique stared at him in shock. 'You must be joking!'

'I lost my sense of humour the second you pointed that gun at me and pulled the trigger. I'll make damn sure I get everything I'm entitled to. If you want to keep your precious company and this house and everything you'll have to buy me out. I won't fuck off and die.'

'I wish I had killed you!' she screamed. Conal started as she cracked a piece of porcelain underfoot.

'And I'll move out, don't worry about that. There's no way I want to be under the same roof as you and the teen witch up the stairs any longer than necessary. I'll find another place in the next day or two. I'll be talking to *my* solicitor as well.' He paused. 'You know, I think I'll tell the police the truth anyway. I don't see why you should get away with shooting me . . . You're dangerous; you deserve to be locked up.'

'You wouldn't – you can't do that! What about Lauren?'

'Oh yeah. Dear little Lauren. Like I'm supposed to give a fuck about her now.'

Monique could not look at Conal any more, could not be in the same room with him. She heard Lauren moving around overhead.

She ran to the door and pulled it open, dashed up the attic stairs and along the passage. Lauren gave a gasp of shock as she burst into her room.

'How many times do I have to tell you? You can't just barge in here whenever you like. Or go through my stuff. I'm entitled to privacy.'

'I'm getting a bit sick of hearing about all the things you imagine you're entitled to.' Monique stood in the doorway breathing heavily. 'Are you ready for school?'

Conal was an older man who had seduced a young girl, exerted undue influence. Or what did they call it now – grooming for sex? Try as she might though, she could not help blaming Lauren as well. Resenting her, hating what she saw as her daughter's betrayal. How could Lauren do this to her own mother? Monique had brought her up single-handed, put her first, loved her most, given her everything. What happened to love, to loyalty? Of course it was stupid to think that way. Why should someone be loyal to you because you happened to love them? Why should they be grateful? Stretch out your hand and get bitten; that was life.

'*Yes*,' Lauren hissed. 'I am ready. At least I can get away from you for a few hours.' She had lengthened her mini-mini into an ordinary mini, and changed into black leather, knee-high boots.

'Then go. Get yourself an education. Believe me, it'll be a lot more use to you than having sex with your mother's husband.' Oh, Christ! Monique thought. I shouldn't have said that. It isn't her fault. I've got to control myself.

Lauren threw her a look of pure hate. She grabbed her rucksack, ran out and down the stairs. A minute later the front door slammed. Monique usually dropped her off at the bus stop and saw her on to the bus, but this morning she couldn't be bothered. Lauren could walk for once, get some exercise. She was more than capable of looking after herself.

Monique went into the kitchen, poured herself a cup of coffee and added a spoonful of sugar for much-needed energy. She felt like having a drink, but it was far too early in the day and she did not want to turn up at the solicitors stinking of alcohol. It was hard enough to keep control of herself without drinking. Everything was falling apart and she felt powerless to salvage any piece of her shattered existence.

Surely Conal wasn't serious about grassing her to the police? But Monique had a feeling he was. She had an even more horrible feeling that he was right and they would believe him. She took quick sips of the hot, strong coffee.

'*Half* of everything?' she whispered, tears dripping into the steaming liquid. That was wrong, terribly unfair. Conal must know he couldn't expect that much. She had built up the company herself, paid for this house, owned both before she even met him. Conal had started working for her because his own job as manager of some import-export company was not going anywhere fast. If she had to give him half of everything she owned it would cause big problems and she would end up a hell of a lot poorer. She might even have to sell this house. It was adding insult to injury. Monique had not even considered getting a pre-nup. She regarded such things as unromantic, nasty and mean, a deeply cynical admission that you were not certain your marriage would last. If you felt like that, why bother to get married?

She banged the cup down on the draining board. She had to take a shower, get dressed in something severe to make it look as if she was a normal person in control of her life, and drive into Liverpool to the solicitors. She would take Conal's Jag because he wasn't driving himself anywhere today, not with his injured arm and shoulder, and her Lotus wasn't yet back from the garage.

And why not? Monique could not even remember to which garage it had been towed the other day. She needed her own car back. Of course she couldn't just have one or two big hassles, there had to be lots of little ones as well. She phoned the AA and eventually managed to get through to a man who seemed to know what she was talking about. He gave her the number of the garage and she phoned them.

'Mrs Thorn, we were about to call you. Yes, your car's been repaired now. But the mechanic who carried out the repairs thinks it could have broken down because someone tampered with it.'

Monique got a cold flush. '*What*?'

'He said there was something wrong with the suspension and steering. I won't go all technical on you–'

'Thanks for that.' Patronising bastard.

'–but were you having any problems with the car before it broke down?'

She tried desperately to think. She had not noticed very much at

147

all that day because she had been so preoccupied with Lauren. Well, she knew now who her daughter's secret lover was!

'I – I can't remember anything,' she stammered, in shock again. 'What do you mean exactly, what problems?'

'Well, that the steering didn't respond, especially at higher speeds. You might also have noticed it didn't respond at low speeds. Actually, you were lucky. The car could have veered across the road and hit an oncoming vehicle. You and any passengers might have been seriously injured. Or killed.'

She gasped. 'Are you sure about this?'

'Well–'

'But hang on. If someone wanted to tamper with a car, wouldn't they nobble the brakes rather than the steering or suspension?'

'Not necessarily. If the brake fails you just take your foot off the pedal and the vehicle comes to a stop by itself.' The man's voice took on a smug tone. 'That's why all those Hollywood films in which characters career along in speeding cars while jamming their feet on brake pedals that don't respond are totally unrealistic. You just wouldn't do that.'

'I've learned something new today, isn't that great. Look, are you *sure*? I can't believe this.'

He sounded annoyed now. 'The mechanic says your car *might* have been tampered with.'

Monique was finding it hard to breathe. 'You mean somebody wanted to kill me?'

'I wouldn't go that far.'

'But there's no way they could be certain I'd get injured. Or killed.'

'You're right, they couldn't.'

Monique hung up on him. She sat at the kitchen table and buried her head in her hands. She was shaking. The coffee machine gurgled in the silence and puffed out a little cloud of steam.

Someone had tampered with her *car*? Who? The day it broke down she had dropped Lauren at her friend's before driving on into Liverpool to the hairdressers. That meant her daughter could also have been injured or killed. It was supposed to look like an accident, but the accident had not happened. Did that mean whoever was behind this was prepared to try again, perhaps with some other method? Did they want Lauren dead as well as her? *Who*? *Why*?

'Oh, my God!' Monique whispered. She raked her hands through her hair. She had to call the police right now, get a detective or somebody to accompany her to the garage and talk to the mechanic in question. She should have asked his name.

She picked up her mobile then put it down again as another terrifying thought occurred. She groaned and tried to push it out of her head. But the thought wasn't going anywhere. It burrowed deep into her brain and lodged there, stuck like candy floss around teeth.

Monique got up, walked into the hall and stopped, looking up the stairs. Listening. There was no sound. She went back into the kitchen.

She thought things could not get any worse. But she was wrong. Stupidly, terrifyingly wrong. Conal did not want half of everything she owned.

He wanted it all.

Chapter 17

'It's all right, sweetheart. It's okay. I'll save you!'

She felt overwhelming love and protectiveness as she hugged the baby girl to her, careful not to hug too tight as she felt the rapid, rasping breaths and the growling in the little chest. She had to get the baby to hospital now, or she would die. But no one would listen or help. The people around her in this great big house were laughing, chattering, drinking – men in tuxes and women in swishing gowns and glittering jewellery. She could smell perfume, flowers, cigar smoke. They didn't care. They thought she was stupid to bother, that she should abandon the unimportant child and join the party. Life's party. She felt desperate.

'I'll never leave you,' she whispered, kissing the baby's flushed cheek. She cradled the child in her arms, tears running down her cheeks. 'I'll help you. You're mine and I love you so much. I'll save you.'

Estella woke to find herself gasping, her eyes full of tears. She sat up, one hand on her chest, and stared around Val's guest room. Afternoon sun slanted across the rose carpet and white wall, highlighting dust motes on the dressing table and chest of drawers. A breeze smelling of autumnal fields blew through the open window and she could hear Chanticleer, her unoriginal choice of name for Val's cockerel, crowing energetically. The noisy thing carried on all day, not just at dawn or dusk. Down in the hall the phone rang, and she heard Val answer.

Estella's breathing calmed, but the depression and fear of the dream did not fade. Depression and fear were her main emotions these days, squeezing out anything that could make life bearable, let alone enjoyable, and the dream was another manifestation of

150

her misery, guilt and anxiety. Deep-buried feelings were struggling out of her subconscious and forcing themselves to the surface of her mind. It was torture. Rest, the consultant said. Relax. At least his words gave her a laugh.

She got up, walked to the windows and drew back the heavy curtains, let the breeze cool her sweaty neck and face. She looked out over the back garden and fields. She had thought she would be glad to get back to her own home, but the truth was she was terrified. She did not want to be alone there. Val had insisted she stay with her for a week or two, and Estella was glad to acquiesce. She knew Val was surprised because she had expected her to argue about it or refuse outright.

Was this what it was going to be like for the rest of the time she had left? How long did she have? The consultant, Mr Stand-Up Comic, also said she might need a pacemaker when she was ninety. Estella could not imagine living until eighty, let alone ninety. But it was possible; she came from a long-lived family. She did not have the courage to try to kill herself; knowing her luck she would not die, just end up maimed and helpless. Besides, there was Frankie. She had to keep going for her daughter. Frankie's life was falling apart, and she needed her mother. Had there been times in Alyssa Ward's life when she needed her mother? Estella turned away from the window and buried her head in her hands.

'No!' she mumbled. 'Forget about her. You did it then, you can do it now. You have to. It's too late, too late.'

But her lost baby's presence hovered, wraithlike. Only Alyssa Ward was no ghost. She was real and terrifying, a woman with a history, dreams, desires, ambitions. Images flashed through Estella's brain, images she could not banish of the baby lying in her cot, her solemn, grey eyes following her restless, unhappy mother as she moved around the room. Her crying, as if she knew she was not loved, realised she would be abandoned. That final sight of her, sleeping at last, downy head to one side, her tiny fingers curled as if trying to grasp life and hold on tight, make sense of the world into which she had come. Her little breaths, her warm, baby soap and powder smell, the flutter of her unbearably delicate, shell-pink eyelids. What kind of world had three-month old Alyssa woken up to after the night her mother had left?

'Stop,' she whispered. 'Stop. *Now*.'

151

Estella walked into the adjoining bathroom and splashed cold water on her face and wrists. She felt her pulse – not too rapid, surprisingly – and studied her gaunt, anguished reflection in the mirror. She thought she looked like a corpse. She dusted blusher across her sharp cheekbones and painted her lips red, making the effort for Val and Colin rather than herself. The lipstick and blusher gave her the look of a made-up corpse. Estella combed her hair and smoothed her trousers and sweater. It was no use. She couldn't kill herself because she was a coward and because she could not do such a terrible thing to Frankie, so she just had to endure. This torture wouldn't last, it couldn't. Bad as well as good things came to an end. She would either stop feeling this way, or she would die. Until then she had to go on as best she could. She opened the bedroom door and went slowly downstairs. Colin was snoring behind the sitting-room door, the television was on, and in the kitchen teaspoons clinked against china. There was a smell of baking. Val hurried into the hall and stopped.

'Oh, hello. I was just coming to knock on your door. I've baked some lemon shortbread biscuits and made a pot of tea. Assam, your favourite. Frankie phoned from Holland, about ten minutes ago, but she told me not to disturb you. She says not to worry, she's all right and she'll call again tonight or tomorrow. And she'll be back soon.'

'Oh.' Estella nodded. 'Right.'

'Poor girl,' Val went on. 'What a thing to happen. It just shows, you never can tell. But she's a toughie, your daughter, isn't she? She'll sort herself out, get through the divorce and be happy again one day.' She paused, smiling. 'So how are you? Did you have a good nap?'

Estella, clutching the banister, nodded and forced herself to smile back. Now she thought she looked like a grinning, made-up corpse.

'Lovely, thanks.'

'Are you sure no one followed you here?'

'As sure as I can be.' Gasping and grimacing, Joe eased himself on to the bar stool and ordered a beer. 'Not a bloody undercover agent trained in counter-surveillance techniques, am I? You could have come to the apartment, you know. You don't have to stay at the Bel Air. I only left hospital this morning; I'm too ill to drag myself out of bed and halfway across town.'

'I'd hardly describe the Frederik Hendriklaan as halfway across town. And never mind ill,' she muttered. 'You might be dead soon. We both might be.'

'Cheers for that.'

'You know I wouldn't feel safe going to the apartment. With good reason.'

Frankie took a gulp of white wine and glanced around the crowded bar. Three more men entered and sat at a table near the door. They were scruffy, bearded, smoking roll-ups, crumpled shirts hanging loose from their jeans. She looked at Joe again. 'Didn't you get my message? I asked you to bring my laptop and some clothes.'

'Yeah, I got the message, all right. I assumed you were joking. I've got two cracked ribs in case you've forgotten, not to mention my other injuries.' Joe's bruised face darkened with anger. 'I'm hurting all over, my chest is bandaged so tight I can hardly breathe. I'm in no condition to lug around a laptop and a bag of clothes. Sorry, but you'll have to brave the apartment and collect the stuff yourself before you fly back. Oh, and the police will probably want to talk to you.'

She started. 'Why? I've got nothing to say to the Dutch police.'

'They might want a statement. I told them you weren't there when it happened, that you had nothing to do with it. But you're my wife and–'

'Yeah, for how much longer?' Frankie interrupted, her eyes filling with tears. 'Until you divorce me, or that criminal you got hooked up with murders me? What do the police think, that I fixed up the rape and beatings to get revenge on my cheating husband and his bitch girlfriend? Would that simplify the case for them?'

'Don't be stupid. I told you, they think it could be something to do with Lida being a lawyer at the Yugo War Crimes Tribunal. They also want to talk to you because you're Lida's friend as well as my wife.'

'*Was* her friend. And I thought she was mine. So Lida can't – or won't – help you get that money now?'

'Doesn't look like it.' Joe gulped beer. 'I've tried to get in touch with her, but I can't. Haven't got a clue where she is. It'll be her bloody parents,' he fumed. 'They've taken her away, probably to some private hospital. They won't let her contact me, not while she's ill anyway. It's their fault I can't get to see or speak to Lida.'

He could believe that if he liked: Frankie believed Lida had dumped Joe even faster than Joe had dumped her. She swirled wine around her glass. 'I want to talk to Agron Xhani.'

'Christ, not this again.' Joe groaned. 'How many times do I have to tell you that's an insane idea? *Beyond* insane.'

'Have you got a better one? I think not. This is desperate. What the hell am I – are we – going to do? If we can't get that money, and I don't see how we can, we don't have any choice but to throw ourselves on the mercy of the police and tell them we need protection. Before it's too late.'

'If we do that we're fucked. I told you. They can't protect us.' Joe banged his empty beer glass down and signalled to the barman. He lowered his voice. 'And they won't, not unless they particularly want to arrest that bastard – out of all the other bastards! – and think I'd be enough use to them as a grass. If they do and I agree – like I'll have a choice! – I'll be dead anyway. So will you.'

'For God's sake, if you go to the police and tell them your life's being threatened, they have to do *something*.'

'And what do you think they'll do? Take a statement and tell us to be careful. Drive past the apartment a few times a night, maybe. That's it. They won't take us into protective custody. Even if they think we're important enough for that, what then? How many times, Frankie? We can't go to the fucking police.' He leaned on the bar and buried his head in his hands. 'Jesus *Christ*.'

Frankie thought of Alyssa and her cockroach-ridden flat overlooking the bombed-out church. Maybe she could hide there, although the idea did not appeal. But what about her mother? 'You could have put my mother in danger as well as me,' she hissed. 'Haven't you done enough damage without that?'

'Yes.' Joe sighed and wiped his forehead. 'I've done more than enough damage. I never meant any of this to happen. I've been a stupid, crazy bastard and I wish I'd never started gambling or got a coke habit or–'

Frankie put down her glass and stared at him. 'You as well as Lida?'

'That's another reason the debt's so huge. It's not just gambling.

But I stopped it.' Joe shrugged again and winced. 'Okay. You know everything now.' His frightened dark eyes met hers. 'I'm a total arsehole and I'm very sorry about everything. You're caught up in all this through absolutely no fault of your own. That doesn't alter the fact that our lives are in danger.' He gulped more beer, his hand shaking.

'I'm going to talk to Agron Xhani.' Frankie was not going to ask Joe about a coke habit he no longer had. Or said he no longer had. She wasn't even interested. Alyssa was right, she did not know the half of it. And she no longer wanted to know. What she did want was to get her life back. 'Phone him, set up a meeting. Or give me his number and I will. I'll talk to him alone; you don't have to be there.'

'What's the bloody *point*?' Joe banged his glass down. 'Like you said, how the hell are we going to get that money? There's no way.'

'We're wasting time.' Frankie was not going to tell him her purpose was to try and extricate herself from this mess. Persuade Agron Xhani to go after Lida, even Lida's judge father if necessary. Just because Lida appeared to be letting Joe down big time did not mean he wasn't still in love with her. Anger and pain gripped Frankie. She took a breath. 'Let's get out of here.'

They pushed their way out of the hot, crowded bar and walked up the Frederik Hendriklaan past closed shops and an ABN bank. It was dark now and the autumn air was cool. She could smell the sea. A few cyclists whizzed past, avoiding the gleaming tram rails in the middle of the street. The Fred-laan, as most people called it, was one of Frankie's favourite streets in Den Haag, with its lovely shops, restaurants and the best delicatessen in town. She usually came here at lunchtime on her break from the embassy, and she and Joe had often dined in the various restaurants. From now on her memories of this place would be sad ones. Broken marriage, broken life. Danger. Fear. Joe walked slowly along beside her, gasping with pain, hands in the pockets of his black jacket. She stopped and took out her mobile.

'Give me the number.'

'Frankie.' He stared down at her. 'Are you *sure* this is a–'

'If you can't get yourself out of this, you can at least let me try.'

'Hey, sexy lady!' Neither of them had noticed the black Mercedes with tinted windows draw up alongside and two men

155

get out. They came towards them, grinning, arms spread wide. Frankie recognised the men from the bar.

'Oh, brilliant.' She started to tremble. 'You're right, you're not trained in counter-surveillance techniques,' she whispered to Joe as she backed away. She glanced around. The street was quiet and there was nobody nearby. Not that she could have counted on anyone's help if there had been. Especially not when these men had guns. She was dry-mouthed, paralysed with shock and fright. The men came closer.

'In the car,' one of them ordered. 'Get in.'

The doors were open, a third man at the wheel, the engine running. Frankie felt Joe's hand on her arm. To her astonishment, she realised he was shielding her.

'Leave her alone,' he shouted, his voice hoarse with fear. 'This is my problem, it's got nothing to do with her.'

'In the car, or we kill you now.'

Were these the same thugs who had beaten up Joe and raped Lida? Frankie wondered as they grabbed her and Joe and manhandled them into the car, guns pressed to the backs of their necks. We can't get the money, so they're going to kill us anyway. Better to let them shoot us here than in some secret place where they might do other things first.

In that moment, however, Frankie knew she did not want to die here. Or anywhere. She would do anything to stay alive, would cling to hope, the slightest chance. She heard Joe groaning in pain, pleading with them as she was blindfolded and pushed down on her knees, her face pressed into one of the men's crotches and her hands tied behind her back. Her jacket and top rode up. She struggled, terrified, as rough hands moved over her breasts and buttocks and between her legs, pushing and prodding, then tugged at the belt of her jeans.

'Nice ass,' someone laughed. 'Good tits.'

'Get off me! Get *off.*'

'Leave her alone,' Joe gasped. Frankie winced at the sound of a blow followed by another grunt of pain. The men started to talk in a language she could not understand. The car was speeding along, swerving around a corner, and of course she had no idea where they were now, or where they were going. She was hot, her hair over her face, gasping for breath. She could smell sweat, petrol, the car's leather seats. She tried to think straight, think what she could possibly do to escape or persuade these bastards to let her go. But her mind was blanking out with shock. She imagined the police informing Estella that her daughter had been murdered. Thought of Alyssa, her brand-new sister. Alyssa, looking down into the ruins of the bombed-out church, trying to think how to build a new life. Was she really innocent? And what did that matter now?

'Frankie.' Joe's voice was choked with terror. He was close by, so close that she could feel his body trembling against her left shoulder. The man's hand weighed her head down, playing with her hair. The gun pressed into the side of her neck.

'Frankie, I'm sorry!' Joe sobbed. 'I'm so sorry for everything.'

Chapter 18

This is crazy. I'm stunned, I'm shaking. It's unreal.

My father's house – that sounds like the title of a novel – is an exact replica of the house in my dream that starts off beautiful and mysterious then turns to nightmare. Red-brick Georgian, down a cinder path between fields. The fields are even misty, like in the dream, because there's a chilly, autumnal drizzle today. I stand and stare, mist and gentle rain clinging to me like a shroud.

How can this be? I've never seen the house, not even a photo, never been here before. I know my father moved well before I was convicted of Vivienne's murder and sentenced to all those years. He couldn't bear to stay in that house of horror and death. He was also sick of people strolling past then stopping for a good gawp, and reporters phoning him or ringing the doorbell to ask for interviews. It was a house of horror to me long before Vitriolic Vivienne was murdered.

Why – how – could I dream in such detail about a place I've never seen, even down to the dark-blue, shiny paint on the front door? Well, lots of front doors are painted dark blue. Georgian is dear old Daddy's favourite architectural period. He always liked living in the country. And he would have had the money to buy a place like this. Good career, plenty of bonuses, private work on the side, murdered wife's life insurance. Compensation for wife's murder, given that the State had failed in its duty to protect that individual's destructive existence. Wonder what the going rate for murder of a loved one was – is? Not that much, I bet. Still, Daddy would have had more than enough money to afford anything his cold heart desired.

So there's the perfectly rational explanation. Or part of it. I'm unnerved, nevertheless, even more unnerved at the prospect of meeting my father for the first time in more than a decade. I didn't dare turn up on spec – although I would have, if that had been necessary – so I phoned him to ask for a meeting. He refused at first; I got the impression he was frightened as well as shocked and angry. But I persisted, said it was something important that I couldn't talk about over the phone. I promised this meeting was a one-off and that I wouldn't bother him again. He agreed eventually, with great reluctance.

He made it abundantly clear that he doesn't require his only daughter's comfort in his advancing years. So he or the cleaner won't be hoovering the red carpet right now. God almighty – my father doesn't want me, my mother doesn't want me; I dream about a house that turns out to be real! It's enough to make me run screaming to throw myself at the feet of the nearest psychotherapist. And that's what I'll do if I discover a box of wriggling, venomous snakes in the house. I don't think that will happen though. You see, Doctor, I believe the snakes are purely symbolic. Of what, I have no clue. My own demons, perhaps. Poor Alyssa, what a twisted little mass of psychoses. I feel like giving myself a hug.

I walk up the cinder path and stop at the foot of the scrubbed front-door steps. They're worn down in the middle, from centuries of boots and shoes. I'm so nervous I want to turn and run away. But I can't – I've got a higher purpose, a goal to fulfil. I'm conscious of my scruffy jeans and sweater, the second-hand leather jacket I picked up for a tenner in Paddy's Market. It's several days since I washed my hair; it feels lank and heavy, doesn't smell too fresh. The trickle of lukewarm water from the shower in my delightful little city centre des res makes it difficult and time consuming to rinse out all the cheap shampoo and conditioner, so I can't be bothered to wash it more than once or twice a week. I know I've got the time, but I don't care to spend it shivering under lukewarm showers on chilly autumn mornings.

I didn't want to – don't want to see my father. I'm upset already, full of dread, the gleeful demons gathering. I have to force myself not to run away. Maybe he's watching from one of those polished, sparkly windows, or about to open the door. I've got to see him now, though, I've got to do this, no matter how hard it is. I'm doing this for Frankie. I can't bear the fact that she's in danger, that she could be murdered. I can't let that happen.

I gasp and step back as the front door opens. He must have been watching out for me. A second later he's standing there staring down at me with that same old expression: cold, critical, what's-that-nasty-smell, fuck-off-and-die. Well, Daddy, there were times when I wanted to die. But I didn't. And I'll be glad to fuck off, but not just yet.

He's wearing a posh suit and a dark-blue silk tie patterned with tiny . . . God almighty, they're puppies! *Not* really him. What can he be thinking of? He's still tall and arrogant looking, a lot more wrinkled than when I last saw him, and completely grey now. His look still shrivels me, but I tell myself it's not having any effect. All the lies I have to tell myself to get through each day!

'Come in,' he snaps, as if I were the plumber late for my appointment to check out the whiffy drains. 'And make this quick. I've got a lunch to go to.'

'Would that be a charity lunch?' I emphasise the word 'charity'.

My first words to my father in more than a decade. He flushes with anger, and I know I've hit the rusty old nail on its head. Not a brilliant idea to start by antagonising him when he's already pissed off big time. I go up the steps and walk past him into the hall, which has a slate floor, grey-carpeted stairs and a curving, oak banister that no doubt some pleasant woman comes in three times a week to polish vigorously. I catch smells of beeswax, soap, his pricey aftershave. There's also a smell of coffee, but he doesn't offer me any. I don't know if it's the long walk from the train station, or the stress of seeing my less-than-loving father again after all these years, but suddenly I don't feel very well. I go cold and a bit faint. I know I've turned pale.

'D'you think I could have a glass of water?'

He glares at me as if he thinks this is some sort of ruse, and presses his lips together. Glances around like he's wondering what ex-con daughter might try to nick while his back's turned. 'Just a minute.' He points. 'Wait in there.'

'Thank you.'

Wow, what a welcome. I walk into a large, light, sitting room. It's not empty, like in my dream, but tastefully furnished in keeping with the character of the house. There is no box of wriggling, poisonous snakes in the corner by the window. There's a chandelier and a marble chimney piece, but most houses like this would have such things. The chimney piece is grey marble though, not red like in the dream. Phew, I got something wrong. *Result*. I sink on to a yellow-and-white striped silk sofa that looks far too pristine for a scruffball like me. But if I don't sit down I might collapse. I'm shivering and my ears are ringing. A minute later I hear his returning footsteps. Long strides. Always in a hurry. He comes in and stops when he sees me sitting on his posh sofa.

'Oh. Made yourself at home, I see.'

'Sorry, but I had to sit down. I feel a bit faint.'

Now he thinks I'm trying to elicit his sympathy. He walks forward and hands me the glass, careful that our fingers don't touch. That hurts. It shouldn't but it does.

'So what do you want?' he snaps when I've taken a deep, shaky breath, a couple of sips of water and smoothed back my hair. My forehead and the palms of my hands are clammy and now I'm starting to feel sick, for God's sake. I take another sip of water. Better not vomit over all this beautiful, expensive, carefully arranged period furniture. Although that might be fun.

'Don't think you can just turn up here whenever you like,' he says when I don't answer immediately. 'Or treat this place as your home. It isn't and it never will be.'

'Don't worry. I've got no delusions in that direction.' Can't he see I'm ill?

'I told you on the phone, I don't want any contact with you. I didn't before, and I certainly don't now that you're out of prison. Tell me what you want and then go back to this new phase of your sordid, pointless existence. Don't bother me again.'

Worth every penny, that charm school. I put the glass on a little round polished table and look up at him. 'Don't you care about me at all?' Why do I ask such a stupid question? What am I, a bloody masochist? 'I'm your daughter, I haven't seen you for more than ten years.' Stop it, Alyssa, stay cool. No use, I can't. 'Don't you want to know how I am?'

'No, I damn well don't. Why should I? You tortured and murdered my wife.' He steps back. 'I cared about *her*. And yes, more than I did about you. That's what you could never stand. Years and years of resentment and jealousy, which culminated in that vicious, horrific–' He stops.

161

'I didn't do it.' My voice is faint. 'I didn't kill Vivienne.'

He flushes again. 'Did you insist on coming here and intruding on my privacy just to tell me *that*? As if I hadn't heard enough of your lies at the trial.' He points to the door. 'Get out.'

'No, please! Just give me a minute.' I want to stand, but my legs are too weak. 'That's not why I came. But it is the truth and I want you to know, I want you to believe me. Didn't you ever wonder all these years? If I was guilty, why would I have gone to the police after I'd found her dead?'

'Because that way you thought you could deflect suspicion from yourself.'

'No. I took a huge risk. I was afraid the police would blame me, and they did.'

'Maybe your fingerprints being on the murder weapon had something to do with that! Plus the fact that you'd threatened to kill Vivienne only hours before.'

'I never threatened to kill her, she lied about that. Don't you have any idea who did it?' I go on before he can speak again. 'The life she led – her affairs – you must–'

'Shut up. I won't have you talking about my wife, and certainly not like that.' His fists are clenched, as though he's making a big effort to stop himself landing me one. Which he probably is. His eyes are dark with rage and hate. And fear. 'Get out now. Don't ever come back here or contact me again. If you do, I'll tell the police you're stalking me. I'll make sure you're put back in jail where you belong. I can't believe they let you out; they should have thrown away the key. The bloody police didn't even warn me you were out. The first thing I knew about it was when you phoned. I would never have agreed to this meeting if I hadn't been in shock at hearing your voice after all these years.'

I manage to stand, hoping my legs won't give way. 'You can't really believe I killed her.' I try to stop my voice shaking, rising hysterically. 'You know me; you know I'm not a murderer. Look, maybe you don't care who did it; maybe you were so freaked out at the time that you just wanted a scapegoat. But you've had a decade to think about this. Deep down, you don't really believe I'm guilty. Do you? *Do* you?'

Why do I plead like some pathetic little girl who needs stern Daddy's approval to feel like a whole person? This wasn't supposed to happen. I was going to be cool and calm and tell him what I wanted. I've got to get a grip before I lose it completely. I think of Frankie, of her desperate situation. Then I think, so fucking what? She doesn't care about me, doesn't even trust me. She's got no idea what I'm doing for her and wouldn't give a damn if she did. She'll let me down, like all the rest. But I can't allow myself to believe that, not yet. I need a shred of hope to cling to. And something much less abstract than hope ...

'I need money.'

He looks startled. Then relieved, full of comfortable contempt. His shoulders droop and he lets out a long breath.

'So now we come to it.' He nods and puts one hand on the mantelpiece, stroking the smooth marble. 'Yes, I thought it might be this. Why didn't you tell me straight away instead of making me listen to all that rubbish?'

'It isn't rubbish.'

'I suppose you still have a taste for drama. You must miss being a barrister and getting the opportunity to pontificate in court and browbeat witnesses.' There's even the trace of a smile around his thin lips. He despises me more than ever now, if that's possible.

'I need a hundred thousand pounds.'

'*What?*' His smile disappears and he looks furious again. 'You seriously imagine I'd give money – especially an amount like that – to my wife's murderer?'

'I'm not a murderer, I never murdered anyone.' I swallow hard, force back tears. The last thing I want is to start crying in front of him. 'And I don't want you to give me the money, I want you to lend it.'

'Oh, really?' He shakes his head in angry disbelief. 'Ten years in prison hasn't made you lose your nerve! Even if I agreed to this incredible request, how do you imagine you'd repay such a sum? It would take you the rest of your miserable life – several life-times! I'd be pushing up daisies long before you could pay back a tenth of it. Or is that what you're counting on?'

'No,' I whisper. My strength and resolve is draining, leaving me exhausted and full of despair. I thought I was up for this, but I'm not. The trauma of the confrontation, his contempt and hatred, his refusal to believe I'm innocent, has gone straight to my stomach. I clap one hand over my mouth and glance wildly around. Daddy looks alarmed.

'In the hall.' He points and I make a run for it, find the downstairs loo with its mahogany seat and dried flower arrangement on the tiled windowsill just in time. There's a little washbasin and mirror; after throwing up all the bitter bile I rinse my mouth and hands, wipe my forehead and look at my ashen reflection, my pale lips and the shadows beneath my haunted eyes. I pause to lean my forehead against the cool tiled wall and catch my breath. It's so quiet out here. Through the frosted glass of the window is a blur of green, brown and gold foliage. I stagger out and across the hall and back into the sitting room, where he's standing waiting. I sink on to the yellow sofa and close my eyes again. Wishing I wasn't alone in the world, that there was somebody, just one person, who cared. Does Frankie care?

His whiplash voice again. 'I suppose you're a drug addict.'

I open my eyes. 'What?'

'Most prisoners are drug addicts, aren't they? If not when they go in, by the time they come out. Is that what you want the money for? Have you got yourself into debt to some dealer already?'

'I'm not a drug addict.'

'Hmph. What do you want the money for?'

I sit up and reach for the glass of water. 'To help somebody.'

'Who?'

'A very close friend.' I'm not going to tell him about Frankie. Any more than he's going to give me that money.

'Kept in touch with an old cell mate, did you?'

'No.' I've had enough of this. 'Did my mother abandon me because she couldn't stand living with you any more and couldn't support me on her own?'

'Your *mother*?' He stiffens, stares at me, and I get the impression he's frightened again. But of what? Then he smiles and shakes his head, relaxed and contemptuous once more. 'Oh. I see. Been trying to trace her, have you? Well, you won't get any joy there. She won't want to know any more than I do.'

'Or ever did.'

'Ever did. Quite right. Yes,' he muses, 'that sort of thing's all the rage these days. Me, me, me, I've got my rights and I don't care who else's life I intrude on, especially if my own doesn't amount to much.'

'It isn't like that.' He has no shame, no respect. He doesn't care how much pain he causes me.

'Well, I'm not interested. I've heard enough rubbish for one day. And don't think I'm going to talk about *her*, because I'm not. That particular unfortunate chapter in my life closed a very long time ago.'

I put the glass down, making a wet ring on the polished table. 'Your life's just one unfortunate fucking closed chapter after another, isn't it?'

'It certainly is in your case.' He glances at his watch. 'Wait here. I'll be back in a minute.' He strides out and goes upstairs. Floorboards creak overhead. I lean against the yellow silk cushions and rest, trying to gather strength for the walk back to the station, because I know he won't offer me a lift or pay for a cab. Nothing can ever be easy for me, can it? Absolutely bloody nothing.

It's all too hard, too much. I get that feeling again, the feeling that I just want to lie down and give in, fade away. I was crazy to come here. I've done myself a lot of damage. More damage. My life's never going to get better. What was it Schopenhauer said? *'We can regard our life as a uselessly disturbing episode in the blissful repose of nothingness.'* My father comes back into the room and tosses a brown envelope on to the sofa.

'What's that?' I get up, ready to leave.

'Six thousand pounds. It's all the cash I've got in the house. You won't get a penny more from me – ever. So take it and get out, stay away. I never want to see you or hear from you again. If I do, I'll get the police on to you. And you know what'll happen then.'

'Six thousand?' I open the envelope and finger the stack of notes. They look new, have a good smell. Six grand is by no means a huge sum of money, certainly not these days, and it's nowhere near the amount I need to save Frankie. It would come in very handy for day-to-day expenses though, and there's a lot I could do with it. But I know I'm not going to do anything .

'Six thousand pounds?' I repeat, staring at him in shocked, unbelievable hurt. The dreaded tears start to flow then, warm on the chilled skin of my face. 'I'm your daughter,' I whisper. 'You brought me up, I lived with you, I tried to love you. I wanted you to love me. I tried so hard. I didn't kill Vivienne, although God knows, yes, I had a motive all right! There were times when I longed to blow the face off that cruel bitch. But I never hurt her, I never hurt anybody. You must know that.' I look at the money again. 'Is this all I'm worth to you?'

'Actually, no. You're worth a lot less.' He looks angry again, as if he was expecting me to be grateful for his nice present. 'Take it and go. Use it to buy drink, drugs. Take an overdose. I'll come and identify your body in the morgue, and pay for you to be cremated. I'm happy to perform that final duty as your unfortunate father.'

His words leave me gasping. I thought he couldn't hurt me any more, but I was so wrong. The old wound has cracked wide open.

'I don't want your fucking money,' I scream, tears pouring down my face. Well, not strictly true, given that I just asked him for a hundred thou. But I won't let that spoil my grand gesture that I'm in no position to make. I fling the envelope back at him and the unbound stack of notes falls out and scatters, tenners and other denominations see-sawing through the air and fluttering to the carpet. He flinches and moves away, puts up one arm to shield himself. 'Hey, Dad, what's wrong?' I mock. 'Don't be scared. It's only paper, it can't hurt you. It can't hurt you the way somebody tortured and killed Vivienne, the way that same person tortured me and ruined my life by making me do the time for their crime.'

'Get out!' he yells. 'Go! Leave me alone.'

'I'm going.' He's just a blur through my tears now. 'I don't want your filthy, stinking, rotten money. Keep it. Keep it all. I hope it makes you happy. I didn't murder Vivienne! And I won't take an overdose, so you can just *fuck* off for ever!'

I turn and stumble sobbing out of my father's house.

Out of the house of my nightmare.

Chapter 19

'We're going to kill you. And your man.'

'He's not *my man*, not any more.' Frankie felt sick with terror as what she presumed was a gun was jammed against her right temple. 'He owes the money – it's nothing to do with me.'

She was blindfolded, tied to a chair, her clothes in disarray. She didn't know how many men were in the room. There was a smell of sweat and cigarette smoke. If these bastards were going to kill her, why didn't they just do it? Were they going to rape her first? Slash her face, like Joe said they had done to Lida?

Where was Joe? They had been separated after being dragged blindfolded from the car. It was quiet in this room, but in the background she could hear voices and laughter, taped music, the clink of glasses. Was this a club, a casino? Agron Xhani owned a casino. People were out there gambling with money; in here she was gambling with her life.

'I want to speak to Agron Xhani,' she repeated.

'Shut up.' The gun was withdrawn and the man hit her across one side of her head. 'You don't tell us what you want. We tell you!'

She felt a draught as the door opened and closed. A minute later the blindfold was pulled off. She shook back her hair, blinked and looked around. She was in an office, tackily furnished with a red carpet, mirrored walls, a table crowded with bottles and glasses, and furniture that looked as if it came from Ikea. The chair she was tied to was uncomfortable enough to have come from there as well. Two men stood by the door and another man sat at a desk in front of her. He was youngish, dark-haired and wore a dark-blue suit with no tie. He looked colourless, ordinary, boring even, like any businessman you could walk past in the centre of The Hague on any weekday.

'I'm Agron Xhani. You're Francesca Sayle.' He seemed calm, matter-of-fact. 'Where's my money, Francesca?'

'Look – you don't understand.' Frankie swallowed, cleared her throat. 'My husband dumped me – we're separated. I tried to explain that to –' She glanced back at the other men. 'All we have to do now is sort out the divorce. It's no good you coming after me, threatening to kill me, because he doesn't care. Joe's only concerned for his girlfriend – Lida van der Graaf, the woman your men attacked at our apartment.'

'I know that now. You were in England at the time. With your sick mother.'

Frankie gasped. 'How do you know?'

'Never mind.'

Joe must have told him. 'You should go after Lida – she's a lawyer, she's rich. She's got a hell of a lot more money than I have. And her father's a judge.'

'I know all about Lida.' His eyes darkened. 'We used to be … close.'

Oh my God. Frankie stared at him in shock. 'But I thought you were –'

'Her friend? Her supplier?' He shook his head. 'No, no. Much more than that. Your husband stole her from me. I don't want her any more – she is damaged, finished. She has paid. Now your husband must pay.'

'But why should *I* ?' So Lida had been Agron Xhani's girlfriend. This made things worse, if it was possible for them to get worse. 'I didn't even know about any of this!'

'Shut up.' Xhani leaned back in his chair. 'You've had a lucky escape so far. You still have a pretty face.' His eyes flickered down. 'And body.' He lit a cigarette, and one of the men brought him a drink. 'Don't you want to know where your husband is right now?'

'Why should I care?' Frankie's eyes filled with tears. 'He dumped me.'

'Why did you meet him at that bar? What did you talk about?'

'The divorce – and how he could pay you your money.' She flexed her wrists and ankles against the thin rope that bound them. 'He's been ignoring me, leading his own life for months now. I

168

had no idea he gambled, owed you money – I didn't know anything! I only just found out about his affair with Lida. And the coke habit. I'm the classic stupid wife who's the last to know. You've got to believe me. Let me go – I won't say anything about this to anyone. I won't go to the police. I just want to get on with my life. This is all Joe's fault!' Her heart pounded with terror. 'His and Lida bloody van der Graaf's. Ask *her* for your money!'

He smiled. 'You hate Lida.'

'And you don't? I just want you to understand that this debt is not my problem.' Frankie cringed as he grabbed a gun, got up and came around the desk.

'You don't understand.' He grasped a handful of her hair and twisted it, making her cry out in agonised shock. 'In my country, a man must pay his debt. If not him, his wife or his family. Otherwise we kill him and them. Honour is everything.'

Oh God, Frankie thought despairingly. Unreconstructed, with knobs on!

'They have to know they must pay. Or die. I don't care what you tell me.' He ran the gun barrel over her face and neck, then down and around her breasts. 'But I'm patient, I am a reasonable man. So I'll give you one week from today.' He twisted her hair harder and pulled her head back. She couldn't move, despite the agony she was in. Her body was drenched in sweat. 'You or your man – get the money or you die. We keep watch on you – whether you stay here or go back to England. I have contacts there; I know where your mother's house is.' He recited the address just in case she didn't believe him. 'If you go to the police, you die. You understand me?'

'Yes!' she sobbed. All she wanted was for the pain to stop. He let go of her hair.

'You know Scheveningen boulevard? Kurhaus Hotel?'

'I . . . yes!' Her scalp was burning. Frankie had never been inside the big, posh Kurhaus Hotel with its wedding cake architecture, but the Scheveningen boulevard was a great place to eat ice cream, drink coffee, buy shells, souvenirs and cool swimwear, people-watch, and dine in one of the many seafront restaurants.

'The fountain outside the hotel?'

'Yes.'

He sat on one corner of the desk, keeping the gun pointed at her face. 'You be there.' Frankie tried not to struggle or turn

169

her head away. 'One week from today – be waiting there. With my money.'

'Me?' She stared at him. 'But it's Joe who owes you. Why not him?'

'Because I say so!' He slapped her. 'Don't question me. Be at the fountain seven o'clock in the evening. Somebody will be waiting; they'll bring you to me. You give me the money, you're free. Free to live your divorced life. If you're not there, I come after you. Here or in England. Your husband, you, your sick mother. You all die.' He paused. 'Understand?'

'Yes.' Frankie felt powerless, collapsing with shock and terror. Agron Xhani stood up, laid the gun on the desk and gave her another backhander.

'I think you're laughing at me, you bitch.'

She shook her head, her eyes full of tears. 'Do I look like I'm laughing?'

'You don't show enough respect. Women in my country have more respect. You know what happened to Lida. You will get worse – much worse. *You understand*?' He hit her again.

'Yes!' Frankie sniffed and felt warm blood trickle from one nostril. She tasted blood in her mouth. Why were his type always obsessed with respect? Probably because they knew they did not deserve any.

'Then goodbye,' Xhani said. 'For now.'

The blindfold was put back and she was untied and dragged to her feet. It was difficult to walk. The voices and music became louder, then faded away. A minute later she felt cool air on her face as a door opened. Someone shoved her; she stumbled forward and fell on her hands and knees. The door slammed. Sobbing with fright, she tugged at the blindfold.

'Frankie? *Frankie*.' Joe was beside her, helping her untie the blindfold. 'Did they hurt you? Christ, I thought they'd kill me. They told me they'd kill you. Can you get up? Are you all right?'

'Oh, I'm cool. I love being abducted and slapped around and having my life threatened by a gangster. . *No*,' she screamed. 'I am *not* all right.' She stared around. They were at the back of some building near a row of wheelie bins overflowing with smelly garbage bags. The moon and stars were out and she could hear the sea close by. 'Where are we?'

'This is his – Xhani's – casino. I've been here a few times.'

170

'Yeah, I bet. Got thrown out with the garbage before, did you?' Rage blew up in her. 'After you'd swigged champagne, snorted Columbia's finest and groped that bitch Lida while you ran up a debt that's going to get me murdered unless I can think of a way to save myself. Which right now I can't.'

He was pale and stricken in the gloom. 'I'm sorry.'

'Not good enough!' She shoved him in the chest, forgetting his cracked ribs. Joe gave a cry of pain and staggered back. 'He knows I was in England, he knows about my mother, even that she's been ill. How? Did you tell him?'

'I never even mentioned . . . I don't know how he knows. He must be having you – us – watched. Proves my point about how we can't go to the police, doesn't it?'

'And I don't know why I'm even bothering to ask this, but if you wanted an affair why did you have to pick his bloody girl-friend?'

Joe tensed. *'What?'*

'Lida was Xhani's girlfriend. That's what he meant when he said you'd stolen something from him.'

'No!' He looked sick. 'Xhani was her supplier, that's all. Oh *shit*. No, it can't be–'

Frankie grabbed her bag and started to walk away, wiping her bloody nose with a tissue. Joe followed, his arms across his sore chest. They came around the corner of the building onto a deserted, narrow stretch of road. Across the road was the beach, dark sands and a moonlit sea stretching to the horizon. In the distance the lights of Kijkduin's boulevard, smaller than Scheveningen. A man walking an alsation gave them a curious stare. Frankie ignored him.

'Xhani wants you to deliver the money,' Joe said in a low voice when man and canine had passed. 'That's crazy, it's bizarre. I told him – again – that it was nothing to do with you. But he wouldn't listen. I tried. Christ, I had no idea Lida was his–'

'Oh, shut up.' Frankie stopped. 'Where can I find a cab?'

Joe gave a sob. 'What the fuck are we going to *do*?'

'It's *we* now, is it? Go to the police, of course, try and get that tosser arrested.'

'For Christ's sake, I've told you, we can't–'

'Well, what do you suggest? We can't get the *money*.' She looked down the road and started to tremble. 'Oh no.'

A car was cruising towards them, a familiar black Merc. One of the men who had kidnapped them earlier stuck his head out of the passenger window.

'Hey, lady. Want a lift?'

'Fuck off.' She started to walk again, faster, Joe limping along after her. The car trailed them until they had reached the end of the road and turned into a street full of bars and cafés. Further on in a little square they found a cab. Joe gave the address of their apartment to the driver, and Frankie did not argue. She wasn't in any more or less danger there than anywhere else. She looked back; the Merc was behind them in the stream of traffic.

They did not speak again until they were inside the apartment. She walked into the sitting room and dropped her bag on the sofa, sat down and buried her head in her hands. She heard Joe moving around the kitchen. The coffee grinder whizzed. He came back into the sitting room and poured himself a cognac.

'D'you want a cognac with your coffee?'

'No.'

One week to live, unless she could find a hundred grand. It was impossible, incredible. Wild thoughts ran through her head. Could she steal some money from the embassy? The Consul had a safe in his office that he often left open; she knew it contained cash, although its chief use was to store cartons of cigarettes. The chauffeur regularly drove him to the ABN-AMRO bank to withdraw cash for various things, including the monthly salaries. Joe said it was retarded that she got paid in cash and of course it was, but Frankie never minded. Sometimes the chauffeur was sent to the bank alone if the Consul was too busy. He had once come into her office with a sealed brown envelope stuffed with money and asked her to look after it until the Consul returned, because he did not want the responsibility; Frankie refused, because she didn't either. She remembered the time he had gleefully shown her a great wad of notes, thousands of euros, intended to pay for an antique dressing table the ambassador's wife had ordered from Italy. Frankie could never understand why they preferred to deal in cash.

She might be able to steal some money, but nowhere near enough. And as local staff, she would be one of the first suspects. Even if she somehow managed to evade Agron Xhani, she would be looking at a prison sentence: stealing from a diplomatic

172

mission would mean a longer sentence. People might joke about Dutch prisons being like five-star hotels, but that did not mean they cared to serve a stretch in one. Although it was better than being dead. What a choice.

Joe put a cup of coffee in front of her, took his own and sat down on the opposite sofa. He slipped off his jacket and took a gulp of cognac.

'Frankie?'

She looked at him. 'What?'

'I'm sorry I–'

'Oh, save it, will you? Just bloody well save it.'

He tried again. 'I don't suppose you – that we – could forget about the divorce?'

She was silent, staring at him. She was thinking so hard about ways to get her hands on impossible sums of money that his words took a few seconds to sink in. When they did she laughed.

'Forget the divorce because we'll be dead, is that what you mean?'

'No. I – I went apeshit for a while. But that's over.'

She nodded. 'It certainly is.'

She had no interest in whatever he might be trying to come out with now. She picked up her coffee and put it down again, really saw him for the first time in weeks. Joe had lost weight; his face was thinner and he looked older, suddenly seemed to have a lot more grey in his hair. His dark, frightened eyes stared back at her.

'Don't fly to Liverpool in the morning, Frankie. Stay here. Your mother's all right now – or she will be. Please,' he urged. 'Not long ago you were telling me how much you loved me, begging me not to leave you.' He got up, sat beside her and took her hands. 'God, your hands are freezing.' He kissed her cheek.

'What the hell is this?' Frankie pulled away sharply. 'Have you gone loopy? All I can think about,' she said, 'is how I could be dead this time next week.'

'You won't be. I won't.' He grabbed her hand again. 'I don't want a divorce any more, I want us to stay together. I love you, Frankie.'

She looked at him in alarm. He really had lost it. .

'Listen to me, okay? I've got a plan.'

She did not know whether to laugh or cry, so she just sat there looking dumb and feeling numb. 'What might that be? And do I even want to know?' She picked up the cup to warm her hands, took a sip of coffee and winced. It was horribly strong, and because Joe didn't take sugar himself he had forgotten to put any in hers. It was pathetic to feel annoyed about such a thing, especially at a time like this, but she did. So many acts of thoughtlessness, large as well as small.

'We get together all the money we can.' Joe looked excited now, hopeful. 'It could be a lot. There's a good few grand in the bank. I can sell the car and hi-fi and some other stuff. I might be able to fiddle something at work. And I'm sure you could nick a good chunk from that embassy. You're always saying how careless those knobheads are, leaving safes open and envelopes full of cash lying around.'

'I've already thought of that. It won't–'

'The ambassador even gave you his credit card a couple of times when he wanted you to order books for him because his secretary's Dutch wasn't good enough. You might be able to nick that as well as a load of cash, and we could use the card until it gets cancelled. Which probably won't be for ages. The silly old bastard's got loads; he won't even notice one's missing.'

'Just as we have to hope no one notices and becomes suspicious of two Westerners using a credit card with a Korean name.'

Joe took no notice. 'You said his secretary told you he never checks the bills. We get all that money together and just take off.'

'Take off?' Frankie put down the cup. 'Where?'

'France, Spain, Portugal. Or Eastern Europe . . . no, maybe not there. The US, Australia or New Zealand! I don't know – who cares? We'll decide that later.'

'Just take off,' Frankie repeated. She stood up. She wanted to strip and get under a hot shower so she could wash away the vile touch of Agron Xhani and his thugs. If being slapped and manhandled made her want to scrub her body until the skin was raw, how the hell must it feel to be raped?

'What about the lovely Lida?' she asked. 'You wouldn't think of deserting her in her hour of greatest need?'

'She deceived me.' He shrugged, glanced away. 'I would never have had anything to do with her if I'd known she'd had a thing with Xhani. And there's no way she'll come up with any money now.'

'You really know how to flatter a girl.' Frankie looked at him in

174

disgust. 'So that's your bit on the side dispensed with. Running away always looks so easy in movies, doesn't it?' she remarked. 'Couple fly off into beautiful blue yonder, happy ever after. We don't see them struggling to get visas, residence and work permits, jobs, food, a place to live. Having rows, paying bills. Or not paying them. In addition to all that, we'd be on the run from a gangster who wants to murder us. We'd also be on the run from the police if you've defrauded your company and I've stolen cash and credit cards from my diplomatic employers. It won't work, you moron. We won't make it as far as the club class lounge at Schiphol.'

'Of course we will!' Joe frowned. 'Neither the cops nor Agron Xhani and his thugs will get us. We'll think of some ruse to evade them.'

'You couldn't think of a ruse to evade them when you turned up at that bar this evening. So that's your solution, is it?' Frankie laughed because otherwise she would have wept. 'Get the Dutch police, not to mention Interpol, on our trail as well as Mr Xhani. Absolutely brilliant.'

'Well, if you've got a better idea I'd love to hear it.'

'I often thought Lida seemed hyper.' Frankie knew there was no point to this, but she could not stop herself. 'I put it down to her general exuberance. Or was it the kick she got from secretly shagging her best friend's husband as well as a psycho gangster? Likes life on the edge, doesn't she? Well, now she's fallen off.'

'Lida was a mistake.' Joe got to his feet, his colour deepening. 'Okay, a big mistake. Can't we forget about her?'

'I'm afraid not. You only want me back – or say you do – because you're terrified and need my help.'

'No.' He took a step towards her. 'Okay, I am terrified. Or course I am. So are you. But I do love you, Frankie, I swear.'

'If Lida was a mistake, you won't mind that I told Agron Xhani to go after her.'

Joe flinched, swallowed. 'No. I don't mind. As a matter of fact, I told him the same thing.' He shrugged. 'What else could I do?'

Frankie looked at him with contempt. 'Am I supposed to believe anything you say? Even if I go along with your Great Plan, how do I know you won't fly off into the blue yonder with all the loot and leave me to stop Xhani's bullets?'

Joe clenched his fists. 'How can you even think I'd do that?'

175

'You want a list?'

'I wouldn't go off and leave you to get murdered by Xhani!' Joe shouted, his face crimson. 'There's no way! For Christ's sake, Frankie, I love you.'

'Not long ago you were definite that you didn't.' She wiped her eyes. 'I won't steal anything,' she cried. 'Or go anywhere with you. What about my mother? I can't leave her. And –' She stopped. She could not even begin to tell Joe about Alyssa Ward.

'What about your mother? I think she'd prefer you to be on the other side of the world rather than dead. Don't you?'

Frankie turned and walked out, hurried upstairs.

'Where are you going?' he called, following.

'Leave me alone,' she cried. 'That's what you planned to do, wasn't it? Nothing I said mattered. You didn't want to know, didn't care how freaked I was. All you cared about was yourself and what you wanted.'

'*Thought* I wanted. Frankie, please. I was going through a crisis, I didn't mean it.'

She glared at him from the top of the stairs. 'Go away! 'He stared at her, then turned and disappeared.

She got a suitcase from the attic, took it into the bedroom and filled it with clothes, leaving the black dress and expensive shoes. She got her laptop, some papers and a few books from the study, and put them in a bag, then carried the luggage down the narrow stairs. In the sitting room Joe was sprawled on the sofa drinking cognac, his expression sullen and frightened. He got up when she came in.

'Don't go, Frankie, please. It's better if we stay together.'

'No it isn't.' She looked at him, her eyes full of tears. 'I'm going back to England for a few days. I can't stay here. I'll try and think of some other way to get the money, although God knows–' She shook her head. 'Otherwise we have to throw ourselves on the mercy of the police. We've got no choice. And I'll have to tell my mother. Prepare her.' The thought of telling her mother about the danger she was in filled Frankie with horror. Estella might have another heart attack. Fatal this time.

Joe put down his glass and came towards her. 'I am sorry.' His eyes were wet. 'The way I've treated you . . . there's no excuse. But despite what I've done, how thick I've been, I do love you. That's not a lie.'

176

Frankie thought for a second that he was about to try and take her in his arms. But he made no move. 'I need a cab,' she whispered.

'Sure. Want me to call you one?'

'Thanks.'

'I will try and get some money from work,' he said as he went towards the phone. 'A legitimate loan. Maybe you could get a loan too.'

'From the embassy? Forget it.'

'I mean from the bank. You've got a separate account in the UK. Or borrow a few grand from your mother – you don't have to tell her the real reason. We might be able to scrape together most of the money that way. It's just possible.'

She sighed. 'I'll try.'

The cab took her back to the Bel Air Hotel near the Catshuis, the prime minister's official residence. As the cab dropped her and moved off she spotted the black Merc again. One of the tinted windows was open, a man talking on a mobile. Yes, what to do now? Stay and keep a watch on Joe, or follow her? Both? Mr X would have to get more thugs on the case. At least she wasn't making things easy for him.

Next morning, a beautiful autumn day, Frankie checked out after breakfast and took another cab to the airport. The half-hour journey was an extravagance, but she did not fancy struggling on and off the train with heavy luggage, and what the hell anyway if she was going to be dead in a week? She sat in the back and kept looking around, but there were so many cars on the motorway that she could not tell if they were being followed. At Schiphol she boarded a flight to Liverpool.

She was surprised at how calm she felt. But that wouldn't last. It felt better to get out of the Netherlands. Frankie thought of Alyssa as the 737 descended through scattered cloud and flew over the city with its two cathedrals, the river and long, ragged lines of sprawling docks. Alyssa had said she would try to help – had she come up with anything? Probably not. She would visit her, but not today. At the airport Frankie hired a car, a red Ford Mondeo. Another extravagance, but what did that matter?

177

She did not notice anybody tailing her as she drove off and followed the signs for the A59. She felt exhausted from getting up early after a sleepless night. The sky was cloudy here, and it felt colder. She tried not to think about Joe. She had to protect herself as best she could. If that meant she and her mother going to the police, maybe even going into hiding, so be it. Joe would have to look out for himself. He did not deserve any more consideration.

Her mother's house was silent and chilly. Frankie struggled in with her bag and suitcase, dumped them in the hall by the telephone table, and went back to lock the porch door. She stooped to gather the accumulated mail: a parish newsletter, phone bill, a colourful brochure for some new pizza place, and two white envelopes postmarked Liverpool. Addressed to her.

'Oh God,' she whispered, staring at them. 'Now what?'

Were they from Alyssa? But Alyssa did not own a word processor. Maybe she had access to one, probably in a library. Why would she write two letters? Frankie did not want to open the envelopes immediately. She took them into the kitchen and left them on the table while she made coffee. When it was ready she poured a cup, stirred in sugar and took it up to her bedroom. She looked out of the window, down the road and across the field towards St Michael's spire, searching for whoever could be watching her, watching the house. Again, she could not see anybody.

She sighed and sipped the coffee. She sat on her bed and opened the first letter, postmarked the day before yesterday. It had no name, address, date or signature. Just a couple of lines printed in Times New Roman font on a sheet of white paper.

> *You need a hundred grand. I've got it.*
> *Meet me at the abbey ruins at ten tonight.*

She gasped and her heart began to race. Who was this person, how did they know about the abbey ruins? More to the point, how the hell did they know she needed a hundred grand? She had not told anybody. Except Alyssa.

What was this? Panicked, she grabbed the other envelope and ripped it open. Had Alyssa told somebody that she was desperate for money? Somebody she had known in prison, maybe? That was all she needed, Frankie thought, an ex-con on her case. A *guilty* ex-con. She slowly read the second note.

You didn't turn up. Are you scared? Shouldn't you be more scared of what will happen if you don't get that money? Same place again, same time. Tonight.

Last chance.

Chapter 20

'Why didn't you turn up, Alyssa? Did you forget our appointment?'

Damn. I only answered the door because I thought it might be Frankie. Where is she, what's she doing? Is she safe? I can't reach her and it's driving me mad. I'm also crushed after the experience with my father; that really ripped the guts out of me. I came straight back here, got into bed and stayed there for the rest of the day, all night, and most of this morning. I had over ambitiously planned to find and confront – if that's the right word – Tomás after seeing my father, but I was in no fit state. Now I've lost my bottle completely. What if Tomás rejects me as well? So yes, of course I forgot the appointment with my probation officer.

'You all right?' Carl asks as he walks in uninvited. It's cold today and he's wearing a red padded ski jacket and one of those horrible black woolly hats that make people who wear them look like muggers. Or so I think. His brown eyes are curious and disapproving as they take in the state of the living room, my lank hair and dingy, white cotton bathrobe. I haven't eaten since breakfast yesterday, or even drunk anything since the glass of water my father so grudgingly handed me. My mouth is dry, my head aches, my stomach is hollow with hunger and despair. I looked – and smelled – better in prison.

'I don't feel too good,' I understate. 'Think I might be coming down with something.'

He sits on the sofa as if he owns the place. 'How did the interview go?'

What interview? 'Oh. They wanted a junior secretary. I wasn't junior enough.'

'I see. Anything else lined up?'

I'm too weak and depressed to argue. Or lie. 'No.'

'Hmm.' Carl purses his lips as if he's about to whistle. 'So many interviews. So little result.'

'If you can tell me who's queueing up to employ a thirty-eight-year-old, female ex-con, I'll give it another shot.' I sit in the armchair because my legs are trembling.

He sighs and sticks his hands in his pockets. 'I've told you before, Alyssa, you can't take that attitude.'

I'll take whatever attitude I like. 'You mean I should ignore reality?'

'It's not reality. Or it doesn't have to be. My other clients are in the same boat as you and despite the difficulties, quite a few of them have managed to find jobs.'

I wonder what sort of jobs. 'That's really encouraging. I'm very happy for them.'

Carl frowns. 'Look, I realise this isn't easy, but you've got to accept the fact that you can never again practise as a barrister.'

Patronising bastard. 'I know *that*.'

'But do you accept it? Or accept that whatever job you do get won't be as well paid or interesting? I don't think so. It's difficult for you and, believe me, I do sympathise. It doesn't mean you can't still get something reasonably good. But you've got to make an effort. Like I said, change your attitude.'

I wish he'd fuck off. I hate that he can just turn up here, question and lecture me, think he's got an inalienable right to violate my privacy. Unfortunately he has, however, so I've got to take this crap. For now, anyway. I stand up. 'I'd like to go back to bed, if you don't mind. I told you I don't feel well, and it's the best way to keep warm since I can't afford to have the gas fire on for long.'

He ignores that. Of course he doesn't want to hear about such things. And he wouldn't dream of making me a cup of coffee or offering to pop out for a few groceries. 'So.' He glances around again. 'How's life in general?'

What? I think of my empty fridge and bare cupboards. I look out of the window at the ruins of the blitzed church. 'Terrific.'

Carl knows I don't like him or confide in him any more, and that annoys him. He thinks he should have a guru-acolyte relationship with his so-called clients, with him as guru. Most people want you to like them, even if they don't feel they can return the compliment. My father being an exception, of course. And perhaps Frankie. I'll try to call her again later. I remember my empty fridge. If Carl won't offer, I'll ask. It's his job to guard my welfare, after all, not just bore me with patronising lectures.

'Could you perhaps nip out and buy me a loaf and some butter and a couple of cans of veggie soup?' Oh, wretched pride – I should never have flung Daddy's six grand back in his kisser. Wonder what he'll spend it on? An electrified fence and gates in case I decide to pay a return visit? A couple of rottweilers would be cheaper, although the cost of the doggies' food and keep over several years would certainly add up.

'Butter?' Carl's eyebrows lift.

I know. Somebody of my lowly status has no business to be hankering after butter. My late paternal grandmother taught me to hate margarine though, and some things just stick. I can hear her now. *'Hydrogenated muck! Tarted-up candle grease'*.

'No time. Sorry.' Carl glances at his watch and gets to his feet. At least my request has the desired effect of persuading him to piss off. 'I've got to be somewhere else in about ten minutes. You'll have to ask one of your neighbours.'

'I've never met them. There's not much social cohesion around here.'

'There must be someone you can ask.'

'I'm afraid not.' How could I ever have liked this prick from hell? 'But hey, don't worry. I'll drag myself out later, get some fresh city air.'

He nods. 'A walk will do you good.'

Such concern, such compassion. I'm overwhelmed. When he's gone I collapse on the sofa, my body trembling, heart pounding as if I've got iron-deficiency anaemia. I could end up with that if I don't start eating properly. I've got to go out and get something, especially coffee. But first I have to make myself look human.

I drag myself into the cold bathroom, brush my sticky teeth and take a shower, wash my hair. I have to dry it as best I can with a towel because I've got no dryer. I dress in jeans and the sweater Frankie asked if I'd worn when I was first taken to prison, and slip on the beige, non-lace trainers with thick black soles that I picked up the other day in a sale for two quid. Cheap, but they look cool. I apply some make-up that wasn't cheap – not by my out-of-date standards – but is still nasty, and fluff out my damp chestnut locks.

My hair could do with a trim, but what would that cost? I go down the stairs and hear the baby crying again behind the closed door. The desolate wails give me the creeps.

I wish I had a mobile phone as well as a hairdryer, but I can't afford it. Everybody's got mobiles now, that is, everybody who wants one. Especially kids; wherever I go there are loud brats in sports gear having self-important conversations; sometimes I feel like snatching a phone and giving its owner a good smack. Lots of people go round in sports clothes, adults as well as children, it's amazing. I don't think society has changed for the better since I was put away. I know that makes me sound more like a hundred than thirty-eight, but so what?

Being out in the city streets amongst people who have lives to live, places to go, things to do – I'm sure a lot of them don't, but it seems that way – makes me feel more isolated than when I'm in the flat. I feel illegitimate, a fraud, an alien who's just landed on a new planet. There is nobody in this city, country, continent, world, who gives a toss – except possibly Frankie. I need to talk to her again, tell her what happened with my father. I need to know she's okay. I hope she wasn't serious about trying to confront that gangster.

I'm starving and dehydrated but I walk down Bold Street, manage to find a rare phone box and dial her number. The mobile seems to be switched off, so I try her mother's number and hope Estella is still staying with that friend of hers. I don't want to give her that creepy feeling you get when some mystery caller hangs up on you. Ring ring. Come on.

'Hello?' Her voice is low. Wary.

'Frankie, at *last.*' The rush of relief brings tears to my eyes. 'Are you okay? How are things? Where have you been?' I'm shaking.

'I'm okay.' She doesn't answer the last two questions. 'Did you – or somebody you know – send me two letters?'

'No. Why?'

'Are you sure?'

'Of course I am. What's going on?'

'Did you tell anyone about . . . you know? What we talked about last time?'

'No way.' I get a flash of shock. And insult. 'I wouldn't!'

A pause. 'You said you were going to try and help me.'

'Yes, I know. I'm sorry, Frankie. I did try, but I failed pathetically. It was a long shot, and like most long shots it didn't bloody work. But I never mentioned you or your predicament to the person I hoped might help.' *Person*. Is my father actually human?

Another pause. Then a sigh. 'I see. All right.'

'You do believe me?' I can't control the tremor in my voice. 'You can trust me, I swear. What are those two letters about? Is it anything to do with–'

'I can't talk now. I'll come to your place tomorrow, okay? Around noon.'

'That's fine. That's great.' I stare up the long, narrow street towards the blitzed church. St Luke's is starting to get on my nerves because it looks like a stone metaphor of my ruined life. I'd prefer to have a shopping mall or multi-storey car park as the view from my window. 'I'll wait for you. Just tell me – how's Estella?'

'She's getting better. She's going to stay with her friend another week or so.'

Frankie hangs up without saying goodbye. I walk to the end of Bold Street, ignoring shop windows full of furniture, art materials, books, CDs, clothes and shoes, cross a busy road – so much more traffic now – and find a café. A normal café, not a Starbucks or Coffee Republic or God knows what. And as for McDonalds or Burger King – do not get me started. The place is clean, warm and cosy, with friendly staff; I order a bacon buttie, toasted teacake and cup of coffee. After I've eaten and ordered a second coffee, I start to feel human again and the world seems a marginally less hostile place.

I think about what Carl said. He's right, of course, there's no way a convicted murderer can resume practising her former profession of barrister. Unless she could somehow be proved innocent, but that's another story. It's the way he says it, with a kind of smug satisfaction as if he wants to bring me down, emphasise that my place is at the bottom of the heap. I think of my father's words: '*Take an overdose. I'll come and identify your body in the morgue*'. The look in his eyes when he said it.

I'm not hungry any more and I can't finish the second coffee. It's hot in here and I need some air, so I get up, pay and leave. Out in the street I soon feel cold again, despite walking briskly. The grey autumn air is raw and my thin leather jacket's not warm enough. I try not to imagine how I'm going to cope in that flat with winter coming. I can't ignore the tempting consumer goods in shop windows, goods that would make my benighted life more bearable. There's a big new mall now, cutting across part of what used to be Casey Street. I do want a job, and I'm not being toffee-nosed about what I won't accept. Well, okay, maybe I am a bit. It's just that I don't see the point in doing something that pays barely enough to survive, let alone have a life. I won't waste my energy like that. If I do I'll be more lost than I am now.

I find myself walking towards the business district, a part of town I've avoided so far. It reminds me too forcibly of when I had a career, friends, a man I loved. When I'd phoned Tomás's old place, pretending to be a long-lost friend from abroad, they kindly informed me he'd moved, and to where. His new place is in Castle Street near the Town Hall, a big, posh firm. I'm impressed. Wonder where I might be now if my career hadn't been so brutally cut short? I don't imagine I'd be a QC but I think I'd be doing okay. Maybe I'd be trying to juggle my brilliant career with a couple of children, mine and Tomás's. No. Can't think like that.

Tomás is probably in court now. Unless he's away on a case, gone to London or some other city for a couple of days. I long to see him again, hear his voice, and yet I'm terrified, even more terrified after the way my father treated me. Then again, might as well get all the rejections done with at once. When you're at rock bottom you can only go up, or at least that's the theory. I'm not sure I believe it.

I won't write to Tomás in case a wife intercepts and perhaps even destroys my letter, or orders him not to have anything to do with me on pain of lots of aggro. I don't think phoning is a good idea either. If I confront him, I'll get the most immediate – and honest – reaction. Tomás might even be able to help Frankie. Can't imagine how, but you never know. I'll have to do it. I will. But first I need to psych myself up.

The cheering effect of having coffee and food inside me wears off, and I start to feel desperate again. For myself and for Frankie. What the hell's going to happen to us? She's in danger of being murdered, and I'm walking cold city streets alone with only four quid in my nasty green nylon wallet. That pathetic sum of money has to last another four days. Can anyone in the UK survive on a pound a day? I could ask Frankie for money but that seems too deeply ironic, given her situation. Besides, I haven't paid back that fifty quid. She said she didn't want it, but I consider it a loan I want to repay. Alyssa and her grandiose ideas.

I cross another hectic road at the junction of Whitechapel and Paradise Street. Liverpool is still recognizable, but it's changed a lot. Demolished buildings replaced by new and uglier ones, new roads, a different traffic system. Yesterday I came across a big, elaborate gate at the entrance to Chinatown, built by authentic Chinese craftsmen, so an old man told me. He probably thought I was a tourist. Chinatown has fewer shops and restaurants and doesn't seem so lively any more. Tomás and I used to go there after a night's clubbing, and gorge on crispy duck. I still can't get used to not being locked in at night. It seems unreal and frightening that I can open my front door and go out whenever I want.

The exhaust fumes are so strong they make my eyes water and the back of my throat sore. I'm getting dangerously close to the Crown Court, Derby Square and Castle Street. Not as many tracksuits and trainers around here. I turn into quiet, narrow Temple Court and stop, overcome by a sudden choking, panicked sensation. I feel as if I can't get my next breath. I've had this before, usually at night in my cell. It's horrible, but I've learned that if I make a big effort to just go with it, not panic, breathe ultra-slowly and quietly, it goes away.

A prickly feeling starts at my head and sweeps over my body. I break out in an icy sweat. The longed-for breath comes at last, and I take another one and another. Slow, slow. I sink down on the steps of the entrance to some elegant building, several polished brass plaques on the wall above. My eyes fill with tears. Behind me a door opens; quick, light footsteps click out and stop. I shift, turn and glance up.

A slim, blonde, forty-something woman in a pinstripe trouser suit has got a real gob on as she steps around me, like I'm something you really don't care to get stuck to your shoe. She probably thinks I'm drunk, a dosser or on drugs. Or all three. She doesn't dare look me in the eye or voice her irritation in case I attack her. Her expression is enough. I feel hurt, humiliated. I want to explain.

'I had to sit down. I wasn't feeling well.'

What does she care? She doesn't even believe me. What happened to all the friendly Scousers?

Well dressed, professional, no money worries. That could have

186

been me now. Although I don't think I would have worn bright-red nail varnish or quite so much make-up. And if I found someone languishing pale and wan on my smooth, scrubbed doorsteps I like to think I'd ask after their welfare. Anger overtakes my humiliation. She walks off without a backward glance, black leather handbag swinging over one shoulder. I get up and move on as well, before someone else walks out and calls the police. Can you still get done for loitering, or do they call it something else now? I suppose the law's changed a lot since I last stood in a courtroom.

I follow the haughty lady out of Temple Court. Well, I don't follow exactly, I happen to walk in the same direction. She doesn't go far, just turns the corner and goes into some crowded Italian place where people are having lunch. I watch through the window. She air-kisses some similarly dressed, dark-haired woman who's been waiting for her at a table by a big yellow and gilt pillar with a coat stand next to it. They sit down and start talking. And I stop thinking. Or do I start?

I go in and manage to find a table on the other side of the pillar, which two men have just vacated. I pick up the menu and pretend to study it. I can't see her unless I twist around, but I can hear her going on about some man, Greg, and a place on the Côte d'Azur where they've just been on holiday. She orders spaghetti alla carbonara and Pellegrino. When the same waiter steps around the pillar to my table I order an espresso. I can't see much on that menu for under four quid and besides, I haven't gone in there to eat. I hear her friend say she's dying to see the holiday snaps.

I turn my head slightly and see Blondie's blood-tipped, beringed fingers delve into her bag. The bag was on the floor, between one table leg and the pillar. She probably thinks she's being security conscious by not slinging it over the back of her chair. And maybe this is a place she often comes to and feels safe in. She pulls out the yellow-and-black envelope containing the snaps. Leaves the bag open.

I put down the sticky plastic menu card and glance around as if I've lost something. I push my chair back and bend down, groping around on the uneven wooden floor, coat hems brushing my face. It's too easy really. My hand creeps beneath the unfastened flap of her bag and my shaking fingers close around what feels like a leather wallet. I slide it out, stick it in my jacket pocket and sit upright again. My face is burning and I'm sweating all over.

I want to run out there and then, but that would look suspicious. I glance around, but everyone seems to be busy eating and talking, not taking any notice of the lone woman at her table by the pillar. The waiter brings my espresso and I pay immediately. I force myself to swallow the strong coffee, like I needed anything else to make my heart beat faster. When I've finished I get up and walk out. At the door I glance back; they're still laughing over the snaps.

How long before Blondie discovers her wallet is missing? Probably not until she's eaten her spaghetti, drunk her bubbly Pellegrino water and perhaps an espresso, and has to pay the bill. If her friend insists on treating her she won't discover her loss until she gets back to the office. I walk and then run down the street, duck into an alley and check the wallet's contents. It's a beautiful piece of work, burgundy leather with a tiny gold buffalo on the flap. Shame I can't keep it. It contains three credit cards and various customer cards for big stores in town. Two hundred and eighty-five quid in cash, plus assorted coins. I reckon I've got a good hour, maybe more, before Mrs G. Heyworth, the name on the cards, discovers her loss and freaks.

I'm too rushed and nervy to enjoy my first shopping spree in more than a decade, but I nevertheless manage to buy clothes, underwear, shoes and boots, and the much-needed hairdryer. I also buy body lotion, face cream, eye balm and some good make-up to replace the nasty stuff. I'm shocked by the prices. I remember I've got no perfume, so treat myself to big sprays – seems you can't get ordinary bottles any more – of my old favourites, Diorella and Chanel No. 5. The packaging is different, but they smell as fabulous as ever. I take a cab back and get the driver to drop me around the corner from my flat. I dump all the stuff in the bedroom and go out again to stock up on a load of groceries from Marks & Sparks.

After that, with much regret, I decide it will be prudent to dump the cards. I slip them back in the wallet, wrap that in a plastic bag and shove it deep into a waste bin amongst cold, greasy chips, crumpled newspapers and empty hamburger cartons. I transfer the rest of the cash to my own wallet. Finally I go into a hairdressers and say, 'Please do something.'

The man who cuts my hair says wow, it's time, and even though

It's a gorgeous colour how about a rinse to cover those few stray grey hairs? I agree. I'm amazed at the result – the sophisticated new style seems to lift and brighten my face, make my eyes more animated. I feel less alien, almost like the old Alyssa. I thought she was gone for ever. I blink away tears as I smile at my reflection. The man pats my shoulder and looks pleased, says there's no need to ask if I like it. I pay with Mrs Heyworth's cash. Forty-five quid! But it's worth it.

It's late afternoon now, and I'm getting tired. I go back to the flat, unpack all my purchases and put them away, tear up the receipts and flush them down the loo. I take another shower and make up my face, dress in clean, new underwear, black trousers and a soft, short, clingy lilac sweater. New black Mexx shoes with a chunky heel. I fluff out my hair and spray myself with Diorella. That beautiful perfume is so evocative of my past life – the happy part – that it almost makes me cry again. I must stop being so fragile. I'm standing there admiring my brand-new self when the enormity of what I've done suddenly hits me. I start to gasp and shake with panic.

Suppose Mrs G. Heyworth connects the disappearance of her wallet with the scruffball on her steps at lunchtime, and decides that it's been stolen rather than lost? Someone in that restaurant might remember me and give a description, tell the police they'd thought at the time I was acting suspiciously. If I get sent back inside I won't come out for a long time. I run to the window and stare down into the street, terrified that a police car might draw up and stop any second. The irony of the situation doesn't escape me either; I have committed a crime, the first of my life, after serving more than a decade in jail for something I didn't do.

I go into the kitchen, pour myself a glass of the Cabernet Sauvignon I've bought in Marks & Sparks, and gulp it down. I want to dump all the stuff I've bought, but of course I'd be bound to meet one of my new neighbours for the first time just as I'm staggering back downstairs with the bags. Besides, where can I dump all that stuff, and without being noticed? I tell myself to calm down. I've destroyed the receipts. There is nothing to worry about.

I pace the flat, trying to talk myself out of my panic. There's no reason for Mrs Heywood to think of me, let alone recognise me; she didn't even look at me, not directly anyway. I didn't touch her,

189

and she can't have known I followed her. She *would* think she had lost the wallet, although she would soon know somebody had taken ruthless advantage of her carelessness. And that restaurant was so busy, people concentrating on stuffing their faces and babbling at one another, how would any of them have noticed me? Most people are notoriously unobservant, and hopeless at accurately describing who or what they have seen. I knew that from the time of my brilliant career.

My panic subsides. The wine warms and comforts me. I move to the window and look out over crumbling St Luke's and its overgrown gardens. The sky is clearing, turning violet, with pink-tinged streaks of cloud on the horizon. It will be dark soon. I think of people hurrying home to be with loved ones, share meals, talk about their day. I'm sure they haven't all got loved ones to go home to – some of them might be worse off than I am – but standing here feels like being the loneliest person in the world. I thought of my father. Of Frankie. My mother, who was so freaked at the idea of seeing me again that she had a heart attack.

Suddenly I have to get out again. I need to walk. I put on my new, warm, lined, black suede jacket and go. I pause on the stairs. I can't hear the baby crying. I hope it's asleep. Warm, fed, feeling secure and loved.

I know where I'm going but don't want to acknowledge my destination to myself. I'm not sure it's a good idea. It's probably a really bad one. But I can't resist. By the time I get to Castle Street twenty minutes later, it's almost dark. The Town Hall windows are lit up; chandeliers blaze in its elegant upper rooms. I once went to a reception there, met the mayor and a couple of high-ranking police officers. Those were the days. I reach the Victorian office building with steps going up to the entrance, and scan the large board with the names of all the firms based there. It's after six; he might have already gone home to share his dinner with loved ones. But he never usually left until six-thirty. Of course he might not even be here. I'd like to go in and ask, but don't dare. So I hang around outside.

Ten minutes later I'm shivering with nerves. And cold, despite the new jacket. Several people hurry in and out of the building, but they don't give the new scrubbed-up Alyssa suspicious or disgusted glances because I look the part now. One man, balding and middle-aged, smiles at me; I don't return the compliment.

After another five minutes I'm starting to lose my nerve. He's left already, or he wasn't here in the first place.

What shall I do now? I can't bear to go back to the flat yet. I could go and have a drink, get something to eat. Yes, great fun by yourself. I could go to the cinema; something else I haven't done for years. I'm struck by desolation as I realise again that no matter what I tell myself I've still got all these crazy hopes and dreams. How many more times do I have to burn my wings and crash back to earth?

I stare through the glass doors into the bright, cosy interior beyond, my eyes blurring. Always on the outside looking in. A tall, dark man wearing a black overcoat and carrying a briefcase is coming down the flight of grey marble stairs. He nods and smiles at someone to his right, someone I can't see. He pushes through the doors and pauses at the top of the steps to peer at his watch. I blink. I want to speak, call out, but I can't because my mouth has gone dry and my heart's racing.

He looks up, sees me standing under the lamplight à la Lily Marlene, and stiffens. I long to do something, say something, but I'm powerless. We stare at one another. The suspended moment seems to go on and on. The chatter of passers-by and the roar of traffic recedes, and it's like we're in our own silent world. He slowly descends the steps and walks up to me. Stops.

His face is the same, lean and fine-boned. He looks older. I want to touch his wavy black hair, which has a bit of grey in it now. But I restrain myself. I look into his eyes. What do I feel? What does he feel? The last time I stood this close to him was – no. I don't want to think about that.

'Alyssa? I don't believe it. It is you. *Alyssa*?'

'Yes,' I whisper. 'Hello, Tomás.'

Chapter 21

'Oh, my God,' Frankie whispered as she parked the car on the grass verge by the little stone bridge, and got out. 'I must be insane.'

No. Just desperate. She walked slowly down dark, narrow, winding, Abbey Lane towards the white cottage on the corner, and turned on to the path that ran alongside the cottage and various scattered farm buildings. A few minutes later she reached the field where the abbey ruins lay. She walked through the damp grass. The moon and stars were out, and the night was cool. There were country odours of earth, herbs and wild garlic. She swore as she stumbled over a tussock. All she needed now was to twist her ankle.

Who had sent her the notes? Was this some kind of trap? She did not believe it had anything to do with Agron Xhani. But Frankie was not sure she believed Alyssa when she protested she had not told anyone about her urgent need for one hundred grand. Alyssa might have lied, realised she had made a mistake and be trying to cover herself. What, after all, did she know about her new half-sister? Except that Alyssa was a convicted murderer. But Alyssa would hardly know about the abbey ruins, somewhere Frankie had played as a child, hung around as a teenager, and where she had experienced her first less than satisfactory snog one sticky, starlit July night with a nervous boy whose name she could not remember.

The high walls and broken arch that formed the ruins of the priory, once a fine specimen of early Gothic, were hardly abbey proportions, but had always been known locally as the abbey ruins. The priory had been founded in the twelfth century by

Augustinian monks and destroyed during the dissolution of the monasteries in 1537 on the orders of Henry VIII. In 1454 three of the canons had been sacked for allegedly practising Black Magic.

Trees surrounded the field. In another field was a caravan park, used only in summer. Frankie glanced round fearfully as she heard dogs bark in the distance. They were probably from the farm. She slowed as she reached the ruins. The crumbling, moonlit walls and gaping arch resembled a film set. They looked as unreal as she felt.

She stopped. 'Hello?'

No answer. She was not early or late; it was one minute past ten. She looked around, her eyes straining for any sign of movement. Her fear increased; she was taking a risk coming alone to this dark, isolated spot. But what choice did she have?

'Is there . . .?' She paused. It sounded stupid to ask if anyone was there; she wasn't playing the Ouija board. 'It's Frankie,' she called, her voice sharp. 'I got your notes.'

Still no answer. Her fear escalated. 'Listen – I've got better things to do than hang around here all night. Come out. I'll count to ten. After that I'm going, and sod you!'

She had reached number three when someone stepped out from behind a wall. The figure was slim and of average height, wrapped in a long, dark coat. Moonlight glinted on pale hair; the face was in shadow.

'I didn't think the two of us would ever meet up in our old secret place again.'

Frankie gave a violent start. 'Monique! What the–'

Alyssa had not lied. That thought caused her a rush of relief, which disappeared instantaneously. But why on earth Monique Thorn?

'Was it you who wrote me those notes?' she stammered.

'It was.' Monique came closer and stopped, pulling the coat tighter around her. 'I'd practically given up on you. Thought you were too frightened. Or maybe not so desperate after all.'

'The hospital,' Frankie said, remembering. 'You heard me talking on my mobile.'

'Right. The only part I was interested in was when you said you needed a hundred grand. I wondered why you needed so much. Although I wasn't that interested. But my life's taken a different turn since the night we bumped into one another.'

193

Frankie was trying hard to recover herself, get over the shock of finding out that Monique Thorn had written those notes. She also felt somehow let down. Whatever, whoever she had expected, it certainly was not this part friend, part thorn in the flesh from way back. 'You always had a twisted sense of humour,' she remarked. 'Is this one of your crap jokes, to get me here like this and promise me money you haven't got?'

Monique raised her head. She looked tense, her complexion washed out by moonlight. 'The last thing on my mind is humour. And I haven't promised you any money yet, although I most definitely have got it. Tell me, Frankie, what do you do with yourself these days?'

'What's that got to do with anything?'

'Just tell me, okay? It's relevant.'

'I live abroad – in the Netherlands. That's why I didn't turn up here before. I went back – briefly. I didn't read your notes until this morning.'

'I see. So our ships could have passed in the night and continued on their separate courses. But they didn't. You don't believe in fate, do you, Frankie?'

'Did you drag me here for a cosy existential discussion? Because I'm not in the mood.'

'Nothing existential about what I've got in mind. Are you married?'

Frankie hesitated. 'Yes.'

'Any kids?'

'No.'

'And you were always so fond of puppies and kittens. What do you do?'

'I work as a translator at an embassy in The Hague.'

'So you're not in the police. Good. Are you and your husband happy?'

'Deliriously. Monique, what do you *want*? I can't believe you've got a hundred grand going spare, or even if you have that you'd give it to me for old times' sake.'

'Definitely not for old times' sake. Are you really happily married?'

'Bloody hell.' Frankie looked down. 'All right, no. He's dumping me. Or was. He seems to have changed his mind now.'

'Sounds a bit one-sided. Why do you want a hundred grand so badly?'

'Does that matter?'

'Yes.'

'To pay off a gambling debt. To a gangster. It's my husband's debt, but this gangster's after me for it too. We've got a week to find the money.'

'Wow. He's really landed you in it, hasn't he? Thought you'd be far too clever to marry a nightmare bloke like that.'

'Joe wasn't a nightmare,' Frankie whispered. 'Not until recently.'

'Still, all good things come to an end. Can't you go to the police?'

'If either of us do that we'll have *less* than a week. We've had one warning already.'

Monique stiffened and glanced round. 'I hope you weren't followed here.'

'Don't worry. I made sure.'

'How?'

Frankie glared at her. 'I made sure. Even if I was followed, it doesn't matter. As long as that guy gets his money, what does he care? But if I can't get it I'll just have to risk trying to fling myself over the threshold of the nearest cop shop. Now, what do you want?'

Monique stepped closer. 'I have definitely got one hundred grand. Plus a lot more where that came from.' She folded her arms. 'Since you've been dwelling across the grey North Sea with the Calvinist clog and cheese people, you probably won't have heard of Thorn Communications?'

Frankie thought. 'I have, actually. Read something about it in the *Echo* once. It's a very successful company. Why? Have you got some connection with it?'

'I own it, darling. I may not have left our sad old Catlick comp with as many qualifications as you, but I've done all right for myself. I'm good for several million.'

'Well. Congratulations.' Frankie felt startled then resentful. 'So Sister Maria Magdalena got it all *so* wrong when she said a flighty trollop like you would never amount to anything?'

'Yeah, dead wrong. She can eat my shit now. D'you know, the school governors of that place had the nerve to write to me when

195

I was crowned North-West Businesswoman of the Year, and ask me to go back there and give a role-model talk to the kids? As well as buy them a new science lab, if you please. I gave a talk, all right, but it wasn't what they expected. You should have seen their faces. I ended by telling them they could whistle for their lab.'

'Good for you. Are you still with Gerry?'

'Nah. Dumped him years ago. Anyway.' Monique turned and picked up an attaché case half hidden by damp grass, which Frankie had not noticed before. 'This nostalgia stuff is delightful, but it's time we got down to business.'

Frankie stiffened. 'I can't wait.'

Monique laid the attaché case on the grass, fumbled in her coat pocket and pulled out a torch. She snapped the locks open, switched on the torch and shone it on the contents. Frankie gasped at the bound stacks of notes.

'There's fifty grand there.' Monique switched off the torch and snapped the locks shut. 'I've got the other fifty in a secure place. It's half now, half later. That's if you decide you're up for this.' She sounded breathless now, more nervous. 'How far will you go, Frankie? To get that hundred grand?'

Despite the tension, Frankie started to laugh. 'Who do I have to kill?'

She was joking, of course, because it couldn't be that. You could have someone killed for a hell of a lot less than a hundred grand. Human life was chillingly cheap. She guessed Monique wanted her help with some corrupt business deal, although she had no clue what that would entail. Some dodgy people and considerable risk to herself, probably, for such a sum. Well, how much more danger could she be in?

'I'm up for it.' She shivered. 'As long as I can do it and get the money within the next few days.'

'No worries. You can do it tomorrow if you like.' Monique glanced around again and her voice dropped low. 'I want you to kill my husband.'

'What?' Horrified, Frankie took a step back. She too looked around the dark field. 'You . . . *what*?' she hissed. 'Are you serious?'

'Of course I'm bloody serious. What's wrong with you?'

'What's wrong with me?'

'You just asked who you had to kill.'

'I was joking! I thought . . . I thought it was some corrupt deal . . . I don't know!'

'So you're not up for it. Well, I hope the condemned woman eats a hearty breakfast. Oh, and just in case you feel like telling the cops about this intimate conversation, I'll deny it took place. You can't prove I sent those notes either.'

'Why ask *me* something like this?' Frankie was stunned. Dodgy business dealings were nothing compared to this. 'And why offer a hundred grand? You can get somebody murdered for a fraction of that amount. Murder is what we're talking about here.' She couldn't believe it. 'Why don't you . . . I don't know . . . hire a hit man, contract killer, whatever?'

'I don't have a clue how to do that. It's not the sort of thing you can go round asking people, is it? Even if I did know, it's too dangerous. I could get myself into a lot of trouble. Whoever I hired to do the job – and I'd just have to hope I'd got the right person – might blackmail me. He might even turn out to be an undercover cop. I've heard about a lot of cases where that happened.'

'Done your research then, have you?'

'And God knows *how* it happened,' Monique went on, 'because they never tell you that crucial bit. So I wouldn't know how to avoid it. I want someone with no criminal record and with whom I've got no obvious connection. That's why I thought of you. I haven't seen you for years, you're not in my life any more – and you won't be again after–' She stopped, chewing her lip. 'I told you I'm not short of a quid or two. If I divorce my husband I'll have to give him at least half of what I've got. So a hundred grand is cheap at the price.'

Frankie's eyes filled with tears. 'Monique, this is crazy. I can't *kill* someone. I can't just murder another human being, especially someone I don't hate or feel any anger towards – don't even *know*. You have to have a screw loose to be able to do that. My husband – he hurt me, wanted to dump me, he got me into this terrible mess. But despite all that, it doesn't make me feel like I want him dead!'

'So Saint Francesca will ascend to heaven with a pure soul.' Monique's voice was angry, malicious. 'And that's due to happen next week, I believe, isn't it?'

Frankie turned cold. Murder someone, or be murdered. Was that the only choice she had left?

197

'I look on it as self-defence,' Monique went on. 'I don't expect you to get all upset about this – or even believe me – but the fact is, the bastard cheated on me. I loved and trusted him, I thought we were solid. For life. I was so happy – should have known better, shouldn't I? Conal's been screwing some girl. I walked in on them. Of course that doesn't justify killing someone – not a *woman* killing a man anyway, according to our great legal system. But I found out Conal's been screwing my daughter too.' Her voice faltered. 'My own daughter. *She's fourteen years old*! And Lauren's on his side. She loves him and hates me. He's destroyed us. I thought this was as bad as it could get, but I was wrong. Wrong again, Monique.' A tear rolled down her cheek, glittering in the moonlight. 'Now I've found out he wants to murder me. He's already made one attempt. He thinks I don't know.'

Frankie did not know what to believe. 'How can he think you don't know if he's already tried?'

'It was meant to look like an accident. He did something to my car. Tampered with the steering. I could have veered off the road and crashed, or collided with some oncoming vehicle. Lauren was in the car with me when that was supposed to happen. I couldn't believe he'd do something so terrible. I didn't want to believe it.' Monique was crying now, her voice high and shaky. 'But it's true. He wants Lauren dead as well, the bastard. I didn't work my arse off for years building my company so that he and his whore can step over my corpse – my daughter's corpse too! – and get their filthy, betraying hands on all my money, on everything I bloody own. That is *not* – no way! – going to happen.'

Frankie was silent, staring at her. Was any of this true? Monique certainly seemed upset enough. ' Why don't you go to the police?'

'Well, as in your case, things are complicated.' Monique wiped her tears.

'Even if I agreed –' Frankie fought to think '– how would I do it? I mean, for Christ's sake, it's not like I'm some contract killer who despatches several poor bastards a week and thinks it's a job like any other.' She covered her face with her hands. 'What if I tried to do it but screwed up?'

'I know you, Frankie. If you put your mind to something – one hundred per cent – you won't screw up. But you don't necessarily have to do this yourself. Let your husband do the dirty work – he got you into this mess, he needs the money as much as you do.

198

Just make sure it gets done. Make it look like an accident – or murder in the course of a break-in, things getting out of hand. Use your creative imagination.' Monique laughed suddenly. 'That reminds me, have you started writing those novels yet?'

'No. Got some great material now though, haven't I?'

'You'll have to change the names.'

'If I do it – if your husband dies – you're going to be the major suspect. And if what you've told me is true you'll have had more motive, opportunity and a better method than most. The police will go through your life with a nit comb. Investigate your finances and everything. How will you explain missing a hundred grand shortly before the – cough, cough – *tragedy* occurred?'

'What do you know about finances, Ms Embassy Translator? Ms Wannabe Novelist? You don't just withdraw a big chunk of money from one account! I've always kept lots of cash, spread everything around. I'm not so thick that I don't have that covered. Think you're so clever. You've got no fucking idea, have you?'

No, Frankie thought, she had no idea. About anything. She had messed around, done nothing with her life. What was the use of having a writing talent, any talent, if you didn't have the confidence and determination to try to make something of it? She had spent too much energy being afraid, too much time waiting for things to happen. She had allowed herself to get sidetracked into marriage with a man who didn't care about her, had put her fate squarely into his hands. She had even been afraid to lose a crap job she hated. And where had all this passivity got her? About to be murdered in a week's time if she could not come up with an impossible sum of money. But now it looked as if she just might be able to come up with it, however terrible the means. Frankie remembered reading an interview with an author, a female author who said, 'Courage is the first essential'. She was referring to writing, of course, but that applied to just about everything.

Monique was staring at her, puzzled and aggressive. 'What are you thinking?'

Frankie took a breath. 'Give me that money.'

Monique gasped. 'You'll do it?'

'Obviously.'

'Why have you changed your mind?'

'I haven't. I hadn't made it up.'

'You could have fooled me.'

'Just hand over your dirty money, Monique.'

Monique picked up the attaché case and hugged it to her, hesitating. 'How do I know you'll do it?'

'And how do I know you'll pay me the rest? We have to trust each other, don't we? Otherwise we both go down. Come on, Monique. You got me here, you started this.' Frankie sensed she was gaining the upper hand. 'If you're not up for it any more, just tell me and I'll walk away. And don't worry, I've got no intention of telling the cops – or anyone else – about this conversation. What would be the point?'

'Right. You could be dead by this time next week anyway.'

'Oh, I don't think that will happen.'

'No? You seem different all of a sudden. Harder. Purposeful. What's changed?'

'Let's call it a reality check.' Frankie held out her hand for the attaché case. Monique gave it to her with obvious reluctance. 'Thank you.'

'That's a posh one and I want it back. Don't scratch the leather.'

'Wouldn't dream of it.' Frankie moved into the shadow of one of the crumbling walls and seated herself on a pile of ancient stones, the attaché case between her feet. She felt numb. It was as if some other person she did not know, someone calm and ruthless, had taken over.

'Okay. We've got a few other vital matters to discuss now. Like how we're going to communicate with one another until this is done.' She looked up at the nervous Monique. 'Seeing as you're not thick, I take it you've brought a photo and all the necessary information?'

Monique nodded. 'She drew an envelope from her pocket. 'Here's a couple of recent photos. You'll destroy them, of course, after–'

'After.' Frankie took the envelope. 'So tell me everything.'

Chapter 22

'I wondered when you'd be released – that's if you weren't out already. Wondered where you might be, how you were doing. I didn't think I'd ever see you again.'

Tomás Slaney sipped his coffee but left the rest because he felt another mouthful might choke him. He leaned back in his armchair.

'I had to find you, Tomás. I wondered how you were too.'

He watched Alyssa finish her cognac. She had drunk a lot of wine during their subdued dinner in the half-empty restaurant, subdued because of their mutual shyness at seeing each other again after so long, and because both of them were thinking of the anguished circumstances of their last meeting.

Tomás remembered Alyssa's cries and screams after the appeal failed, her trembling body as she clung to him for that last goodbye, the terrified, despairing look in her eyes as the three pissed-off prison warders dragged them apart and marched her away in handcuffs. His own anguish, his fear and helplessness, his shouts echoing along that cold stone corridor beneath the court-room: '*I love you! I'll save you, I'll get you out of this. Don't give up. Alyssa, I'll never let you go!*'

He had not been able to keep those wild promises. Alyssa had been refused leave for a second appeal. Soon afterwards she had stopped writing to him and refused to see him again. Tomás kept her letters for several years, then burned them one night when he was drunker than usual. At first that felt like the lifting of a burden – then a betrayal. It had, however, proved something of a defining moment. He realised he had to put the horror and despair behind him and go on with his life.

201

'That's an amazing story,' he remarked. 'About your mother and sister.'

'Yes.' Alyssa nodded. 'I'd love you to meet my sister. That's if ...'

Her voice trailed off. Tomás wished he could say how glad he was that she had found her mother and discovered this sister, but from what Alyssa had told him it was very early days and was not exactly proving a fairy tale reunion so far. Unless the troubled mother underwent a sudden and drastic change of heart it did not look as if there would be any fairy tale. At least her sister, Frankie Sayle, sounded all right. There seemed to be hope for that relationship.

He felt awkward at seeing Alyssa again and knew she felt the same; it was difficult to break the silence of years. Too much talk initially would not have been desirable. They needed silence and long looks to grow accustomed to one another's presence again, absorb the shock of their meeting, gauge each other's feelings and reactions. But Tomás could not gauge Alyssa's feelings, any more than he was capable of gauging his own right now.

He could not begin to imagine what she must have gone through in prison. All that torture, and for a crime she was not guilty of. How had such suffering marked her? It would have marked her, he was certain ... She had changed, but in ways he could not define. Or not yet. The thought made him uncomfortable. Tomás was also afraid. He did not know what to expect.

'This is a lovely apartment.' Alyssa got up, taking her drink, and strolled to the windows. She gazed out over the city lights and the orange-lit bulk of the Anglican cathedral. 'You should see my place – or maybe not.' She laughed. 'Funny how we've both got views of churches.'

'Practically impossible not to have a view of some church in this city.' Tomás studied her slim figure in the clingy sweater and tight trousers, her dark, glossy, well-cut hair falling over her shoulders. She was bright-eyed, flushed, full of vitality. 'I can't believe how good you look. Sorry,' he added hastily. 'I didn't mean that to sound–'

'It's okay.' Alyssa smiled at him, walked back and reseated herself on the sofa in front of the fire. He was sitting in an armchair. 'I don't blame you for thinking I'd emerge hollow-eyed and twitchy, with knackered hair and a prison pallor. I expected that myself. Must be my pure soul and the fire within that kept my looks – and me – from falling apart. I was determined not to give up – well, most of the time. I had my little lapses.' Her smile wavered, and her eyes were suddenly full of tears. 'But in the end I was determined not to let *them* win.'

'Of course you were.' Pity for her, horror at her ordeal, pierced his whole being. Tomás was about to sit beside her and put his arms around her when something stopped him. He got up, poured more cognac into her glass and laid one hand on her shoulder, gave it a brief squeeze. Alyssa gripped his hand, then let go. She sniffed, tossed back her hair and took a sip of cognac.

'How long have you been living here?' Her voice shook slightly. 'The Electoral Register gave your address as some village on the Wirral.'

'I bought this place about eighteen months ago. After my marriage broke up.'

'When did you get married?'

'Seven years ago.'

Alyssa shifted forward, frowning as she stared into the fire. 'That would have been a bit more than a year after they refused me another appeal. After I'd told you I didn't want to see you again. Why did your marriage break up? If you don't mind my asking.'

'I don't mind.' Tomás sat down and stretched out his legs. 'We should never have done it,' he sighed. 'It was my fault, not hers. I just – I don't know–' He shrugged. 'Too rash, too unadvised, too sudden and all that.'

'Any children?'

'A daughter. Claire. She lives with her mother. She's seven.'

'*Seven.*' Alyssa smiled. 'Who did you marry? Anyone I know? I can't imagine you'd have met her unless it was in the course of your work.'

'Right.' He hesitated, watching the firelight play across her rosy face. 'Mary Vance.'

'Oh my God.' Alyssa leaned back, laughing. But somehow Tomás did not think she was amused. 'The loyal, admiring colleague. She was always sniffing around. I suppose she was there to hold your hand and mop your fevered brow just when you were at your most vulnerable.'

He winced. 'I know it's sad.'

'It isn't. At least you had somebody. I'm glad. Even if it didn't last.'

'I wasn't fair to her,' he said in a low voice. 'I was selfish. I thought the best thing I could do was try to forget you. Marry, have kids, settle down. I should have known it wouldn't work. I didn't love Mary enough. And I was a mess. I wasn't fit to be with anyone, let alone get married.'

'Are you seeing someone now?'

'I have the occasional night out with a woman I met about three months ago – a solicitor. She does family law. I like her, she's nice. But you couldn't say I was *seeing* her. We're just friends really.' He shrugged. 'There's no one special.'

Alyssa wiped another tear. 'You were a mess because of me. I really fucked things up for you, didn't I?'

'*No*.' Tomás suddenly felt furious. 'Someone fucked things up for *you*, remember? For both of us. The murderer.' This evening was resurrecting unwelcome memories, emotions long buried. 'Now that you're out–' He hesitated again. 'D'you want to try and discover who did kill Vivienne?'

'Yes. I'd like to clear my name. But I'm not under any illusions. It's so long ago, which means it'll be even more difficult. If not impossible. But I think the immediate thing is to try and build some kind of life for myself.'

He nodded. 'It must be very difficult being back in the world. A changed world.'

'It is.' She looked at him, her eyes shining. 'Tomás, I'm sorry I turned up like this. It must have been an awful shock for you when you saw me standing there.'

'It was certainly a shock.' He smiled. 'Not an *awful* one. Far from it.'

'You're very kind. You always were. That's one of the things I loved – love – about you.'

'Alyssa ... ' He felt nervous again. 'I want to help you. Criminal law's not my field, as you know, but there are some people I can talk to about you. About your case.'

'That would be great. But what I really need at the moment, Tomás, is a job.'

'A job?' he echoed. 'Well, yes. Of course.'

'Obviously I can't be a barrister again. Not unless or until I clear my name, anyway. Even then it wouldn't be easy. But right now I need something I can exist as opposed to subsist on. You can imagine the sort of crap I've been offered.' She glanced away, her expression bitter. 'My probation officer really likes to rub my nose in my severely limited options.'

'Well, hopefully you won't have to put up with her much longer.'

'It's a him. Smart arse Carl with the mean little snarl.'

'Whatever I might be able to get you – it'd only be receptionist or secretary work. Not much of an intellectual challenge, to say the least.'

'That's still a hell of a lot better than a dry-cleaning or cardboard box factory.'

He frowned. You don't have to take *that*. Give me a couple of days to sort something, all right?'

'Thanks. Tomás, I really appreciate this.'

'It's no problem.'

Lucy Frost might take Alyssa on, he thought. She was incandescently pissed off with work-shy, barely literate teens, even if they were cheap and easily dismissable. Mary needed someone too, but that might be pushing it. Another thought struck him. 'Let me give you some money.' Not that Alyssa looked as if she needed it. How did she afford those clothes? Her beautiful hair seemed newly cut; she certainly couldn't have got that style in prison. He felt a sudden twinge of unkind suspicion, but dismissed it as quickly as Lucy's latest teen.

Alyssa shook her head, embarrassed. 'You don't have to give me money.'

'I want to,' he interrupted, ashamed of his suspicion. He got up. 'Relax, finish your drink. I'll be back in a minute.'

Tomás went into the room where he kept his word processor and papers, opened the desk drawer and took out his cheque book. Then he realised Alyssa probably didn't have a bank account. He unlocked the wall safe and took out a thousand pounds. Keeping cash handy always made him feel more secure. He slid the money into a brown business envelope.

In the sitting room doorway he hesitated. She was still hunched on the sofa, staring into the fire, clutching the cognac glass. He noticed it was empty again. The light from the flames picked out warm, gold glints in her chestnut hair.

Tomás remembered running his fingers through that hair,

smelling its fresh scent, burying his face in its thick softness when they made love. He stared at her slim shoulders and back, the outline of the bra beneath her sweater. He tried to analyse what he felt.

Shock mainly, of course. Pity. Shame, as if he had let her down, not fought hard enough for her. Most of all, unease. Alyssa was an unknown quantity now, this situation full of somehow threatening possibilities. He knew her and yet he did not. Tomás suddenly felt completely out of his depth, on the verge of making what he thought could prove to be a terrible mistake. Sensing his gaze Alyssa turned her head, revealing the curve of her firelit profile. She smiled.

'What are you thinking? Can't get over the shock of seeing me again, I suppose. I don't blame you.' She stood up, staggered slightly, and looked longingly around the big room. 'I should go,' she yawned, arching her slim body. Her breasts stood out. 'I've pestered you enough for one evening.'

Tomás knew she did not want to go. And he wasn't sure he wanted to let her. He came forward and handed her the envelope.

'Here. Put money in thy purse.'

'Tomás, I really don't–'

'Want to argue. Quite right. Let me be master in my own home, will you?'

He thought of the house on the Wirral, surrounded by trees, the views of Thurstaston Hill from the front bedrooms. Mary kept saying she was going to move, find somewhere smaller, but she hadn't done anything about it yet. Too busy, as usual. Was Claire asleep? Tomás missed hearing about what his daughter and her friends had got up to at school that day. He missed reading to her at bedtime. Being a weekend father wasn't very satisfactory, but what else could he hope for? It was his fault; he should have expended more time and effort on his marriage. He suddenly felt tired and very depressed. He needed to make a new beginning but the effort, as usual, seemed beyond him.

'I'll pay you back,' Alyssa was saying.

'Don't be daft. Look on it as a gift.' He paused. 'From a friend.'

'A best friend. That's what you are, Tomás.' She stared up at him, laid one hand on his shoulder and kissed him very lightly on the lips. Tomás smelled the cognac on her breath. 'Thanks so much for this evening, for …' She paused, biting her lip and blinking away more tears. 'I don't know what I would have done if – if you hadn't wanted to know.'

'Were you afraid of that? You shouldn't have been.'

'I know, but I couldn't help it.' She hesitated again. 'I went to see my father the other day. Just to tell him once more that I didn't murder Vivienne, to ask how he could ever have believed I did? And to ask him … well, never mind. He was horrible, but I suppose I should have expected that. He said he never wanted to see me again.' A tear ran down her cheek. 'Unless it was to ID my body in a morgue.'

'Jesus Christ, Alyssa!' Tomás wrapped his arms around her and held her close.

'I don't know what I was thinking of.' Her face was against his shoulder, her voice muffled. 'I must have been crazy.'

'Fucking old bastard. He doesn't – he never deserved you. You don't need him. Don't go back there, okay? Ever again.'

'No worries. I'm sure he's got the rottweilers and electrified fence in place already.'

Her soft hair tickled his face. It had the fresh scent he remembered, mingled with some citrus shampoo or conditioner. Tomás lifted a silky strand and let it fall. His heart began to beat faster.

There were no warders to drag them apart now. They could stay here like this all night if they wanted. He gently tilted her chin, stroked her face and looked into her eyes. Rainy day in Liverpool, he thought, remembering how he used to tease her about their lovely grey colour. Mist on the river. Clouds over Lake District fells. They continued to stare at each other, Alyssa's lips slightly parted. But neither of them made any move, and the dangerously intense moment passed. Tomás let go of her. She was disappointed, he guessed, and so was he, obscurely.

'Better get you home,' he said, too briskly, with what he knew was a false smile.

Alyssa took a deep breath and nodded, turned away and picked up her jacket. She slipped the envelope of money into her bag. Her expression was calm now, carefully neutral. When he talked about what jobs he might be able to find her, she listened and smiled politely. Like a friend grateful for the favour. A few minutes later they were in his car, driving across town to her flat.

Tomás knew the place was a depressing dump, despite Alyssa's good clothes and cool hair, and he decided to make some excuse not to go in because he couldn't face seeing it now. And he did not want another dangerous moment. His desire to help Alyssa was suddenly tinged with boredom and resentment, and felt horribly like duty. He just wanted to go home and be alone with his thoughts. After all these years of putting his life on hold he had finally managed to get over Alyssa. His mistake of a marriage – a mistake except for Claire – had broken up. And now here Alyssa was, back in his life again. Tomás was not at all sure he wanted this. He guessed she hoped for more than friendship from him, despite what she said. There would come a point when he had to tell her he couldn't give her any more.

He was ashamed of himself for thinking this way. But his life, such as it was, had to go on even though this bombshell had exploded. It was late, he was exhausted, and he hadn't had a chance to look through those papers ready for tomorrow, his original plans for the evening.

Yes, he needed a new beginning.

Alyssa Ward was not it.

Chapter 23

Dear Mum,
This is a letter I hoped with all my heart that I'd never have
to write . . .

'Didn't want to worry you, but now I'm dead. *Shit.*' Frankie
pressed the delete key then 'Close' and shut down the laptop. 'Is
that the best you can do?' she muttered. 'If you live, you can take
up comedy writing.' She stared out of the window across the
grassy field towards the church tower.

There was no way she could write this terrible in-the-event-of
letter. Estella would be even more devastated because she would
blame herself: for being ill, for not selling the house, for not being
confided in, for not getting a loan or doing anything else she
would imagine she could have done to save her daughter's life.
Frankie also knew she could no more bring herself to tell her
mother about the danger she was in than she could write the letter.
Or any more than she could contemplate murdering Monique
Thorn's husband Conal in the next day or so.

By some horrible coincidence she had seen an item on last
night's regional news about women who murdered their husbands.
Or had them murdered. Monique must be one of that growing –
according to the media – band of wives who wanted their
husbands disposed of for one reason or another, many such
contract killings being disguised as suicides or road traffic acci-
dents. Of course the papers said feminism was to blame for this
phenomenon, as it apparently was for so many others. And now
here she was finding herself a hired contract killer for one of these
murderous wives. The phone rang.

Who was calling? Agron Xhani? Joe, to tell her he'd scraped together the rest of the money? Somehow she didn't think so. Alyssa? Frankie got up and went into the front bedroom to answer it, automatically checking the road for cars with thuggish-looking men seated in them. She still could not see anybody. Her watchers could be very good. She didn't imagine they were the elderly couple getting out of the white Ford Escort though.

'Good morning, Madam, and how are you today?' The man's voice was full of false cheeriness.

'Like you care. Are you selling something?'

'Well ...' Strangely enough, he did not seem to have been trained to respond to that question. 'I'm just calling to inquire–'

'Fuck off.' She crashed the phone down. Some people you wouldn't think twice about murdering. She sat on the bed and covered her face with her hands.

Conal Thorn might be a cheating bastard, seducer of his under-age stepdaughter and would-be wife murderer, but Frankie had only Monique's word for that. Even if it was all true it wasn't her job to play judge, jury and executioner. She had taken the fifty grand because she had not been able to resist. Talking to Monique in the moonlit abbey ruins, she had believed she could do it. Now Frankie knew she could not. More to the point, did not want to. Crazy to have such scruples, when her life depended on not having them. She had no scruples about keeping Monique's dirty money though, even trying to get the rest without killing the husband. But how the hell could she do *that*?

She thought about her appointment with Agron Xhani in five days time. Even if she could hand him the money she no longer believed he would just take it and let her walk away. People like that never let anyone walk away. He or his men would kill her. And Joe. *Joe.* She went downstairs, got her mobile and dialled his number. No answer. She tried his mobile, the apartment and then his work number.

'Joe isn't here,' said Martijn, one of his colleagues. 'We haven't seen him for a couple of days. He stormed out after a bust-up with someone in personnel. He wouldn't talk about what had happened, but he was in a terrible state. Joe's been acting weird for weeks, now I come to think of it. One or two of us have tried to contact him, but he's not home – not answering the phone or door bell, anyway. His bosses aren't happy, I can tell you. If he doesn't come back and sort things soon, he won't need to bother at all. What's wrong with him, Frankie? What's happening?'

She hesitated. 'I'm sorry, Martijn. Joe's got some problems, yes, but I can't talk about that now. I'm trying to find him myself.'

'Okay. Whatever.' Martijn's voice took on a sharp note. 'If you do manage to find your husband, tell him he'll have another problem – a big one – unless he sorts himself out. Namely, unemployment.'

'I'll pass that on. ''Bye, Martijn.'

She hung up and tried to call Joe again, swearing as the apartment phone rang and rang, and then his voice mail came on the mobile. She left a terse message. The bust-up with personnel probably meant his request for a loan had been rejected. Was Joe home and just not answering, or had Agron Xhani's men done something to him? Or... she went cold. Had Joe lost his nerve, wiped out their joint bank account and done a runner? He might be on a plane right now, leaving her behind to take the rap for his mess. Frankie did not want to believe that, but there were lots of things she didn't want to believe.

Useless to hope for anything from Joe now. It might be his debt, his problem, but it was hers too, and now she was on her own. She had been from the start. If he were to surprise her and phone she would not tell him about the fifty grand she had hidden in the attic, in an old tea chest beneath stacks of old story and school books. On top of the books was a child's nurse's kit and a naked blonde doll the size of a toddler, with blank blue eyes from which the thick black lashes were unevenly snipped, dusty bandages hanging off her moulded flesh-coloured plastic limbs. No wonder I turned out warped, Frankie thought. She dialled another number.

'Val? Hi. It's Frankie. Is Mum around?'

'Yes, love. I'll get her for you. She ate a good breakfast this morning.'

'Not a fry-up, I hope.'

'Joker. Toast, cereal and a banana. She's looking a lot better. And–' Val paused '–she's told me,' she said, her voice hushed. 'Last night.'

'Told you ...?'

'About the poor baby she had to abandon. To think she's been keeping such a shocking secret all these years. I can't even begin to imagine what a terrible burden it must have been. She was so frightened – she still is. But I think talking about it did her some good. Oh, here she is. Yes, it's your darling daughter.'

'Hello, darling. How are you?'

Her mother's voice sounded lighter. As if a burden really had been lifted. It broke Frankie's heart to imagine what Estella might be feeling this time next week. I can't do this to her, she thought, squeezing her eyes shut for a second. I just can't.

'I'm okay,' she lied. 'Got a lot of stuff to get on with, though. New life, etcetera.'

'Of course you have. And me to worry about on top of everything else. You mustn't, you know. I'm getting there.'

'You told Val about Alyssa.'

There was a brief silence. 'The way you say her name. Sounds as if you know her.'

Frankie was glad her mother could not see her face. 'How could I?'

Estella didn't answer that. 'I'll come home in a few days. Val's been wonderful, of course. But I'd like to be back in my own place soon. Have you decided what you'll do yet? Where you'll live, I mean?'

'I – I don't know. I haven't really made any decisions.' You didn't think about a future you weren't sure you had. Frankie gazed out of the window. The clouds were parting, weak sunlight breaking through. 'I'll look for a smaller apartment,' she said, trying to think what she might have done if she'd only had being dumped and divorced to worry about. 'On my own. I don't fancy sharing. And I'll carry on working at the embassy, for now at least. That'll give me time to save money while I think about what I want to do eventually.'

'That sounds sensible. Very sensible. I'm proud of you.'

'I'm proud of you as well.' Tears stung Frankie's eyes. 'You're the best mother in the world.'

'Given my history, that's hardly a compliment I deserve.'

'You do deserve it. Mum, you've taken the step of telling someone else – Val – about Alyssa Ward. That's a big step. Do you think you might–'

'Confront my demons and meet her? No. One day, maybe. And that's a big maybe. But not yet. Not for a long time.'

Frankie did not push it. It was beyond insane to expect her mother to meet Alyssa and form a close relationship within days, so that Alyssa would be there for her in case something terrible happened to her other daughter.

'How's His Lordship behaving?' Estella never referred to Joe by his name any more. 'Mister Midlife Crisis?'

'Oh – he's being civilised. A bit fraught.'

'I should damn well think he is fraught. You're better off without him now, you know. When all this is over you're going to have a lovely new life.'

'Yes.' *No*. Frankie wanted to end this conversation. She glanced at her watch. It was quarter-to-twelve; Alyssa was expecting her. How would her mother feel if she knew the two of them were meeting in secret?

'Val says come and have your dinner with us this evening. Get here about six.'

'Well – tell her thanks very much. But I've arranged to meet a friend, so we'll probably have a bite together later.' Frankie needed to keep her time free, and if anyone was tailing her she did not want to lead them to where her mother was staying. Alyssa was safe enough. If Xhani's thugs saw her they would think she was just a friend. 'Carol Hudson, remember her?' She hadn't seen Carol for ages. Too late now.

'Oh yes. That's good. You need your friends around you. All right, love, I'll see you soon then. Take care.'

Frankie hung up, imagining the police coming to tell her mother she was dead, murdered. She could not bear to imagine Estella's reaction. She would have nothing left to live for – probably would not live. So, she would be dead, her mother dead, innocent victims of crime, a vicious maelstrom of circumstances that had swept them up and crushed them. Such injustices happened every day all over the world to lots of people.

Except it wasn't going to happen to her. She had been dumped in this situation without having done anything to deserve it, and she had a right to use any means possible to get herself out of it. Frankie's dream of the previous night came back to her: in the dream she had been looking at a newspaper article, an article she had written, with a photo of her next to it. She was smiling, looking happy and full of confidence. The title of the article was 'How Evil Can Improve You'.

What was that trying to tell her?

*

'Mum, is it true?'

'Is what true?' Monique snapped, suspending operations with the lip brush as Lauren came into her bedroom. 'You're always complaining about me failing to knock on your door.' She glared at her in the dressing-table mirror. 'Why don't you try doing it for a change?'

'Is it true that you and Conal are getting divorced?'

'No, of course not.'

Monique resumed painting her lips a soft, shiny red. Best to try and pretend everything was going to be hunky-dory. When your beloved husband was going to die horribly in an accident or push up the victims of fatal crime statistics any day soon you didn't want to admit to anyone, not even your own daughter, that you had planned to get divorced. Monique wondered if Frankie would do the job herself or hire someone. She didn't care as long as it was done soon, because her nerves were stretched to breaking point and she couldn't take much more. It had to happen in the next two or three days. She had delivered all the info about Conal and his movements; now she had to sweat it out while she waited for the phone call, on a specially bought pre-paid mobile that she would immediately dispose of after the event. Calls made on pre-paid mobiles were more difficult, if not impossible, to trace. In the event that the police felt they needed to trace any of her calls.

'Then why's he moved out?' Lauren asked. 'Where's he gone?'

'He hasn't moved out – he's just away for a couple of days. We needed some space.'

'Where is he?'

'Like I'd tell you.' Conal was staying at their apartment in town while he looked for a new place. Little did he know, he needn't bother. Monique glared at her daughter again. 'It's none of your business. And I'm not going to have a conversation with you about this – or anything – first thing in the bloody morning. I've got things to do. So have you. Get your stuff – you'll be late for school if you don't hurry up. Always the same.'

'What about me?'

'What *about* you?'

'Mum! Can't we–'

'Just go, will you?' Monique's simmering anger and despair, stoked with fear, bubbled up. 'Get out. I don't want to look at you

214

right now, never mind talk. Go to school and have a fab day snorting to your mates about your bitch mother.'

'You are a bitch.' Lauren's green eyes filled with tears. 'I was going to tell you something, but now I won't. I'll tell you this though, I don't want to stay with you any more. I hate you. I want to go and live with my Dad.'

'*What?*' For the first time since she couldn't remember Monique started to laugh. 'Well, that's a good one. Best I've heard in a long time. You're welcome, my dear. You'll have to find him first, of course, and persuade him to take an interest. Seeing as he didn't do that years ago I hardly think he will now. But hey, good luck.'

Lauren slammed the door and pounded down the stairs. The front door slammed, so hard that the ancient oak ceiling beams creaked in protest and the Constable reproduction on the wall wobbled perilously. Monique got up and watched her daughter half walk, half run down the drive, corn-blonde hair flying, the heavy black rucksack bouncing. It looked too heavy for Lauren's thin shoulders.

'I'm sorry,' she groaned. 'Oh God. Sorry, Lauren.'

Adversity was bringing out the worst in her rather than the best – she was finding out what she was capable of, and it wasn't pretty. It was even less pretty to discover what her supposedly loving husband was capable of. She turned away, her glance resting on the little pink-and-purple mobile on the dressing table.

Conal was going to pay for destroying their relationship. For everything. But Monique was terrified he would get to her first. Being alone here, except when Lauren was home, alarms switched on, doors locked and bolted, watching her back the whole time whenever she was out, felt like a half-life. What a gruesome spectacle this was, she and Conal wanting each other dead! How could she have been such a fool? Her marriage to Gerry seemed blissful compared to this. And now her relationship with Lauren was ruined. Was there no way back? Was she never again to be allowed happiness or peace of mind?

Monique felt like collapsing again, not moving for the rest of the day, but she couldn't allow herself to fall apart. She froze as the phone rang, then realised it was the phone on the bedside table and not the new mobile that she had morbidly programmed to play Chopin's death march.

215

'Mrs Thorn, we phoned the other day to tell you your car was ready. Can I ask when you'll be–'

'This morning, all right?' Fuck's sake. 'I'll be there in half an hour.' She slammed the phone down. She never wanted to set eyes on that bloody Lotus again. She would buy another car. Monique tried to think. She had cancelled her appointment with the solicitors. Had Conal seen one yet? Why would he bother, if he planned to have her killed? Of course that could be a front.

She shut her eyes as fear and grief threatened to overwhelm her. Then she took a deep breath and dialled the apartment number. She had to try and pre-empt Conal. Surprise him, outmanoeuvre him, keep him off balance. Until . . . *until*.

'Hello?' He sounded depressed, wary. Monique swallowed. Her mouth was dry.

'It's me.' She paused. 'How are you?'

He took a few seconds to answer. 'How do you think?'

'Is your arm – your shoulder – getting better?'

'What do you care?'

'I do care, Conal. Can you drive again yet?'

'Just about. Had a go yesterday, but nearly ran myself off the road a couple of times during the first ten minutes. Wasn't too bad after that. I have to take it slowly though. No sudden movements.'

'Have you seen a solicitor?'

'Yesterday afternoon. Davenport Chapman & Gale in Church Street, if you want to know. They'll be contacting your bunch of cut-throats shortly. Selina Davenport's dealing with me, she thinks I've got a strong case.'

Monique shivered. 'What did you tell her – them?'

'Don't worry, Monique.' Conal's voice was weighted with contempt. 'You're safe from the long arm of the law – the criminal law, anyway. All I'm interested in is getting the divorce settlement I'm entitled to.'

'I've been thinking about that.'

He laughed. 'I bet you have.'

'I may have acted a bit hastily.'

'Don't make me laugh, please. It hurts. I'm trying to cut down on the painkillers.'

'Can't we talk, Conal? I don't want this divorce. I want to do everything I can to try and save our marriage.' Monique looked at herself in the mirror as she spoke the lies, at her smooth blonde

216

hair and young-looking, made-up face, the glossy red lips that suddenly resembled a wound.

'You've changed your tune big time.' He was silent for a few seconds. 'What's brought this on? Lauren confessed she lied, is that it?'

'Not exactly.' Monique controlled a surge of anger. 'I just want to talk. You said there wasn't a way back, but I'm hoping that's not true. If we talk and you decide there still isn't, then okay. I won't fight you. You can have whatever settlement you want and I won't contest it.' She paused. 'This is my fault after all.'

Another silence. 'What are you up to, Monique?'

She felt sick. 'I'm not *up to* anything. I just want to–' her voice wobbled '–talk.'

'All right,' he sighed. 'Come to the apartment after work. I'll be there.'

'Can't we go out for dinner?' Monique wanted Mr and Mrs Thorn to be seen dining happily together before the tragic event.

'Yeah, okay. I suppose I've got to eat. And maybe it's safer for me not to be alone with you.'

She cringed. 'I'll meet you down in the lobby, at six-thirty, is that all right? We'll decide where to go then.'

'Whatever. Okay, six-thirty.' Conal hung up.

He had none of the barely controlled anger of a few days ago. Monique still could not believe he really wanted her dead. Well, she had launched her pre-emptive strike. She put on a black linen trouser suit, drank another cup of coffee and called a cab to take her to the bloody garage.

When she arrived she looked over the canary yellow car in disgust. She hated the thing now; could not think why she had ever bought it. Worst of all, it was the car she and Lauren could have been killed in.

'Glad you could make it,' the red-haired, blue-overalled mechanic grinned. He swept out one arm. 'All present and correct, Madam.'

'I hope the bill's correct,' Monique snapped. 'No lone female surcharge stuck on it.'

He looked blank. 'You what?'

'Never mind. Is it safe to drive now?'

'Safe?'

217

'Yes, *safe*.' She glared at him. 'D'you need a dictionary – an English lesson?'

'That car always was safe. I'm surprised you managed to do more than thirty in it.'

'What?' Monique smelled petrol fumes and autumn woodsmoke. 'I was told I could have veered over the other side of the road and hit an oncoming vehicle, or gone off the road altogether and crashed.' She tried to keep her voice steady.

'Well, anyone can do that, can't they? Especially when they've had a few.'

'Where's the manager?' She was sweating. 'I want to speak to him.'

The manager was bored but busy. 'Yes, Mrs Thorn, there was a problem with the steering and suspension. Which we've fixed. I can't imagine someone would have messed about with the car though – done it deliberately.'

'But I was told–'

He shrugged. 'There'd be no point.'

'There might be a point if someone wanted to cause me to have an accident. Look. Someone from this garage told me that the mechanic who repaired my car said someone could have tampered with it.'

'Oh. Well.' The manager loosened his horrible striped tie and shuffled papers on his desk. 'That would be my colleague you spoke to the other day. The mechanic you're referring to doesn't work here any more.'

'Why not?'

'We had to let him go.'

'*Why?*'

'Well – his work wasn't quite up to standard. Unreliable too.'

'You mean he made a mistake?'

The manager looked embarrassed. 'Overactive imagination combined with inexperience, you could say. I'm sorry about that.'

'Sorry?' Monique stared at him. 'I've been through hell. I thought someone was trying to kill me!'

'Now hang on a minute.' He looked startled. 'I'm sure nobody here said *that*. Saying your car might – *might* – have been tampered with isn't saying it *was*. You're the one who's jumping to all these conclusions here.'

'What bloody conclusions do you expect me to jump to?'

Monique didn't like the way he was looking at her. She could hardly breathe. 'How could you nobble a car if you wanted to kill whoever was driving it?'

'You couldn't. Basically. Even if you disable the brakes a vehicle comes to a stop by itself eventually. Of course you could crash, but –' he shrugged again '– that wouldn't guarantee a fatality. You can't really do anything to a car to make sure it'll kill the driver. If you want to kill someone with a car it's best to arrange a collision, preferably head-on. Or a hit-and-run.' He shook his head. 'I don't believe I'm having this conversation. Would you like to settle the bill, please, Mrs Thorn, and take your car? I've got a lot on.'

Monique was finding it hard to control herself. 'I was going to call the police!'

He looked annoyed. 'It's taken you long enough to get here, Mrs Thorn. If you really thought someone was trying to kill you, wouldn't you have called them before now? They could have taken a look at the car before we repaired it. But I doubt if they'd have found anything.'

She stared at him. Of course, she couldn't tell him why she hadn't called the police. She pulled out a credit card and slapped it down.

He and the red-haired mechanic stood watching as she drove off. In the driving mirror she saw the manager shake his head again and make a familiar gesture.

'Okay, I'm a loony,' she spat. 'So fuck you, you moron.'

She was trembling all over, could barely handle the powerful car. The thought that she was a paranoid bitch and that Conal might have no intention to murder her after all buzzed around her brain, arousing horrendous doubts just when she desperately needed not to have any. This did not mean he had not tried. But it was impossible to tell one way or the other.

She drove on towards Liverpool. In the end, she reasoned, this did not change things. Even if he had not tried to murder her Conal still wanted a divorce, wanted to get his hands on half her property. She would lose out big time. There was that tart she had caught him with. Worst of all, he had seduced Lauren, turned her against her own mother. Monique could not let him get away with that unforgivable act of ultimate cynical treachery and outrage. Conal had destroyed everything she loved, and now it was too late.

219

She had set things in motion and she had to follow through. Stay cool. She would be fine as long as she kept her head. It was the waiting that freaked her, not knowing how and when 'it' would happen. That was what she couldn't stand. Once it was done she would feel much better.

She could start again, get a new life. The trauma, misery and bitterness would fade, although the damage would leave its mark. Monique did not expect to find happiness again, certainly not with some other man. But maybe she could achieve a kind of peace. She would have the satisfaction of knowing she had dealt with the awful situation, not allowed Conal to get away with his crimes. And she would still be rich. She would get to keep everything she had worked for. That wasn't nothing.

Driving into Liverpool she pulled over in a street of red-brick terraced houses and got out the pretty pink-purple mobile.

'I can't wait any longer,' she snapped. 'You have to do it tonight.'

Chapter 24

'Tomás, you're a gorgeous man and I adore you,' his friend Lucy Frost laughed. 'But I'm afraid I won't consider employing a convicted murderer as a receptionist or secretary, even if she is your ex-fianceé. I'd do anything for you, but not *that*.'

Tomás glanced around the lobby of the Queen Elizabeth II law courts. 'Lucy, Alyssa Ward was – *is* – the victim of a terrible miscarriage of justice.'

'That may well be.' Lucy shrugged. 'So are lots of people.' She gripped her briefcase, the bundle of briefs under her arm, and smoothed one hand over her dusty black suit. 'And after all those years in the nick she's bound to be psychologically damaged – that's unavoidable. It's just a question of how much damage. If she wasn't a murderer before, who's to say she won't become one now?'

He frowned. 'Not funny.'

'I wasn't joking. Look, I'm sorry. But you can understand my reservations, I think.'

'I suppose. It's just that there's nothing going at my place now, and you're on the hunt for a new receptionist. I thought you might give Alyssa a chance.'

'I'm afraid not. I'll stick to the illiterate, inarticulate teens. I know where I am with them. Have you asked any better person than me to give this lady a job?'

Tomás shook his head. 'You're the first.'

'Well, I'd make me the last if I were you. If it gets around that you're trying to find a convicted murderer – even if she is innocent – a job, and for deeply personal reasons, it might just ever so slightly tarnish your impeccable reputation.'

Tomás's frown deepened. Lucy was right. But he had to ask a few other people before he gave up. He wondered if he could get Alyssa work somewhere else. But the legal community was his sphere of influence, in theory at least.

'Did you know she was out and look her up?' Lucy asked. 'Or did she contact you?'

Given the cynical look in Lucy's bright brown eyes, he did not want to admit that Alyssa had found out where he worked and waited for him outside his building. 'She, er . . . she contacted me.'

'Hmm. Thought so. Tomás, I know you. You're kind and very loyal; you feel sorry for her. Protective. I can understand you want to help. And if she was innocent then yes, of course she must have suffered terribly. But none of that was your fault. Just be careful, okay? You might be getting yourself into some scarily deep waters here.'

'Come off it.' He felt on the defensive. 'Alyssa's trying to start again and she needs a break. I only want to help her find a job. Something a tad better than the kind of crap she's been offered so far. You can imagine.'

'Yes. And that's very noble of you. But like I said, be careful.' Lucy adjusted her specs and tossed back her long, dark hair. 'She must be incredibly fragile. Vulnerable. She might want a lot more from you than you realise. More than you might care to give. Life's tough, and you must look like her knight in shining armour right now.' Lucy paused. 'Know what I mean? Nothing personal, but you guys can sometimes be a bit dense about these matters.'

'And you girls can be a bit bloody cynical.'

'I know. Women are nearly always harder on other women. Watch any jury.' She laughed and glanced at her watch. 'Got to run. See you, Tomás. Take care.'

'Yeah. See you, Lucy.' Tomás's smile faded as he watched her hurry towards the exit and be waved through by the security personnel. He recalled last night, Alyssa trembling against him. The scent of her hair, her tears, the look in her glittering eyes. He felt uneasy to think how he could have let himself go at that moment, plunged head first into those scarily deep waters.

And drowned.

*

'Was that Lady Macbeth?' I ask.

Frankie nods as she slides the mobile back into her bag. She looks pale and very preoccupied. As you would. So preoccupied that she doesn't appear to have noticed my cool new hairstyle, new clothes and expensively subtle make-up. Just as well, because I wouldn't fancy explaining to her how I acquired them. Not that she'd disapprove strongly, I imagine, in the circumstances. Or even care. She's got much bigger issues to worry about. Maybe she assumes Tomás bought me them. I was so excited that I started telling her about meeting him again, about last night, before I realised what a state she was in.

'Monique wants me to do it tonight.' Frankie rakes her hands through her hair. 'Jesus Christ, this is –' She shakes her head, her eyes full of tears.

'Well, you knew you'd have to do it soon.' I adopt a brisk, businesslike tone, as if icing some unsuspecting guy on the instructions of his missis was just any old job. Okay, I know it is to some people.

'Not this bloody soon.' She looks at me. 'I can't do it. I don't want to.'

'So what will you do, give back the fifty grand and say sorry but?'

She glances away. 'No.'

'Then *what*?'

Frankie frowns. 'I'm not sure.'

'Why the hell did she ask *you* to stiff her husband? Why not hire a pro? She'd save herself a lot of money. Millionaires love to save money, don't they?'

'Monique doesn't have a clue how to find a hit man. Even if she did, that's too risky – he might blackmail her or turn out to be an undercover cop. That's why she's willing to pay well over the odds for–'

'Some freaked-out amateur,' I finish, seriously worried. 'Look, I don't want to sound hard, but it's not like you have a choice here, is it? You've taken half the cash, so you've got to do this. Be bloody, bold and resolute, like Lady M. Bottom line – if you don't get the money, you're dead. What's this Conal guy to you anyway? Even if he hasn't committed all the heinous crimes his missis accuses him of, so what?'

'I hate the idea of murdering someone, that's *what*. Especially

223

someone I've got nothing against. Who could be innocent. I can't stand injustice, Alyssa.'

'Good job you didn't become a lawyer then. But no.' I feel my face get hot. 'I can't stand it either. Unfortunately you don't always have a choice.'

'No. Sorry,' she sighs. We both don't know what to say for the next few seconds.

'So,' I resume, 'it should be someone evil and guilty for whom you feel deep personal hatred?'

Frankie gives a wan smile. 'Preferably.'

'How are you ... have you thought how you'd do it? If you did.'

'I can't overpower a strong man and manually strangle him or bludgeon him to death, even if I wanted to. So I thought shooting or a hit-and-run. Shooting might be best. But I've no idea where to get a gun, and I'm sure I'd need a lesson on how to use it.' She shudders. 'I know it's not as easy as it looks on telly.'

I think of the revolver with its box of bullets, concealed behind those stones in the wall of St James' Cemetery. Is it still there after all these years? It was well wrapped with thick plastic, so it should still be in good condition. And as Danny Paglino taught me how to use it, I can certainly give someone a lesson.

'I know where there's a gun – a revolver. And I can show you how to use it.'

Frankie stares at me, shocked, and I can guess what she's thinking. 'I bought it from an ex-client,' I quickly explain, 'the day Vivienne showed me my birth certificate. I was in a terrible state. I got pissed, hardly knew what I was doing. It was all very stupid. But I calmed down. I didn't seriously believe I'd use it. I couldn't give the gun back though, as I knew it'd have a history. And of course I didn't want the police to find it in my possession. So I hid it.'

She swallows. 'Where?'

'St James' Cemetery. Ever been there?'

'A few times. Years ago. It's a spooky place, but I liked it. I used to try and decipher the names and dates on the old gravestones. I'm not sure I'd go there now though. Certainly not alone at night.'

I get another idea. It frightens me, but I'm prepared to follow through. 'I'll do it,' I say quietly. 'I'll kill Conal Thorn for you.'

'No.' Frankie turns white. 'This is my problem.' She stares at me again. 'Why would you do it anyway?'

'Because you're my sister.' I hesitate. 'You're my sister and I – I love you. Besides, you've got a lot more to lose than I have.' Bitterness sweeps over me, so strong that I can almost taste the wormwood. 'I've spent more than a decade in jail for a murder I didn't commit. If I go back there it's damn well going to be for something I *did* do. I don't care, Frankie, really I don't. My life's ruined.'

She gets up. 'Don't say that.'

'It's the truth.'

'*No.* You've had a terrible time. But you're still young, you can start again.'

'How?'

'Well – for one thing, you've got Tomás to help. Haven't you?'

She sounds doubtful, as if she's not even sure a person named Tomás Slaney exists. Maybe she thinks I dreamed him up as part of some warped self-protection mechanism. My excitement about Tomás suddenly plunges back to despondency.

There was a moment last night when I thought he might kiss me, when I felt we could have been right back where we were before all the shit happened. He sensed that too, I know. But I was too scared to make a move, and so was he. We let the moment pass. Will there be another? How does he feel? It's terrible and I know I shouldn't hope for this, definitely not expect anything, but I want him again. Not just as a friend, but as a lover. Tomás is the man I love. I'll always love him.

'And . . .' Frankie hesitates. 'You've got me.'

That's a big thing for her to say. The biggest. And at a time like this. I glance away, out of the window at the gold autumn sun shining on St Luke's crumbling stonework, then look back at her, biting my lips, trying to contain the rush of emotion. My emotions are so strong they frighten me. I know how fragile I am. They're dangerous, they could overwhelm. Look what's happened so far: I confronted my father because of Frankie; I want Tomás back; Now I'm offering to kill for her. I'm serious, I am prepared to do it. That's what love means, being willing to kill or die for someone.

'I won't have you,' I hear myself croak, 'by this time next week, if you haven't sorted this mess you're in.'

225

Frankie clenches her hands. 'I can't let you do my dirty work. What kind of person would that make me?'

'A live one. With a future. I'll deliver that money for you as well.'

That makes her laugh. 'What, in the Netherlands? You don't have a passport, and you couldn't get one in time. Besides, people on probation aren't allowed to leave the country.'

'Lend me yours. We've got the same eyes, same hair. Who looks like their mugshot anyway? Who looks *at* a passport photo, really *looks*? And that Xhani bastard, what does he care who delivers his money as long as he gets it?'

'He'll probably kill you. Or me, if I–' Frankie stops, grimaces. 'Being a bit previous, aren't I? I haven't even done the dreaded deed and collected the remainder of my contract killer fee.'

'Yeah, when exactly are you supposed to get that? How long after the–'

'I'm supposed to give Monique a call once it's done.' Frankie takes a couple of sips of lukewarm coffee then moves into the kitchen and pours it down the sink. 'She's got the money ready. We meet at a pre-arranged location after the police have given her the tragic news, and thereby proving to her I've done the job.She hands over the fifty grand then rushes back home to play grieving widow.'

'Grieving Black Widow.' I stand aside as Frankie comes out of the kitchen; it's so tiny we can both barely fit in at once. 'How can you be certain she'll hand it over?'

Frankie shrugs. 'We have to trust each other. Not entirely satisfactory, I know. But we're dependent on one another – if either of us screw up, we've both had it.' She goes to the window and looks out at the people, the traffic and the old man selling the *Echo* at the foot of the church steps. 'God. How can everything look so *normal*? Maybe I should go and pitch a tent in the middle of that nave amongst the trees and bushes and tombstones. Agron Xhani couldn't find me there.'

'Or here. As long as you're not followed.'

'I keep checking if I'm being tailed, but I can't see anyone. The road behind me was empty practically all the way into town. I never see anyone outside the house. Of course that doesn't mean they're not there, at least some of the time. And Xhani knows where I live. He knows about Mum. He can pick his moment.' She

226

glances at me over her shoulder. 'I've been thinking.' She hesitates. 'Maybe I could get the rest of the money without killing Conal Thorn.'

Now it's my turn to laugh, although I'm not really amused. On the contrary; maybe the tension and fear is getting to her and she's losing it.

'I'd give you a glass of wine if you weren't driving. You need it.'

'I'm serious.'

'Okay. Frankie, look. Whatever you decide to do, I'll help. We'll do this together. I can't believe I've found you, and there's no way I want to lose you now.'

She turns, as if about to say something. A puzzled expression comes into her eyes.

'You look different. Your hair, those clothes ... like you've had a make over.' She grins. 'Was it the social services, trying to make you more fit to compete in today's cut-throat job market?'

I grin back. 'Well, someone did me a social service. Do you mind if I have a drink?'

'Of course not. Go ahead.'

I pour myself a glass of velvety red wine, take several sips and look down into St Luke's nave. The sun makes the stone look mellow. I'm starting to think it's quite cool to live next to a bombed-out church. 'So how do you reckon you're going to get the other fifty grand from Lady Macbeth without stiffing her allegedly errant spouse?'

'I'm not sure it'll work. It's probably crazy.'

'All the best plans are crazy.' I take another sip of Aussie Shiraz. The quality of wine on offer in Britain has certainly improved a lot since I got put away. 'Go on.'

The ring of the doorbell interrupts us. I slop Shiraz over the rim of my glass.

'Shit. It must be Carl, the nosey, interfering bastard.'

'Your probation officer? What does he want?'

'To check up on me, of course. Invade my privacy. Make sure I'm miserable enough, continuing to be fully cognisant of my position at the bottom of the food chain.' I'm furious, floundering around, in a panic at the thought of him seeing my new hair and clothes, the wine and food in the kitchen; he's quite capable of just barging in there and opening the fridge. He'll suspect the worst and he'll be right. Maybe he's heard about some member of the local chattering classes who's making a big fuss because she lost her wallet and some lowlife went on a jolly with it.

'He sounds a right bastard,' Frankie says. 'Don't answer the door.'

'I have to. I'm supposed to be ill at home.' I drag off my trousers, sweater and boots and pull on my scratchy old bathrobe, shove the soft, thick, new, cream-coloured cotton one beneath the bed. Mess up my hair. 'Could you hide in the bedroom?' I beg a surprised Frankie. 'I don't want him to find out about you; he'll only start asking awkward questions that are none of his damn business.'

'If he asks me any questions I'll tell him to fuck off. He's got no right.'

'Not where you're concerned, no. But it'll be another black mark against me. He'll get suspicious. Please, Frankie.'

'Okay.' She comes in and sits on the rumpled bed, switches off her mobile. 'You're sure he won't walk in here?'

'I don't think so. I hope not. If he does, don't tell him who you are. Can you hide the rest of those clothes for me? Shove them under the quilt. Thanks.'

The bell goes again and I rush out swearing and sweating. I can hear him coming up the stairs; someone's left the street door open again. I long for a place with intercom phones, CCTV, good locks to make you feel safe and private. The flat doorbell rings. I drag a tissue over my face, wiping off lipstick and blusher, shove it in my pocket and open the door, hoping he'll piss off within ten minutes like he did the other day. I smell of Diorella and my breath must smell of wine. Shit.

'Hi, Alyssa. How are you today?'

'Tomás!' I'm stunned. I didn't expect to see him again already. I'm delighted and hugely relieved, although now of course I'm ashamed of my threadbare appearance. He's wearing a cool suit, a black overcoat and he smells of the cold outdoors and of something fresh and citrus-like. He smells of another world.

'Can I come in?'

'Of course. Excuse the state of this place. And my appearance. I–'

'Don't worry. It's fine. You look fine.'

'You always were kind.' I feel too shy to kiss him, so I wish he'd kiss me. But he doesn't. He looks a bit awkward. My shyness increases as I'm reminded of the great gulf between our two worlds: his of money, security, a good career and the confidence that brings; mine of probation officers, income support, sordid flats, depression and fear. When can I claw my way out of my world back into his?

'Can I get you some tea or coffee? A drink?'

'No thanks.' I feel hurt as he glances at his watch. 'Haven't got time, I'm afraid. This is just a quick visit. You don't have a phone, so I couldn't call.' He walks into the living room and stops, doesn't even put his briefcase down. 'I've come to tell you there's a job going, if you're interested, but–'

'Already? Are you joking, of course I'm interested!' I pause. 'What's the 'but'?'

'It's secretarial work, that's all. In a solicitor's practice. Salary's not great, but it's okay. You answer the phone, deal with clients who come to the office, type letters and other stuff. Even make tea and coffee sometimes. Way below your capabilities.'

'That doesn't matter.' But it does. Very much. I should feel grateful and excited, but my heart sinks. I realise I've been hoping – unreasonably, I know – that Tomás could get me something a bit better. Me and my hopes, when will I ever learn? It's still better than a dry cleaning factory though. Welcome to the real world, Alyssa, this is how it's going to be. In case you didn't know. 'When do I start?'

Have to keep a window of a couple of days to help Frankie with her plan, whatever that turns out to be. I will kill Conal Thorn if I have to; I feel quite cold-blooded about that. It's almost a relief to get the chance to be guilty of something. Of course if I get caught it's throw-away-the-key time. And I'll lose Tomás, for ever. Frankie too. I might lose her anyway.

'Start as soon as you like. I suppose you'll have to clear it with your PO first, but that shouldn't be a problem. You can have a chat with Linda this afternoon. Phone or go round to her office.' He hands me a slip of paper. 'Here's her address and phone number. I hope you don't mind, but I had to give her a quick summary of your, er . . . history.'

'Of course I don't mind.' Liar, liar. 'She'd have to know anyway. I'd rather you told her than someone else. So who is this lady brave enough to employ me?'

'Linda Nichols, she's a family law solicitor. The woman I … see sometimes.'

'Oh.' My dismay increases. 'So she's doing this at great personal favour. She must like you a lot.' Maybe Tomás is more friendly with her than he lets on.

He shrugs. 'We're friends, really, more than anything else. Like I said last night.'

I don't want to talk about the damn job any more, don't even want to think of it. And it's stupid, but I already hate this Linda Nichols. I recall Frankie lounging on my wrecked bed with her switched-off mobile. 'Tomás, there's someone I'd like you to meet.'

'Well, sure. But right now I'm a bit pushed for–'

'No, it's okay. She's here.' I turn. 'Frankie? You can come out now.'

'Frankie?' He looks surprised. 'Your–'

'Yes, my sister. I asked her to hide because I thought you were Carl.'

Frankie appears in the doorway, holding her mobile and pushing back her mass of dark hair. Her grey crystal eyes look cool, so cool that you wouldn't guess her anguish, the danger she's in. I feel pride, admiration.

'Frankie, this is Tomás Slaney, my … friend. Tomás, this is Frankie. My sister.'

There's a startled expression in his eyes as he looks at her. He moves forward and stops. Frankie takes his outstretched hand. She doesn't smile or say anything either. She seems as startled as he is.

I get a horrible flash of unease, ice on the nape of my neck. It's an effort for me not to snap at him to let go of her hand. She seems equally transfixed.

If Frankie thought Tomás was a figment of my wild imagination, she knows better now. He's not a dream, but real.

Very real.

Chapter 25

'We specialise in communication solutions – communication design. From browser-based e-business solutions to more traditional media, such as promotional activities. On paper or video. Yes. You're more than welcome. 'Bye.'

Monique crashed the phone down and buzzed for her secretary. Samantha came in smiling, smoothing her shoulder-length brown hair and short blue denim skirt as if rearranging herself after a quick sex session.

'Why was that call put through to me?' Monique snapped. 'It was just someone inquiring about the business. There won't be a business for much longer if I have to spend all day doing the bloody receptionist's job. Or yours.'

Samantha's bright smile faded. 'But this man said he wanted to speak to you specifically–'

'Yeah, a lot of people want to speak to me. Specifically.'

'Sorry, Monique.' Samantha looked dismayed. 'The truth is, it's been a bit unorganised here since–.'

'*Dis*organised. Can't you speak fucking English? Can't I take some time off without everything falling apart?'

'Well, of course. But Conal's been off too, what with his injury, and he was handling most of the big accounts. How's he doing after his accident, by the way?'

Monique tried to calm herself. 'Conal's fine now, thank you.'

'I'm so glad. It was an awful thing to happen; we've all been really worried. It must have been a terrible shock for you as well. When's he coming back to work?'

'I – I'm not sure. Soon. Sam, look, I'm sorry I snapped. I've been a bit on edge since Conal's accident. You're right, it was a

231

big shock.' And things were going to get much worse before they got better. Monique trembled at the thought of what was to come.

'Of course. It's all right, I understand. Here's some mail that's been lying on his desk. I wasn't sure whether to leave it or send it on, but now you're here ...' Samantha paused as Monique closed her eyes and put one hand to her forehead. 'Are you okay? Can I get you some water or a coffee or something?'

Monique took a deep breath. 'Coffee would be good. Thanks.' Camomile tea or something else non-caffeinous would be better, but she couldn't stand herbal muck. She had to stay calm and polite, control this terrible jittery feeling. Having one's husband killed – she didn't want to use the word 'murder' – was not as easy and straightforward as she had imagined. It would be easier when it was over. When she was free. But it was impossible to imagine life without Conal. She felt as if she was already mourning him. There would be a period of mourning for what she – what they – had had together. It was heartbreaking. She could never love or trust another man.

She felt like cancelling the dinner with Conal. How could she sit there eating and talking, trying to pretend things were normal or getting back to normal? Knowing it was the last time she would see him alive? And that bloody garage, the business with her car! What a bunch of wankers. It had upset her terribly. Conal was still guilty of the other things though. Monique would not lose half her money and property to him in a divorce settlement – no way was that going to happen. And Lauren. The thought of him touching her ...

No. This had to be done. She would go through with the dinner. And she should make more effort with Samantha and everyone here, try to appear more her normal self. How would it look if they told the police she had seemed jittery and freaked the day before her husband's untimely death?

'One cup of fresh ground coffee coming up,' Samantha sang. 'Would you like a sandwich as well? It's after three and you didn't have any lunch. You've got the meeting with the building society man soon, then the people who want us to help promote their new scooter. And Stephen wants to talk to you about the website design for that garden centre. You'll be starving.'

'No, I–' Monique paused. Acting normal meant eating. 'You're right. I'd love a baguette with smoked salmon and salad,' she lied.

'No tomatoes, just lettuce and cucumber.' She could always wrap it in the napkin, smuggle it out in her bag and chuck it in a bin. To have to think of such ruses now!

Samantha waltzed out and Monique picked up Conal's mail. The few envelopes seemed to be letters from clients. Conal had shouldered a lot of the workload, work for which she would now have to take responsibility again. Just when she had thought things were getting easier. More work, more heartbreak. Monique sighed, then stiffened. One envelope, baby pink with tacky sprays of roses at each corner, was handwritten and marked 'Personal and Confidential'. She picked up her sharp, polished steel letter opener and sliced blade through paper.

Dear Conal,

Your secretary says you're ill, but she won't tell me anything else except that you'll be back soon. So I hope you're better now. I won't phone or send this to your home address because I know you don't want me to, and don't want the missis to get the wrong idea again. I'm really sorry about what happened that day. I shouldn't have crept back in and flung myself at you. My only excuse is that even though we're mates I always fancied you rotten as well! Anyway, obviously you don't want that, at least not for now. I hope you're not angry any more. I want to ask again, won't you please spare me that fifteen grand? I'm desperate. My ex-boyfriend cheated me, took my money, that's why I had to come back to the UK. You've certainly fallen on your feet, fifteen or even twenty grand must be a piss in the ocean to you. I'll pay you back, but that'll take time. I just need help to get myself together. Please, Conal, for old time's sake. Call me soon.

Love ya for ever!

Linds-y. XXXXXXXXXXXXXXXXXXXXXXXXX

Monique read the letter a second time, her heart pounding. Lindsay Roberts ran a bar in Spain, and came back to the UK when things didn't work out. Looked Conal up through old friends in Liverpool. Threw herself at him. It all checked out.

233

'Oh my God!' she whispered.

Conal had not lied. She had accused him wrongly, shot him because of this fucking, gold-digging bitch. Two things Conal was innocent of now! But there was still Lauren. And holding on to this company and all her money – that was for Lauren too, for her future. She was doing the right thing, and she musn't lose her nerve now.

Monique felt a surge of fury; it would be a lot easier to murder *Linds-y*. No problem with that at all. She dialled the phone number scrawled at the top of the letter. Lindsay's address was a street in Kirkdale, an area not noted for its prime real estate, if you wanted to describe it in such snotty terms. Which Monique did.

'Hello, yeah?'

'Could I speak to Lindsay Roberts, please?' This nasal snarl did not belong to her.

'Hang on, luv. *Lindsay*!' the man bellowed. 'Phone.'

'Thanks, Dad.' Feet pounded down stairs and a breathless, hopeful voice answered. 'Hi! Who's this?'

'Monique Thorn. Or Conal's *Missis*, as you prefer to obliteratingly label me.'

Of course Lindsay was home in the middle of the afternoon. What else did she have to do but chill out, refurbish herself in between forays where she attempted to lay her sticky paws on other people's hard-earned money?

There was a brief silence, during which Lindsay was perhaps trying to figure out what 'obliteratingly' meant. 'What do you want?' she demanded, her voice sullen. 'How do you know my name – my phone number?'

'Conal told me about you. He showed me your letter.'

'He . . . *what*?'

'He doesn't think of you as his mate – in any sense of the word. I believe you need fifteen to twenty thousand pounds.'

Another silence. 'Yeah, I do. To get back on my feet. So?'

'And that's a piss in the ocean to the likes of us, right?'

Lindsay's voice hardened. '*So*?'

'So I'm going to give away twenty grand. Conal's happily married – he loves me and I love him. He wants nothing to do with you. Not now, not ever. He asked me to give you the message. He thought it might have more effect that way.'

Lindsay gasped. 'You're going to *give* me twenty grand? On

234

condition I don't see Conal again? Well, okay,' she laughed. 'That's cool.'

'Friendship obviously means a lot to you. This is the deal. If you turn up at our home or work place again Conal or I will get the police on you. And yes, I'm going to give twenty grand.' Monique paused. 'To a dog's home.'

'*What*? You–'

'Better stay on your back, darling, because it's going to take you a long time to earn that money. Now get lost and don't bother us again unless you want to end up in jail for stalking.'

Monique crashed the phone down. Putting Lindsay Roberts in her place made her feel better, but not much. She gasped as the phone rang again.

'Lauren for you on line two,' Sam chirped.

'Oh. Right.' Monique didn't feel like speaking to her daughter now, but she couldn't just hang up. 'Lauren?'

'I'm calling to tell you I'll be going home with Karen and spending the night at her house. Just so you know.'

'Such consideration. Thank you. Actually, that's fine, because I'm dining out myself this evening.'

'Who with?'

'*With whom*.' God, Monique thought, what's wrong with me? 'Conal.'

'Oh. You're going to talk about ... everything?'

'I imagine so.'

'Mum, I–'

'Yes?'

Lauren's voice sounded wobbly, little girl instead of over-confident teen. 'I wish things could be different.'

'So do I.' There was a silence. 'Were you serious when you said you'd like to go and live with your father if you – we – could find him?'

Another silence. 'No.'

'Good. Well, have a nice time at Karen's. I'll see you tomorrow.'

Monique hung up, swivelled round in her chair and gazed out over the roofs of Liverpool. She could see the Anglican cathedral in the distance and the Catholic one, Paddy's Wigwam, nearby. Other church spires, including that bombed-out place that was kept as a monument to the 1941 May Blitz. She flexed her hands and studied her smooth, manicured nails, gripped the arms of the comfortable leather chair. She was trembling and she wanted to cry. Wanted to scream, shatter the quiet of the large, cosy office. The smell of brewing coffee drifted in.

Lauren would get her wish, although not in any way she could have anticipated.

Things were going to be very different.

'*Kidnap* Conal Thorn?'

Alyssa stared at Frankie then glanced across Canada Boulevard towards the glittering, sunlit River Mersey beyond the Pier Head. The breeze ruffled her hair and the sun picked out coppery glints. 'I got it wrong when I said the best plans were crazy.' She looked back at Frankie. 'In the immortal words of that tennis player, you cannot be serious!'

'Kidnapping's better than murder. Okay, not much.' They started to walk down Canada Boulevard past the Cunard Building and Liver Buildings in the direction of St Nicholas' Place. 'I haven't got time for this,' Frankie said, angry and desperate with impatience. 'You told me you wanted to help. Was that true or just bullshit?'

She put Tomás Slaney out of her mind because she had to. And because she refused to believe what had happened, refused to even acknowledge her reaction to him. Or his to her. He was the man Alyssa – her sister! – was obviously still crazy about, however much she tried to pretend their relationship could never be the same again and that all she hoped for from Tomás was friendship and some help. Frankie herself might be dead in a few days. The timing, the circumstances, could not be worse. Nothing was ever so impossible.

'It wasn't bullshit,' Alyssa flared, turning pink. 'Of course I'll help. I'm up for it. But I thought there might be some other way ... I don't know! Why do we have to do *that*?'

'I want Monique to think I've done it. For a while, anyway. I have to make it look real. We stage what looks like his killing, then tell Monique it's done. Telling her won't be enough, of course – she'll want proof. So we'll give her what looks like proof – the police calling on her to tell her Conal's dead. Or so they think. He won't be, of course. But by then I'll have got my money

236

and run. Monique can't exactly complain to the police that she's been ripped off, can she?'

'I'd love to see her face when she finds out hubby wasn't stiffed after all. Talk about a surprise. Although I can't really savour the humour of that just now. And we kidnap Conal Thorn to stop him reappearing inconveniently soon?'

'Exactly. Keep him out of the way until it's time for him to come back from the dead.'

'So how are we supposed to do this? I'm sure two girls kidnapping a big, strong guy isn't going to be quite as straightforward as you make it sound.' Alyssa shook her head. 'Christ. I don't even want to think about what'll happen if it goes wrong.'

'So don't. It isn't going to go wrong.' Frankie stopped. 'Are you sure you're up for this?'

She was surprised to find that her fear had gone, for now at least, and had been replaced by desperation. Pure and simple. This horrible act that she loathed the mere thought of was the first in a chain of events that had to bring her to where she wanted to be. Time to think later – if she survived.

'Of course I'm up for it.' Alyssa's grey eyes were calm again. 'Only, it's like I said – you make it sound so terrifyingly easy. What if he fights us off and escapes? I'm also thinking witnesses, general mayhem.' She paused. 'Being caught.'

'I'm not saying it'll be easy.' Frankie's lips tightened. ' I have to do this. And I need to know I can rely on you. I've involved you, told you so much.'

'I won't let you down, Francesca. I promise.'

Frankie searched Alyssa's face, her eyes. 'Good. Tonight, okay?'

'So we wait until dark. In the best tradition of grave robbers, kidnappers and highwaymen. How are we going to do it?'

'Big, strong Conal Thorn can't fight us off or escape if he's unconscious, can he?'

'Oh, I see. One or both of us has to accost him in a bar or club and slip something into his Babycham? Suppose he doesn't drink? Or just wants a quiet night in? And we might not be able to catch him alone.'

'We'll tail him, see where he goes and what he does. There's bound to be some opportunity. If not, I'll make one. The immediate thing is to get hold of some GHB.'

237

Alyssa grimaced. 'That shouldn't be a problem in a modern-day British city. You have to be careful with that stuff,' she warned. 'Don't give him too high a dose, or you might end up murdering him after all.'

Frankie looked scared. 'I'm not that stupid.'

'You're not a medical professional either.'

'It'll be fine. I've read everything about it on some websites.'

'The wild, wicked web.' Alyssa sighed. 'Okay. What do we need to do now?'

'Find our supply of that stuff. And buy some rope. Plus a few other things.'

Alyssa linked her arm through Frankie's. 'Just a cosy afternoon's shopping then.'

Chapter 26

'Gold-digging bitch.' Conal screwed up Lindsay Roberts' letter and tossed it across the table.

'I phoned her.' Monique put the letter back in her bag. 'I couldn't resist. Told her I'd give twenty grand to a dog's home, in her honour.'

'That must have delighted her no end. From what I remember, she's not just a gold-digger, but vindictive with it. Better watch your back for a day or two.' He paused. 'It still doesn't explain why you've changed your mind about the divorce.' Conal took a gulp of deep red Burgundy. 'You were even more incandescent with murderous rage when you accused me of knobbing your precious daughter.'

'That's an extremely crude way to talk.' Monique flushed. He was drinking more than usual, seemed almost as on edge as she was. Conal was certainly angry. He wasn't wearing the sling any more, but his bandaged upper right arm looked bulky beneath the black jacket and blue shirt.

'Well, why don't I say it like it is?' He emptied his glass and signalled to a passing waiter. 'You were so incandescent I thought you would have shot me again if there'd been another gun in the house. And finished the job this time.'

'For God's sake!' Panicked, she glanced around the candlelit restaurant. His words, the smell of food and the tension churning her stomach made her feel sick.

'Oh yeah, sorry. I'm not supposed to mention you winged me in a fit of jealous rage. It's our dirty little secret, isn't it, darling?'

'Conal, *please*.' This dinner had been a really bad idea. The boy waiter approached and looked at Conal apprehensively.

'Yes, sir?'

'If you're going to put that wine bottle on a table where I can't reach it, you can at least keep my glass refilled without me having to attract your attention every time.'

'Yes. Sorry, sir.' He fetched the bottle, refilled Conal's glass and turned to Monique, who shook her head.

'Not for me, thanks.' She felt like drinking herself stupid but she had to drive home, out of the city and then through all those dark, twisting country lanes with ancient oaks as menacing sentinels at every blind corner.

Conal looked so handsome sitting there, so full of life and anger, passion. Impossible to believe his life was about to be snuffed out, and that just a few hours from now he would be dead, cold. She wanted to hate him, longed to, because it would make things so much easier. But she couldn't. Get revenge, exult, move on: If only it could be that simple. Monique was pierced with guilt and shame, heartbreaking pity for him. And herself.

Lauren *was* telling the truth, wasn't she? She couldn't lie about something like this; it was not in her character. She knew her daughter, as much as any parent could know their child. She shivered and took a tiny sip of her wine. She couldn't keep thinking like this or she would go insane.

'I'm very uneasy.' Conal looked at her, his eyes narrowed. 'Uncomfortable about all this. You say Lauren hasn't confessed she lied, so why do you believe me all of a sudden? Or *say* you do. What are you up to?' He laughed, but he wasn't amused. 'And why do I even ask? Like you'd tell me.'

'I'm not up to anything!' Monique twisted her napkin under the table. How insistent he was that he hadn't seduced Lauren. Well, of course he wasn't going to admit he had. 'So much has happened,' she stammered. 'I just think we should all try to stay calm. Slow down. Think, talk.'

'Calm down and think?' He laughed again, louder. 'I love it. That's good, Monique, that's rich coming from you. Have you really got no sense of irony, or is it that you need time to think how you can cheat me out of a fair divorce settlement? The longer you delay, the more time you and your bloodsucking lawyers get to find loopholes for you to wriggle your cute little arse out of.'

'It's not like that, I promise. I told you, I don't *want* a divorce any more.'

'Always about what you want, isn't it?' Conal leaned back, shaking his head. 'So what's supposed to happen now, according to you? Because if you think I'm going to move back to the cosy, rural idyll of Bay bloody House and live under the same roof as your scheming, lying, teen witch daughter again, you've got it dead wrong. Even if she admitted she'd lied – which she hasn't – and apologised, it wouldn't make any difference.'

'But Conal–'

'I'd be crazy to put myself in that situation again after what's happened. Christ knows what she'll dream up next time she gets the raving hump about some perceived injury to that scarily fragile pride. Has she done *Macbeth* in her English Lit class yet? That's if they still do English lit in schools these days. Might be daggers at midnight, or a lethal dose of some Class A drug in my Bombay Sapphire with full sugar tonic.'

Monique felt furious at this attack on Lauren, even though she herself had barely managed to keep her temper with the girl lately. She tried to control herself.

'Look – Lauren's fourteen. I'm her mother – I can't just send her away. Or abandon her. That won't solve anything.'

'Oh, it would solve a lot.' Conal thumped his glass down on the white cloth. 'But no, of course I wouldn't expect you to choose between me and your daughter. Even though I think she's more than capable of fending for herself in the big, wide, wicked world. You wouldn't be afraid for a lion in a deer park, would you?'

'Let's forget Lauren for a moment. Concentrate on us.'

'I loved you,' Conal's eyes glistened with tears. 'You'll never know how much. We had everything, Monique. Didn't we?'

'Oh, *Conal*.'

She decided she could not go through with her plan. She could not just have her husband murdered; she might be crazy and fucked up, but she wasn't evil. She had made more than enough terrible mistakes already; she didn't want to make another. What if she got caught, arrested? She had to call it off right now. Monique got to her feet, gripping her small evening bag.

'Excuse me a minute. I just have to nip to the Ladies.'

He nodded heavily and she walked off, unsteady on the high heels, threading her way between tables, conscious of curious glances from other diners. She made sure the toilets were empty before shutting herself in a cubicle and dialling Frankie Sayle on

241

the special mobile. No answer. Frankie's phone must be switched off.

'*Shit.*' Monique closed her eyes. She wanted to stop this now, she had to, but how could she? She had no idea where Frankie was. And how could she tell Conal that she'd planned to have him killed but had changed her mind, and could he please be careful until she'd called off the hounds? No way! She was finished then.

There was only one thing to do. She had to stay with Conal until she could contact Frankie and call off the killing. Where and when tonight was it supposed to happen? What did Frankie have planned? Monique started to shiver with panic. She put the phone back in her bag, wrenched the cubicle door open and hurried out. She caught a glimpse of her white, strained face in the oval, gilt mirror. The face of a killer? It better not be.

At first she couldn't locate their table. Or Conal. Where was he? Had he gone to the loo as well? Or given up on the waiter and got up to help himself to more wine? She hurried forward, skirting around a waiter with a tray of coffee and cognac. She reached the table and stopped, staring down at the red wine stains and plates of crumbled bread rolls. .

'No.' Her breath came out as a sob. '*No.*'

Conal had left her a note, scrawled in biro on his crumpled white linen napkin.

Sorry. No way back.

Conal slouched out of the cinema halfway through the film he didn't understand and couldn't concentrate on or care less about: Nicole Kidman, not looking herself, wearing a frumpy dress and funny nose. He had wanted somewhere dark and quiet where he could sit and think, but the noisy bastards in the audience were a worse irritant than the film. His injured arm and shoulder were starting to hurt more, and he needed another painkiller.

He should not have drunk all that wine in the restaurant, but seeing Monique again and talking to her, knowing his marriage was in ruins, was more pain than he could handle right now. He still loved her, would go on loving her for a long time. But, as he had scribbled on the restaurant napkin in his fit of agonising self-pity, there was no way back. At least there didn't seem to be. Conal felt he could never trust Monique again, feel safe or comfortable around either her or her brat. A surge of hatred for Lauren rose along with bitter bile and he stopped and swallowed, wiped his sweating forehead. His arm and shoulder throbbed. Sod the painkillers, he needed another drink. Alcohol would do the job just as well and be a lot more fun. There was a pub further up the street.

Conal decided he did not want to think any more, at least not for now. He did want to get off his face. But he had a headache, and his stomach didn't feel too good either. This was hopeless. Might as well go home and lie on the sofa, fall asleep in front of the telly. He paused to take a few breaths of cool night air, and hailed a black cab.

He leaned back and closed his eyes, felt tears start. He thought of Monique – her face, her voice, her green eyes. His little green-eyed monster. The truth was, he wanted her right now. Naked and perfumed, hugging him close, telling him how much she loved and needed him. It wasn't entirely her fault she'd got the wrong idea that day when she had walked in on him and that bitch Lindsay. Lots of people would have. But why couldn't Monique have loved him enough, trusted and believed him when he told her he was innocent? It was as if she had been determined to believe the worst. As if misery, however bad, was a familiar and comforting refuge from the terror involved in allowing herself to love and trust. Okay, she'd had a hellish first marriage. But you had to put that sort of stuff behind you, regain perspective, move on. Conal dreamed of her body, her eyes, the last time they had made love.

He wanted to slide into deep sleep, but the cab driver's nasal voice was cutting into his dream of love and sex, saying hey mate we're there and it's four pound sixty, please. Conal sat up and fumbled for his wallet, pressed a fiver into the man's hand and got out. It felt colder now.

The cab pulled away, leaving him shivering in the quiet street of terraced Georgian buildings, feeling more alone and unhappy than he had ever felt in his life. He smelled the distant sea and glanced up at the sky; a few stars glittered. *To him that overcometh, I will give the bright and morning star*. Who said that? Someone in the Bible? Monique would smile and say, why's it always a 'him'?

No point standing here like the prick at the wedding. Keys, where were his bloody keys? Conal groped in his pockets, found

243

them and turned towards the entrance door of the apartment building. His Jag was parked nearby in its reserved space. He didn't want to go into the apartment and spend a night alone, lie in that great big bed without Monique, see her creams and perfumes in the bathroom, her clothes in the dressing room. He sniffed and wiped his eyes. He had to find a place of his own soon, somewhere without memories. And another job. He couldn't work with Monique any more.

'Conal Thorn? Mr Thorn?'

He turned, blinking. A woman walked out of the darkness towards him, slim and dark haired, wearing trousers and a short leather jacket.

'Who the hell are you?' She had wide cheekbones, a sexy mouth, cool eyes beneath dark, straight brows. 'Have we met?'

'No.'

'Because if you want money ...' Conal started to laugh, but he really wanted to cry again. 'Forget it.'

'I don't want money, Mr Thorn.' She stepped closer. 'Not yours anyway. I'd like to talk to you. It's about your wife.'

'My *wife*?'

'Yes. You see, I'm a private detective. Mrs Thorn hired me to follow you.'

'She ... *what*?' His head reeled with shock and wine. 'Having me *followed*. Why?' The woman was closer now, almost as if she wanted to kiss him. He could smell her perfume, recognised it as one Monique used to use. Diorella. 'Why?' he repeated, mystified, pierced with new hurt.

His question went unanswered. The woman brought up her right hand and he heard a hiss. Suddenly he was reeling backwards, blinded, his eyes stinging, gasping for air. He fell across the bonnet of a car and slid to the pavement, half choked, crying out in agony. What was this, a mugging? She didn't look like a mugger, but what did he know? Hands grasped his arms, helping him to sit upright, sending shafts of lightning pain through his injured shoulder.

Was this help? Someone -- not her -- was telling him the pain would go soon, to try and drink some water because that would make him feel better. Did they think he was drunk? Conal wanted to tell them he wasn't drunk, but the neck of a plastic bottle was being gently pushed between his lips. He took one gulp then another, coughed and retched, gasped for breath.

'A bit more,' a woman's soft voice urged. 'Just a bit more.'

He opened his streaming eyes, but the agony was too great. He caught a glimpse of orange street lighting and the dark blur of figures in front of him, he could not tell how many. The water tasted unpleasantly warm and slightly salty. He felt sick and dizzy.

Monique, he thought. Where are you? Why don't you help me? Why wouldn't you love me enough?

Conal passed out.

'Oh, God. Where is he, where's he *gone*?'

Monique sat panicking in her car, parked near Slater Street and clubland, after her failed attempts to locate Conal or contact Frankie Sayle. Groups of laughing, mostly young, people strolled past. She had been driving around the city for over an hour after checking the apartment. Conal wasn't there, and his Jag was missing from its parking space, unless he had parked it somewhere else. She couldn't see it. Had he driven off in it, despite telling her his arm and shoulder hurt too much to drive? And after drinking that wine?

He was not at the office or in any of the few bars he sometimes visited. His mobile was switched off. She did not dare call any of his or their friends and be obliged to admit there was a problem. Hopefully he was with a friend, because he would be safer then. Monique could not bear to think Conal might already be lying murdered somewhere. There was still time, there had to be. But what could she do now? How could she stop this, without revealing herself as the instigator of an attempted murder plot? She started to cry.

Could Conal have gone to Bay House? That was highly unlikely, after what he'd said about no longer wanting to be under the same roof as Lauren. Lauren was not there tonight, but he wouldn't know that. Monique phoned; there was no answer. Desperate, she drove back across town to the apartment, went in and checked again. Conal was not there and there was no sign that he'd been back. She scribbled a note asking him to please phone her the minute he got in, and left. Outside she stared up and down the street, willing him to walk up to her or get dropped off by a cab. A cab did draw alongside the line of closely parked cars, but only to disgorge a bunch of laughing women.

'Cheer up, love,' one of them shouted at her. 'It might never happen.'

Monique turned away, got back into her car and drove off, barely able to control her shaking hands, her tortuous thoughts. She decided to drive back to Bay House. It was just possible Conal had gone there. He might have wanted to collect some more of his stuff. Or changed his mind and decided to talk after all. She prayed that was the case. Several times along the way she pulled over and tried his mobile, kept trying Frankie Sayle. Nothing. She even broke the no-contact rule and drove to Frankie's house – her mother's house – stopped and rang the doorbell a few times. The place was in darkness, and there was no one home. She got back in her car and drove off again. This was going to be one long night.

Monique again felt a stab of disappointment not to see Conal's Jag parked at its usual careless angle on the gravel by the front door. She went in, dropped her keys and bag on the hall table and paused, breathing hard. She longed for a drink, but she would probably have to drive again tonight.

She glanced around and stiffened as she suddenly realised that the hall light had been on when she came in, and that the sitting room lights were on, also lights upstairs. Why? She had not been home all day. Lauren was staying with her friend, so she hadn't been home either. Could Conal be here after all? He might have put his car away in the garages behind the house.

Monique gasped with delighted relief and started towards the stairs. He was here, he was safe! She would put the alarm on and barricade the house, get through to Frankie bloody Sayle and tell her the job was off. Frankie could whistle for the rest of her money, and Monique didn't give a flying damn if that gangster murdered her. Frankie's story might be all bullshit anyway.

'Conal?' she called, her voice shaking. 'Where are you?'

'He isn't here.' Lauren appeared at the top of the stairs. She wore her lurid turquoise towelling bathrobe with the hood, and her long curly hair hung in damp ringlets around her face.

'What are you doing home?' Monique stared at her in shock, gutted with disappointment. Her heart started to pound with terror again. 'I thought–'

'I wanted to come home; I couldn't stay at Karen's. Oh, Mum, I'm so sorry. I never meant any of this to happen.'

'What are you talking about?' Monique felt totally unable to cope with a burst of teen angst, especially tonight. What had Lauren done now, got herself pregnant? Whatever it was, it would just have to wait until she could resolve the immediate crisis. Where the hell *was* Conal? She had to find him! Let him be alive, she prayed, let him be all right. 'How long have you been home?' she snapped.

'I don't know – about an hour, I think. Why?'

'I rang. Didn't you hear the phone?'

'Well, yes, but I was in the bath. I didn't think it would be you, because I'd told you I'd be at Karen's. Oh, Mum, please don't look at me like that.' Lauren ran down the stairs and flung herself sobbing into Monique's arms. Monique smelled thyme and lavender bath oil, the damp perfume of her daughter's hair. She remembered how Lauren had smelled as a baby. She still missed that baby smell.

'I never meant it to go this far,' Lauren sobbed against her shoulder. 'But I felt so hurt, so rejected. He really hurt me.'

'Who did?' Monique made a monumental effort to be patient with her daughter. She had to phone the apartment again, then drive back to the city. She would wait there for Conal, keep phoning him, sit up all night if necessary. She felt she would never sleep again. 'Who hurt you?' she repeated.

'That boy. I did have sex,' Lauren sobbed. 'But it wasn't with Conal. He wouldn't touch me, even though I wanted him to. He told me not to be so stupid, said how hurt you'd be if you knew. He said he wouldn't tell you as long as I promised not to try it again, and I said I wouldn't. But I felt so angry, so hurt that Conal didn't want me. Oh, it's all horrible. I've ruined everything.' She raised her reddened, tear-drenched face, her green eyes frantic. 'Mum, I'm so sorry! I lied about Conal.'

'What?' Monique pushed her away and stepped back. She felt herself blanch.

'I lied about Conal.' Lauren was all tears, flying hair, panicked eyes. 'He never touched me – except to push me away! I can explain. I only did it because …' Her voice tailed off when she saw her mother's expression. She cringed. 'Mum, no! Don't!'

Monique raised a hand and slapped her across the face. She was

247

drowning, suffocating, frozen with horror. Lauren staggered backwards and collapsed whimpering against the banister.

'You don't know,' Monique screamed. 'You don't know what I *did* for you!'

She couldn't think what the sound was at first. Some electronic tune, impinging on her consciousness. Chopin's *Death March*. She rushed to her bag and scrabbled furiously in it, pulled out the special, pretty, pink-purple mobile. The murder mobile. Only one person who could be calling her on that secret number. Lauren dashed back upstairs, sobbing wildly. Monique raced into the sitting room and slammed the door.

'I want to call it off!' she gasped into the phone. 'I've changed my mind.'

There was a silence. 'Too bloody late for that,' Frankie Sayle said, her voice icy.

'No!' Monique screamed. Tears poured down her face. 'Oh God, *no*!'

Chapter 27

'Couldn't get close enough to toast a marshmallow,' Alyssa murmured, the flames from Conal Thorn's blazing Jaguar reflected in her eyes. She jumped back as the petrol tank exploded, totally destroying the burning car. The fire lit up the deserted stretch of dockland.

'What the hell do you mean, you didn't want me to do it?' Frankie shouted into her mobile, shocked and enraged. Of course she knew what Monique meant. She just couldn't believe it. Especially not after having gone to all this trouble and risk.

'No, no, no, I didn't want you to kill him! Oh God, Conal, oh God, what have I *done*?'

'Get a grip on yourself, you moron!' Monique couldn't lose it now, or Frankie was finished. She had only one thought in her head – to get the other fifty grand.

'I want my money,' she shouted. 'Monique, are you listening?'

No answer, only hysterical crying. 'Jesus Christ.' Frankie raked one hand through her hair. Her hands, clothes and hair reeked of petrol, and she was pouring sweat. 'You're not helping yourself, carrying on like this. Get yourself together. I want the rest of the money. Forget about later. I want it *now*, Monique.'

But how was she going to get it? Frankie tried not to catch Monique's panic. 'Have you got the money?' she asked. 'Get it and go to our meeting place. I'll see you there in half an hour.'

'No! I never want to see you again. Go away, *go away*! When the police come I'm going to tell them what I did. What *you* did, you murderous bitch. I don't care what happens to me. I've done a terrible thing. I deserve to be punished!'

Frankie hung up on the incoherent wails, trying to control her rising panic. She hunted on the rubbish-strewn ground, grabbed a large chunk of cement and used it to crush the mobile. She gathered the pieces, ran to the edge of the quay and threw them in the river. Acrid, oily smoke stung her eyes and irritated the back of her throat, and she could feel the heat from the burning Jaguar. She ran back to her own car, calling to Alyssa, who stood gazing into the flames as if using them as a focus for meditation.

'We have to get out of here,' she shouted.

Alyssa turned and came running up. 'Did you tell Lady Macbeth the police will be paying her a visit soon? When are you going to collect the rest of the money?'

'Good question. The stupid bitch has lost it big time. The minute she picked up the phone she started screeching about how she didn't want this and what had she done. She changed her mind.'

'Bloody hell.' Alyssa stared at her in shocked dismay, her face glowing in the light from the flames. 'But she can't!'

'She just did. She says she's going to confess all to the police.'

'*What*?'

'I don't know if she's throwing a temporary wobbly, or if she really means it.'

'Lady M can't lose it now, or you're fucked. We all are ... You have to get the rest of that money.'

'Tell me something I don't know.' Frankie opened the glove box, took out the plastic bottle of water that contained the dose of GHB, unscrewed it and emptied the contents over the stone flags. She ran forward, tossed the empty bottle into the flames and ran back, wiping her hands on her trousers. 'Monique can't ruin everything now. I won't bloody let her.'

'So what do we do ?' Alyssa opened the back door of the car. 'And what about our handsome hero?'

'I checked him a few minutes ago. I think he's okay.' Frankie stooped, ducked inside and leaned over the unconscious Conal Thorn, who was sprawled on the back seat, his head lolling to one side. Conal's mouth was open and he was drooling slightly. 'I kept checking his pulse and heartbeat and they're fine. His breathing's all right too. And I bathed his eyes, or tried to. He'll just have a headache and sore eyes when he wakes up in a few hours.'

'He could have had a lot worse than that if you'd decided to do what his missis wanted. Or thought she wanted.' Alyssa looked at her, shaking her head. 'I don't believe that stupid bitch. What the hell do we do now?' she repeated.

'Hurry up and get in.'

'Where are we going?'

'To pay Monique bloody Thorn a late-night visit.'

Frankie drove out of the abandoned dock past two low stone towers from which the wooden gates were long gone. Near the right-hand tower was a tiny, dilapidated wooden hut, once occupied by a police constable whose duty had been to check exiting dock workers for illegal contraband filched from unloaded ships and bonded warehouses. She drove down the dark, narrow road and turned on to a bigger, lighted, dual carriageway.

'What are we going to do with him?' Alyssa looked back.

Frankie glanced at Conal in the driving mirror. He looked pale, washed out, and she felt frightened again. *Would* he be all right? She had smelled alcohol on his breath before she sprayed pepper spray in his face then got him to take some gulps of the GHB-laced water. He was young though, and seemed healthy. She hated to do this to someone. But as Alyssa said, Conal could have suffered a much worse fate. 'We'll find somewhere safe to leave him.'

'Like where?'

'I'm trying to think.'

'I take it you're not going to make that anonymous call to the police about the Jag now, and tell them you think Conal Thorn's dead?'

'No point.' Frankie slowed the car; she didn't want to get done for speeding. 'Monique already thinks the worst. The longer they take to find it now, the better. I don't want them paying Monique a visit until I've seen her. My God, what am I going to *do* if she won't listen to me? Me and my sodding plans.' She blinked back tears. 'Everything's falling apart!' She turned on to the Dock Road and headed back to town, past St Nick's church and the old White Star Line building on the corner of James Street. The name James triggered a memory, and she glanced at Alyssa.

'You said you knew where to get hold of a gun.'

'Yes.' Alyssa looked startled. 'So?'

'I think we'd better make a little detour and see if that weapon's still where you hid it all those years ago.'

'St James' Cemetery? Well, okay. Park somewhere discreet and look after our sleeping friend in the back while I get it.'

'Be careful. You don't know who might be hanging around there at this time night.'

'Don't worry, I'll be fine. You really think we need the gun then?'

Frankie nodded. 'Just to focus Monique's mind. Make her see sense.'

She could not let herself think about what she was doing.

Not yet.

Conal was dead.

She had murdered him. And he was innocent. He hadn't cheated on her, hadn't tried to have her killed. He had not seduced Lauren. She had built up a twisted, stunted tree of lies in her mind because she had no trust, no faith, and because she was nothing but a wobbling mass of freaked insecurity. How could she bear this? How could she go on living now? Monique could not think straight, could not pull herself together. All she could do was panic. She felt like she was going mad. She lay curled on the sitting room sofa, crying hysterically.

'Mum.' Lauren was standing over her crying too. 'Calm down, please, you're scaring me. What's happened?'

'My life's ruined, that's what's bloody happened,' Monique sobbed. 'I've lost the only man I ever loved.' She turned over and sat up, tears streaming down her ravaged face. 'Go away,' she shouted, 'go to bed, get out of my sight. I don't want to look at you or talk to you.'

Lauren ran out and she thought the girl had obeyed her for once. But she was back within a minute holding a big, crystal glass full of what looked like Coca-cola.

'What's that?'

'Southern Comfort and coke, your favourite.' Lauren held out the glass, her tearful eyes pleading. 'Drink it, Mum, it'll help you feel better.'

Nothing would ever make Monique feel better again, she was certain of that. But she took the glass and drank; it was about 90 per cent Southern Comfort and 10 per cent cola. She gasped and coughed, drank more. The drink went straight to her head and

252

stomach, making her warm and dizzy. She shoved the glass back at Lauren.

'Another.'

Lauren looked alarmed. 'Are you sure?'

'Just get it.'

How had Frankie Sayle killed Conal? Or had him killed? How was she going to explain things to the police? And there was Conal's shooting, that so-called accident. They had been suspicious of her then, and they might be more so now. She was supposed to get the rest of the money, take it up the road to the ruined priory and leave it under the pile of stones for Frankie to find. She should do it now, before the police contacted her as Frankie said they would. But Monique could not bring herself to do anything except drink and cry. When the police came she would give herself up, confess everything. She didn't care about going to prison, didn't care about anything any more, not even Lauren. She deserved to be punished. Although no punishment could make up for what she'd done.

Anguished, pierced with unbearable grief, she thought of Conal sitting opposite her in the restaurant just hours ago. The look on his face, the tears in his eyes.

'*I loved you, Monique. You'll never know how much.*'

He was telling the truth. He had been telling the truth all along. He had loved her, had never done anything to hurt her. She had destroyed that love. Destroyed him. She couldn't believe she had done this, that he was really dead. Monique gulped the drink, wishing she had a bottle of sleeping pills to swallow along with it.

'There was this boy at school.' Lauren stood there twisting the belt of her bathrobe. 'Everyone fancied him, including me. To cut a long story short, we – we had sex. Here, one afternoon when you and Conal were at the office. But–' She stopped, her eyes flooding with tears. 'It was horrible, it hurt and – it was just awful. And he was awful. He told everybody. Told them I was crap, rubbish, rancid, a stupid virgin. You're either a virgin or a slapper! All his mates were laughing at me. Everyone was, except Karen. I wrote that stuff in my diary because I wanted to try and imagine how my first time could have been, *should* have been, with someone who cared about me. I'd had a crush on Conal, and it sort of grew until I felt like I was crazy about him. I really wanted him. I felt guilty about you, but I couldn't help myself. One day when you were

253

out, I – I told him how I felt. I tried to kiss him, I wanted him so much. He got hold of my wrists and held me away from him. Then he pushed me away.' Lauren started to cry again. 'He was angry, Mum. Scared. He told me never to try that again, because he loved you and didn't want you to get hurt. That it was just a teenage crush and one day I'd find someone my own age who I really liked. He told me he wouldn't say anything to you as long as I promised not to do it again. I promised, but it made me angry. I thought, what about me, what about *my* hurt? What's wrong with me? How dare they reject me? I felt like I was nothing, a nobody. I wanted to hurt someone too. But I never meant for things to get this bad. I didn't think, didn't realise what I was doing. I couldn't bring myself to admit I'd lied. But then I thought, I have to. I can't let this go on. I tried to tell you yesterday, but we had that argument.' She paused to wipe her eyes. 'I suppose I was taking everything out on Conal. I wanted him to know how it felt to be hurt. I wanted to teach him a lesson for rejecting me.'

'Oh, you've taught him a lesson.' More tears rolled down Monique's face and dripped into her drink. Her body shook with sobs. 'You've done that, no worries.'

Lauren stared at her, stricken. 'This is all my fault. Mum, you'll get Conal back, won't you? You won't get a divorce. I'll tell him I'm sorry; I'll do anything to make it up to you both. I'll go away somewhere so that you and he can be alone together. I can understand he won't want me living here any more.'

If Lauren blamed herself now, how would she feel when she found out Conal was dead? Monique got up, trying desperately to control herself. What use was shouting, rage, recriminations, now? The fault lay with her, with her hideously flawed nature. She was too gutless to kill herself, but she was determined to confess all and spend the rest of her sick life in prison. She could never atone for what she had done. She could not live with this. It would be terrible for Lauren, but she was better off without such a mother. She would see that eventually. She would grow up, make a life of her own.

'We'll talk in the morning,' she managed to whisper. 'Go to bed now.'

'No, I want to stay with you.'

'Please, Lauren. Please go to bed and don't come down again tonight. I really need to be alone.'

'But you're terribly upset, you–'

'I'll be all right. Like I said, I just *really* need to be alone. If you want to help, you'll do what I say now. Promise me you'll go to bed and get some sleep.'

'Okay. If you're sure.'

'I am. Just go.'

'Mum?' Lauren backed away, her eyes locked on Monique. 'Everything's going to be okay, isn't it? It's not too late. You haven't really lost Conal; you can get him back, can't you? You do still love him?'

'Yes.' Monique stifled an enormous sob, forced back a wail of pure anguish. 'I still love him.'

'Do you ... do you still love me?'

The sob came out as a groan. '*Yes*.'

All she had left now was her bloody money. The money, the property, the company she had been so desperate to protect. Monique dragged herself up from the sofa, followed Lauren into the hall and watched as she trailed up the stairs, the long, hooded bathrobe dragging behind her like some mediaeval lady's gown. A minute later Lauren's bedroom door closed. Monique went into the kitchen and sat sobbing at the table, paralysed with grief and remorse. The house was silent, spookily silent except for her crying and the creak and crack of ancient beams. She could not believe Conal was dead, that he would never walk in here again. She knew she should get herself together, but all she could do was get herself another drink.

She was pouring it, tears still streaming down her face, when she thought she heard footsteps outside. She gasped and stiffened, holding the Southern Comfort bottle poised over her glass. Was this the police coming to inform her of Conal's death? Conal's *murder*. She hadn't heard a car or siren. But there was no need for them to use a siren. A jail term, even a life sentence, seemed like nothing compared to the real life sentence which was going on inside her head right now, and would go on torturing her until the moment of her death. Maybe even afterwards. Monique's long-lapsed Catholicism surfaced – murder was a mortal sin and could never be forgiven. She was stained for eternity. She would lose her soul.

She dumped the bottle on the counter, hurried out of the kitchen and across the hall, desperate to reach the front door before they rang the bell; she didn't want Lauren coming down again. Let her sleep while she could.

Monique felt desperately sorry for Lauren. The girl had been stupid, selfish, cruel, but she had had troubles of her own and none of this was really her fault, even though she had lied about Conal. She had been – she would be – punished enough. Lauren did not deserve a mother like her. Monique flung open the heavy front door, ready to confess. She realised she was holding out her hands to be cuffed.

No grim-faced police officers stood there, and there was no car with flashing lights. Only Frankie Sayle, pale faced, her crystal eyes that had broken a thousand hearts now glittering with rage and fear. There was a moment of shocked silence. Then Frankie spoke.

'I want the rest of my money. Where is it, you bitch?'

Chapter 28

'I thought your old friend Alyssa was desperate for a job.'

She did not want to say *ex-fianceé*. Linda Nichols poured herself another glass of golden, perfumed Gewurztraminer seeing as she was home for the night, and looked across her dining table at Tomás, who was hunched over his barely touched plate of Chicken Catalan. He looked tired, stressed; she didn't think he'd stay. 'I waited all afternoon for her to call me or turn up at the office for a chat, but she obviously had better things to do. Well, so did I.'

Linda didn't like her sharp tone, but the evening wasn't going well and she was irritated by Tomás' preoccupied air. She already regretted her stupidly impulsive, generous offer to give this ex-con Alyssa Ward a job. It had been worth it at the time just to bask in the fantastic smile of delight and gratitude that had lit up Tomás' handsome face and made her think maybe, just maybe she meant something to him after all. Now Linda was starting to wonder what she could have let herself in for.

'I'm sorry,' Tomás sighed. 'I know you're busy. And yes, she is desperate for a job – I can't understand why she didn't contact you either.' He leaned back and looked at her. 'You're having second thoughts?'

'Well – a bit.' A *lot*. Linda hated the way her fair skin blushed so easily. Of course drinking two big glasses of wine didn't help. She got up, smoothing the tight black dress which had seemed so sexy before, but which now made her feel like a fool, not to mention physically uncomfortable because she had to keep remembering to pull in her stomach when she got up and moved around. Rushing to the supermarket and spending too much money, cooking exotic meals, getting tarted up. That was okay, but in this instance it just didn't feel right. Not any more. It all felt like one huge waste of time and energy.

'It seems bizarre,' she said, clutching her glass. Linda glanced at herself in the big mirror over the mantelpiece; her hair had gone flat now, ash-blonde strands limp around her face. 'Having a convicted murderer answer the phone and type stuff, show clients in, make appointments. It's just … I can't really explain … it gives me a creepy feeling. I know you say she's innocent,' Linda added hastily, 'and I believe that.' Did she? Weren't they all bloody innocent. 'But like I said, it just seems bizarre.' She took another swig of wine and faced him. 'Are you sure she hasn't still got feelings for you? She is your ex-fiancée after all. Does she have dark hair?' Linda suddenly wanted to know.

'Well, yes.' Tomás raised his eyebrows. 'Dark chestnut brown, like bitter chocolate.' That was the colour of Frankie's hair too. Long, thick, silky, smelling faintly of perfume. He had to try and get Frankie Sayle out of his head, get over his stunned reaction to her. Nothing could ever happen between them; it was impossible. He dragged himself back to the present … 'What's the colour of Alyssa's hair got to do with anything?'

'I know I'm being stupid.' Linda shrugged. 'I know we're not exactly – well, having the love affair of the millenium.' There, she had said it. 'But suppose she hates me? It could be like light and dark, good and evil, Odette-Odile.'

'Wow. Second thoughts with knobs on.' Tomás got up, came over and kissed her lightly on the mouth. 'I always said your imagination was going to waste and you should take up writing fiction in your spare time.'

'Spare time. I remember that.'

'Look, it was very kind of you to offer Alyssa a job, and I appreciate it. But you're right, it is a bad idea. Forget it, okay? I'll explain to Alyssa. She won't mind.'

He had a feeling she really wouldn't. Alyssa had loved being a barrister – it must be bitterly frustrating to her not to be able to take up her old career again. Tomás could not imagine her working as a receptionist or secretary. He could not imagine what she would do, how she would adjust to her new life. She was like a lost soul.

Linda frowned. 'To be honest, Tomás, I'm having second

thoughts about everything.'

He stroked her cheek. 'You mean us?'

'It's no good, is it? It's not happening. Whatever's supposed to be there – it isn't.'

'You know I like you a lot, don't you?' His voice was gentle. 'That I've got a lot of respect for you?'

'Yes. And that's very nice. But it's not enough.'

'I know. You deserve better. Much more than I can give you.' Tomás took her hand, ashamed of the relief he felt. 'If I can ask the ultimate cheesey question, can we still be friends?'

Linda suddenly found it difficult to speak. 'Of course.' She paused, waited for him to let go of her hand. 'It's been a long day,' she whispered. 'I'm very tired.'

'Let me help you clear up. You've gone to all this effort and expense, cooking a dinner I didn't eat.'

'No, really. I'm just going to dump everything in the dishwasher and go to bed.'

'Are you sure? Well, okay.' He kissed her again. 'I'll push off.'

Linda knew this was right, for both of them. She was being sensible, saying what needed to be said. She nevertheless felt hurt at the relief in his eyes that he could not quite conceal, the quick, almost light-hearted way in which he kissed her one last time and turned to throw his coat over his shoulders.

'See you,' he said. 'Be in touch.'

'Yes. Goodnight, Tomás.'

When the door closed behind him Linda started to cry.

'Get out of here!' Monique spat. 'Or I'll be going down for double murder.'

'Neither of us are going down for anything, Monique. Just give me my money and I'll go. I haven't got time for this.'

'I've got all the time in the world.' Tears streamed down Monique's face. 'The rest of my life without the man I love!'

'Why did you change your mind?' Frankie stared at her. 'I don't get it.'

'Leave me alone, you murdering bitch.' Monique brushed a hand across her eyes. 'What do I care what you don't get? All you're going to get is what's coming to you.'

'You'd better care. We had a deal.' Frankie did not glance at Alyssa, standing silently nearby in the dark shrubbery.

'I tried to call you.' Monique sniffed and wiped her eyes with the back of one hand. 'Tried to call it off, tried to tell you I didn't want you to do it. Why didn't you keep that bloody phone switched on? Where the hell were you, what were you doing?'

'What do you fucking think I was doing? Earning my money. Now I've earned it and I want the rest.' Was there someone else in the house, Frankie wondered? She remembered Monique had a daughter, but not her name. The girl had to be into her teens now.

'It's all a terrible mistake. I didn't want you to do it.' More tears streamed down Monique's face. She looked like she had been crying for a long time. 'Oh, Conal, Conal ...!' She covered her ravaged face with both hands.

Incredible that Monique had changed her mind and was in this state after being so cool and determined about the whole thing. She really had lost it big time, Frankie realised with dismay.

'Why the fuck did you change your mind?' she asked again.

'He didn't cheat,' Monique sobbed. 'He didn't do any of those things. It was me all the time. Getting the wrong end of the stick, being a stupid, jealous, fuck-up. I didn't love him, didn't trust him enough. I've ruined everything and now it's too late.' She took her hands away from her face. 'I can't believe you did this.'

Frankie was starting to feel hysterical herself. 'You're blaming *me* now? Look, it's a bit bloody late to say you made a mistake and wanted to cancel. Will that form part of your defence?' Her anger increased. 'Will you amuse or piss off the judge with that little gemmie before he sends you down for life? And it *will* be life. You won't be able to plead provocation and get the charge reduced to manslaughter, like all those men who murder their wives and girlfriends.'

'I don't care if I go to jail for life. I'll take you with me. You're not getting any more money,' Monique hissed. 'I hate you; I'd like to kill you myself! Just get out of here and leave me alone.'

'I'll be delighted to do that once you've paid me.'

'Fuck off. I told you, I won't–' Monique broke off, gasping with shock as Alyssa stepped forward, the ugly revolver in her hands. She pointed the gun at Monique's heart. 'Who the hell are *you*?'

'Get the money, Monique.' Frankie stepped forward. 'Before

she blows your face off. Before your beautiful daughter's bright future gets cut tragically short.'

'My–' Monique's tear-washed, reddened face turned ashen. 'She's not here.'

'No?' Frankie stepped closer and shoved her in the chest, making her stumble backwards. Alyssa followed, keeping the gun levelled. 'We'll find out, shall we? Take a look round.' She shoved Monique again, noted with relief the first flicker of returning sanity in her terrified eyes. 'Go on, give us the grand tour. I'm sure you're used to doing that for admiring visitors. I'm surprised *Lancashire Life* hasn't done a colour spread on the successful local business lady posing around her prime piece of real estate.'

'No!' Monique gasped, trembling. 'My daughter's upstairs asleep; I don't want her disturbed. She's been through enough – she'll be devastated once she finds out about Conal. Don't touch Lauren, please! Please don't hurt her.'

'Lauren?' Frankie smiled. 'Oh yeah, that's her name, isn't it? After that drippy seventies film star you used to like.' She glanced around the hall with its ornate furniture and grandfather clock. 'Posh house. Not minimalist enough for my taste though.' She was startled as Alyssa rushed forward, grabbed Monique by the hair and pressed the gun barrel to her smooth throat. 'Where's the money?'

'I'll get it, I'll get it,' Monique groaned. 'It's in my bedroom. But please, you have to be quiet! I don't want Lauren to hear you.'

Frankie did not like the remote, unfathomable look in Alyssa's eyes. 'We don't want Lauren to hear us either.' She prayed that would not happen, because she did not have a clue what she would do.

They went quickly up the stairs and along a passageway. Monique opened the door of her bedroom and they crept in, Alyssa holding the gun to her head. Monique moved aside an armchair in one corner and lifted the carpet to reveal a floor safe. She was trembling, breathing heavily. Frankie and Alyssa stood over her as she crouched and opened it. The safe was stuffed with money.

'It's all in there,' Monique gasped. 'I already counted it.' She glanced around. 'I need a carrier bag.'

Frankie found one in a drawer and shoved it at her. Monique

began to cram it with money. A minute later she held up the black-and-gold bag. 'Fifty grand.'

Frankie snatched the bag. 'We don't have time to count it.'

'It's all there,' Monique repeated. 'Maybe more. I swear.'

'If it isn't . . .' Alyssa grabbed Monique's hair again, forcing her head back and making her gasp in pain. 'We'll be back. For your daughter as well as you. You won't escape.'

'Used notes,' Monique went on. 'I've had them for ages. I always keep lots of cash.'

'Very wise.' Frankie looked inside the bag, unable to believe she had actually got her hands on a hundred thousand pounds. It was even more unbelievable to think she now had to hand it over to Agron Xhani. She wondered again if Joe was still safe. 'Oh, and your special little mobile,' she said. 'Where's that?'

'In my bag.' Monique took it out and gave it to her. Frankie shoved it into her jacket pocket to get rid of later.

'Mum?' a sleepy voice called from the floor above. They froze. Monique's eyes were wide, terrified, pleading as she stared at them. Frankie motioned to her and she moved to the door, Alyssa close behind.

'Mum, are you okay?'

'Yes.' Monique stood on the landing, looking up. Frankie could not see the daughter. 'Lauren, I asked you to please stay in your room and go to sleep.'

'I was asleep. Then I woke up.'

'Go back to bed. We'll talk in the morning.'

A big sigh. 'Okay.' A second later a door closed. Monique turned back to them. She looked as if she was going to faint.

'You've got your money,' she whispered to Frankie. 'Now get out. *Please.*'

'I hope you care now.' Frankie pointed to the ceiling. 'I hope you've come to your senses. If you tell the police what happened it's not just you and me who'll suffer the consequences.'

'I know.' Monique nodded, biting her lip. 'I realise that now. Don't worry,' she whispered. 'I panicked, but I've got myself together. I won't tell them anything, I swear. I won't be that crazy.'

They went back down the stairs and across the hall. Frankie cringed as the clock made a whirring sound, struck and began to chime the midnight hour. The chimes were probably not as loud as they seemed. They went outside. It was densely dark and still, a few stars pricking the blackness, the distant horizon orange-grey. There was a smell of grass and decaying vegetation. Frankie turned to look at Monique. They had blown into each other's lives one last time, in this extraordinary, incredible way. She would never see Monique Thorn again and she was glad. This was over now; she had to try and put tonight behind her. The worst danger lay ahead.

Time seemed suddenly suspended. The bloody clock was still chiming and Monique stood there in her black, sleeveless dress, her feet bare. The overhead light shone on her silky blonde hair, in disarray around her ruined face. Frankie recalled how she had once been jealous of Monique's green eyes until some man she had had a passionate fling with told her how beautiful her own were and how much he loved them.

She cringed and cried out in shock as an explosion shattered the peace of the cold autumn night and set rooks in nearby trees cawing wildly. Monique was crumpling, collapsing, one arm flung up, her legs buckling. The hand she had clamped to her chest came away drenched with blood. She fell against the door post and lay still, her head lolling to one side. Strands of blonde hair fell across her face, hiding her eyes.

Frankie stared at Alyssa who stood gripping the gun, her hands shaking. She could smell cordite, like fireworks, and imagined she could smell Monique's blood, now flowing out of her awful chest wound over the scrubbed, worn doorstep.

'What have you *done*?' she whispered, overwhelmed with horror. 'Are you crazy? For fuck's sake, why did you *do* that? There was no need, no … she gave us the—' Tears filled her eyes and she started to tremble.

'She was a threat to you – to us.' Alyssa's eyes were frightened, exultant almost, but her voice was cool. 'Now she isn't.'

'You shouldn't have done it.' Frankie glanced at Monique's inert body. 'Oh, my God. Quick, we have to call an ambulance.'

Alyssa grabbed her wrist. 'Joking, aren't you?'

' I don't plan to hang around until it gets here.'

'Look at her!' Alyssa flung out one arm. 'Look at all that blood. It's too late, she doesn't need a fucking ambulance. Come on, you've got the money. Let's *go*.'

'No. I can't just leave her!' Frankie was shivering and crying. A scream came from inside the house.

'Mum? *Mum?* Where are you – what's happened?'

'Oh, God.' Alyssa was pulling her by the arm now, dragging her. 'Come *on*. Frankie, please. Listen, there's a car in the lane. Someone's coming!'

Terror made Frankie run. They raced down the drive, keeping to the shelter of the trees and shrubbery, crouching in rhododendron bushes near the gates as a Land Rover turned into the drive and swept past. They ran out and down the lane to the tree-lined track where Frankie had parked the car. She did not know how she got the engine started, reversed and drove away past the ruined priory, ghostly in the moonlight. Alyssa's white face looked equally not of this world. She put the gun in the glove box and fastened her seatbelt.

'Wonder who that was? A concerned neighbour, perhaps.'

Frankie's face streamed with tears as she drove. 'Why did you *do* that?' she cried. 'For God's sake, why? There was no *need*.'

'She was a threat,' Alyssa repeated. 'Unstable, unreliable. You saw the state she was in. She said she'd got herself together, but she hadn't.'

'She had. She did come to her senses! She wouldn't have told the police anything.'

'Monique Thorn had to die, Frankie. Don't you see that?'

'No! You shouldn't have killed her. You've done a terrible thing.'

Alyssa laughed. 'Deserve to go to jail now, don't I? I've done the crime for the time. Most people do it the other way round.' That made her laugh harder.

Frankie drove down the dark, winding lane, trembling with shock and revulsion. She did not care any more that Alyssa Ward was her sister.

She never wanted to see Alyssa again.

Chapter 29

Done the crime for the time.

I couldn't stop laughing at that, even though it was obvious Frankie was definitely not amused. I knew it was a shock reaction, of course, and that I'd feel terrible later when it sank in. I hadn't meant to shoot Monique Thorn. I just wanted to threaten her with the gun and thereby help Frankie force her to hand over the money and then run. But when I saw the flaky state Lady M was in I got very scared. Even more scared – and furious – when I thought of how my and Frankie's fragile freedom had to depend on a nut job like that keeping her gob zipped. Monique Thorn reminded me in some chilling way of Vivienne my Wicked Stepmother. The rich, blonde bitch in her big house, nothing to do except think about who or what she wants next, believing her money gives her the power of life and death over people. Jealous, paranoid, totally selfish.

All that rage and pain I'd felt about Vivienne, the terrible fear, came rushing back so that I almost panicked and put the bullets in Lady M while I was following her up to her bedroom. I tried to control myself, God knows. I didn't want to do it. Unlike Vivienne's mystery murderer, I don't take pleasure in torture or killing. I hate to even read or hear about it.

I could understand Frankie being shocked and upset. But not *this* upset. For Christ's sake, I did it for her! Can't she see that? Maybe she will when she calms down. She drove me back to my flat last night, or at least around the corner, dropped me off, wouldn't come in. I tried to talk to her during that dark, fast, tension-filled drive, but she wouldn't listen. I'm worried about her because I don't know what she'll do now. She shouldn't be alone, she needs me. I even tried to persuade her to forget about giving the hundred grand to that gangster in the Netherlands, to keep it all so we could go off together, just the two of us, somewhere the bastard would never find us. I'd even give up Tomás for her sake.

Frankie got furious then. Go on the run – was I crazy? Who did I think we were, bloody Thelma and Louise? (Who were they?) How could she go off and leave her mother in the lurch? Estella was my mother too, or had I forgotten? One hundred grand might seem a lot, but not if you considered two people had to live on it indefinitely. Agron Xhani *would* find her one day and she wasn't going to keep running and looking over her shoulder until that happened. And what the hell did I mean, I'd *give up* Tomás? He wasn't mine to give up, was he, or had she missed something? I needed a reality check. I retorted that she did too if she planned to go back to the Netherlands, hand over that money and risk getting herself murdered all because of a cheating husband who'd dumped her in a mountain of excrement.

Frankie went quiet then and concentrated on driving through the city streets, which were busy even though it was after midnight and mid-week. I keep hearing about the twenty-four-seven society, and it's true. I can't get used to it ; my body clock's still on prison hours and I think it will stay that way for a while. Most of the cars seemed to contain young males in baseball caps. There's something about baseball caps – or is it their wearers? – that I hate. I can't explain; it's emotive not rational. Carl wears one occasionally – that could have something to do with it. I kept thinking of Lady M, Monique Thorn, collapsing in slow motion, blonde hair flopping over her eyes. That slim, helpless arm flung up. The blood, all that blood. Shakespeare's Lady M was right on that one – incredible, mind-blowing, to think that one human body can contain so much of the stuff.

Around the corner from my flat Frankie stopped the car but left the engine running. She turned to me. She looked washed out, done in, crushed. I felt the same way. Her big, grey eyes were full of tears.

'What I do is no longer any of your business.' She flipped open the glove box and tumbled the heavy, plastic bag-wrapped revolver into my lap, making me jump. 'I suggest you put that

266

thing back where you got it. Or dump it somewhere it'll never be found.'

'This *thing* helped you out of a lot of trouble tonight.'

'No, it didn't. You know I only meant you to threaten her with it, not–' She put one hand over her eyes. 'Oh my *God*.'

'What's the use of threats if you don't back them up with action?'

'Your *action* wasn't necessary. Even if Monique had told the police everything, so what? I didn't do what she wanted. Okay, I took her money on false pretences, but she could hardly sue about that in the circumstances!'

'You're right on that one.' I couldn't help laughing again.

Frankie glared at me. 'Get out.'

'What?'

'I said get out, get out of the car. Go. Goodnight, goodbye.'

'Hang on . . . we can't leave it like this. You're upset, we need to talk.'

'There's nothing left to say. You shot Monique Thorn, you killed her. It was stupid, crazy.' She shook her head, despairing. 'What the hell's going to happen now?'

'Nothing. Not to us, anyway. You met her in secret and no one but me knows about what happened between you two. You don't have any obvious connection with her – and I certainly don't.'

'I'm not frightened about that. I'm thinking about the terrible thing you've done.' More tears flooded her eyes. 'You may not have been a murderer before, but you are now. It's finished – I never want to see you again.'

I panicked then. 'You can't just dump me like this. It's not fair!' I sounded pathetic, like a little girl. 'We've been through so much together. You don't think I enjoyed killing that mad woman, do you? I did it for you; I only wanted to help you.'

'I don't need any more of your help. Now get out of the car.' She shoved me, punched me on the arm. 'Get out, get out!' She was gasping, almost hysterical. I realised it was no use, that there was nothing I could do while she was in that state.

'I'll talk to you tomorrow,' I said, scrambling out.

'You fucking won't. Stay away from me,' she shouted. 'Stay away from my mother too. She was right about you all along. I should have listened to her.'

'*Right* about me?' I stared down at her, panicking and desperate with hurt.

Frankie leaned across, wrenched the passenger door shut and accelerated away, leaving me standing on the street corner clutching the wrapped gun. The look in her eyes made me think she wouldn't have cared if she'd trapped my fingers in the door or run over my foot. Run over me.

I was shivering uncontrollably, my teeth chattering. The orange-lit shell of St Luke's towered over me. I wanted to be inside the dark nave, curled up in one of those abandoned vampire coffins. I was certainly sated with blood tonight. I skirted the three graceful flights of steps that surrounded the closed-off entrance to the church, and turned into my tiny street, let myself into the silent house and climbed the dark, narrow stairs. Cold, ancient, evil-smelling damp settled on me like a shroud.

In my flat I put the gun in the bottom of the wardrobe, opened a bottle of Aussie Shiraz and downed two big glasses in five minutes. I sat on the sofa, cradling the bottle between my knees. I was still shivering, freezing cold, so I got up again, boiled a kettle and filled a hot water bottle. I couldn't undress and get into bed as I felt too restless. I knew I wouldn't sleep that night. I wanted to pick up the phone and call Frankie, but of course I didn't have a bloody phone. I'd have had to go out again and walk down Bold Street to find a call box, brave gangs of drunken clubbers wandering from Slater Street and its environs. I thought about taking a cab to her house, and tried to persuade myself that was a good idea. Even after three-quarters of a bottle of wine, however, I knew it wasn't. I had to leave Frankie alone, at least for tonight. Give her a chance to calm down, get some sleep. She was in shock, she didn't mean what she'd said. She couldn't. We had a connection now. She would realise I was right about Monique bloody Thorn. In my heart though, I knew I'd shot Lady M because she reminded me of Vivienne, and had brought back all those feelings I'd believed were long buried. I didn't want to admit they had barely sunk below the surface of my mind.

I finished the bottle and opened another. I started to cry and couldn't stop. I was shaking, sobbing, bawling, screaming. Having a real pity party. No one came up on to my landing and knocked at the door, not even to shout at me to keep the bloody noise down. I stopped after a couple of minutes, because you can't go on bawling indefinitely. It tires you out. I staggered into the tiny bedroom and collapsed across my wrecked bed. Maybe I'd feel better if I tidied up a bit more. But what's the point of trying to improve a hole like this? There were damp patches on the walls, layers of old wallpaper peeling off. Mould on the bathroom ceiling, the kitchen a disaster area. I thought of my father living in his big, beautiful, clean house with original period features. Blanking me out, pretending I didn't exist. Okay, he believed I'd murdered his wife.

I lay staring at the scabby ceiling, my head whirling. If I closed my eyes it felt as if I was flying backwards at a hundred miles an hour. It was no use, I didn't understand anything and perhaps I never would. Why neither of my parents wanted me, who murdered Vivienne, how my sister who I loved and wanted to help could push me away and decide she didn't want to know any more. I felt like getting up and going out then, taking a cab to Tomás' apartment, throwing myself into the warmth and comfort of his embrace. But I couldn't do that because Linda might be in his arms at this moment. Oh-so-friendly Linda, who was kindly going to permit me to skivvy for her. Well, she could stuff her job. I'd rather clean bogs than be someone's bloody secretary or receptionist. It's more honest. I'm sure Carl could get me a job cleaning bogs.

The only thing that made me smile – albeit with great bitterness – was the thought that Linda was wasting her precious time trying to please Tomás. I'd seen the look he'd given Frankie. It was useless to pretend. Tomás would help me out of loyalty, a sense of duty. But that was all. He didn't want me any more, not as a lover. I was sure he wouldn't make a move on Frankie, any more than I believed she would make a move on him. But it was there – that thought, feeling, connection. Even if nothing happened, it was there. And it made me sick.

Two bottles gone now. I rolled over and crawled off the bed, crawled on hands and knees to the wardrobe and reached inside for the wrapped gun. I took it out of its carrier bag and held it, feeling its coldness. Opened the cardboard box of bullets. I couldn't believe I'd shot Monique Thorn twice, spilled her bright blood all over that nice scrubbed doorstep. It seemed unreal.

I wondered who else besides Monique Thorn had been shot with Danny Paglino's gun. A piece with a history. I went on thinking about my history, about how everything had gone so wrong. I didn't think about the future, because I couldn't imagine it. I had no idea how I was going to get through the night, let alone tomorrow or the day after.

I held the gun to my right temple, then my throat. Put the barrel in my mouth; it tasted nasty. I shifted and my left knee knocked the box, spilling bullets over the smelly, stained, cigarette-burned carpet. There were plenty left. Enough to kill a good few more people.

But I only needed one bullet.

He awoke, nauseous and shivering violently, to a grey dawn, the long grass around him soaked with dew. He groaned and blinked hard to produce more tears to soothe his burning eyes. There was a salty taste in his mouth. In the distance he could hear dogs barking, and a police siren wailing along a road. He glanced at the low, steel-grey sky. A long, straggly V-line of clacking geese flew overhead.

Conal blinked hard again and looked round. Big stones, crumbled walls, a broken arch, ruins in the middle of a field. Of course. The abbey ruins. What was he doing here?

What had happened and how did he come to be in this place? The cries of the geese died away; he thought they'd be heading for ... where? Marton Mere. Yes. He was lying in the abbey ruins and his house – his and Monique's – was just up the road. He felt dazed, sledgehammered, his head ached like hell and he could not remember what had happened. Why were his eyes so sore? As if he'd gone swimming in a pool that contained too much chlorine. Conal could remember a time he had done that, years ago. So why couldn't he remember what had happened last night?

His body felt strange, stiff and painful, and his arms were trapped. He wriggled, and realised that his hands were tied behind his back. He looked down; he was wrapped in a thick, blue sleeping bag and bound with rope, tied to what remained of a stone pillar. He wriggled harder but could not free himself. Someone must have put him here during the night, wrapped him in this sleeping bag so that he wouldn't freeze to death. But Conal felt as if he was freezing now. And he was desperate for a pee.

'Help!' he shouted, his hoarse voice cracking. 'Help me.' His shout seemed to go nowhere, suffocated by the flat, grey morning air. He remembered there was a farmhouse not far away. Would they hear him? The dog's barking seemed louder.

If he could remember who he was and where he lived, that he was married to Monique and that they had problems that could lead to divorce, why the fuck couldn't he remember what had happened? Had he seen Monique last night? Had he been drinking? Conal thought he probably had drunk quite a lot. But that didn't explain his sore eyes or why he was dumped here and trussed up with rope. He took a deep breath, opened his mouth wide and yelled again.

'Help me! I'm here in the ruins, help me. I'm tied up, I can't move. *Heeeeelp.*'

Nothing. Nausea overwhelmed him and he vomited, retching down his front and over the sleeping bag. It was ugly. Exhausted, he leaned his throbbing head against the stone and closed his eyes once more, trying to gather energy for the next effort. He felt frozen and knackered. He wanted hot coffee and a litre of water – if he could keep it down. Then he wanted to get into a warm, soft bed and sleep for hours. How long would he be stuck here before someone discovered him? People didn't often come here. Monique liked to visit on her walks. She thought of this place as hers, believed she was the only person around here who appreciated the abbey ruins. She liked to sit among the stones and pillars and broken arches thinking and dreaming God knew what.

A thought occurred to him. Had Monique put him here? If so why? It didn't make sense. And she couldn't carry him by herself; she would have needed help. Conal groaned. A shaft of pain through his arm and shoulder brought back another memory – Monique had shot him! She thought he was cheating on her with another woman, but he wasn't. And something else. *What*?

He tried to wriggle out of the sleeping bag, struggling against the ropes. It was no use. Panicked, he started to yell again.

'*Help me.* Somebody help. I'm trapped, I can't move. *Help me, for fuck's sake!*'

If he stayed here all day and perhaps another night, he *would* freeze. Or die of pneumonia. The grey sky was darkening, not getting lighter. It would rain soon. A movement in the grass startled him. A family of wild rabbits appeared, nibbling their breakfast and pausing to look at him and wonder who was the big,

271

rough-looking eejit in the sleeping bag? They weren't that interested because a minute later they dashed away, leaping high in the air. The dog was barking again. Why didn't someone shut it up? He'd never be able to make himself heard above that racket.

Conal tried to twist his body around as he heard a scrabble and hoarse panting behind him. It was the dog – or a dog. A border collie with angry brown eyes, probably after the rabbits. The dog stopped and looked at him, barked again then started to growl low in its throat. It moved forward and stopped. Conal's mouth went dry with terror.

'Hey boy,' he managed to whisper. 'Good dog.' If the bloody thing went for him there was nothing he could do, trussed up like this. 'Good dog,' he repeated. He didn't dare shout again in case it jumped on him and ripped his throat out.

'Hey!' a man's voice shouted. 'Come here, you! Where are you?'

The dog turned and barked furiously, ran backwards and forwards. Conal cringed at the sight of its teeth. Footsteps swished through the grass and a man appeared, tall and fair haired with a ruddy complexion, wearing a thick brown jacket, jeans and green wellies. The farmer, presumably.

'Shut up, will you?' he said to the dog. He stared down at Conal. 'What the bloody hell are you doing there?'

'I wish I knew.' Conal was shaking, nearly crying, feeling sick again. 'Look, I'm ill. Can you help me, *please*? Call that dog off, for a start.'

'Oh, he's a softie. He won't do you any harm.'

'That's what all dog owners say.'

The man crouched and started to fiddle with the rope knots. 'Someone's trussed you up good and proper. A joke, was it?'

'I don't know. Somebody must have dumped me here while I was unconscious. I don't know what happened; I can't remember anything. I feel terrible.'

'Yes, you look it – and smell it. One of those nights, eh?' The farmer laughed. 'Who needs enemies when you've got friends who'll do this to you? Hey, hold on, don't I know you? You live at Bay House, right? With that blonde woman, whatshername?'

'Monique Thorn. Yeah. I'm Conal Thorn.'

'Pleased to meet you.' The man stood up. 'I can't undo these knots. I'll need a knife.'

'Hurry it up, will you? Please!'

'I'll be back in a couple of minutes. Take it easy, okay?' He strode off, the dog following.

The first thing Conal did when the farmer came back and freed him was to vomit again and take a long pee against an arch wall. His head swam when he stood up and his legs, his whole body, felt weak. He could not stop shivering, had never felt so ill in his life. The farmer gave him a lift up the road and turned into the drive of Bay House. The tall gates were open.

'Haven't been here since I was a boy,' he said as the van bumped up the drive. 'The owners who were here then, an old couple, used to give garden parties. Bloody hell,' he commented, seeing the two parked police cars and people in white jumpsuits milling around. 'What's going on here? Come to think of it, me and my wife got woken up a couple of times during the night by police sirens. Looks like some crime scene from the telly. Wonder if all this could have anything to do with you being trussed up at the abbey ruins?'

Conal could not speak. He climbed out of the van and walked slowly towards the open front door, ignoring a brusque question from a woman in white. He was dazed, exhausted and confused, his heart thudding. He knew he'd have to be sick again soon. He badly needed to sit down, lie down preferably. But what the bloody hell was going on here? He stopped, astonished as a wildly sobbing Lauren dashed out of the house and threw herself into his arms. Two uniformed police officers, a man and a woman, followed her.

'What's happened?' Conal tried to free himself, but Lauren clung to him. He didn't want her clinging to him, didn't want her to even touch him. Something had happened to make him wary of Lauren, to hate her even, but he couldn't remember what that was. 'What's up?'

'Are you Conal Thorn?' the policewoman asked.

'Yeah. So?'

'Mr Thorn, where have you been? Where were you last night?'

Conal ignored her question because he could not give an answer. 'What's up?' he repeated. He tried again to push Lauren away but she clung on like a dead weight, sobbing and screaming. He glanced up at the house. Where was Monique?

'Mr Thorn, your wife–'

'My *wife*?' He noticed a big stain spread over the doorstep. Dried, rusty. Red. Was it blood?

Icy horror seized him. He made a big effort and shoved Lauren off. She stumbled away, screaming something he couldn't make out. He wished she would shut up, because she was more noisy than the farmer's dog and her screams were getting inside his head and driving him crazy. The policewoman tried to put one arm around Lauren's shoulders, but she pulled away.

'What about Monique?' Conal stared at the rusty stain. His stomach contracted again, and his mouth filled with saliva. 'What's happened? Where is she?'

Chapter 30

Dear Frankie,
I can't get the money, or nowhere near enough. I don't suppose you can either. Time's almost run out. I've no choice but to take off before Xhani kills me.
PLEASE do the same – even if you won't go with me.
You don't deserve this. I'm sorry for everything.

Love, Joe.

He left the note on the dining table, anchored beneath the empty fruit bowl. There was mail for Frankie, from what he already thought of as their old life – a writers' magazine and a letter with some London literary agent's address on the top left-hand corner of the envelope, probably another rejection. Like that mattered now. Frankie had always been sad for a day or so after a rejection, but then she cheered up and got on with writing her stuff. Joe had never read any of it, and she never offered to show him. He liked newspapers and magazines but books, especially novels, bored him.

He glanced at his two suitcases, stuck with labels and security tags from previous trips, dumped in the middle of the sitting room. Maybe Frankie had already done a runner; he had tried to call her several times, but got no answer from her mobile or her mother's phone. He had given up trying to contact Lida. She must be traumatised after the rape and other appalling violence Xhani's men had inflicted on her. She would be scarred for life, physically as well as psychologically. But at least Lida was safe now. She didn't owe a huge sum of money she could not pay, and no one wanted to kill her. She would get the help she needed from her family and friends, recover in time, go back to work, meet new people. She would never forget him – for all the wrong reasons.

Joe went to the windows and peered into the sunlit street. There were so many parked cars he didn't know which was The One. Which was the quickest and safest way to get to Schiphol airport – train or cab? Although what did that matter, because if they spotted him coming out of the apartment lugging a couple of suitcases they wouldn't need to be *Mastermind* contestants to guess where he was going. Best if he left the luggage and went out with only his rucksack, as usual. He would just have to buy stuff when he got to his final destination.

He glanced at his watch. Ten-to-nine and time to get going. He was booked on the twelve noon Malaysian Airlines flight to Adelaide via Kuala Lumpur. Joe had chosen Adelaide because it was on the other side of the world, he had been there a couple of times for work, thought it one of the most beautiful cities on earth, and knew several people there who, although he had neglected them somewhat, hoped they would be happy to see him again.

The palms of his hands were sweaty, his stomach was rumbling and he needed another pee. Frankie sometimes joked that he needed to pee more often than a woman in the last stages of pregnancy. When packing Joe had tried not to look at her clothes hanging in the wardrobe or sniff the perfume that lingered on them, and had shut the door of the study so as not to see her books and papers. It was too weird and upsetting, as if she had just died. He went to the toilet, came back and picked up the phone, put it down again. Forget the cab. Best to get a bus to The Hague Central Station, nip down one of the escalators and disappear into the crowds, then hop on a train for Schiphol. Xhani's men couldn't follow the bus into the station; they would have to get out of their car, and it would be too late because by then he would have lost them. At least that was the theory. Once he had picked up his ticket at the Malaysian Airlines desk, checked in and gone through Passport Control, he was safe. They couldn't follow him airside. In the Departure lounge he would head straight for the nearest bar.

Joe did not think about what he would do in Australia or how long he would be able to stay there, or what would happen when his money ran out and he overstayed his tourist visa. The urgent thing now was to get out of the Netherlands. There was no way Frankie could have got that money, so surely she would now have the sense to hide somewhere. Agron Xhani couldn't pursue them for ever. Frankie would be all right; she had to be, because Joe could not bear to think she would be killed because of him.

He opened the suitcases, rummaged through, and crammed a few more clothing items into the rucksack. He slipped his arms through the straps and hoisted it on, jammed the black baseball cap down over his forehead. He didn't normally wear those things, but hopefully this would give him anonymity. Joe did not take a last, lingering glance around the silent apartment, think about what he had destroyed or wonder what would happen now. He strode out, double-locked the door, pushed the keys through the letter box and heard them drop. Who would pick them up next? Frankie? The house owner, concerned about the non-appearance of her latest month's rent? Xhani's thugs bursting in?

It was a beautiful autumn morning. He walked down the street and headed for the bus stop, skirting the Frederik Hendrikplein; the small park was deserted except for two children with a red-haired woman. The bus stop was outside a travel agent and near the Ethiopian Consulate where Frankie had once briefly worked. Joe tried to put her out of his mind, at least for now. He looked up and down the street, feeling vulnerable and frightened, wishing Bus 4 would hurry up. Maybe he should have taken a cab.

Stay calm, he told himself. An hour tops and he'd be at Schiphol, drinking that first beautiful, cool, double vodka and tonic in the departure lounge. Bus 4 came and he got on and sat down, glancing around, sweating with impatience and anxiety as it crawled the length of elegant Groot Hertoginnelaan towards the centre of town. At Central Station he jumped off and ran down the escalator, bought a first-class single to Schiphol and was on a train ten minutes later.

He had to change at Leiden, something that normally irritated him, but this time Joe didn't mind because it gave him an extra evasion opportunity. When the Amsterdam train arrived he raced down the long platform and got into a first class section, empty except for a couple of businessmen playing on laptops. He was out of breath, his heart thudding. The double-decker train was modern, fast and very smooth on the tracks. He gazed out at flat fields, brown cows, rows of poplars bent by years of wind, old

277

farmhouses, the occasional windmill and new roads-in-progress. His last sight of the Netherlands.

He liked the country and had been happy here. Until recently. Until he had fucked up his life big time. A majestic blue KLM Boeing 757 descended slowly, flying low over the ploughed fields on final approach, and a minute later blackness engulfed the windows as the train entered the Schiphol tunnel. Joe was shivering with nerves now, even though each passing minute brought him closer to safety. The conductor's voice came over the intercom, in Dutch and then in English.

'Ladies and gentlemen, Schiphol airport. Schiphol airport. This train is now going on to Amsterdam Sloterdijk and Amsterdam Central Station.'

He got out, the heavy rucksack chafing his shoulders, pushing past people and bags on the escalator. The airport was busy as usual, baggage-laden passengers forming straggling queues at check-in desks and KLM ground staff, mostly female, walking around in their blue uniforms. He had to walk what seemed like miles to find the Malaysian Airlines desk.

'No baggage to check in, sir?' The clerk smiled. 'That's unusual.'

Joe shrugged and smiled back, hoped it wouldn't make her suspicious. His heart was thudding, palpitating as if he was coked up, and he felt worried. Cocaine could cause a heart arrythmia even after you'd stopped taking it. He dismissed the fears; it was anxiety, nothing more. He would be fine once he was airside. He collected the ticket, nodded as the clerk told him the gate number and boarding time, and walked off again.

He could see a long line of passengers, passports and boarding cards in hand, queueing to go through to the departure area. Damn. Joe glanced around as he walked, scanning faces, searching for anyone who might be watching him. Beyond that gate and those desks, the blue-shirted immigration officers and security personnel, lay safety. Freedom. For now, anyway. He walked faster. He was a few metres away from the end of the queue when he felt a gun – he presumed it was a gun – jam into the small of his back beneath the rucksack. A dark-haired, dark-eyed man, shorter than him, blocked his path.

'Airport security,' he grinned.

'Yeah, fucking *right*.'

278

They were going to kill him; if not here, somewhere else. While he was in a public place with people milling around he still had a chance. If they shot him now, so what? He had nothing to lose. Joe moved so fast he surprised himself. He realised he had been expecting this. He punched the man in the face, hurting his knuckles, and watched him stagger back, blood running from his nose. He kicked behind him and made contact with someone's shin, jabbed his right elbow into their solar plexus and heard a grunt of pain. It happened like in a movie fight, everything going according to the director's carefully choreographed plan.

People around them scattered, called out in alarm, abandoned their baggage and ran when they caught sight of the man with the gun. The only difference between life and the movies here was that no women screamed. Joe raced to the straggly passport control queue, shoving past frightened, protesting people who were asking no one in particular what the hell was going on. A security guard grabbed him as he tried to force his way past the desk and metal detector.

'Where do you think you're going, sir?'

'Let me through.' Joe shoved him away. 'I've got a plane to catch.'

'So have a lot of people.' Another guard grabbed him. 'You have to wait your turn. Do you have a passport and boarding card?'

Their stubborn stupidity in the face of his fear and shock enraged him. 'For fuck's sake!' he shouted, struggling. 'Of course I've got a–'

Where was his bloody passport and boarding card? He felt in his jacket and jeans pockets, glanced around in despair. He must have dropped them. Christ. He tried to turn, struggling and terrified in their arms. Some yards away the two men lingered, watching him, menacing and enraged but also helpless and uncertain. They couldn't do anything now, but were reluctant to abort their mission and get the hell out.

'They're trying to kill me,' he yelled, wrenching one arm free and pointing. 'Those two – there. Help me.' He saw the look of disbelief on the guards' faces. 'It's true!'

Drunken Brit, said the glance they exchanged, although he didn't stink of booze because he hadn't had time to get any of the lovely stuff down his neck. They grasped him more firmly.

Another guard came running up, shouting into a walkie-talkie. He gestured to them, interrupting his conversation to tell them someone had seen a man with a gun in the terminal. Joe looked back and saw the man running for the exit, colliding with startled people, shoving them and their baggage aside. A couple of armed policemen appeared. Of course they wouldn't risk tackling him here in the terminal where someone might get shot; they would wait until he was outside.

'So – who wants to kill you, eh?' one of the guards asked Joe angrily.

Joe knew he was out of danger, for now at least. He forced himself to calm down and stop struggling. His objective now was to find his passport and boarding card and be allowed through to the departure area.

'Nobody.' He swallowed, shook his head, even tried to smile. His mouth was so dry he could barely speak. 'Sorry. I just – I thought – I saw that guy with the gun and I panicked. So did a few other people, I guess. I mean, look at them.'

The boarding card and passport had to be lying somewhere nearby. No one would pick them up, surely; they were no use to anyone but him.

'I've dropped my boarding card and passport,' he explained. 'It must be over there somewhere.' He pointed. 'Please, I need to get it. I'm checked in on the Malaysian Airlines flight and it leaves at twelve. I haven't got much time.'

'Okay.' They let him go. 'But hurry. This area will be closed off in a minute.'

More armed policemen appeared. Joe took a deep breath. He was shaking, his body prickling with sweat. He walked along, scanning the ground as he went.

'Anyone seen a passport and boarding card?' he called. People stared stupidly or ignored him. 'Anyone seen a passport?'

'Passport?' A tall, thin Japanese teenager turned. 'You lose?'

Joe grabbed the document the boy held up and opened it. His black-and-white mug shot of six years ago stared back at him. 'Yeah.' Delighted and relieved, he clapped the boy on his sweat-shirted shoulder. 'Thanks! Thanks, mate.'

'No problem.' The boy nodded politely, turned away and merged into the crowd.

Nice one. Now for the boarding card. If he couldn't find it he would go back to the Malaysian Airlines desk to check if someone had handed it in. God almighty, did he need a drink. Joe moved slowly, staring at the clean, shiny floor. Boots, trainers, and elegant stockinged legs beneath blue hems, the feet encased in black pumps, filed past. He paused to do the classic thing and ask a policeman.

The officer shook his head and brusquely informed him that the area was being cleared and passengers were being directed to another section of the airport. Joe hurried up, desperate to find the boarding card before he was moved on. He was close to one of the revolving doors now. Outside the terminal was a long line of parked cars. Cabs moved slowly along, looking for places to stop and unload their passengers. Groups of people stood around chatting, getting in other people's way.

Joe gasped as he noticed what looked like a boarding card lying crumpled on the ground, half trapped between the non-revolving part of the door and the black rubber groove. Was it his? He started forward and stooped to retrieve it, trying to keep out of the way of the revolving door and the people streaming past.

In the stunned seconds that followed the blow to his head and the terrible feeling of pressure, as if someone was kneeling on him, Joe thought he must have been hit by the door and trapped. Dizziness overwhelmed him, and he thought he was going to black out. He was gripped under the arms and hauled to his feet, propelled through the door and out into the cold air. He smelled coffee mingled with aviation fuel. His head was down, his eyes half closed; he would have fallen but for whoever was holding him upright and helping him to walk.

By the time he realised what was happening Joe was blindfolded and his hands tied, the rucksack pressing down on him, half suffocated and freaked with terror as the car the men had forced him into drove off at speed.

I woke up on the bedroom floor, the stink of vomit in my nostrils, shiny bullets tangled in my hair and lying scattered around my head. I still held the gun in my right hand, the heavy weapon numbing my fingers. I let go of it and slid my hand away. I was cold, my body stiff and aching, and the pain in my head was so bad that I could barely sit upright, let alone stand. Once I managed to attain the horizontal position I had to stumble to the toilet to throw up again.

When you feel like this you want to die. And the means of death were right there on the floor by the wardrobe, just in case I didn't croak it from this mother of all hangovers. But my hands were shaking so much I thought I'd certainly muff the job and end up a maimed vegetable at the mercy of carers. Yes, things could be worse. Coffee, water, two paracetamol and a lie-down later, the headache had more or less gone, but I was still weak, shaky and felt generally rotten. I knew I needed to get something in my stomach, even though eating was the last thing I wanted to do. First I had to clean my teeth and take a shower, get dressed and put on make-up. After that I tried to clean the carpet in the bedroom, spraying the stinky spot with a bit of Chanel No. 5 for good measure. I forced myself not to think about last night. The flash-backs kept intruding nevertheless – Frankie snarling at me, spitting her hateful, hurtful words, me firing the gun and watching Lady M collapse on her door step. My father joined in, shouting at me to get out of his house, that he never wanted to see me again unless it was to ID my body in a morgue. I gasped and closed my eyes. Don't even *go* there!

I picked up the bullets and dropped them back in their box, wiped the gun and re-wrapped it in its carrier bag, returned both items to their place at the bottom of the wardrobe. I had a stupid urge to load the gun, put it in my handbag and go out with it, but resisted. I didn't plan to shoot anyone else. I tried to analyse my psyche dispassionately. I was shocked at what I'd done – I suppose the archetypal guy on the Clapham omnibus would call it murder – and I wasn't proud of myself. I was afraid of being caught, although I couldn't see how that was going to happen. But I didn't feel guilty or stained, the way murderers are said to feel.

I was different somehow though. I had crossed some invisible line that had changed me forever. I wasn't me any more; I had lost something. All those years in prison I'd survived on the thought that no matter what happened they couldn't take away my integrity, the fact that I was innocent. It had kept me intact, given me a prop to cling on to. Now that prop was gone. I wasn't innocent any more. I was as evil as Judgie said. A lost cause.

Burning tears flooded my eyes, my image wavering then dissolving in the toothpaste-spotted bathroom mirror. I thought of the gun and bullets as I blotted my eyes with a tissue. Death was there if I wanted it. If I really couldn't take any more, I could check out. The thought was comforting.

The doorbell rang and I felt a rush of relief, renewed hope. It must be Tomás. I didn't fool myself it would be Frankie – not yet. She needed time to come to terms with what had happened. Lady M's death was for the best; she would understand that soon. It was the only way I could justify killing Monique Thorn. It wasn't normal murder. I had done it to help my sister.

I'd forgotten Carl existed, but there he stood looking like a befuddled hippy in a woolly black hat and long, dusty black coat with wide lapels. And oh God, he was growing a beard. I bet he refused to listen to any music post-1973, and probably raved about ancient bands long consigned to obscurity for very good reasons.

'Hi.' His little rodent eyes flickered over me. 'Feeling better this bright, sunny, autumn morning, are we?'

The sight of him pissed me off, and I wasn't in the mood to take any smart remarks either. 'All the better for seeing you, Carly.'

He was disconcerted at my contemptuous new tone. 'Aren't you going to let me in?' he asked when it became obvious that I wasn't.

'Actually, Carly, I'm just on my way out. I'd love to chat, but I don't have time.' I wonder what he'd think if he knew I had a gun in the wardrobe.

'It's Carl, if you don't mind. Alyssa, why are you smiling?'

'Was I? Oh, sorry, Carly. I realise I'm supposed to look permanently crushed, as befits a despicable ex-con at the bottom of the food chain. Have you seen that painting called *The Angelus*?'

'The what?'

'*The Angelus*. Can't remember the painter's name. Two depressed peasants in the middle of a ploughed field break off from their hard labour when they hear the church bell, and bow their heads to give thanks for their tragic life. That's supposed to be me, isn't it?'

He shook his head. 'Are you on something? And where are you going?' He'd noticed my new clothes now, the virgin wool trousers and expensive jacket, and I'm sure he'd caught a whiff of Chanel No. 5. 'Is it a job interview, by any chance?'

'Yeah. I'm going to be president of a multi-national. And Miss

World in my spare time.' I step back, ready to shut the door. 'See ya, wouldn't wanna be ya.'

'Hold up. You can't just–! If you've really got an interview, where is it? And shouldn't you have told me?'

Enough already; I'm no longer amused. 'Just fuck off.'

Carl stiffened and turned red. 'Maybe you don't realise, Alyssa, but you're not in a position to speak to me like that. What you do is very much my business. My opinion of you has a lot of influence with–'

'So what d'you want, a shag? Sorry Carly, you're not my type.' I slammed the door on him and went back into the bathroom to repair my make-up. He rang again twice, shouted my name. I ignored him. After a minute I heard him go downstairs.

Carl was right, of course; his opinion of me does have a lot of influence with the great and good people who frowningly wonder if they did the right thing to grant me my relative freedom. I left the flat and walked down Bold Street, stopped off at a burger place to buy coffee, chips and a large coke. The combination of salty chips and bubbly, full sugar coke was fantastic, instantly dispelling what remained of the headache and nausea. I felt full of energy, ready to walk all day. But what should I do with this brilliant day?

I decided Linda Nichols didn't have to stuff her job after all. It might not be as bad as I'd thought. And at least I'd get to keep an eye on the competition. Carl, however annoyed he might be at me right now, couldn't complain if I got a respectable position in a solicitor's office. Especially as said solicitor knew about my past and was still willing to hire me. I found a phone box and made the call; Ms Nichols had just got back from court.

'Alyssa Ward?' Her voice was soft and light; she sounded nice. I wondered what she looked like. A pang of jealousy stabbed me. 'You didn't phone or come to see me yesterday. I thought you weren't interested.'

'I'm sorry I didn't turn up. I meant to, but I was busy.' And how.

There's a silence and I guessed Linda was wondering what the hell an unemployed ex-con had got to keep her busy. 'I am interested.' I'm suddenly desperate for the bloody job. 'I'd like to come and see you now, if that's all right. Or later today – whenever's convenient for you.'

'Tomás didn't explain yet then?'

She sounded embarrassed and I didn't need to be Einstein. 'You've changed your mind.' My energy and optimism plummeted. The world was once more a cold, cruel, terrifying place.

'I'm afraid I had second thoughts and decided it wasn't a good idea after all. I told Tomás and he said he'd tell you, but he obviously hasn't got round to doing that. I'm sorry. He said you wouldn't mind.'

And he would have been right then. But not now. It's my fault. If I'd gone round there yesterday and snapped up the job Linda wouldn't have had time for second thoughts. And I'd have proved myself a model employee from day one. Alyssa screws up again.

'Okay. Thanks for your time.' I call Tomás's office next, but he's in court. His mobile is switched off. I thought, what's the point of arguing with him? It wasn't his fault. He did his best. He couldn't call me because I've got no phone, so he was probably planning to come round at lunchtime. It was approaching noon now.

Suddenly I couldn't wait any longer. I wanted to see Tomás, but wanted to see Frankie more. I had to talk to her. I hoped she'd be feeling better after a night's sleep. I went to Central Station and bought a ticket, looked at the newsstand before passing through the barrier and taking the escalator down to the platform. But it was too early for the *Echo* and Monique Thorn's killing wouldn't have made any national dailies yet. If it did at all. I mean, people get gunned down every day all over Britain. There might be something on regional telly or radio, although I dreaded finding out, because what I'd done would hit home harder then. I wondered if Frankie had seen or heard anything.

Travelling out to the sticks again made me think of my father and his Georgian pile, the house in my dream. I hadn't had the dream since that terrible day I'd gone to see him. Reality had turned out to be more of a nightmare.

I was nervous and frightened as I got off the train and walked down the narrow road leading from the station, crossed the main road and headed along the tree-lined lane, gradually walking uphill past detached Edwardian and Victorian residences with long drives and big front gardens. The church tower came into view. I went down the cinder path and across the field. A black cat shied away as I approached and gave an aggrieved yowl. Animals didn't want to know me any more than people did. I paused and looked across the green field at the blank windows of Frankie's mother's – my mother's – house. Wondered how Estella was doing.

God, I hoped Frankie would talk to me! She had to, she couldn't just push me out of her life. Not now. I crossed the field, passing the trees and bushes at the edge where I had stood that dark night which seems so long ago now. The leaves were turning autumnal colours, starting to drop and pile in drifts along the gutter. I went up the path to the house, hesitated, then ring the bell. A shadow appeared through the porch door and front door. My heart was thumping.

It was not not Frankie who answered the door, but a smart, friendly-looking woman with silver hair who I guessed was some-where in her sixties. But who the hell was she? I checked the house number – of course I've got the right one.

'Yes?' She smiled politely.

My shock was so great that at first I didn't know what to say. Had something happened to Estella? Where was Frankie? The woman's smile faded. 'I – I'm looking for Frankie. Francesca.'

'Oh, I see. And you are?'

'I'm her – a – a friend.'

'Who is it, Val?' The voice from down the hall was not Frankie's. Panic seized me. How stupid was it to just turn up here like this? I should have phoned first. Why the hell didn't I phone?

'A friend of Francesca's.' Val looked back at me and I could tell she thought me rude when I still didn't give my name. But how could I?

This was the moment I had dreamed and fantasised about, alter-nately longed for and dreaded all these years: My mother coming to the door and finding me there.

'Francesca isn't here,' were the first words she said to me.

I gasped. '*What*?'

'I said, she isn't here. She's not available.'

'Where is she? Where's she gone?'

'To stay with a friend.'

'What friend?'

A pause, during which we stared at one another. Estella sensed my tension and looked puzzled and annoyed, then uneasy. Val wanted to take charge, but seemed at a loss. She's realised there's something she doesn't know.

'Who are you?' Estella asked finally. 'What do you want?'

I couldn't answer. I didn't know what I'd say next, what I would do. What my mother would do.

Like in my dream, it stopped here.

Chapter 31

Cut the head off the monster.

The sentence kept running through Frankie's mind as she stood at the hotel suite window watching a clear violet dusk descend over the Amstel river, Amsterdam's lights glittering in its dark waters. Robin Seiffert had just left, not having bothered to lug her black case of murderous hardware with her for one small delivery. Robin was the same as Frankie remembered, only more sun burnished and leathery, with a few new silver hairs in her bushy gold mane. Her long, sharp, über-cool nails looked more lethal than the weapons she flogged.

Frankie had never dreamed she would ever use that phone number; she had kept the woman's business card purely as a memento of an intriguing, sinister experience that could prove fab grist to any wannabe fiction writer's mill. Robin remembered her, although not her name. Which was just as well because Frankie had given a false one.

'Sure,' she laughed when Frankie called. 'The cute girl with the crystal eyes and hair the colour of my favourite chocolate. What can I do for you, honey? Jesus,' she exclaimed in dismay when they met later, 'what did you *do* to that gorgeous hair? Blondes don't always have more fun, y'know.'

'It was necessary. I'm travelling on a different passport.'

Finding Monique Thorn's passport in the carrier bag of money had been too good an opportunity to resist; Monique must have slipped it in accidentally. Frankie did not exactly resemble Monique, but the blonde hair and light eyes, which could have been grey or green in the black-and-white passport shot, had been enough to satisfy the cursory glance of a bored, busy immigration

288

officer. Who looked like their passport mugshot anyway? Taking such a risk seemed like nothing compared with the risks she had already taken. Or those that lay ahead.

'Oh, sure.' Robin nodded, as if travelling on false passports was a normal everyday thing to do. Frankie could have used a wig, but she couldn't find any blonde wigs that looked natural enough or matched her skin tone, and in the end she decided that was too melodramatic anyway. The hairdresser had been horrified but knew the customer, however deluded, was king.

Frankie turned away from the window, startling herself again with her new reflection in the dressing-table mirror. She felt like a different person. That made it easier somehow, as if someone else was travelling on a stolen passport and meeting with arms dealers. The gun, a Browning 9 mm pistol, lay on the bed. She picked it up and examined it again. It was just under 200mm long and weighed about a kilo.

Robin had talked at length on the advantages of various handguns, going on about calibre, operation, feed, effective range, higher rates of fire and swift reloading with simple magazines instead of loose rounds, single or double action and how automatics or semi-automatics possessed greater ammo capacity. This one had a thirteen-round magazine. Thirteen. Unlucky for some.

She glanced at her watch. Time to get ready. She was nervous and a drink would have helped – although not much – but she had to drive. She put on make-up, brushing shadow and pale gold highlighter around her eyes, painting her lips a shiny red. She went to the wardrobe and took out the little black dress of her dreams, or so the shop assistant had described it, and slipped it on. Tights, shoes, coat, and she was ready. She put the loaded gun in her handbag. Robin had loaded it for her at her request, and shown her the basics. She had smiled as she left.

'Good luck, babe. I like you. Call me again sometime. Not just for – you know. Maybe we can have a drink together.'

Frankie smiled back. 'Love to,' she lied.

She put Monique's passport in the small safe at the bottom of the wardrobe, plus most of the cash she had brought with her. She took her car keys and handbag and buttoned the coat. Then she paused, trying to fight her way through another tidal wave of panic. She had run out of options – if there had ever really been any – and she had to do this. Or try. She had no choice. Frankie left

289

the room and walked down the corridor to the lift. Then she changed her mind and took the stairs, even though she was on the ninth floor. She hated lifts.

It was Ladies' Night at the casino. Free entry and a free drink. The lion's den. The last place Xhani would expect to find her.

Cut the head off the monster.

'I'm sorry there's nothing good I can tell you. About me or your father. About anything, really.'

Estella leaned back in her armchair, exhausted and trembling, her fingers closed around the glass of white wine. Val had gone home, reluctant and angry, with repeated promises to be back first thing in the morning and instructions that Estella was to phone her if she wanted anything. She had taken an immediate and deep dislike to Alyssa Ward, and once she found out who she was had tried to send her on her way like some importunate seller of double-glazing or conservatories. Estella had been tempted to let Val do that. But this unresolved matter had been preying on her mind, looming larger and larger until she felt she could not bear the pressure any longer. She needed closure. One way or another. The best way to get that was to square up to her demons. This particular demon sat across the room from her, pale-faced, perched on the edge of the sofa. Estella had no doubt Alyssa Ward was her daughter and Frankie's half-sister. The hair, those eyes, the features. Even the way she sat. There was almost nothing of *him* in her.

'My friend means well,' she remarked. 'She's concerned for me, that's all.' Not that Estella felt she had anything to apologise for. If anyone should apologise it was Alyssa Ward, for turning up like this.

'Of course.' Alyssa nodded. 'I understand. I'm glad you've got friends who care about you.'

'You haven't told me much about yourself, except that you've been living abroad for the past ten years. And that you're not married and don't have any children.' But did she really want to know? Estella paused. 'Was it you I saw that night I had the heart attack? Standing outside on that field watching the house?'

Alyssa nodded again, averting her eyes. 'I just wanted to see where you lived. I wasn't going to knock on the door or try to speak to you. Then I saw the ambulance.'

'So what made you come here today? And why did you ask for Frankie? Why did you tell Val she was a friend of yours?'

'I know, I didn't handle that very well. I found out I had a half-sister as well as a mother.'

'How did you know we call her Frankie rather than Francesca?'

'I guessed.'

Estella sighed. 'You've had contact with her, haven't you?'

'No! I–'

'Listen. I may be getting old, but I'm not stupid or senile.'

'I never thought you were.'

'Then don't insult me with pathetic lies. If there's going to be any point to this, we have to be honest with one another. Have you and my daughter already met?' Estella felt a sudden pang as she noted the flicker of pain cross Alyssa's features at the phrase '*you and my daughter*'. That was clumsy. But what was she supposed to say?

'All right, yes, we have. Several times.'

'I see.' Estella was silent. Of course Frankie had kept the meetings secret because of her illness and because she knew how her mother would react. Slow anger invaded her, and she tried to stay calm. She was not angry at Frankie, but at Alyssa Ward. She was right; the woman had played on Frankie's vulnerability. Alyssa suddenly seemed threatening, a sinister stranger trying to worm her way into the family, taking advantage wherever she could.

'I don't know what my daughter has said to you.' She leaned forward and put down her wine glass. 'But she's going through a very difficult, traumatic time just now, and even though she's a strong person it's made her vulnerable. She's got a lot to do, a lot to think about, and I'm afraid she may not be in any position to judge whether or not your coming into her life is a good thing.'

Alyssa drained her glass, put it down and clasped her hands tightly. 'That sounds a bit clinical.'

'It's the truth. And your behaviour – just turning up here – you must see that's not the best way to handle things.'

'I know. It was stupid and I'm really sorry. But I was – I'm desperate. Frankie's told me about her problems and I–'

'You see?' Estella was shocked. This had gone further than she realised. 'That's exactly what I mean when I say she's vulnerable.

She doesn't realise what she's doing, what she could be getting herself into.'

'Please, you don't have to worry. I want to help her, be there for her. Don't you think it's great for Frankie to know she's got a sister who'll stand by her? Especially with what she's going through? And great for you, to have another daughter? I'd really love to get to know you.'

Estella's anger increased. 'You're an adult and you seem reasonably intelligent, although what you've just said makes me wonder. You must know you can't expect a fairy-tale reunion in which we all live happily ever after. You can't be that naive. As I said, you haven't told me much. I haven't pushed you to because I'm not sure I want to know. I'm sorry if that sounds cruel.' She clenched her hands. 'You have to understand – it's just not that simple that I'm reunited with my long-lost daughter and it's all wonderful! To be honest, this is a nightmare for me.'

'I know. And I'm sorry.' Alyssa put up one hand and wiped a tear. 'I don't expect a fairy tale either.'

'If it's an apology you want, you can have it. You deserve that. Yes, I'm sorry. I'm sorry I had to leave when you were a baby; it must have been terrible for you growing up with that knowledge.'

Alyssa sniffed. 'I didn't grow up with–'

'Let me finish. And if it's any comfort to you, life wasn't much fun for me either. You'll never know how guilty I felt, how ashamed. I thought I was the most worthless person alive. I never even told my husband about you – or Frankie. I never told anyone. I thought I didn't deserve Jack's love. Or Frankie's. For years I was terrified that you'd turn up – perhaps like this – and blow my life apart. Now it's happened. I'm just glad my husband isn't here to witness this, to realise I betrayed him and that I wasn't the person he loved and trusted.' Estella put up her hands as she felt tears run down her face. 'I'm sorry,' she muttered, 'but it's too late. At least I think it is. I don't want you in my life. I don't want you in my daughter's life either.'

'Well.' Alyssa Ward's voice hardened. 'Maybe Frankie will have something to say about that.'

Estella sensed a stubborn determination. Alyssa Ward did not care what she or Frankie wanted, she thought. She only cared about herself. She had been right not to want contact; she was only sorry that Frankie hadn't heeded her warning.

'I had to leave your father,' she said. She hadn't been going to say this, had intended to spare Alyssa's feelings. Alyssa wasn't concerned about her feelings though. If she wanted the truth she could damn well have it. 'I couldn't stay with him – or you – even if I'd wanted to. I certainly could never have married him. There's something I haven't told you. I haven't even told Frankie.'

'There's a lot you haven't told Frankie.' Alyssa stiffened. 'What is it?'

'Your father was violent. A sadist. He–'

'Hang on!' Alyssa jumped up, blushing crimson. 'Frankie told me he gave you the odd slap now and again, and of course that's not nothing. But–'

'I see you and she have got through a lot in your several meetings. It was rather more than the *odd slap*.' Estella gripped the arms of the chair. 'D'you think I'm making this up to justify leaving him and you?'

'Very possibly. I notice you won't say that word.'

'What word?'

'*Abandoned*.'

'Do you want to hear this or not?'

Alyssa hesitated. 'Go on.' She sat down again, perched on the edge of the sofa, her body tensed as if ready to run away.

'As I said, he was violent. A sexual sadist. Not immediately, of course, not while we were in the first flush of romance. He wanted to get me hooked before he tried anything. Initially I thought he was just being a bit rough. But it got worse and worse until I was so terrified I didn't want any more sexual contact with him. He was also insanely jealous, even though he had no reason to be. He never showed it, never made a scene – except when he was alone with me. He was what my mother used to call a street angel. She should have known, she was one herself.' Estella paused. 'Most people who knew Philip Ward would be as incredulous as you are now at hearing this. And it wasn't enough for him to hurt and humiliate me. He liked to take photos of his handiwork. I wouldn't be surprised if he's still got them.'

'*What*? That's crazy!' Alyssa was stunned, shaking her head, her eyes wide with shock and disbelief. 'I can't imagine my father being like that,' she gasped. 'He never hit me or ... anything. He was too bloody uninterested. He never hit my stepmother either,

293

or hurt her in any way. He loved her. *She* was the sadistic one in our holy family trinity.'

'You've got no other brothers or sisters then?'

'Only Frankie.'

Estella let that go. 'If you've never seen that side of your father's personality, you're very fortunate. Do you have contact with him?'

'Not any more.'

'Don't worry.' Estella watched her. 'I won't ask why.'

'I know you won't. It's not because he was violent towards me, if that's what you're thinking. It's like I said, he never wanted to know. I often wondered why he didn't put me in care. I suppose he was worried about the negative effect that might have on his public persona.'

'I thought someone your age would say "image".'

'Whatever.' Alyssa shook her head again. 'I'm *sure* he was never violent towards my stepmother. He loved her, I know he did.' She twisted her hands together. 'That's just one reason why he never had any time for me. And she had all these flings. You couldn't call them affairs; they were too short for that. I don't know if my father knew about any of her men – or suspected. I don't think he did. He never stopped loving her.' Alyssa broke off, agitated and trembling. 'You're talking about someone I don't recognise.'

'What did he tell you about me?'

'Nothing. He never mentioned you. He never even told me my stepmother wasn't my real mother. I tried to tell you that before. I didn't find out you were my real mother until I was twenty-seven.'

'My God!' Estella stared at her, shocked. 'How on earth–'

'My father made sure I never saw my birth certificate until then. But sooner or later you do see it. I needed it because I was going to get married.'

'I'm sorry,' Estella heard herself say. 'That's terrible. It must have been very tough for you. What did you do when you found out?' she asked, curious for the first time. 'I mean, don't mind me saying this, but it's quite some time ago you were twenty-seven, isn't it?'

Alyssa stood up again. 'I know he was – that he's a bastard. Or he was to me. But I can't believe – I can't imagine he's like you make out.'

She wanted to ask questions but not answer any. Estella's brief feeling of sympathy died and she felt angry again. 'You think I'm lying.'

'Not deliberately lying. I can understand that you built all this up in your mind over the decades, to try to justify your actions to yourself because you felt so guilty and ashamed, and that now maybe–'

'Maybe I've come to believe my own fantasies?' All right. Fine. Alyssa Ward had asked for this. Estella got up, pulling her cardigan around her because the room felt chilly. 'Wait here.'

'Don't worry.' Alyssa tried to smile but it didn't work. 'I won't run off with the silver.'

'I haven't got any bloody silver.'

Estella walked out of the sitting room and went upstairs. She knew where it was, in the old brown leather attaché case with the rusted locks, containing all the documents you'd want to grab and escape with if your house caught fire. She had kept it in different places over the years, secret places where Jack and then Frankie would never look. Of course they didn't dream she had any secrets. Or not one like this. She went into her bedroom and took the case from the bottom of the chest of drawers, unlocked it with shaking fingers and drew out the scuffed white envelope.

It had served its purpose – or almost – and now she could destroy it because she wasn't frightened any more and she finally had closure. She did not want Frankie coming across it after her death. She went downstairs and back into the sitting room.

Alyssa Ward looked as drained as she felt. Estella was sorry she couldn't feel maternal towards her lost daughter, experience delight instead of nightmare at this meeting that had happened at last after so many years of dread. She paused to gather herself again, breathed in slowly, and for a second it was as if she could smell Alyssa as a baby once more, warm and powdered, lying sleepy in her cot. Those eyes, the same clear grey eyes with their long, feathery lashes, watching her.

She took out the hand-made card and gave it to Alyssa, watched her tense expression change to horror as she saw the '*Happy Birthday*' greeting scrawled in faded, rusty blood and the black-and-white photograph of the naked woman bound to a chair and gagged so that she couldn't scream, her tear-filled eyes dilated with pain and terror. She gasped, glanced up.

'Yes. It's me,' Estella said, in answer to her look. 'He – I'm sorry, I can't say his name, I don't want to – pounced on me one night when he was drunk.' She was suddenly afraid for Alyssa. But she had to explain; Alyssa had to know. 'He cut my arm to get the blood to write with. Then he dripped acid on my breasts. He said he liked the idea of knowing the scars were there under my clothes.' Her voice was a whisper now. 'I always told my husband that the burns – the scars – were the result of an accident in the school chemistry lab. Some accident!' She laughed shakily. 'But I didn't want him to know the truth. I couldn't tell anybody the truth.'

'Except me now.' Alyssa stared ashen-faced at the photo. 'Because you hate me.'

'I don't hate you.' Estella's eyes filled with tears. 'But you didn't believe me. I had to prove I wasn't lying or fantasising. I thought – I thought that night he was going to murder me.'

Alyssa dropped the card and turned away. She covered her face with her hands.

'I'm sorry,' Estella groaned. 'I'm sorry. Wait!' she cried as Alyssa grabbed her leather jacket, pulled it on and ran out into the hall. 'Stop! Don't go yet. I–'

The front door slammed and then the porch door. Estella hurried to the window and watched Alyssa sprint down the dark road. She couldn't run after her and she was in no fit state to get out the car and follow. She was filled with remorse at giving Alyssa such a great shock.

She suddenly longed to talk to Frankie. Tell her she loved her, she was proud of her, and that she had been selfish, thinking only about what she wanted. Of course Frankie would be intrigued by the knowledge that she had a half-sister; of course she would want to meet her and talk. Even if it wasn't a good idea, Estella could perfectly understand.

She went into the hall, picked up the phone and dialled. No answer from the apartment or Frankie's mobile. She must be out with Joe, discussing the divorce settlement. The best she could hope for was that he would be civilised about it.

Estella picked up the card and envelope from the carpet and, holding them by the tips of her fingers, took them into the kitchen and dropped them into the wok. She struck a match, held it to the old paper and watched the flame leap up and begin to devour, licking and burning its way through the memory of horror. For a second the blood on the card seemed to melt and turn bright red, as if it were fresh. A minute later everything was reduced to curling, sparking ash. She dumped the wok in the sink and ran the taps.

Closure. Estella felt a sense of lightness, freedom. The worst had happened and she had survived. She poured herself another glass of white wine and slowly sipped it. She would sleep that night.

She was worried about Alyssa Ward though. More than she cared to admit.

Chapter 32

As she rose through the darkness she became conscious of a sound, but could not think what it was. It went on and on. She felt crushing pressure on her chest and it hurt to breathe. The air she did breathe felt cold. She could not move her body. Or speak. She realised the sound was somebody crying. But who was crying? And why?

She opened her eyes, blinked rapidly and closed them again because the light was too strong. She heard voices, male and female, saw moving shadows behind her closed eyelids. She waited a few seconds before trying to open her eyes again. She started to feel very frightened. Where was she, what had happened? Why was she immobilised, and in so much pain? What was the pressure on her chest? Pain and pressure in her right arm too. Someone grasped her right hand and held it too tightly. She tried to wriggle her fingers free.

'She's awake! Look. She's moving her hand.'

'Get Geoff in here,' someone called. Who was Geoff?

She opened her eyes again and managed to keep them open this time. She saw a white ceiling, yellow walls, yellow curtains around the hard bed she lay in, scary-looking medical paraphernalia. Her bed was in a corner; there was a window to her left, darkness outside. Dazzled, she tried to turn her head as someone shone a pen light into her eyes. When they took it away she started to pick out faces. Two people she didn't know, one a young fair-haired man in a white coat, the other a woman smiling down at her.

'Welcome back, Monique,' the woman said. 'How are you feeling?'

Did she seriously expect an answer? Monique wanted to cough, but tried not to because she felt sure it would rip her chest and abdomen apart. The woman wore green overalls and had some sort of white scarf or handkerchief tied loosely around her neck. Monique realised she was a nurse.

'Mum! Oh Mum, thank God! Mum, I'm so sorry for everything!'

She recognised another face, reddened and tear streaked, framed by a hanging mane of roughened gold hair, as belonging to her daughter. Lauren. What was Lauren sorry for? 'Will she be all right now?' her daughter sobbed. 'Will she live?'

'Yes. No need to worry any more, love. Your Mum's going to be fine. Try and calm yourself, okay? You don't want to upset her, do you?' The nurse reached up to adjust the drip. 'Why don't you pop to the canteen and get yourself something to eat and drink now? You could do with a break. Sorry,' she called to someone who appeared in the doorway. 'She's regained consciousness, but I'm afraid it'll be a while yet before you can talk to her.' She glanced at Lauren again. 'Go on, love.'

'I'll be back soon, Mum. I'm not far away, all right?' Lauren squeezed her hand again then left, sniffing into a bunch of damp pink tissues. Monique slurred her eyes to the right and saw that the person in the doorway who moved aside to make way for her was a uniformed police officer.

Disjointed bits and pieces of sounds and images formed in her confused brain, but broke apart before she could make sense of any of them. She only knew something bad had happened. That was why she was in hospital.

'You lost a lot of blood, Monique,' the nurse was explaining, smiling as if that was good news. 'You're lucky to be alive. We had to transfuse you. We had to operate to get the bullet out. We don't think there's any major damage to your heart, liver or kidneys, but you do have a collapsed lung. That's why we had to put the chest tube in. That's what the funny sucking noise is.'

Monique had not noticed the noise before, but she now became unpleasantly aware of it. Why did this grinning idiot have to tell her stuff like this? It wasn't as if she wanted to know. Of course they wouldn't tell her things she did want to know, like when she could get up and walk out of here. She stared at the policeman before he disappeared. The disjointed images returned, like lights flashing on and off, alternately blinding and illuminating. A terrible realisation hit her.

Conal was dead! She had murdered him – or had him murdered. Same difference. But he was innocent; he hadn't cheated on her or tried to have her killed or . . . what was the other thing? What was Lauren sorry for? For lying. Yes. Lauren had lied about Conal seducing her. Oh God, oh *God*.

Monique started to panic. She wished she had not woken up to this catastrophic, pain-filled reality. She wished that woman had killed her. She remembered a flash as the gun was fired, hearing the bang and the startled rooks cawing in the trees around the house as she stumbled and collapsed, the strength suddenly gone from her body. All the blood pumping out of her onto the ground. Lauren screaming. After that, darkness.

Who was the woman who had shot her in the chest? Not Frankie Sayle. Someone else. Monique did not know her, had never seen her before. Why had the woman shot her when she'd already handed over the money to Frankie? Was that why the policeman was there, to protect her? Or did he intend to arrest her for having her husband murdered? But how did they know it was murder? Frankie Sayle had promised it would look like an accident. Or at least a senseless, unprovoked, stranger attack.

It was all too complicated, too terrifying. The doctor and nurse were moving around the bed now, monitoring drip levels and bleeps on screens, doing various unpleasant and painful things to her. She even had a catheter – how horrible was that? Monique wanted to cry, but she couldn't. She closed her eyes, hoping to slide back into unconsciousness. She wanted to sleep and sleep until this nightmare was over, until she could just get up and not be trapped and helpless any more, leave here and go back to her normal life. If that could not happen she preferred to die.

'Monique?'

Another voice. But no, this was impossible, it couldn't be! What did these people have her on? Morphine, muscle relaxants, blood thinners? Whatever drug cocktail was flowing through her veins and arteries, it was making her hear things now. She couldn't bear it. When would this torture end? The voice went on.

'They told me you were awake. Thank God! I'm sorry, I'm so sorry. You didn't deserve this. Joanna saved you; she heard the shots and drove up to the house. The ambulance got there just in time. I'm still not sure what happened to me, and neither are the police. But don't worry. You're safe now. We both are. That bitch won't get away with this.'

What bitch? Had Frankie and her mystery accomplice been caught? Monique didn't understand. She didn't understand anything. Most of all this voice.

'Monique? Can you open your eyes? Look at me?'

She had to make the effort because once she opened her eyes she would see that there was nobody there, and the relentless voice would stop torturing her. If only she could speak, demand to know what the hell was going on. She opened her eyes again, blinked a few times. A vision of a figure leaning over her wavered and became sharp. Excruciatingly, terrifyingly sharp.

No. It couldn't be. Oh God, now she was hallucinating. But when the nurse came back in and smiled at him, told him he could only have another minute, she realised she wasn't seeing things.

He looked terrible, exhausted and ashen with dark rings around his eyes. He was wearing a bathrobe, so he must be in hospital too. He was leaning over her, touching her face, speaking again, but he might as well have been speaking another language for all Monique could understand, her shock was so great. It *couldn't* be. But it was.

Conal was alive.

'Not this way, lady.' The hired thug blocked her path. 'Only private offices up here.'

'Oh, sorry.' Frankie glanced around, clutching her small but heavy handbag. 'I was looking for the–'

He pointed slowly and deliberately to the sign for the Ladies' Room, raising his thick, straight eyebrows to show his contempt because he didn't want to waste any more precious words on her. She turned and walked away, conscious of his stare. She was sure that the corridor he guarded led to Agron Xhani's office, or suite of offices. Even if she could get to them though, would she find the great man alone? He might not even be here tonight.

She went into the Ladies, all blush-pink walls, ornate gilt mirrors and soft lights, and locked herself in a cubicle. She was trembling. She had been here a couple of hours, mingling with the crowd, fending off several chat-up attempts, accepted a free glass of champagne but not drunk it, and had even won at roulette. Gambling in faultless evening dress, like a character in an old James Bond movie. Only this was The Hague, haunt of politicians and non-fast-track diplomats, not Monte Carlo. She stood there, stroking her bare arms, wondering if she should abort this crazy mission before it was too late and drive back to her Amsterdam hotel. But what then? She would only be putting off the evil hour. If she didn't go to Agron Xhani, he would come to her. And no use terrifying herself with her fantasies of pulling a gun on him when she couldn't even find the bastard. Not a bad idea to have a *plan.* Although to plan you needed information.

Two women came in speaking what she guessed was either Russian or some Eastern European language. One sounded angry, the other soothing. She waited until they had gone, then came out of the cubicle, psyching herself up to go back for another sortie.

She had never visited a casino before but had imagined, perhaps naively, that it would be a more glamorous place. Glamorous was the wrong description though. It was full of seedy, dodgy-looking people, women as well as men. Frankie did not feel safe here, especially being by herself. She felt their curious eyes on her and knew they were looking at her because despite the hair and sexy black dress, she hadn't got it right. There was something about her that told them she did not belong. There was a good crowd milling around the tables and bar, but she couldn't blend in. If she didn't find out something soon she might attract more unwanted attention that could land her in big trouble.

She went out of the Ladies and strolled around the tables again, stopping once more by the roulette table close to the corridor where the thug stood guard. A man had just won a few hundred euros and was promising to buy his excited girlfriend a new pair of shoes. Frankie stood watching. She noticed a dark-haired woman in a glittery, strapless dress go up to the thug.

'I want to see Agron.' She spoke English with a foreign accent. Not a Dutch accent, Frankie thought. 'I need to talk to him.'

'He's busy. Not seeing anyone.'

'When can I see him?'

'You can't.'

'How about later?'

'No.'

She pointed a pearl pink-tipped finger. 'You tell him Natasha needs to talk to him. Okay? And he needs to talk to me, so make sure you give him the message. You got that, you big moron?'

Frankie flinched, thinking the big moron was going to give the woman a big slap, but he merely nodded and re-fixed his calm gaze somewhere above her head. The woman walked off, heading for the bar. So Agron Xhani was here. A minute later two men came up and were also turned away by the guard. Frankie could not linger by the roulette table any longer. A man looked at her and smiled when she caught his eye. She went back to the Ladies and locked herself in the cubicle for another think. She was disturbed and angry with herself to realise that she missed Alyssa and wished she were here now. Alyssa cared about her, maybe loved her, and how many people in her life could she say that about? If she had not allowed Alyssa to get entangled in her own mess Alyssa would never have shot and killed Monique Thorn. Alyssa might have pulled the trigger, but the killing was her fault.

How could she get to Agron Xhani? More to the point, get him alone? He was bound to be surrounded by hired help. If only she knew where he lived. Even there, he might not be alone. She hung her bag on the door hook, leaned against the cold wall and covered her face with her hands. She couldn't stay around here much longer, it was too dangerous. She had to try something else.

It was getting on for midnight. Frankie decided to leave – or pretend to – and take a discreet look around outside. Her car was parked nearby. She collected the money she had won at roulette, thinking it might look suspicious if she didn't, got her coat and walked out past the smirking doormen, keeping her head low. She walked down the road away from the lights, and stopped.

It was dark here, and she could smell the sea. She shivered as she recognised the narrow road along which she and Joe had walked while being tailed by the car full of Agron Xhani's men. She walked further down, glanced around to check no one was watching, then retraced her steps and headed around the back of the building. Keeping herself hidden, she approached the wheelie bins full of rubbish that were ranged on either side of the doors from which she and Joe had been thrown out that terrifying evening. She fastened her coat and slung the long, thin handbag strap over her head and across her body. The bag was stiff black leather with a tiny gold 'A' on the flap, and had a magnetic clasp.

The doors were closed, the overhead light shining on a silvery

303

Mercedes convertible parked a few metres away. A short, dark-haired man in a dark suit stood by the car, smoking and talking on a mobile. Frankie waited fearfully, cowering behind a wheelie bin, ready to run away if he so much as glanced in her direction.

She waited for what seemed like ages. Her legs were just beginning to cramp when the doors opened and another man walked out. He glanced up and down and snapped something to the other man, who quickly terminated his phone conversation. Was the man Agron Xhani's driver? Was Xhani about to leave? And what could she do if he was surrounded by helpers? She would have to run back to her car and try to tail him without being spotted. She tried to memorise the licence plate number, which was Belgian, thin red numbers and letters on the white background.

The two men went back inside, leaving the doors open. The driver – or Frankie assumed he was the driver – came out again a minute later, threw down his cigarette and trod on it, then smoothed his hair. He was tense and alert now. Frankie crept nearer, flinching as she clicked open the handbag clasp and reached inside. Her terror increased. She tried to breathe calmly, quietly. She didn't need a shaking hand now, of all times. But would she even get the chance to see Xhani? He might not be leaving yet. Whatever was going on here might be nothing to do with him.

Another long wait, or it seemed long. The driver was less alert now. He lit another cigarette and exhaled, pacing around. Frankie could smell the smoke. He pulled out his mobile then stuck it back in his jacket pocket. The sky was clouding over, the wind rising, the sound of the sea close by.

Suddenly he dropped the cigarette and crushed it, sprang to open the driver's door and the rear, left-hand passenger door. Frankie pulled the gun from her bag and grasped it with both hands, holding it ready. She was sweating, her heart beating wildly. She moved closer, keeping herself hidden, praying no one would come around the corner and find her. She was almost crying as Agron Xhani finally walked out, alone, an overcoat draped across his shoulders.

He stopped by the car, exchanged a word with the driver and got in. She lowered the gun. This was pointless, she couldn't get to him here. She would have to sprint back to her car and try to follow him. Where did he live? The driver was about to close the passenger door when Xhani said something to him and he paused, gripping the door handle. Xhani got out and pointed, muttered something. The driver nodded and disappeared back inside the building, leaving Xhani standing there alone. He walked around the car and stopped, staring beyond the lights into the darkness, as if listening to the waves tumbling on the nearby beach. Frankie gripped the gun. She wouldn't get another chance. Somebody else might come out at any second. It was now or never.

She broke cover, ran forward, stopped and fired at close range because she was terrified she might miss otherwise. The first shot hit him in the lower back. He staggered, and half turned. She aimed for the chest area and fired twice more. Then at his face; suddenly half of it was gone. Blood, bone and flesh spattered one side of the silvery Merc. The recoil went up her arm and across her shoulders, almost making her lose balance. She was deafened by the noise. She smelled cordite, something metallic. Xhani collapsed, eyes staring at the light over the door, at her. He looked astonished. His mouth was a gaping black hole. Frankie turned and fled. It had all happened in seconds.

She shoved the gun back into her bag as she ran, gasping and grunting, her heart hammering. Away from the building, down the dark road to where her car was parked. Behind her she heard panicked shouts, footsteps pounding the concrete. She reached her car, tumbled in and crouched on the floor while she felt in her bag for the keys. She drove off, nice and easy, slow and steady. Just another car passing by. Her ears were ringing, like after a particularly loud concert. She glanced in the driving mirror, saw three men run out the front entrance of the casino and look wildly around. A group of frightened, bewildered people was already gathering.

Xhani was definitely dead. Would his men call the police? The thought of that made her laugh. She had cut the head off the monster. They wouldn't even imagine one of Xhani's victims had dared to shoot him. Or not her anyway, a frightened woman who wasn't even supposed to be in the country. The police would assume it was just another gangland murder. A turf war, maybe, or whatever they called it.

Frankie increased speed as she headed for the motorway and Amsterdam. Once in the city she drove down a quiet, tree-lined street behind the Rijksmuseum and discreetly dumped the gun and box of bullets in a turgid canal before heading back to her hotel. When she walked into the lobby the tired clerk asked if she had had a pleasant evening. She nodded and smiled, then took the lift up to her room.

She was shaking now, her body bathed in sweat, numb and in incredulous disbelief at what she had done, that not only had she dared to do it but had actually pulled it off. Frankie knew this was shock and that she had to take care of herself now, try to remain calm. She took a long shower, remembering Alyssa's talk about gunshot residues, and drank a Cointreau from the minibar because she didn't like whisky or cognac. Still unable to stop shivering, she made herself a cup of hot, sweet tea. She got into bed, switched off the lamp and made herself lie down and try to relax. Amazingly, she fell asleep.

In the morning she ordered coffee and rolls in her room, surprised that she felt hungry. She drank some coffee and forced herself to switch on the television. She flipped channels until she found an RTL4 news bulletin: the lead story was the gangland murder of Albanian organised crime boss Agron Xhani, which had taken place shortly after midnight. The perpetrator must have been lying in wait and had seized their chance when Xhani was standing alone waiting for his driver who he had sent back into the building to fetch some documents he had forgotten.

Agron had so many enemies that the police didn't know where to start, and there was already a debate about the level of crime committed by foreigners and whether such individuals should ever have been permitted to enter the Netherlands and take up residence. Cut to police examining the crime scene at the rear of the casino, forensics people using tweezers to pick up bullet casings and drop them in plastic envelopes. There was a chalk outline where the body had lain. Blood on the ground.

Frankie gasped and clapped one hand over her mouth, shock hitting her again as she recalled firing the gun, the bullets ripping into his body. But Xhani would have killed her; it was self-defence, not murder. Now she was terrified of being caught, however unlikely that seemed. She tried to calm herself and think. Even if the Dutch police did somehow get on her trail, how were they supposed to prove she had even been in the country when the murder took place? And where was the murder weapon? They had bullets but no gun. They were highly unlikely to find it, unless they wanted to go to the trouble of dragging every canal in Amsterdam. There was no way they would do that.

Frankie told herself to stay calm. She was safe now. The debt had died with Agron Xhani. She hoped Joe was safe too. She drank another cup of coffee and ate a roll with butter and apricot jam. Got dressed and checked out, paying cash when she settled the bill. She realised she was quite rich now. She thought about Monique Thorn again. Who would have imagined their long, on-off friendship and rivalry would have led to this? She still could not believe it. She felt sorry that Monique was dead. That would haunt her for a long time. Much more than Agron Xhani's death.

The morning was grey, threatening rain. She was in the car heading for Schiphol airport when she realised she wanted to go back to The Hague and check the apartment one last time, collect some stuff and perhaps pick up a clue as to Joe's whereabouts. Frankie was not sure it was a good idea, but decided to go ahead nevertheless.

By the time she got to The Hague it was raining. She turned off the motorway and drove through part of the city, past the Binnenhof and tree-lined Lange Voorhout, heading for the Frederik Hendriklaan and the Statenkwartier. A few streets away from the apartment she stopped the car and phoned from a call box. Joe did not answer the phone, or his mobile. She didn't dare call his office. She left the car and walked the rest of the way. She hesitated as she turned into the street, frightened just in case Xhani's men might still be watching and might recognise her. She didn't believe they would be there, but she still felt terrified all over again. She hesitated at the corner. The street was empty except for a few cars she recognised as belonging to various residents.

The first thing Frankie saw were the keys lying on the hall floor. She looked at them, mystified. Joe could not get back in now unless he contacted the landlady and asked for a spare set. Had he dropped them here when he came home, drunk maybe? She didn't want to see him; he would wonder why she had turned up without telling him, and why her hair was different. Was he in bed, asleep? She could not imagine him sleeping under these circumstances. Unless he was drunk. Or dead.

The apartment was chillingly silent. She crept into the sitting room and saw the open, half-empty suitcases on the floor, articles of clothing strewn about. The withered, drooping pot plants. And a note, written by Joe, lying on the dining table next to some unopened post. Raindrops spattered the windows and rolled down; the tiled balcony outside was drenched, water trickling down the drainpipes. Frankie picked up the note and read it. She read it a second time. She gasped, felt herself turn pale.

Joe was not dead. He had left her, really left her this time. To face his mess. Danger, death. It hurt terribly, even though she had suspected he might do a runner. Despite everything that had happened, Frankie still imagined her husband retained some vestige of respect and concern for her, maybe even a little bit of love. She imagined Joe would want to save her from his mess, or at least try. He had said he wanted her back. But there was nothing left. She could be dead now, murdered, as far as he was concerned. He might feel bad about it. But not that bad. Where had he gone? And did it really matter?

She laid the note where he had left it, sank down on a chair and burst into tears. She wept for ten years of marriage, for the love she had lost, for Joe's betrayal, her terror, and what she had had to do to save herself. How could she go on now? How could she ever get over all this?

She would get over it. She was alive. That was what mattered. She had to go on. Frankie dried her eyes. She could not be bothered to collect any stuff now, or even glance at the unopened post. It could wait. Everything could wait. She had time.

She left, locking the apartment door carefully behind her.

Chapter 33

'This is crazy.'

Conal sank back on the sofa, the cognac glass trembling in his hand. He glanced out of the apartment window at the dark city vista of rooftops, clear night sky and shining strip of river, dock cranes outlined against the horizon.

He would not move back to Bay House – he was determined not to be under the same roof as Lauren. She could stay there or at the hospital, make her own arrangements. There was no way he'd let her stay here. She might be sorry for falsely accusing him of seducing her, but as far as Conal was concerned it was too late. The little bitch had done enough damage, could have done a lot more. He no longer felt any responsibility for her and he didn't care if the police or anyone else thought him a callous stepdad. He wished Lauren had got downstairs quickly enough to give a description of or possibly even identify whoever had shot Monique; he didn't give a damn what trauma or danger being a witness could have caused her. Unfortunately Lauren swore she had not seen anything or anyone.

'D'you think it was a wise move to discharge yourself from hospital, Mr Thorn?' One of the detectives put down the photograph of Monique she had been examining – with interest but without his permission. 'Or drink alcohol?'

'Thanks for your concern. I'd rather it translated into finding out exactly what the hell happened to me. And to my wife. And *why*. It just feels weirder and weirder.' Conal took a gulp of cognac, which only made him feel more rotten. 'Maybe that's down to the fact that blood tests show I was drugged with GHB,' he went on before either detective could reply. 'And I'm not feeling too great since a doctor told me there's only a minute difference between a dose that knocks you out for several hours and one that sends you into a coma. I could have died as well as Monique. Getting an eyeful of pepper spray was apparently the least of my worries.'

'Yes, and you're still in shock, which is why I don't think you should have left hospital. Right. As I just told you, your car was found burnt out on a stretch of dockland,' the woman detective said. 'Have you any idea who would have done that? Or why?'

'Is it connected to who shot Monique?'

'I'm afraid we don't know that.'

Conal reached forward, put the glass on the coffee table and wiped his tearing eyes, sniffing. 'It doesn't make sense. None of it does.' Fear and shock returned, making him tremble again. He felt like crying. 'Are you sure Monique's safe now? That I am?'

'Can you think of anyone who might want to murder your wife, Mr Thorn?'

'*Yes.*' Fury gripped him. 'Lindsay bloody Roberts. I've already told you she had a motive – with knobs on! But she couldn't kidnap me and shoot Monique all by herself, so she must have got someone to help her. I know her from way back – she's jealous and vengeful enough to do this. And she was desperate for money. You've seen the letter she wrote me, the one Monique found. I told her to go to hell and so did Monique ... in her own creative way.' He paused, breathing heavily. 'What more motive do you want?'

The detective took a small notebook from her trouser suit pocket and flipped it open. 'We've interviewed Ms Roberts and we'll talk to her again, but she swears she knows nothing about Monique's shooting or your abduction.'

'Yeah, well. She would, wouldn't she?'

'Ms Roberts has got an alibi for that whole night.'

'Oh yeah,' Conal sneered, reaching for his glass again. It was almost empty, so he got up to pour himself more cognac. 'I'll bet she has.'

'Her father and a friend, a Ms Annette Arslanian–'

'*Who*?' He picked up the bottle.

'And three other friends with whom she spent most of the evening – until just after three a.m. – in a city centre nightclub. Two of the doormen remember her.'

'So you believe the word of that vicious little gold-digging

310

scrubber's dear old dad, a few of her pisshead mates and a couple of knobhead bouncers?' Conal turned, clutching his glass. 'Good on you. Classic detective work, that is. Should all stand up brilliantly in court. Not a brief on the planet who could blow that lot out of the water.' He raised the glass in a mocking salute. 'Cheers, guys.'

DI Whatserface frowned. 'I was about to tell you Ms Roberts was caught on camera entering and leaving the nightclub. The CCTV has very high-quality imaging and there's no doubt it's her. She was in the club during the time of your abduction and Monique's shooting took place.'

'She could have sneaked out the back and got in again later.' He knew that sounded pathetic. Conal sat down again.

'No. The club's rear doors are kept locked and guarded at all times.'

'Even if there's a fire,' the male detective added grimly.

'Have you remembered anything else about what happened before you were drugged?'

Conal sighed again and rubbed his eyes. If Lindsay Roberts hadn't shot Monique, who the hell had? 'I just remember this woman coming up to me. She had dark hair, she was pretty. Slim. Wearing jeans and a leather jacket. She said something.' He paused. 'Something I thought was weird. I don't remember what. Next thing I knew, I was waking up in the abbey ruins down the road from my house.'

The detectives glanced at one another. 'Would you recognise this woman again?' the man asked.

'Well, it was dark and I was … I'd had a few. But yeah. I think so.' He shrugged. 'I don't know. I was sure I'd never seen her before.'

'And she squirted pepper spray in your face, then got you to drink that GHB-laced water?'

'It was her who sprayed me, but I couldn't say if she was the one who made me drink the water. I suppose it was. I was in agony, I couldn't see a thing.' Conal drank more cognac. 'I just don't get it! What did she … they — *whoever* — want from me? From Monique? Who shot her and why?'

'Maybe they wanted you out of the way. Wanted to make sure you wouldn't be at home. Mr Thorn.' The woman walked around the sofa and sat down opposite him. 'You and your wife had dinner together that evening, didn't you? Do you remember what you talked about?'

'Not really.' Conal felt himself blush. He didn't want to tell them he and Monique had marriage problems, that he wanted a divorce. He was no longer sure what he wanted. Of course he wouldn't start proceedings while Monique was lying in Intensive Care. 'We talked mostly about business, I think. Monique showed me that letter from Lindsay Roberts, told me how she'd phoned the bitch and said she'd give twenty grand to a dog's home rather than her. We laughed.' He blinked back tears.

'Why did you return to this apartment and Monique to the house?'

He shrugged. 'We often did that. I had to keep going back and forth to the hospital to get my wound dressed and checked, so it was more convenient to stay here.' His arm and shoulder ached as he spoke.

'Oh yes. Your shotgun accident. Shot yourself accidentally, I believe?'

Conal was sweating now. 'That's right. It was really stupid.' They would probe and probe, like surgical instruments in a wound. He didn't want to tell them about Lauren's crazy accusation, even though she had retracted it and apologised. They might think there was no smoke without fire. It was best to say as little as possible. He decided to go on the offensive.

'If you don't think Lindsay Roberts shot Monique – and I still think she could have – what else are you doing to try and get to the bottom of all this?'

'Oh, plenty, I can assure you.' The detective tucked a strand of hair behind one ear and flashed him a quick smile. Her grey-blue eyes looked mild, sympathetic even. But that did not fool him. As Monique's husband, Conal was well aware that the police might consider him a major suspect even though he appeared to be an innocent victim. He leaned back on the sofa, overwhelmed with exhaustion again. It went beyond exhaustion; it was leaden, draining fatigue of a kind he had never experienced. Was this still the after-effects of the drug, even though it was supposed to be out of his system by now? He shuddered again to think that it could have sent him into a coma or killed him.

'Of course, what we really need now is some input from Mrs Thorn,' the male detective said, his voice brisk.

312

'Yes. Hopefully Monique will be able to tell us what happened, maybe even identify her attacker. Or give a description.' The woman closed her notebook and slipped it back in her pocket. 'The doctor says she might be able to talk to us tomorrow. Briefly, anyway.' She stood up, smiled her gentle smile again. 'We'll leave you to get some sleep now, Mr Thorn.'

Conal staggered after them because he needed to lock up. He put the bolt and chain on and stood leaning against the door, his legs trembling. He heard them walk away. Their footsteps stopped at the lift.

'Any thoughts?' the woman asked in a low voice.

'I wish!' Her colleague gave a short laugh. 'It's all as clear as mud to me. If the wife can't tell us what happened–' A ping and the sound of the lift doors opening cut off the rest of his sentence.

Conal switched off the lights, staggered into the bedroom and collapsed across the bed, too tired to brush his teeth or undress. The thought of oblivion unnerved him now though, and for a while he fought against sleep. He forced his eyes open and stared at the light patterns flitting across the white ceiling, listened to distant city sounds muffled by the double-glazing. He gave a long sigh and his head drooped to one side. He began to sink down and down. Suddenly the dark-haired woman was standing in front of him and he was looking into her clear eyes. She was speaking and this time he could hear what she was saying.

'Mr Thorn, I'm a private detective. Your wife hired me to follow you.'

Conal gave a groan. Another piece of the memory jigsaw slotting back into place. And this could be crucial, even though he didn't understand it. He had to tell the police, phone them now. He struggled to wake up, move his body. But it was no use.

Oblivion.

'You look terrible.' Estella came into the sitting room where Frankie lay on the sofa wrapped in her blue dressing gown, staring into the glowing coals of the fire she had insisted on lighting immediately after she had got home and unpacked. Two candles burned on top of the mantelpiece. 'You should get to bed.'

'I'll go soon. Oh, thanks.' Frankie sat up and took the cup of tea. 'I should be waiting on you,' she muttered.

313

'No. Someone who can dye their beautiful chestnut locks that appalling shade of blonde definitely needs a lot of looking after.'

'It was a mistake.' Frankie could not of course tell her mother why she had dyed her hair.

'An aberration? Temporary, I hope.'

'I'll dye it back in the morning. I bought some stuff in Boots.'

'Don't you think you should go to a hairdresser instead of doing it yourself?'

'I can't be bothered.'

Estella sat down. 'You're not still cold, are you?'

'A bit.' Frankie was highly relieved to have made it back, and was comforted by her mother's presence. Everything seemed more normal now, recent horrific events a world away. She just wanted to lie on the sofa and not answer any questions. She looked into the fire again; Monique Thorn's passport was burned now. No trace.

'Well, it is chilly this evening. I suppose it's nerves getting to you as well. Can't have been pleasant to see Joe again. I know you're tired, love, but you haven't said much about that. Did you get things sorted out? Nasty, practical things, I mean.'

'Not exactly.' There was no need to lie or conceal this. 'Joe's gone. And before you ask, I haven't a clue where.'

'Gone?' Estella stared at her. 'But why? He asked you to go over there again so that you could both talk. Didn't he?'

'Yes. Well.'

'What an ...! D'you think his lady friend persuaded him to go off with her?'

'Don't know.' Frankie thought of Lida. The rape, the beating that had been meant for her. She wondered if she would ever see Lida again; she thought not. Hoped not. She wondered why she could not feel more angry with Joe. Perhaps that would come.

'How dare he treat you like this!' Estella's face looked flushed in the firelight. 'He turns your life upside down, tells you he wants a divorce, and now he decides to just go off somewhere instead of meeting you to discuss things. What's the point of behaving so childishly?'

'Mum, please.' Frankie sat up and drank her tea. 'Don't get aerated, especially not about Joe. He's not worth it. Nothing is. I've learned that much.' She paused. 'You didn't tell Val or anyone that I'd gone back to the Netherlands, did you?'

'No. Don't worry. Although I don't know why it had to be such a big secret.'

'It's called having a personal life. People not knowing my business all the time.'

Estella was silent. Then she looked at her. 'You don't seem to mind some people knowing your business.'

'What's that supposed to mean?' A frisson of fear ran through her.

'*She* came here.' Estella got up and straightened a photograph on the mantelpiece. 'Yesterday. Just turned up.'

'You mean–' Frankie had thought she was too tired and numbed to feel any more shock.

'Yes. Alyssa Ward. Seems you two know each other quite well.'

Frankie put her cup on the floor. 'What did she tell you?'

'Not a lot, really, considering. She didn't tell me much about herself except that she's been living abroad for the past ten years and isn't married. No children. That was a relief, frankly; I'm glad not to have to face the prospect of grandchildren as well. Although I imagine most people would expect me to be delighted about that. She knew about your situation, about Joe. She said you'd met several times.'

So Alyssa had not told Estella the truth. Or not the whole truth. Frankie did not know whether to be relieved or deeply worried. 'Look.' She scrambled off the sofa. 'I know how you must feel and I'm really sorry. I should never have gone behind your back like that, I shouldn't have–'

'Stop.' Estella held up one slim hand. 'It's all right. I don't blame you,' she said quietly. 'I blame myself. I've been stupid, selfish. Of course you'd be intrigued to discover you had a sister; of course you'd want to meet her. I don't mind any more, really. I'm just concerned for you. To be honest, I didn't like her much and I didn't trust her. I thought there was a lot she could have said but didn't. Of course we were both on edge.'

'It must have been an awful shock for you. Your worst nightmare, what you always dreaded.' Frankie was pierced with guilt and worry, furious at Alyssa. How dare she turn up here like this after what she had told her about Estella! She must have wanted to talk to me, she thought, try and persuade me she did the right thing by killing Monique Thorn. And of course I wasn't here.

'Yes, it was a shock.' Estella nodded. 'But not as bad as I

thought. I realised I'd been half expecting it. Ever since I got that letter. Somehow it was a relief. In the end, I think it was a good thing. I don't feel frightened any more.

'Really?' Frankie's mouth had gone dry. She sat down again. 'Well, I suppose that's something. Do you want to see her again?'

'I'm not sure. I don't think so. Not for a while anyway.' Estella hesitated. 'Do you?'

'I'm not sure either.'

'Actually – I'm a bit worried about her. She ran off in a state.'

'*You're* worried about *her*? She wasn't worried about you, was she, if she could just turn up on your doorstep? I told her not to even think of doing that; I told her you'd had a heart attack and needed rest and quiet, no more shocks – Mum, are you *sure* you're okay?' Fear ran through her. 'I can't believe you're so calm about this.' Her eyes filled with tears. 'I'm so sorry I betrayed you! Alyssa Ward came here before. I'd just got back from visiting you in hospital one day when she turned up. That's how we met. She had the back door key. She sneaked in here the night you were taken ill – it must have been before Carole or Barry had a chance to lock up – and took a look round.'

Estella stiffened. 'She didn't tell me that.'

'I bet she didn't. I don't know why I listened to her. I should have told her to get lost there and then. I should have called the police.' Frankie decided not to tell her mother that Alyssa had spent the past ten years in jail for murder. It would be too much at once. Estella must have been shaken by Alyssa's visit, despite her calm exterior. She looked at her. 'Are you really okay?' she repeated. 'I couldn't bear anything else to happen to you. I love you.' She started to cry. 'And you're the only person in this bloody world who loves me.'

'Come on now.' Estella stepped forward and hugged her. 'I'm fine, I promise you. Worry about yourself, not me. Your old mother's going to be around to nag you for a good few years yet. You're not alone,' she whispered. 'You've got me. And I know it's hard about Joe. So very hard. But you'll get over him. You'll build a new life. You might meet someone else one day, but it doesn't matter if you don't. You'll be happy again, you'll be all right. Hush, darling, don't cry.'

Frankie was not crying for Joe, but for herself. The enormity of what she had done was starting to sink in and it was terrifying, more terrifying than when she had done it. Alyssa did not know she had killed Agron Xhani, but she knew the situation. And Monique Thorn, what about *that*? Alyssa knew so much about her. Too much. What would she do with that knowledge? Frankie drew away, wiping her eyes on her sleeve.

'You said Alyssa ran off in a state. Why?'

Estella sat down and looked into the fire again. 'I told her some things about her father.' Her voice was low, almost a whisper. 'They were unpalatable, to say the least. She didn't want to believe me at first; she preferred to think I'd made it up to justify leaving him – and her. So I had to prove I was telling the truth.'

'About what?' Frankie listened, horrified as Estella told her. 'Oh my God,' she breathed. '*Acid*. Why didn't you …? No. I suppose I can guess why you didn't tell me.'

'I never told your father either. I was too ashamed. I've kept so many secrets all these years. That's why I feel so relieved after last night. But it was a big shock to her. That's why she ran off.'

Frankie wondered. She was no longer sure of anything Alyssa had told her, even whether she was innocent of her stepmother's murder. She recalled the cold-blooded way Alyssa had pointed that gun at Monique and fired twice. Okay, she herself was a killer now too. But that was self-defence. Frankie wished she could forget about Alyssa and never see her again. But she did not think it was going to be that simple.

'I need a big vodka and tonic,' she muttered. 'Do you want something?'

Estella gave a little smile. 'I'll have a lovely, dark, sticky sherry.'

'Coming up.' Frankie was in the kitchen pouring their drinks when the phone rang. She started and put down the vodka bottle, gave a gasp and glanced at the clock. Ten-past eleven. Estella came out into the hall and hesitated.

'Might be Val,' she said. 'Or –'

'Or.' Frankie handed her the glass of sherry. 'I'll get it.' She ran down the hall and picked up the receiver. 'Hello?' Her heart was thudding. She was going to hate answering the phone for a long time to come.

'Frankie? It's me. Joe.'

She sat down on the pile of ironing on the hall chair, wishing she had her own drink in her hand. 'Where are you?'

Estella stood there, her mouth forming the word 'Who?' Frankie grabbed a biro and scribbled his name on the phone pad. Her mother nodded, grimaced and disappeared into the sitting room, closing the door behind her.

'Where am I?' He laughed. 'At home, of course.'

For a second she couldn't think where he meant. 'The apartment?'

'Yeah. Where else?' His voice was high, excited and frightened. 'Frankie, listen. I'm safe. We both are. Xhani's dead – murdered. Someone shot him last night, gunned him down round the back of his casino as he was leaving. One of his gangland rivals, the police think, although they haven't arrested anyone yet. Frankie, did you hear me? We're safe now. His men kidnapped me.' He sniffed, choked back what sounded like a sob. 'Held me for a couple of days, tied up in some dark room, I don't know where. I was terrified; I thought they'd kill me. But this morning they let me go. Took me out in a car, blindfolded, and dumped me out in the sticks. I didn't know what the hell was going on. When I got home a few hours later I switched on the news and found out he was dead.' He laughed. 'Isn't it great? Christ, I'm so happy! I'm sitting here with a bloody big Scotch in my hand. Still in shock, of course, but–'

'They kidnapped you?' she interrupted. 'How? Where?'

He hesitated. 'Near our place. Why? What does that matter?'

She guessed they must have grabbed him on his way to the airport. Or maybe at the airport. 'I hadn't heard from you. I thought you'd done a runner.'

'What? Come on. You didn't think I'd bugger off somewhere and leave you to face the danger all alone?'

Frankie thought of the note he had left her. Of course he did not realise she had seen it; he thought she'd been here all the time. 'Actually, I did think that.'

'Look. I know I've been a bastard, but I'd never sink that low. Did you manage to get together any money while you've been over there?'

'No.'

'Well, it doesn't matter now. Christ, we're safe, it's all over. I can't believe it. Who would have thought somebody would have gunned down the bastard just hours before we were supposed to pay him a hundred grand? Talk about timing.'

'Incredible, isn't it?' She felt numb again.

'You don't sound very excited.'

'I've had just about enough of excitement.'

'Yeah, you've got that right. So have I. By the way, there's a letter for you. From some literary agent in London. He says he loved the sample chapters you sent, and now he wants to read the rest of your novel. Shall I give you his address?'

Frankie wrote it down. Even that did not make her feel excited. 'I take it you're not going to report your abduction to the Dutch police?'

'You must be joking. I'm not planning to get involved with the police in any way. Especially not over this business.'

'What about Lida? I mean, the investigation into her rape and beating?'

'She couldn't identify her attackers and neither could I, even though we knew who was responsible. But if we'd grassed up Agron Xhani we would have been dead sooner. Their investigation won't go anywhere. And it's not like they give a toss about some raped woman. Lida will keep her mouth shut, and so will I.'

'How do you know Lida will keep her mouth shut?'

He hesitated. 'Well, I – actually I spoke to her earlier.'

'You did?' Frankie could not suppress a pang of hurt.

'Not to try and get back with her or anything,' he said hastily. 'Just to make sure she'd keep quiet. There was no answer from her apartment, so I phoned her parents' house, thinking at least they could tell me how she was. Lida answered – they were out. She's staying there convalescing. She said she just wants to get back to work as soon as possible. She's going to have plastic surgery on her facial scar. She wasn't interested in how I was – suppose I can't blame her. But she said to tell you she was sorry.'

Frankie blinked back tears. 'Well, I suppose she's learned a lesson.'

He sighed. 'So have I.'

'I've had to learn some lessons too. Like how someone you love and trust can not only betray you big time, but end up nearly getting you killed. It's no thanks to you I'm safe. You did *nothing*.'

Joe sighed again. 'Of course you're angry. You've every right to be.'

'Thanks for that.'

'Can you get a flight tomorrow? I'll meet you at Schiphol. We've got a lot to talk about, Frankie.'

'I don't think we've got anything to talk about, apart from things like splitting the CD collection. It's all very clear.'

'Frankie, *please*.'

'I'll come back to get the rest of my stuff when I'm ready. That won't be tomorrow. I'm not coming back to you. Not after what you've done. I mean, which bit is any self-respecting spouse supposed to overlook?'

'You're crying, you're upset. Frankie, I've been a total shit, I know that. But I do still love you – very much. We can put this behind us, I know we can. If you'll just give me a chance.'

'You've had all the chances you're going to get.'

She replaced the receiver and ran upstairs. In her bedroom she dragged her battered black suitcase out from under the bed, unlocked it and lifted the lid. She crouched and stared at the neat stacks of money. A bit more than one hundred thousand pounds. She could smell it, and it smelled good.

'Cheer up,' she muttered, brushing away tears. 'Things could be a lot worse.'

She locked the suitcase, pushed it back under the bed and went downstairs. Got her vodka and tonic, drank it and poured another. Estella was sitting by the fire sipping sherry. She looked round and smiled. Didn't ask.

Frankie sat on the sofa again. 'Just bullshit.'

She could never tell her mother what she had done. There was only one person she could tell. One person who would understand. *There is no friend like a sister. In calm or stormy weather.* But she didn't want anything more to do with Alyssa Ward, did she?

'I'll get us some supper.' Estella finished her sherry. 'I fancy a slice of toast. Some cold ham and a bit of that mature Cheddar.'

'Cheese? You'll get nightmares. I'll join you.'

She laughed and stood up. 'Oh, by the way, there's something I meant to show you.' She went out and returned with a copy of the local paper. 'I thought I recognised this woman, although it's years since I last saw her.'

Frankie took the paper and stared at the headline: WOMAN GUNNED DOWN OUTSIDE HER HOME. She gasped and a wave of panic hit her. She glanced up, but Estella had gone out. She heard her put the kettle on and open the fridge door.

Police are investigating the shooting of glamorous local businesswoman Monique Thorn, gunned down outside her country home on Tuesday night.

No motive for the shooting has been established. She was taken to intensive care and was critical for a time, but is now off the danger list. Mrs Thorn's teenage daughter Lauren was asleep upstairs when the attack took place; the person or persons responsible escaped unseen. Police are treating it as attempted murder. Mrs Thorn's husband Conal was also mysteriously kidnapped the same night and ...

Monique was *alive*? Frankie leaned her head back and closed her eyes. A heap of glowing coals settled with a tinkling sound, and a spark hissed up the chimney. She could not think what Monique would do now. Or could do. She could hardly tell the police she had hired someone to murder her husband but got ripped off. Especially after she had decided she didn't want him stiffed after all. Frankie imagined Monique waking up in hospital to find Conal alive, maybe sitting at her bedside. How the hell would *that* turn out now? One thing was sure; she had her hundred grand, and she didn't plan to give back one penny of it. Estella came in from the kitchen.

'One round of toast or two?'

Frankie opened her eyes and sat up. 'Two, please. Hey, I'll make it.'

'No, you sit there. It is her, isn't it? The Monique you used to be friends with?'

'Yes.'

'I never liked her, as you know. Too much of a glamour puss. And a bad influence.' Estella pointed to the fuzzy black-and-white picture of Monique that accompanied the article. 'Terrible what happened to her though, isn't it? And her husband. Maybe it was burglars who shot her and kidnapped him. A gang. Although it doesn't say anything was stolen. I wouldn't fancy living in some isolated house in the country, no matter how beautiful it was.' Estella paused. 'I don't suppose you've seen her for years, have you?'

'No.' Frankie laid the paper down and stared into the fire. 'No, not for years.'

Chapter 34

The acid torture thing.

That's just coincidence of course. It has to be. Ditto the photo taking. My father never took any pictures of me. Or of Vivienne. I don't remember even seeing him hold a camera. He just wasn't interested.

Estella must be lying. Lying when she said my father did that to her, I mean. I realised that once I'd got back to the flat and was sitting drinking a glass of wine and trying to calm myself. Okay, it was her, my mother, in the photograph. No doubt about that. She looked young, much younger; I could see more of myself in her.

Someone did something awful to her; I believe that much. But it wasn't him, it can't have been. I remember Tomás making some quip about how my father could have hired a hit man to kill Vivienne and made sure he was abroad when the murder took place. That seems as ridiculous to me now as it did then. Besides, as Vivienne's husband, he was still a suspect even if the police did believe they had already got their woman. Tomás told me they investigated my father, but didn't find anything suspicious.

I wished fervently that there was someone I could ask, talk to about this. But the only family he'd had left was a sister, my Aunt Katrina, who was killed in a car crash when I was twelve. She was nice and I missed her. Friends? Don't make me laugh. Or go on, yes, do; I need the chuckle. Any friends my father has got left – or made since I went inside – aren't likely to talk to me now, even if I knew where to find them. There was only one person I could talk to – Tomás.

I wanted to go over to his place there and then, but restrained myself. I didn't fancy finding him with the lovely Linda, gate-crashing their cosy evening. I can't stand other people's warmth and intimacy; it's too painful for me. I'm always on the outside looking in. Cue the violins.

I didn't wonder how my mother could do this to me, as if abandoning me wasn't enough. I've given up wondering how people can do terrible things to one another because it's beginning to sound like an incandescently stupid and naive question, especially after everything that's happened to me. People do bad things to others because they can. Because they don't care, and they can get away with it. Someone could make me do the time for their crime. And they did. End of story. Get over it. Trouble is, I can't.

I wondered if Estella would tell Frankie I'd been to see her. I guessed she would. How could she not? Frankie would be furious, of course, and hate me even more.She would regard it as another excuse to shove me out of her life now that I'd helped her and thereby served my purpose. I asked several times where Frankie was, but all Estella would tell me was that she'd gone to visit a friend and was staying the night. That could have been true, of course, but I didn't believe it. Perhaps she and Tomás had got together and he was having the cosy evening with my sister instead of Linda. Nah, not that either. Not yet anyway.

I think Frankie took a short flight across the North Sea to the Netherlands with one very stupid, dangerous idea in her head, i.e. to try and negotiate with a psycho. That freaked me, but there was nothing I could do. I'm sure she didn't tell her mother what she was up to, because she's so big on not worrying her. Wonder how that feels, to know someone loves you, has your interests and happiness at heart? I had that once – briefly – but have practically forgotten how it feels. Oh, pity poor me.

I didn't sleep that night. Or not much; I suppose I fell into a doze now and then. I lay staring at the orange light slanting across the ceiling – my cheap, nasty curtains aren't lined – and thought how if Frankie's crazy plan didn't succeed Estella would not just end up worried; she would have tragedy on her hands. I felt desolate and anguished beyond words, weary and heartsick of all the doors that kept slamming in my face no matter what I did or tried to do. How could I go on? Was I such a wicked person, so repugnant, so unlovable? I suppose I was, especially now that I'd finally done what most people believed I was guilty of all along: *Murder*.

It was murder. What was the point of trying to pretend otherwise? I was crazy to shoot Monique Thorn. Frankie was right; it wasn't necessary. What would the woman have done when she found out she'd been tucked up, complain to the police? Besides, she had changed her bloody mind. Hubby was alive after all, so she'd got what she wanted. Or would have.

What I wanted to say to Estella, what I tried to hint at was, you've got me if you need me. If your daughter – the one you decided to keep – ends up dead, murdered by this gangster because of her shit of a husband's gambling debts, I'm here for you. And if Frankie's done what I think she's done, that's likely to happen very soon. Oh God, my sister! I've got to do something, I've got to help her. But what can I do? I wasn't allowed to go abroad and even if I was I had no passport.

I decided to tell Tomás about Frankie's terrible predicament. Of course I wouldn't tell him what she and I had done, especially what I'd done. I would just tell him she was in great danger and needed help. I didn't know if there was anything he could do, but I was sure he would want to try.

Next morning I felt sick again and had a headache. This drinking doesn't agree with me. Although would it agree with anyone when consumed in these quantities? I showered and slowly got dressed, put on make-up to try and hide my bags and wrinkles, and left the flat. I wanted to get out early and stay out most of the day in case Carl took it into his head to call round again. He had probably written a lengthy report about my bad attitude and was having meetings with various other sanctimonious bastards to discuss it. What a waste of the space-time continuum! I was walking down Bold Street, shivering in the grey frosty morning, when I stopped and ran into an alleyway because I thought I'd have to throw up.

I didn't, but I still felt terrible. Maybe a coffee and some toast would settle my heaving stomach in which nothing but bile and red wine sloshed around. Nerves weren't helping either. I should try to calm down, no matter how freaked and unhappy I felt. I went into a café. The woman smiled at me and called me 'luv'. Almost one of the family. I sat at a table and took a bite of hot, buttered toast. At a nearby table a big, bearded bloke in a denim jacket was leafing through a crumpled copy of yesterday's *Echo*.

I looked at the black hairs that grew over the backs of his hands and wondered if his body was all matted over with thick black hair. Imagine getting a mouthful of it ... oh, don't even go there. He lifted one hairy paw to turn another page, and that's when I saw the headline about Monique Thorn. I could hardly wait for him to wolf his Full English and get out so I could read the article.

She wasn't dead! I felt the burden lift immediately, and my body grew light. Like a dove released from a cage, or a balloon from its string. I couldn't finish my breakfast, could barely pull myself together enough to count out money for the bill. Walking along the street again, I thought of Frankie. If she was in the Netherlands she wouldn't know this great news. I had to find Tomás, had to tell him to help her. There must be something he could do.

He was in his office getting ready for court. The clerk didn't want to let me see him, but I would have punched her, fought my way through and yelled his name until he heard me and came out. She couldn't stop me. Tomás was surprised to see me, but not anxious or embarrassed; at least I didn't get that impression. He drew me away from the clerk's curious, angry stare and ushered me into his office, closed the door. He made me sit down and tell him my story.

I also told him what my mother had said about my father, how she had accused him of torturing her with acid and that was why she'd finally left him. How I didn't believe her. That I was lonely and frightened. So frightened for Frankie. The words spilled out, broken and disjointed. I almost told him about Monique Thorn, but stopped myself just in time.

When I was finished he got up and touched me lightly on the shoulder. Those light touches! I couldn't bear it; I wanted more. I stood up and put my arms around him. I wanted him to hold me, to tell me everything would be all right. I wanted him to tell me he loved me.

That didn't happen. Tomás stroked my hair and kissed my hot forehead, told me to try and calm down. He said to sit here quietly and try to relax while he made a phone call. He'd bring me some tea. He went out of the big, panelled office, leaving me sitting there crying. I realised that no matter what happened with Frankie or with him, I was going to have to do something about myself. Of course I didn't want to go back to prison, but the fact was that after so many years inside I couldn't cope with the outside. I didn't know what to do. It was all too much. I needed help. It gave me some relief to admit that to myself. But not much. Tomás came back a few minutes later. He sat down beside me on the sofa and put a cup of tea in front of me. The cup and saucer were porcelain with a blue-and-gold pattern. Wedgwood, I think. Only the best for a place like that. I didn't want the tea, but I could hardly ask for some hair of the doggie that bit me.

'Who did you call?' I asked, twisting round to face him. 'Someone in the Netherlands?'

'No.' He took my hand. His dark eyes were grave. 'I phoned Frankie's mother's house. I just spoke to Frankie.'

'You *what*?' I gasped. 'But she – she–'

'She's not in the Netherlands and she hasn't been back there. Frankie's all right,' he said. 'She's fine.' He paused. 'But I don't think you are, Alyssa.'

'Can we remember I'm the victim here?' Monique croaked. 'I've had enough of this interrogation.' She was getting more angry and frightened by the minute.

'We're not interrogating you, Monique, just asking a few questions to try and establish what happened.' The fair-haired detective who she hated smiled her false smile again.

'It feels like interrogation to me. I've told you all I remember; now leave me alone.'

She glared at her solicitor, seated in the corner hardly bothering to take any notes, then sank back against the pillows. She was bathed in sweat, tortured by the pain and pressure in her chest. Her collapsed lung was re-inflated now, or whatever the bloody doctors and nurses termed it, and they had removed the tube that had caused her so much aggravation. She was making great progress for someone who had what they revoltingly described as a 'sucking' chest wound. But Monique was frightened, sick and tired of everything and everybody.

Except Conal, of course. She was incredulous, delighted and relieved to discover he was alive after all. She remembered everything now. Not all of it made sense to her, but one thing was sure: Frankie Sayle had tucked her up good and proper. She had never had any intention of killing Conal. She and her mate, whoever that murderous bitch was, had intended to make her think he was dead.

By the time Conal staggered home drugged and dazed from the abbey ruins, Frankie would have taken the rest of her money and disappeared.

Of course things had got out of sync when Monique had fallen apart big time. For a while. That wasn't supposed to happen. She had nearly ruined everything. Monique was certain Frankie had not intended her trigger-happy friend to shoot her after she had finally handed over the rest of the money. But so what? She couldn't grass the pair of them up without landing herself deep in the excrement as well. She had to keep quiet now, and Frankie Sayle knew it.

The only good thing was that Conal was still alive. Monique realised how much she loved him, how her stupidity and paranoia had almost caused her to lose him for ever. She hoped that now she could salvage their marriage. And that no one would guess what had really happened. But that was hardly likely; the whole thing was so bizarre. Even if someone did guess, they couldn't prove anything.

'Okay, let me just recap.' The detective nodded as Monique's solicitor glanced pointedly at his watch. 'You say you answered the front door and an unknown man you had never seen before just stepped forward and shot you.'

'That's right,' Monique whispered.

'And according to your description he was of average height, stocky build, wearing dark clothes. You think he was in his late thirties or early forties. Sparse hair, light coloured, perhaps ash blond or silver, you couldn't tell.' She frowned. 'Your daughter doesn't remember hearing the door bell, Monique.'

'It didn't ring. I heard someone outside, so I opened the door.'

'Was that wise, at that time of night?'

'I deserved to be attacked, is that what you're saying?'

'No, of course not.'

'*Of course not.* I thought it might be a neighbour. Or – or my husband.'

'I see. Did you hear anything? A car, for instance, a motor bike?'

'Not that I recall.'

'It seems very strange that this man would just shoot you without first saying what he wanted.'

'Well, obviously he *just* wanted to shoot me!' God's sake,

328

Monique thought, get me out of this. 'I panicked; I think I yelled something at him. Maybe he panicked too.'

'Bear with me, Mrs Thorn. We really need your help. Anything you can remember. You've no idea why someone would shoot you? Or why anyone would drug and abduct your husband and leave him tied up in those ruins?'

'No idea at all. I don't know anything more than I've told you. Look, I'm in pain and I'm exhausted. I've had enough. Just leave me alone.' Monique turned her head away from them, her eyes full of angry, frightened tears. She was deeply relieved to see the friendly, dark-haired nurse enter. The nurse smiled at her and looked at the others.

'Doctor says that's it for now.'

The girl detective looked disappointed. 'We'll come back later.'

'No, the doctor means that's it for today. Mrs Thorn's making excellent progress, but she's still very weak and not up to extended questioning.'

'Hardly call it *extended*,' the male detective grumbled as they were ushered out. The solicitor nodded to her and followed. A minute later Conal came back in. Monique was relieved to see him. She wished he would stay with her all the time.

'Did Karen's mother come to pick up Lauren?' she asked.

He nodded. 'She's staying the night with them. I told her to go back to school tomorrow and take a cab here afterwards. Hopefully those people will have her for another night. They seem to like her.' Conal shrugged, as if mystified at the idea that anyone would like Lauren. And Monique could not blame him.

'She really is sorry.' She reached out one hand and laid it over his. 'Desperately.'

'Yeah. Well.' He shrugged again, pulled his hand away and strolled to the window.

Monique's heart sank. She longed, however unreasonably, for Conal to be more affectionate towards her. At first she had thought things might be all right between them. But now, especially since the police could find no evidence that Lindsay Roberts was to blame for her shooting or his kidnapping, Conal seemed puzzled most of the time, staring at nothing, lost in another world. He sat silently by her bedside during his brief visits, or stood gazing out of the window. It unnerved her and she wished she knew what was going on in his head. Maybe his behaviour was the result of shock, post-traumatic stress.

Monique was in shock herself. She would never be the same again after this. She would have great big scars across her chest from the bullet wound and subsequent operation. The doctors kept going on about how lucky she was to have no permanent damage to vital organs. Was Conal figuring out what had happened, or trying to? Surely it would never cross his mind that she had planned to have him murdered? Monique could scarcely believe it herself. Thank God Frankie Sayle hadn't done it. Thank God, thank God. She could keep her bloody hundred grand.

Monique wondered if Frankie's story about owing a huge sum of money to some gangster was true. Who the hell was that other woman, the bitch who had shot her? Strangely enough, she and Frankie bore a slight resemblance to one another. As if they were cousins or even sisters. But Frankie Sayle had no sisters, and no cousins either as far as she knew. Well, sod that family tree. Monique looked at Conal again. She wanted to forget all about Frankie Sayle and her sidekick.

'Are you okay?' she whispered. A tear ran down her cheek. 'Conal, please talk to me. Please tell me you still–' No, she thought. Don't push it. He needs time.

'You want me to give Lauren a chance.' He turned away from the window, hands clenched in his jeans pockets. 'But if she'd got me arrested and charged with having it away with a minor, *I* wouldn't have stood a chance. That little cow could have ruined my life.' He paused. 'And you could have ended it.'

She flinched with horror. Her chest, her heart, ached. 'I can't tell you how sorry I am!' she whispered. 'How sorry Lauren is. But look at me now.' More tears flooded her eyes. 'Haven't I paid for what I did? Haven't I been punished enough?'

'I don't know who'd want to punish you,' he frowned. 'Or why. Apart from me, and I didn't shoot you. If the police are right about Lindsay Roberts not having anything to do with this, I just don't …' He paused again. 'I remembered something else last night. About that woman who drugged me. Or who I think drugged me. She told me she was a private detective who you'd hired to follow me.'

'What? That's – that's *rubbish*.' Monique stared at him,

330

horrified. 'I never hired anyone to follow you, I wouldn't! You don't believe it?'

'I don't know what to believe any more. Why would she say that?'

'I don't know! It doesn't make sense. Are you sure you've remembered right?'

'Yeah. Well . . . I think so.'

She scarcely dared ask the question. 'Have you told the police?'

'I was going to. But now – I dunno. I could have got it wrong. I still feel like crap, tired all the time. I don't even trust my own judgement or memory any more. This is all so–' He sat down and buried his head in his hands. 'What the *fuck* happened?' His voice was muffled, choked. 'It's doing my head in.'

Why had Frankie Sayle or her companion said *that*? Was it a ploy to get his attention, draw him in, put him off guard? Probably. Monique hoped Conal would not tell the police what he had remembered. She felt desperately sorry for him. But she could never tell him the truth, not if she didn't want to go straight from here to a maximum security jail. The thought that she might have confessed to murder – or attempted murder – horrified her now. She stretched out one hand and touched his hair, but Conal jerked away.

'Look, I need some help to cope with all this,' she said. 'I think you do too.'

'Help? A shrink, you mean?' Conal raised his head and stared at her, his eyes full of tears. Monique thought again how gorgeous he was, how handsome. She wished he would take her in his arms – not that that was possible right now. Another disturbing thought struck her. When – if ever – would they make love again? Would Conal want her any more? The future was looking darker and darker.

'I don't need a shrink.' He jumped up, suddenly furious. 'What I need is to find out what *happened*. Why would some guy shoot you like that, for no reason? It doesn't make sense. Didn't he want money? He must have wanted something.'

'I don't know.' Monique suppressed a sob. 'He might have been going to tell me, but I panicked. Like I told *them*. I should have stayed cool, I realise that, but it's not every night you open your door to find someone pointing a gun at you!'

'I get kidnapped and you get shot – in one evening. Why? What was the plan?'

331

'I don't know. Whatever it was, maybe it went wrong. Don't go,' Monique begged as he strode towards the door and pulled it open. 'Conal, please don't leave!'

'I have to get out of here.' He turned, wiping his eyes on his sleeve. 'I need to be alone. Try and think.'

'I don't want to be alone. I'm frightened, I'm in pain. I need you. Please don't go.'

'Sorry. I'll see you tomorrow.' The door swung shut behind him.

'Conal!' Monique started to panic again. She could have been at home now instead of stuck here helpless and in pain. Drinking champagne, wearing a sexy dress over an unscarred chest. Making love with Conal. Laughing with him. Loving, trusting him, knowing he loved her. This horror could have been avoided if only she had trusted and believed in his love. But oh no. If anything good came into her life she had to destroy it. What the hell was going to happen now? Monique pushed the sheet back because she felt hot and sweaty. She was terrified to see dark red blood spreading, staining her blue hospital gown.

'I'm frightened,' she whimpered. She started to cry. 'Help me. Somebody please help me!'

Chapter 35

'Alyssa just ran off?'

'Yes. She was hysterical. I ran after her, but by the time I got downstairs she'd disappeared. I went to her apartment, but she wasn't there.'

Frankie watched Tomás Slaney pick up his coffee cup and put it down again without drinking, play with the spoon, and elaborately fold the multi-coloured paper strip which had contained 5mg of demerara sugar. She glanced at his hands, his mouth, his broad, straight shoulders beneath the black coat, and tried not to look into his expressive, dark eyes too often. She imagined what he would think if he knew she had killed somebody. People never knew who they might be talking to.

'Thanks for meeting me.' Tomás looked at her again. 'I didn't know who else to call. Not Alyssa's father, that's for sure. Or her PO.'

'Her what?'

'Probation Officer. Carl something. She hates his guts.'

'Oh yes.' Frankie smiled slightly. 'I remember. Don't blame her, from what I've heard of him.'

'I could hardly take in what Alyssa said. She seemed so confused, jumping from one thing to another. Then she started crying. She told me she loved me, that she wanted us to be together again.' Tomás looked down at his cooling coffee. 'But I'm afraid that can't happen. It's too late, too long ago. I don't feel the same any more. I'm her friend, and I'll do whatever I can to help her. If that's not enough, I'm sorry.'

Frankie thought he was about to say something else but he was silent, staring out of the café window at passers-by in the busy street near Liverpool Town Hall. A minute later he turned back to her. 'So it wasn't true what she said? You're not in any danger?'

'I was.' It was Frankie's turn to stare out of the window. 'Or could have been. But not any more. It's true my husband owed money to a gangster. But now that this guy's dead ...' She could not finish.

'You're safe? Really?'

'Yes.' She took a sip of coffee.

'Thank God for that. I suppose getting shot is an occupational hazard for gangsters. And you haven't been in the Netherlands the last few days, like Alyssa thought?'

'No.' Frankie blushed. 'My husband phoned a few times, and we've talked. He wants to get back with me, but it's too late. After what he did, there's no chance.'

Tomás did not take his eyes off her. 'I'm glad. To say he doesn't deserve you is the understatement of the millenium.'

There was a silence that went on a bit too long. Frankie laughed awkwardly. 'That's what my mother said. Or words to that effect.'

'She's right.'

Tomás Slaney wanted her and she wanted him. The fact that it seemed a really bad idea from whichever way she looked at it only made her want him more. But the shadow of Alyssa hovered between them. She had brought them together and she would keep them apart.

Tomás stirred his coffee again. 'So you've no idea where Alyssa might be?'

'No.' Frankie hesitated. 'To be honest, this is all a bit difficult. I've been trying to keep my distance and so has my mother. It's getting too intense. I'm angry that Alyssa just turned up on her doorstep the other day – my mother must have been affected by the visit, even though she seems fine. Neither of us are sure what we want to do. The only thing we *are* sure of is that we want to take this very slowly. Alyssa doesn't seem to understand that. She says she does, but–'

'I know what you mean. She can be impulsive.'

'She's been through a terrible time, she's very unhappy and life's very hard for her, but–' A cold finger of fear ran down Frankie's spine. 'Do you think she really is innocent of her step-mother's murder?'

'Definitely.' Tomás nodded. 'She had good reason to hate

334

Vivienne, but she'd never have done all those things … well, you don't want to know. She was so upset that night – the night of the murder, I mean. I wanted to protect her. I told her to go to the police,' he said slowly. 'I thought that was the right thing to do. But it wasn't. I should have known better. If she hadn't listened to my bad advice she might never have gone to jail.'

Frankie resisted the urge to blurt out that it was not his fault and he shouldn't feel guilty. 'Have you any idea who the murderer is?' she asked. 'Although even if you had I suppose it would be incredibly difficult, if not impossible, to get new evidence after all these years?'

'Yes, it would.' Tomás shook his head. 'Unfortunately I've got no idea who murdered Vivienne. I suspected Alyssa's father initially. Well, the husband or partner is often the guilty party when a woman is murdered. But the police didn't find anything on him. I must admit, I wanted him to be guilty – I think I felt he should be punished for being such a crap father to Alyssa. Philip Ward played the harassed, grieving widower to perfection. And maybe his grief was genuine. He'd always seemed to love Vivienne. Alyssa didn't think he even knew about his wife's flings. Or didn't want to know. He travelled abroad a lot for work, and when he was home Vivienne took care to act the model wife.'

'And model Wicked Stepmother,' Frankie murmured.

She suddenly felt desperately sorry for Alyssa. What a life. And after all that suffering to have her chance of happiness snatched away. She felt guilty about telling Alyssa she didn't want to see her again. No wonder her lost sister was needy, intense, unhappy. Who wouldn't be? And who was she to judge? The ironic thing now was that she was the one who had killed. Not Alyssa.

'Alyssa ran away from my mother's house the other night.' She pushed away her coffee. 'After she heard some horrible story about her father. My mother was – is – quite worried. I was going to go round to Alyssa's place this afternoon, to see how she was doing. Then you phoned.'

'Horrible story? You mean – about Alyssa's father burning her mother with acid?'

' Alyssa told you that?'

'Yes. But … is it true?'

'Of course it's true!'

'Alyssa said she thought your mother invented the story to try

335

and justify abandoning her as a baby. Because she felt guilty.' Tomás shrugged. 'God, I don't know. Alyssa sounded so confused I didn't understand what she was trying to say.'

Frankie glared at him. 'My mother didn't lie. She wouldn't.'

'I'm sorry, I don't mean to imply she's a liar. Please don't be angry. Actually, *I* thought Alyssa had invented or imagined the story about the acid because of–' He broke off.

Frankie felt nervous. 'What?'

'One of the things the murderer did to Vivienne Ward before he shot her was to pour sulphuric acid on parts of her naked body.' Tomás did not say which parts.

'Oh, my God!' Frankie put her hands up to her face, the tips of her long, shiny nails sharp against her skin. 'I didn't know. But if Alyssa's father did that to my mother ... and he was married to this Vivienne Ward and ... oh my *God*. Do you think he could have killed her?'

'As I said, I wondered that at the time.' Tomás had turned pale. 'But if there had been any shred of evidence to link him to his wife's murder I would have found it even if the police hadn't.'

'Are you sure?'

'As sure as I can be. I did everything I could to try to save Alyssa. The police and her solicitors and counsel thought I was a pain in the arse, but I didn't care. I never stopped, I never gave up until – until her appeal failed. She gave up then as well. At that point it seemed like there was nothing more I could do.' Tomás shook his head again. '*He* couldn't have murdered her. It's not possible. He was out of the country at the time, on a business trip; that was never in doubt. And there was absolutely no evidence to prove he hired anyone to kill her.'

'Even if Philip Ward didn't kill his wife, maybe he knows who did.'

'Then why wouldn't he have turned them in?'

'I don't know. Blackmail – lots of reasons. Maybe he didn't love his wife as much as everyone thought. You must have asked yourself the legal question: *cui bono*?'

'Who benefits? Well, as Vivienne's husband, Philip did of course.' Tomás frowned. 'There was an insurance policy. And they – he and Vivienne – were well off before her murder. Several months after her murder he bought a beautiful Georgian place in the country. He retired a good few years early, too. Travelled a lot.

336

Always kept himself to himself, except for his precious charity work. The way he treated Alyssa, allowed that bitch Vivienne to treat her ...! She was always so desperate for his love, so grateful for any spark of interest. It was pathetic. He never could get his head around the fact that charity begins at home.' Tomás sat back, drumming his fingers on the table. 'Not that any of that's necessarily relevant to the murder. But the thing about the acid, that's—'

'What is relevant is that Alyssa shouldn't be alone right now. She must be in a terrible state.' Frankie stood up. 'She needs me. I've got to find her.'

Tomás got up too, and took her hand. 'I'm coming with you.'

'Conal, how are you feeling now?' The reporter pressed her face to the car window, leaving a greasy smear of red lipstick that resembled some squashed insect. Conal wished she was an insect he could squash. 'Do you and the police know any more about what really happened that night? Is Monique out of danger?'

'Conal?' A man banged on the car roof. 'Have you got any comments about—'

The only comments Conal had were unprintable. But he wasn't going to lose it and start yelling abuse at this rabble, because of course they'd love that. He pointed the remote control at the gates and pressed the button to raise the windscreen, not caring if one of them got their fingers or hair or bloody note pads trapped. He sat grimly at the wheel waiting for the gates to swing open wide enough for him to drive through.

What irritated the hell out of him – although he couldn't think why, because it was the least of his worries – was the way they kept calling him Conal. They had addressed him by his first name right from the start. They had no respect, no manners. It would never occur to them to say Mr Thorn, Mrs Thorn.

There should be a law against harassing innocent people on their doorsteps. But these scum had the voice; the country was run by them; they were a threat to the democracy they were supposed to help preserve. No wonder everything was going to hell in a handbag.

The gates swung shut behind the baying hacks and he sped up the drive and lurched to a stop outside the front door, the tyres spraying gravel. He got out of the car and quickly let himself into the house and out of their sight. He imagined he could see a faint bloodstain on the doorstep. Of course stone was porous. The old oak door closed and he was alone. He collapsed on to an overstuffed chair in the hall, feeling weak and shaky after the drive from Liverpool, and the bruising encounters with journalists.

The silence of the house closed around him. The only sound was the grandfather clock ticking. Conal could feel his heart beating uncomfortably. The place smelled of beeswax, underlaid with a mingled bouquet of the various perfumes Monique used. He could feel her presence, her spirit.

A nurse from the hospital had phoned last night when he was in bed to inform him that Monique had suffered an unexpected bleed from an artery, and that although the doctors had repaired the damage and assured her everything was fine, she was still upset and very frightened and asking for her husband. Conal said he was too ill and tired to drag himself out of bed, and he had refused to speak to Monique on the phone. He resented her desperation and suffocating neediness, especially after what she had done to him, and to their marriage. She had no right to expect him to be there for her now. He was finding it difficult enough to cope himself.

Today he needed to look around the house while the teen witch was safely out of the way. He was also short on funds; he could take some cash from the safe. Come to think of it, why not help himself to the lot? Conal had a feeling he might not be back here for a while.

He stood up and walked slowly across the hall to the kitchen. He hoped this tired, dazed feeling would disappear soon, because he was fed up with having no energy. It was an effort to do anything. Except sleep, of course. His arm and shoulder ached. He wanted a drink, but that wouldn't be a good idea. He could have got someone to drive him, but did not fancy a driver waiting around, knowing where he was going, wondering about his private business.

In the kitchen he poured water into the filter and spooned in ground coffee, then sat at the table and stared out across the back garden and field. The long, high brick wall that ran around the property was topped with broken glass; he would have preferred an electrified fence. The kitchen filled with the smell of coffee. He poured himself a cup, added sugar and milk, and walked back into the hall. The silence seemed unnerving and oppressive now, as if

338

something was about to happen. But it already had. Conal shuddered as he glanced towards the front door and imagined Monique being shot, collapsing, bleeding all over the doorstep.

He still couldn't make sense of it all. He and Monique, Thorn Communications, had no great rivals or enemies as far as he knew. At least no one who would do anything like this. There wouldn't be any point in someone hiring a hit man to kill Monique, not that he could see. Of course there might be something he didn't know; Conal was starting to think there might be a hell of a lot he didn't know.

Whoever pointed that gun at Monique must have wanted something from her. The most likely thing, the only thing he could think of, was that they wanted money. So they wouldn't just point and fire. Even if Monique had panicked, even if her attacker had panicked, surely at some point he would have told her what he wanted?

Most people froze when confronted with a gun. Wouldn't Monique just do what the gunman told her? What choice did she have? It would have been crazy to try to fight back; Conal was certain she would not have done that. Right now she could be too shocked and traumatised to remember everything. Or she could be lying. But why? Conal could not think of any reason.

He drank the coffee and a glass of mineral water, then strolled around the downstairs rooms. Everything looked normal and tidy except for some trainers and sports gear of Lauren's thrown in a heap in a corner of the dining room. The silence began to freak him.

He was still unsure what to do about his marriage. Monique no longer wanted a divorce, that was obvious. But he felt totally confused. Outbursts of frustration and fury alternated with periods of numb, dazed hopelessness and lethargy. He wished to God he or the police could get to the bottom of all this because he was sure that would make him feel better. It struck him, not for the first time, that Monique did not seem bothered about finding out what had happened. It was as if she wanted to forget the whole thing as soon as possible. Of course her injuries, the fact that she had barely escaped death, would be uppermost in her mind. But Conal had a feeling his wife held the clue to this mystery. Whether she realised it or not.

He went upstairs and paused on the landing, recalling the day

Monique had shot him. He was just as lucky to be alive as she was. Why hadn't he told the police, got her locked up? It was because he felt sorry for his wife, despite what she had done. Her nightmare first marriage had left her spooked with insecurity. He loved her. And Conal blamed himself to some extent; if he had walked into the bathroom and caught Monique naked in the shower with some guy who also had his kit off, what would he have thought? Although he did think he would have listened to what Monique had to say. And he knew he would never have reached for a gun.

What hurt him even more was how Monique had believed Lauren's crazy accusation. That she could believe he had so little regard and respect for her, so little *love*, that he would mess with her daughter! He might come to forgive that one day, given a lot of time and effort. But he would never be able to forget. It poisoned everything. Conal wanted to see a way round it, he really did, but he just couldn't. It was there, and it would never go away. No matter how sorry Lauren said she was, or how much Monique said she loved him.

Deep sadness overwhelmed him as he stood in the bedroom, and tears filled his eyes. He sniffed and wiped them away. Being here was pointless; it wasn't helping, only made him feel worse. Better to just get some cash and go. He knelt, lifted the carpet and uncovered the floor safe, swore as he realised he couldn't remember the combination. He squatted on his heels, closed his eyes and tried to relax. A minute later it came back to him.

'Not completely lost it,' Conal murmured, relieved. He lifted the lid and stared in disbelief. 'What the ...?'

There was no cash. Nothing. He didn't understand. There had been over a hundred thousand quid in here. What the hell had Monique done with it? She wouldn't have spent it or deposited it in the bank; he could check, but he was sure she hadn't. Lauren did not know the safe combination. He got to his feet, went all the way down to the cellar and checked the wall safe there, which was concealed behind a wine rack.It contained various sized black and blue velvet boxes of Monique's jewellery and a thick brown envelope of documents relating to the house. No money there either.

If the mystery gunman had stolen the money, why would he have left the jewellery? And why wouldn't Monique have told him and the police? Or was this just something else she didn't bloody remember? Conal stood there in the cool, dim cellar breathing hard, filled with suspicion. He might still be confused, but one thing he was certain of now – the reason behind everything that had happened was down to Monique. He knew it.

He left the house, braved the gaggle of reporters a second time, and drove back to Liverpool. When he entered her hospital room Monique's anxious, exhausted expression brightened as she smiled, relieved and delighted to see him. She does love me, Conal thought as he approached her bed. Unfortunately that didn't bloody matter any more. He waited until the nurse had left and they were alone. Monique's smile faded; he knew she was disappointed that he didn't kiss her. But at that moment it would have been easier for him to snog a slab of raw liver.

'Where's the money?' he asked quietly.

'What ... *what* money?' She started, turning pale.

'The money that was in the floor safe in the bedroom. There was over a hundred grand in there. You know what I'm on about, so don't try to tell me you don't, or don't remember. I want to know what's going on, Monique. I want the truth. No more bullshit. Otherwise I'll walk out of here and I won't come back. You'll never see me again. The police will be even more suspicious of your strange little story then. And they've got good reason to be.' He paused. 'Haven't they?'

Monique's green eyes were shocked, terrified. 'Conal, please! I – I love you.'

'Yeah. Right. Cool.' He gazed down at her, without pity. '*The truth.*'

She started to cry.

Chapter 36

I pause on the cinder path and look up to watch the long, straggly V-line of clacking geese cross the clear, dark-blue sky. Is that what I'm on here, a wild goose chase?

A few stars glitter near the horizon and a pale moon rises between bare tree branches. It's cold and the air smells of autumn. An ideal day to go for a long, country walk and head home afterwards for tea, cakes and rampant sex beside the log fire, while in the kitchen a casserole slow-cooks for a cosy dinner later.

The house of my nightmare. He hasn't had an electrified fence installed since my last visit, and I can't see or hear any rottweilers either. His car's parked outside. The hall and drawing room lights are on, also lights upstairs. What does he do with himself when he's not at charity lunches, dinners or funerals, rattling around in that big house all by himself? I know he likes reading biographies of historical personages, but you can't read all the time. What does he think about? Well, I know what I've been thinking about ever since I had that illuminating little chat with my dear mother. I have to face it – she doesn't want to know. Nobody does. Not Tomás, not Frankie. It's just me, baby. Me against the world.

I don't care any more. I've given up the struggle, and it almost feels like a relief. There's only one last thing I've got to find out. I open the gate, walk along the path, go up the steps to the front door. Ring the bell. He takes a while to answer, but the door finally opens and there he is, disarmingly casual in brown cords and a soppy beige cardigan.

'Hi, Dad. How's it going?'

I wasn't scared before, but I am now. I feel myself start to tremble. He stands there shocked and, like last time, I get the sudden feeling that he's as frightened as I am. Now why would that be? He quickly recovers himself though, and reverts to that olde worlde charm with which I'm so familiar.

'I told you not to come here again!'

'Well, I know, but you see I really need to talk to you about something.'

'If it's money you want, forget it. That offer's been permanently withdrawn.'

'I don't want money. Not your sad six grand anyway. I reckon I'm owed untold thousands in compensation, given that I've done so much time for your crime.'

'My–' He flinches. '*What*?'

'Let's see,' I go on. 'Loss of earnings alone must be huge. I mean, I was a barrister and good at what I did – if I hadn't been jailed for the murder you committed I might be about to make QC by now. Damage to my reputation, loss of freedom … the list of injury and insult is infinite.'

He takes a step backwards. 'You're mad.'

'I've never been more sane.'

'I told you I never wanted to see you–'

'Unless it was to ID my body in a morgue,' I interrupt. 'I know. I especially remember that part.'

'I warned you what would happen if you pestered me. This is stalking. If you want trouble you can damn well have it. I'm calling the police.'

He's about to slam the door on me when he sees the gun in my hand. Danny Paglino's gun that I bought all those years ago, the same gun I used to shoot the lovely Lady M. It feels heavy but I hold it steady. I point it at his stomach and grip the weapon with both hands. He takes another step backwards and freezes like a frightened animal.

'Go on then.' I kick the door open, step into the hall and kick it shut behind me. 'Call the police. Well, try. See how you go on.'

He backs further away towards the telephone table. 'You won't shoot me.'

'Why are you so certain? Because you know I'm not a murderer? You're right, I'm not. You've known that all along. But you don't know what ten years in jail has done to me. I've had enough. It's all too difficult and I don't care any more. I've got absolutely nothing left to lose.'

343

'Except your new-found freedom.'

That makes me laugh. 'What freedom?' I raise the gun so that it's pointing at his face. 'Freedom to rot on income support in some mouldy old flat next to a bombed-out church? In between visits from a Probation Officer who writes reports about my bad attitude towards all the lovely people who only want to help me?'

'This is stupid.' He seems about to reach for the phone, but wisely thinks better of it. He's really frightened now. 'This won't do any good, Alyssa.'

'Wow. Daddy said my name. Did you call Vivienne by her name when you poured acid on her tits before you shot her?'

'*What*?' He gasps. 'That's–'

'Insane? You took pictures of her last agony, didn't you? I never realised you were interested in photography, Dad. Where are those pictures? I've got a feeling you kept them for your private enjoyment.'

He's gone white. 'That's rubbish! You *are* insane. You won't go back to jail, you'll be put in a psychiatric unit. Or Broadmoor. That's where you belong.'

'Do you think you should talk this way to an insane person who's got a gun? I don't think it's a great idea, myself.'

'If you leave now, I'll overlook this. It's not too late. You can walk away.'

'Now you're giving ultimatums to an insane person with a gun. Where are the photographs you took of Vivienne before you murdered her?'

'I didn't take any bloody photographs!'

'Aren't you supposed to say you didn't murder her?'

He clenches his fists, pale and trembling. 'I didn't! Of course I didn't.'

'Now *you* look.' I move forward, still keeping my distance because I don't want him getting any ideas about rushing me. 'I can use this thing, but I'm not a terrific markswoman. I could just wing you to prove I mean business, but I might kill you instead. I don't care. You let me, your only daughter, take the rap for a murder you committed. You ruined my life. How am I supposed to feel? Fuck it.' I take aim at his chest area, my finger tightening around the trigger. 'Fuck everything.'

'No!' he yells. 'Stop!' He throws up one arm in a pathetic attempt to protect himself. 'I'll tell you. Don't, *don't* kill me!'

344

'So you do believe I'll shoot. Very sensible.' Who says violence or the threat of it never solves anything? He backs away and stumbles into the big, posh sitting room. 'Sit on your pretty yellow silk sofa,' I order. 'And keep your hands up where I can see them.' God, I sound like Dirty Harry. 'Now tell me the truth.'

'All right. I did kill her.' He collapses on to the sofa, his face ashen. He looks so shocked and frightened that I wonder if he's going to have a coronary and save me a bullet. 'I murdered my wife.' He heaves a big sigh as he says that, and slumps. He looks smaller suddenly, shrunken.

'Couldn't say that to anyone all these years, could you? Feel better now? Confession's good for the soul.' I'm shaking again. Hearing him say it is still an enormous shock. It's one thing to suspect, another to know. I'm horrified to feel tears streaming down my face.

'It was that fine line between love and hate.' He rubs his eyes. 'I loved Vivienne, I really did. She was intelligent, vivacious, sexy, full of fun.'

'Younger.'

'She knew how to handle me. I loved her more than any woman I'd ever known.'

'More than my mother?'

'Oh yes.' He shoots me a look of hate. 'By the way, tell me how the hell you knew – or guessed – that I took photographs before I shot her? Nobody knows that. Of course I never told anybody.'

'Don't you remember what you did to my mother? My real mother, the one you never told me about. Before she left you? You were in one of your punishing moods. You tied her up and poured acid on her. Took a souvenir photo and gave it to her as a birthday card. She kept it all these years – although you'd think the scars would be enough to remind her – and looked at it whenever she felt guilty for having abandoned me in order to save herself. When she told me all that and showed me the card, I remembered how Vivienne's murderer had poured acid on her. I've been thinking about that for the past two days, trying to tell myself it was just coincidence because I couldn't bear to think you'd deliberately let me, your own daughter, take the rap for murdering Vivienne.'

'Don't cry,' he says, his eyes full of the old contempt. 'At least you were good for something.' He gasps and cringes as I raise the gun again.

345

'You really shouldn't talk like that. The main reason the police didn't suspect you was because you were in Madrid at the time. And there was no proof you hired a hit man. How did you manage to be in two places at once?'

'That was the easiest part, although boring and time-consuming. It involved a false passport and some quick flying from different airports. I planned it all well in advance. If it's any comfort to you, I didn't intend you to take the rap. It was supposed to look like one of those rare, stranger murders that most of us dread. Psycho breaking into country house and murdering lone woman. Shocked husband returns to face tragedy. But you turned up before I could escape.' He pauses. 'You know the rest.'

'You *did* intend me to take the rap after that though. You told the police Vivienne had phoned you the night before and told you she was terrified because I'd threatened to kill her. That was a lie.'

'All right. But I didn't originally intend you to get the blame.'

'Why did you murder her?' I swallow salty tears. 'And like *that*? I thought you loved her. I thought that sadistic bitch was the one thing in your life that you loved.'

'Now we're back to the fine line between love and hate.' He nods. 'Yes, I loved her. Devotedly. But after some years I found out she was cheating on me. I'm afraid Vivienne wasn't as clever and discreet about that as she liked to think. I was terribly hurt. Angry, devastated. But I tried to understand. I realised she had needs I couldn't satisfy. I was away a lot too, and she must have been bored and lonely. She was getting older and needed to prove to herself that she was still attractive. A fragile personality. I was prepared to tolerate her pathetic flings for a while, because I thought Vivienne would come to realise the stupidity of what she was doing and stop. Before it was too late. But when she told me she wanted a divorce, that was it. I couldn't believe it. Couldn't believe her ingratitude, her contempt, her total lack of respect and decency. I realised she was worthless. I started to hate her. I was determined not to let her divorce me, be forced to hand over half my worldly goods to that vile slut. Let her discard me like some old dog you have put down.'

'So you thought you'd put her down. How could you go on letting me think she was my mother? All those years!' A sob bursts from me. 'For Christ's sake, how could you *do* that?'

'Yes. That was wrong of me.' He shrugs. 'But it never seemed

346

particularly important. I wasn't a good father, I know that. The time children require, the constant care and attention – I found it tedious, draining. An investment that brings no reward. I wished your mother had taken you with her, or that I'd had the guts to dump you on the social services. I don't know why I didn't. I suppose I left it too late.'

'And it wouldn't have been good for your precious image.'

'No. There was that. I had a lot of other things to think about, and so did Vivienne. To tell you the truth about your mother, to do something – it would have all proved too complicated. Anyway, you've found your mother now.' He tries to smile. 'How is it? Fairy tale reunion?'

I blink away tears, shake my hair back. My expression must tell him.

'No. I can imagine. Not exactly the fairy-tale perfect mother type, Estella, is she?'

'Any more than you're the perfect father.'

'Touché. Has your search revealed any other family members? Brothers, sisters, cousins?'

I don't want to answer that either. I want to just end it here and now. For him and for me. The pain is too much.

'I need a drink,' he said. 'And I'm sure you could do with one.'

'I won't, thanks. Not while I've got someone at gun point.'

He sat up, slowly so as not to alarm me. 'I'm not *someone,* Alyssa. I'm your father. I won't try to pretend there's any love lost between us, because that would be stupid and insulting. I know I've done you a great deal of harm, and I'm very sorry.'

'Are you? Sorry doesn't quite cover it.'

'I realise that. It can't have been much fun spending ten years in jail for a murder you didn't commit. I read the rubbish those appalling tabloid hacks wrote about you. But now you know the truth. You know I murdered Vivienne. Where do we go from here? If you shoot me, kill me now, it might give you some fleeting satisfaction. But it won't be long before they're locking you in a cell again. And this time you won't come out. So please think very carefully before you pull that trigger.'

I was silent, blinking away tears. I know he's right. I also know I shouldn't let him take charge like this. Yes, I can kill him now and I'd get a lot more than fleeting satisfaction. But revenge is the dish best served very cold.

'I can give you money,' he went on. 'Thousands. A lump sum and a generous allowance. I'll make a new will. I'll leave you this house, everything I own. You won't need to rot in that flat or take some dead end job. I can make life a lot easier for you.' His frightened eyes stare at me. 'Think about that. Think hard.'

'The photos of Vivienne ... what did you do with them? Don't lie,' I hiss.

He flinches as I make another threatening gesture with the gun. 'I kept the negatives in a secret safety deposit box until after you'd been convicted and sentenced. Then I learned how to develop them myself.' He smiles. 'It wasn't the kind of thing you could take to Boots.'

I feel terrified, even though I've got the gun. I'm in the presence of evil. 'I never knew you were interested in photography.'

'Well, not the kind a father can share with his daughter. Yes, I know.' He holds up one hand. 'I never shared anything with you.'

'I can't believe you destroyed such exciting material. Where are the photos now?'

'In the priest's hole.'

'The—'

'That's what I believe it to be. This house looks Georgian, and most of it is. But there's an older, mediaeval part. To cut a long story short, I had some work done when I moved here. I was poking around one day while the builders had their tea break when I discovered what seemed to be a hiding place in one of the bedrooms, behind some panelling, right next to the chimney. Of course the family wouldn't have had to light a fire in that particular chimney when Father Bunloaf was in residence, not if they didn't want to cook or suffocate him.' He smiles again. 'I dismissed the builders at once. The priest's hole made the perfect hiding place for my collection. Of course I realise I should destroy the photographs. I'm getting to the age where anything can happen, health-wise. I don't want some new owner stumbling across them after I've croaked it. Although I shouldn't care what happens once I'm dead.'

'Get them.'

'Oh, I see. It's justice you want, not money.' He looks scared again. 'They won't prove I murdered Vivienne. They won't prove *you* didn't. But all right. I'll confess to the police if that's what you want – I'll show them the photos. They won't believe me. It won't

348

change anything. It won't do you any good and it may do you a lot of harm. It's really best if you keep quiet and accept my offer of money.'

'I'll be the judge of that.' I step back, keeping the gun levelled. 'Get them.'

'All right,' he sighs again. 'Do you mind if I have that drink first?'

'Just *get* them. Now. I won't tell you again!'

He stands up slowly and awkwardly, and moves towards the door. I follow. I know he's got no intention of confessing to the police. He's only told me all this because he doesn't believe it'll come to that. Why not? I shouldn't have come here. Or not without telling someone. But who could I tell? Who cares? Good question, Alyssa.

We go up the stairs and across the landing into one of the bedrooms. Lovely house, albeit a sinister atmosphere. That's probably down to him. It's so damn quiet. The mahogany panelled walls seem to close in around me; I never liked panelling. He goes to the fireplace, stoops and reaches inside and up. There's a click, creaks and a whirring sound; a little panel door to the left of the fireplace springs open, revealing dank, cold blackness. I feel sick with terror.

'It can only be opened from the outside,' he explains. 'From a lever in the chimney.'

'Forget the history lesson.'

He stands still, arms by his sides. 'I need to get the torch from the drawer.'

'Do it.'

His movements are slow and careful, designed not to startle. He gets the torch, goes to the door and shoves a heavy, carved chair out of the way, pulls the door wide open. The dank, dusty blackness yawns out at me like some mediaeval person with rotten teeth and foul breath.

'They're in there.' He shines the torch. 'Couple of feet down. You have to reach. Alyssa?' He turns. 'Please think about my offer. You can walk out of here with a few thousand pounds cash right now. I'll write you a cheque too. I'll phone my solicitor first thing in the morning and get him to draw up that new will. I know money can't make up for what I've done to you, but now I really want to try and make amends.'

'Save it.' I'm shaking. I have to get those photos and get out of here. I'll borrow his flash car. It's years since I've driven, so let's hope I don't kill myself or anyone else.

'Actually, I'm not feeling very good.' He clutches his chest. He does look grey-faced, but I'm pretty sure I do too.

'Oh, for—' I think I'll lock him in a bathroom or somewhere while I get the photos and make my escape. Should have thought of that sooner, but this is all very unnerving. 'Come on,' I snap. 'Move.'

He drops the big yellow torch and it crashes on the oak floorboards. He sinks to his knees, his face creased in pain. Oh God. I step forward to kick the torch out of the way. But he suddenly makes a remarkable recovery. Before I realise what's happening, he's grabbed my ankle. I stagger, lose my balance and fall, but manage to hold on to the gun.

It all happens so fast. He's on his feet now, kicking and punching, grabbing handfuls of my hair, making me scream. Pushing me. Kicking, swearing. He's much stronger than I imagined, so vicious. Well, he would be vicious, wouldn't he? I don't get a chance to menace him with the gun, let alone fire it. I scream again. '*No. No!*'

Stupid, but I can still hardly believe it's my father doing this to me. Even after everything else he's done. Cruelty to daughters is a long, well-documented historical phenomenon. Why me? Why not me?

I tumble head first into cold, dusty blackness.

350

Chapter 37

'You're telling me that gunman stole the hundred grand and then shot you?' Conal looked incredulously at his weeping, panicked wife. 'Why the hell didn't you say so before? To me and the police?'

'I was in shock,' Monique sobbed. 'I didn't remember until now.'

'Change the record, will you?'

How could she have been so thick as not to realise Conal might go to the house and open the bedroom floor safe? What other vital things hadn't she remembered? She looked at him standing beside her bed, grey-faced and angry, the shadows beneath his eyes. He looked haunted, damaged. As if the horror of his ordeal was just beginning to sink in. She had done this. It was all her fault. Monique longed to make it up to him, but how could she? And would he even let her try?

'We have to tell those detectives. If he's been in the house he must have left fingerprints. Hairs, whatever.'

'He had hardly any hair. And he wore gloves. Latex gloves.'

'Oh really? That's remarkably observant all of a sudden, given the little you've come up with so far. Amazing what you remember when someone asks the right questions, isn't it?' Conal turned and began to pace. 'It still doesn't explain what happened to me. Why someone kidnapped me and set my car on fire. And that woman telling me she was a private detective.' He pushed up the sleeves of his dark-blue sweatshirt and turned back to her. 'You're still not telling me everything. I warned you what'll happen if you don't tell me the truth. Did you think I was having a laugh when I said I'd walk out of here and never come back?'

'No!' Monique tried desperately to think of some brilliant idea with which to extricate herself from this threatening, hideous web of deceit. Of course nothing came. All she knew was that she could never confess to Conal that she had intended to have him killed. Even if she had changed her mind at the last minute.

'I can't tell you anything else,' she whispered, 'because I don't *know* anything else.'

'We have to tell the police that guy came in the house.'

'No!'

'Why the hell not?'

'Because – because they'll think I'm thick.'

He looked at her incredulously. 'After all that's happened to us, you're worried about a couple of plods thinking you're *thick*? You're lying in that bed with what could have been a fatal gunshot wound! Bloody hell. Talk about not seeing the bigger picture.'

'I mean – I could get into trouble for not having remembered sooner. They might charge me with wasting police time – or something like that.' Monique reached for another tissue. 'Those detectives don't like me, Conal. They think I'm a rich cow who's got it all. Especially that woman. I know this doesn't sound very feminist, but women are often a lot harder on other women. She acts nice, but she wants to make trouble for me. I know she does.'

'She – they – only want to find out what happened. As do I.' Conal stood over her. 'What did that guy say to you when he came in the house? You must remember something! And how come Lauren didn't wake up?'

'I think he said he wanted money,' she sniffed. 'Well, obviously he must have said that. I pleaded with him to be quiet, not to wake Lauren. I didn't want her terrified, maybe even hurt.'

'Didn't mind making enough noise to wake and terrify her when he shot you, did he?'

'He'd got what he wanted.'

'Then why would he shoot you? What was the point?'

'I don't *know*.' Monique's sudden fury gave her a surge of strength. 'Does there have to be a *point*? Maybe he was a psycho! You don't threaten someone with a gun, demand money and then shoot them for the hell of it if you're a normal, adjusted, caring human being, do you?' He was worse than the police. The surge of strength disappeared almost immediately, leaving her drained and breathless.

'Don't get sarcastic with me, Monique. And how come he only took money?' Conal demanded. 'You've got jewellery lying about on your dressing table and there's more in the drawers – not to mention the pieces in the safe. Why didn't he take all that?'

'I don't know,' she whispered. Damn, damn, damn.

Conal sat on the edge of the bed and rubbed his tired eyes. He looked at her again.

'Listen,' he sighed, 'forget about the police. This is between us, Monique. No one else, just you and me. I'm giving you one last chance. Now talk to me. Please.'

Tears streamed down her face. She longed to tell him everything, but how could she? If she confessed she was finished.

'I've told you all I know, Conal. I am telling the truth. I swear. Please,' she whispered. 'I love you, I need you. I want us to stay together. Something terrible happened to us, but we're safe now. Can't we *please* start trying to put this behind us and get on with our lives? We were so happy before . . .' Her voice trailed off.

'You know what I wondered when I was in tucked up in bed trying to get through last night?' Conal smiled but his dark-blue eyes were filled with sadness. 'I thought, my wife shot me because she believed I was cheating on her with some tart. Then she believed I'd seduced her teenage daughter. She wanted a divorce because she hated me. And she's impulsive, hot-headed. I should know that better than most.'

'What are you getting at?'

'Suppose she decided divorce wasn't good enough? I'm sure she didn't fancy giving this shit of a husband a mega chunk of divorce settlement with which to send him on his merry way. Especially when there's a much cheaper option available.'

Oh God. Monique stared at him. 'I don't understand!'

'Don't you? You changed your mind about the divorce. Even though Lauren hadn't at that point confessed that she'd lied. Why did you suddenly change your mind?'

'Because I realised you hadn't cheated on me with Lindsay bloody Roberts. You know that, Conal. And I started to suspect Lauren might be lying.'

'Or did you know the divorce wasn't going to happen? Was that why you became so amenable, saying you'd give me whatever settlement I wanted?'

'No. I don't–'

'Did you know the divorce wasn't going to happen because—' Conal paused, his eyes locked on hers '—you thought I'd be dead, Monique?'

She gasped as a knife-like pain pierced her chest, making it difficult to breathe. She couldn't speak for a few seconds. 'Conal, no. *Never.*'

'Something went wrong. Was there an argument about money? Or did you bottle out, try to call it off? They – the people you hired – weren't having that, were they? One of them paid you a visit, forced you to hand over the money and then shot you. I'm not sure why they shot you, and I'll probably never find out. But it doesn't matter because I don't care any more. I don't know if they intended to kill you, but they were hardly concerned for your health and well-being. They could have killed me, but why bother? They'd had enough hassle. And even if you survived you could hardly grass them up. Or complain you'd been ripped off.'

'I didn't want you dead,' she gasped. 'I love you. That's the truth.'

'And I believe you now. That is, I believe you love me.'

'Then let's put this behind us. Conal, please!' Monique was gasping and thrashing around in panic, as much as she was capable of thrashing. It felt like something was pressing on her chest, suffocating the life out of her. Her heart was beating wildly. 'I'm ill, I can't breathe, I'm—'

He stared down at her. 'Dying? You know, this throwing hysterics never solved anything. Most people get their heads around that before their third birthday.'

'Help me, please help me!'

'Yeah. You need help, all right.'

He walked to the door, opened it and called to someone. A nurse came running in, followed by a doctor. Monique's vision started to blur, turn black around the edges. The doctor was taking her pulse, telling her to calm down. He put on his stethoscope and listened to her pounding heart.

She had thought she was dying, but apparently these terrible symptoms were a pánic attack. Not surprising after what she'd been through, the discomfort and pain she was in now with her injuries. She had to try and relax, get as much rest as possible. The nurse took her blood pressure and tut-tutted over the result. The doctor pronounced her heartbeat 'rather fast'. No, she didn't need

354

oxygen. That was the last thing she needed. Ditto detectives and other visitors.

'Where's my husband?' Monique groaned, leaning against the pillows.

What would Conal do now? He could tell the police his suspicions, but suspicions were all he had. He couldn't prove anything and neither could the police. She had to keep on denying, otherwise she was lost.

'I sent your husband to the canteen to get himself a cup of tea.' The nurse gently wiped her tears. 'He wasn't too well either. He looked rotten, actually. Worried sick about you, of course.'

If only that were true. The way Conal had looked at her when she had the panic attack! She could have been dying, and what would he have cared? But she didn't deserve his care, did she? She did not deserve any consideration now. The nurse brought her a cup of tea. Left alone, Monique lay still and tried to rest. She was interrupted by a phone call from Lauren.

'Karen's mum asked me to stay another night. I think she feels sort of responsible for me. We're going to watch a film after dinner, so is it okay if I don't come to the hospital tonight?'

'Of course. They don't want me to have visitors just now anyway. I need the rest.'

'Well, get lots. 'Bye, Mum, see you tomorrow. Oh. How's Conal?'

Monique could not answer for a second. 'He's all right. Getting there.'

'Do you think he'll speak to me again soon? Is he still furious?'

'You can't blame him if he is. He needs time, Lauren. A lot of time.'

'I suppose. I really want to make it up to him. And to you.'

'I know. Look, you go and enjoy your evening. Don't worry too much.'

Lauren's voice was trembly. 'I love you, Mum.'

'And I love you.' Despite everything.

Hours passed and Conal did not reappear. She wondered if he was talking to the police, trying to think of ways to prove her guilt. Dinner time came and went, the tea and coffee trolley was rolled round. Monique heard visitors come and go.

She had never felt so lonely, frightened and in pain. She wished Frankie Sayle's accomplice had killed her. What did she have to

355

look forward to now? A jail sentence? Well, she would make damn sure Frankie Sayle went down with her. If not jail, money? Big deal. It couldn't buy her what she wanted more than anything now – the husband who had loved her. She had destroyed his love. She couldn't blame anyone but her stupid, paranoid self. She lay staring at the wall. The nurse took her blood pressure again and told her to get some sleep.

Just as her eyes were closing Conal walked in. Being a private room, he could visit any time. Monique's heart started pounding again as she struggled to sit up. Conal walked to her bed and stopped. He looked anguished.

'Maybe you're lying,' he said in a low voice. 'And maybe you're telling me the truth. I don't know and I don't care any more. I've thought about what you said. You're right. I need to put all this behind me. Get my life back. That's the only way I can deal with this.'

'Oh, Conal!' She felt a great rush of relief. 'I didn't try to have you killed; I'd never do that! I *am* telling the truth, I swear. Did you . . .?' She hesitated. 'Have you talked to the police?'

'No. I'm not going to. I'll answer their questions, if they think of any more. And you'll have to keep fending them off until they give up. That's it. As I said before, this is between you and me. I've got no more intention of trying to open your Pandora's fucking box of tricks. I've been through enough.'

Monique gasped with joy. She did not deserve this miraculous, this fantastic reprieve. But she would make damn good use of it. She wasn't going to blow this unexpected and fabulous last chance.

'We can put it all behind us, Conal.' She looked at him, her eyes shining. 'We'll have a wonderful life together again. I'll get better, so will you. We can–'

'No,' he interrupted, shaking his head. 'Not together.'

'What?' She stared at him in dismay. 'But I love you! You said you believed me.'

'And I do. But too much has happened. It's too late.' Conal's voice hardened as Monique bowed her head and started to shake with sobs. 'Come on. Don't start that again. You must realise we're finished. Take the consequences of your actions. Be an evolved human being for once in your life.'

'I love you,' she wept. 'I want you! I'm so sorry I misjudged you. It was all my fault, my stupid paranoia. I'll do anything to make up for it, anything. Give me another chance. Don't leave me, Conal! *Please*.'

He glanced around the room. 'Have you got your handbag here?'

Monique looked up, blinking through her tears. 'Yes. Why?'

'Where is it?'

She pointed. 'In the cupboard.'

He walked round to the other side of the bed, opened the cupboard and took out her bag, emptied the contents over the primrose-yellow bedspread. The bag was soft black leather with a gold silk lining. Monique's lipstick and mascara tumbled out, along with her perfume, cheque book, appointments diary and Mont Blanc fountain pen and biro. The bag smelled wonderful, of her perfume and the outdoors.

'We don't need lawyers. Not for this part anyway.' Conal flipped open the cheque book and laid it in front of her. 'Write me a cheque,' he ordered.

She stared at him through her tears. 'How much?'

'Half of everything you own. I calculated it earlier.' He named a sum which caused Monique to gasp again, and not with joy. It was a lot more than a hundred grand.

'Don't even think about giving me any crap. Any *more* crap. Otherwise I'll have to change my mind about talking to our favourite detectives. And just as an added safeguard, I wrote a letter this afternoon and handed it to my solicitor. To be opened in the event of my untimely and unexpected demise.'

'But Conal, for Christ's sake, that's crazy! You don't need to be afraid of–'

'Shut up. And don't you ever, *ever* call *me* crazy.' He stared down at her, his eyes stony. 'Write the cheque,' he repeated.

Monique's hand trembled as she picked up her pen.

Chapter 38

I open my eyes to the darkness of the priest's hole, coughing as several hundred years of dust motes swirl around me after my fall. I can't stretch out, or stand up straight. Father Bunloaf must have been pierced with religious fervour to withstand this level of discomfort. Or terror, more like, at the prospect of being discovered and arrested along with his kind hosts, tried at the nearest assizes and condemned to be hung, drawn and quartered, his entrails tossed on the barbie.

Dazed, my body hurting from the savage kicks and punches, I slowly feel around the suffocating space, my fingers scrabbling over rough, dusty stonework filled with little gaps. Beneath my feet is what feels like a carrier bag containing a couple of thick envelopes. I grab the bag and hug it to me.

How the hell am I supposed to get out of here? I don't think my father plans to let me out. He won't want me to walk away with these envelopes, even if they don't prove his guilt or my innocence. I stretch up one arm. The panel door is to my left. And it only opens from the outside, when the lever in the chimney is pulled. I hear something heavy being dragged across the room and shoved against the door.

'Let me out! Let me out of here!'

No response. I try to control my panic. He surely isn't going to leave me here until I dehydrate and starve? That would be worse than torturing somebody and shooting them. He has to let me out, he has to. I begin to cry. I even pray. Then I really lose it and start screaming.

I scream until the mediaeval dust causes me another coughing fit. Once I calm down I feel ashamed. If my father is standing outside listening he'll be getting a right laugh. Again, I try to think what to do. I suddenly realise that whereas initially I had felt cold, now I was sweating. Was that because of the energy I had wasted? I touch my right hand to the stonework. It feels warm.

A minute later I smell smoke. Woodsmoke. And it isn't coming from the stubbly fields outside. It's coming from the chimney right next to me, filtering through gaps in the stonework. I remember what my father said about the family not being able to light a fire in that chimney when Father Bunloaf was in residence.

Panic surges in me again. My father intends to suffocate me, let me die alone in this pitch-dark, smoke-filled hole. I can't get out and no brave, square-jawed hero is going to turn up to rescue me in the nick of time. This was it. Well, I had considered suicide during some very low moments. Now my own father was about to save me the trouble and do the job for me. One final, caring act. He wouldn't ID my body in a morgue though. He'd drag out my smoke-blackened corpse and bury it in a nearby field at dead of night. An ignominious end to a tragic existence.

I can't hear any more sounds from outside my cramped, dark prison. The smoke thickens and I start to cough again. Whatever gaps there might be in the stonework of the other walls, they can't let in enough air to keep me alive. Another few minutes and I'll be unconscious. Those few minutes are going to be very uncomfortable. My eyes are stinging and watering, my throat is raw. The smoke is constricting my chest, filling my lungs.

I scrabble around frantically again, reaching up to touch stonework and panelling, feeling beneath my feet. I drop the carrier bag. When I reach down to grab it again – why? – my hands touch warm metal. It's the gun. I must have managed to hold on to it and it had fallen into the hole along with me. I was lucky it hadn't gone off. What use was it now though? Unless I prefer to shoot myself rather than croak it from smoke inhalation.

I have to try something. I stick the gun in my jacket pocket and feel around for a hand or foothold. How had the priest got in and out? I manage to haul myself up until I'm standing on a kind of ledge, level with the door. I don't know if it's a man-made ledge or merely stones jutting out. I wrap the carrier bag handle around my left wrist, grab the gun and take aim. I might blast my eardrums if I fire in this confined space, but so what? Better deaf than dead. I wonder where my father is. If he's waiting outside.

I shoot at the panelled door, near where I guess the lock or catch is. The noise of the gun going off is deafening in that small space, and what with that and the suffocating smoke I feel as though I might faint. Ears ringing, I kick and kick at the door until it opens a couple of inches, letting in a draught of desperately needed cool, fresh air.

I have to make sure I stay on the ledge and don't fall back down into the hole. The door shifts a few more inches, and I manage to wriggle my right foot out. As I expect, there is an armchair and a heavy table against the door. I put my face to the crack, gulping air, then use the strength that gives me to shove the door wide enough to squeeze my way out. I'm dizzy and deafened, coughing and choking, my eyes streaming.

The room is empty. Where's my father? Wherever he is, he's bound to be back soon. I clutch the carrier bag to me and make for the door. I get out on to the landing. He's hurrying up the stairs, pale and strained, lugging a couple of heavy logs for the fire that is supposed to cook and suffocate me. When he sees me he stops and gasps, dropping his burden. I must look a smoke-blackened fright, a Georgian chimney sweep back from the dead.

I point the gun. 'Get out of my way!' I want to shoot him, but I can't. Despite everything, I still cannot bring myself to shoot my father. I catch sight of a bathroom on the landing, with a key in the door. 'In there. *Move*,' I wheeze as I get another coughing fit. I'm trembling with shock, fear and exertion. He backs in and I slam the door on him, lock it and throw the key down the stairs. The door might not hold him for long, but it will be long enough for me to escape.

'Where are your car keys?' I call.

'You'll have to find them. Alyssa, wait. We need to talk.'

'You were going to kill me,' I sob. 'There's nothing to talk about.'

He starts shouting and banging on the door as I run down the rest of the stairs. I stagger around, sobbing and coughing, searching for the car keys. I look in the kitchen, dining room, sitting room, coat pockets, table and dresser drawers. I can't find the damn things anywhere. Maybe it's just as well, because I'm in no condition to undertake my first drive in more than a decade. I go back into the kitchen and gulp some water, then run out. Sod the car keys, I'll get the train. I can't stay in that house another minute.

I fling open the front door and run out and down the steps, sprint along the cinder path between the dark fields. The moon is higher now and more stars glitter, just enough for me to see where I'm going. I reach the road and the relative safety of traffic and street lights. I consider trying to hitch a ride, but decide against it. I don't want to get into the car of anyone who will stop for me.

I half run, half walk back to the station and catch a train to Liverpool. Of course I get some funny looks from the few other passengers. The journey is infuriatingly slow, and the train keeps stopping between stations; the nearer we get to the city the more often it stops. The delay freaks me. The conductor passes through the carriage and I feel like asking him if there's an air raid on.

I glance at my reflection in the window. My jeans and black jacket don't show too much dirt, but I stink of smoke and my face is filthy. My hair is a dusty mess. I wonder how long it will take my father to break out of that bathroom. What will he do then? He doesn't know where I live – at least I'd never given him my address. But he can find out if he wants to. Will he call the police, falsely accuse me of some crime and get me arrested? I have to be ready for whatever he tries next. It occurs to me that maybe he will try again to kill me.

The train finally crawls into Central Station. I run up the escalator and take the left-hand exit out of the station, hurry up Bold Street. I'm still coughing, but not as much. I can see the orange-lit shell of St Luke's at the top of the street. For the first time I was looking forward to getting back to my flat. And locking myself in. I'll take a shower, pour a drink and check out the photographs. I'm not looking forward to seeing them because I'm sure my father was right; they will not be pretty. Any more than the real thing was. But I have to do it. A group of girls burst out laughing as I pass. I feel like showing them the gun.

At the top of Bold Street I pause, waiting to cross the busy road. Fear grips me again and I stare round at passers-by. I remind myself that he doesn't know where I live, that he can't know. He's probably still trapped in that bathroom. He might be there all night until the cleaner – of course he'll have a cleaner – lets him out in the morning. If the cleaner doesn't have her own house key the rescue will take longer. He'll have plenty of time to think up a suitable explanation for how he came to get locked in his own bathroom.

I cross the road, skirt the church steps and turn into my little street. It is quiet and deserted as usual, the church looming above. I still haven't met any of my neighbours. Sometimes I think I'm the only flesh-and-blood mortal who lives in this house, and that the rest of the inhabitants are the ghosts of people killed in the Blitz. I approach the house slowly, glancing around as I walk. I hesitate at the entrance, wishing there were other people around. But there is nobody, and I have to go in. I push open the door, step inside and grope for the dodgy, old-fashioned light switch. I press it down. Fuck. The light is knackered again.

It seems a long way up those dark, damp-smelling stairs to my cosy little flat. I feel in the carrier bag for the gun. I draw it out and catch a slight movement at the edge of my vision. A gaunt face of dark hollows, a gleam of silver hair. The face becomes a tall figure which rushes me. Something comes down hard on my hand, making me scream in shock and pain. I drop the gun.

It's him. Obviously he does know where I live. He's known for some time, he must have made it his business to find out. And he must have escaped from that bathroom pretty quickly to get here before me ... Of course his journey to the big bad city would be a lot quicker by car than mine had been on that snail train. I can't look for the gun and try to grab it, and I can't fight him because he has a weapon. When he raises it again, this time to bring it down on my head, I see that it's a big claw hammer. I dodge and he misses.

'Give me the photos,' he gasps. 'Then I'll leave you alone.'

Yes. Right. I can't get the gun back and I have to dodge the offending hammer again. All I can do is run. I fling open the door and dash back out into the street, wondering how the hell this night is going to end. I hope it won't be with my death. But where can I go, who will help me?

The immediate thing is to get away. I'm sure he will have picked up the gun. And there are more than enough bullets left. I flee across Bold Place and come up against the black iron railings of St Luke's. And a notice: KEEP OUT. DANGER FROM FALLING MASONRY.

If I can get in, hide in the church gardens and keep out of the way of any falling masonry, surely he'll give up and go away sooner or later? Then I can get help. I hear his footsteps behind me. A second later there is a crack and a bullet pings against the railings somewhere above my head. Oh yes. Dad means business.

The tall gates, from which steps lead down into the dark gardens, are chained and padlocked. I run up Bold Place and turn into Roscoe Street, go down the alley that stinks of stale booze, in between the church gardens and the empty building which was once a club. I wrap the carrier bag tightly around my wrist, climb up on to some crates stacked against the wall and jump over.

I land badly and cry out in pain. Of course I have to turn my ankle, don't I, like the irritatingly helpless, fleeing heroine with which we're all depressingly familiar. I get to my feet and limp into the centre of the gardens towards the church, gasping with pain. My right hand hurts too; it feels stiff and swollen as well as painful.

Trees and bushes grow around what remains of the walls and inside the nave, and huge blocks of the dangerous fallen masonry lie all around, pale in the darkness. I limp along the nave and collapse on a huge, cracked slab of stone near my abandoned vampire coffin, trying to get my breath back. Through the tree branches and crumbling stone walls I can make out the windows of my flat on the top floor of the house. My little haven.

Where is my father? Has he followed me in here? He might be getting on in years, but he's agile and I remember he always kept himself fit. And of course he has a gun to help remedy any fitness deficiencies. I wonder how long I should hide here before climbing back over the wall – if I can climb back over, with my injured ankle and hand. Will he just wait outside my flat? Maybe I shouldn't go back there. But where the hell can I go?

I glance up at the orange-tinted night sky with its stars and pale-lemon moon, the flashing red lights of an aircraft whose faint drone I could hear. I imagine incendiary bombs falling and crashing all around, that same sky lit by flares and searchlights. All I can hear now is traffic, muffled by the trees and walls; it is quiet and peaceful in here. I listen for the sound of footsteps then jerk upright and cry out in terror as a chunk of stone drops and lands close by. Not a good idea to come right up the nave, but what else can I do? Hopefully he will have seen the warning notices and be too scared to follow.

I stand up and back away as I hear the sound I dread; someone running towards me. I can't run, and my ankle hurts too much. How can I defend myself? I glance around, looking for a hiding place. I get a stupid urge to climb into the vampire coffin and curl up there. I cringe with terror.

'Alyssa? Alyssa! Where are you?'

I gasp and stare into the darkness. The voice is not my father's. It's Frankie.

'You can't go in there, it's too dangerous!' Tomás tried to drag her away. 'That's Alyssa's father we just saw – he's older, but I recognise him – and he's got a gun. He's fired it once already. Keep back, for God's sake!'

'Alyssa's in there. He's after her. She needs help.'

'You can't help her, you'll get yourself killed – either by him or a block of stone crashing on you! There's nothing you can do. Wait until the police come.'

'There's no time. And why the hell are they taking so long anyway? Call them again.' Frankie broke free, ran away and started to climb the wall.

'Frankie, come back, for–'

She heard Tomás groan and swear as she pulled herself up, scrambled over and jumped down on the other side. She had not climbed a wall since junior school, so she was out of practice. She brushed dust off her hands and clothes and ran towards the centre of the gardens.

She had a feeling she knew where Alyssa might be hiding – in the part of the nave near what they jokingly referred to as the vampire's coffin. Frightened, she kept glancing up at the ruined walls, keeping as far away from them as possible. The walls narrowed around her as she went down the nave.

'Alyssa? It's me, Frankie. Do you hear me? Alyssa?' She stopped and turned as a half sob came out of the darkness.

'How did you know I was here?'

'Long story. I'll tell you later. Are you okay?'

'It was him – my father – he killed Vivienne.' Alyssa came limping out of the darkness. 'I went to his house. He tried to kill me, I nearly … Frankie, for Christ's sake, get out of here. It's too dangerous. He's around somewhere and he's got a gun.'

'I know. Tomás just saw him. He's called the police.'

'I can hardly walk,' Alyssa groaned. 'I've knackered my ankle. My right hand too.'

'Don't worry, I'll help you.' Frankie paused. 'What's in the bag?'

'Evidence. It's important. He mustn't get it; don't let him!'

'Okay, okay. Give me your arm, let me help–'

'Never mind me, just get away. He'll kill you too.'

'Just shut up, will you? Come on, we've got to get out.'

Alyssa started to cry. 'Why did you come here? You're in danger, you shouldn't–'

'I *said*, shut up. You don't listen, do you? I'm here because you're my sister. End of bloody story. Now come *on*.'

'You don't hate me for going to see Estella? It was you I wanted to see. I didn't know she'd be there. I'm sorry.'

'You will be if you don't shut up. And no, I do not hate you.'

'Look,' Alyssa gasped. She stopped and pointed. 'Someone's coming. Frankie, it's him, I'm sure. Oh God.'

'It'll be Tomás. Or the police. Just get down, okay?'

'But–'

'Do it,' Frankie whispered. 'You can't run. Let me handle this.' She straightened up and walked forward as Alyssa sank to the ground. 'Tomás?' she called. 'Is that you?' She hoped to God it was.

'So the handsome hero's still in the picture, is he? After all these years. Incredible. I admired his loyalty once, but now I think he must be mentally deficient.'

'The police are coming.' Frankie stepped out of a shaft of moonlight and looked at the dark figure a few feet away. He was tall, well-built. She could see the glint of the gun barrel, a face in shadow, framed with white or silver hair. Philip Ward. She tried not to think about what this man had done. 'They'll be here any minute.'

'You're not ...! Who the hell are you?' His voice cracked with shock. He took a step closer, holding the gun poised. 'Get back in the moonlight where I can see you. As you can see, I've got a gun.'

Frankie slowly obeyed. She stood there looking at him. 'I'm Alyssa's sister.'

'Her *sister*?' Philip Ward was silent for a minute. 'Yes,' he said eventually. 'I can see the resemblance. Well, well. Another family member crawled out of the woodwork. She must have been very busy at the Public Record Office, or wherever people on her kind of quest go.'

'We know what you did.' Frankie tried to keep her voice steady. 'So do the police. As I said, they'll be here soon.'

'Really? I don't hear any sirens. Still, if you – or the capable Mr Slaney – have phoned a police station, managed to explain the situation to some dimwitted, disinterested desk officer and got an armed response team scrambled all in the space of about five minutes, allow me to offer my congratulations on a truly remarkable achievement.' He laughed.

Frankie looked at the moonlight glinting on the gun barrel. 'Just give it up. You're not helping yourself.'

'Save the patronising platitudes, young lady. Where is my daughter, by the way? Cowering somewhere behind you in the shadows, I presume. That's her style. All she has to do is return my property to me, then we can all give this up and go home.'

'Not really. You murdered your wife. And you tried to murder your daughter.'

He laughed again. 'So she says.'

'You've just been seen firing a gun at her.'

'By? Her sister and ex-fiancé.'

Frankie glanced around. 'Give it up,' she repeated. 'This is stupid and you know it.'

His response was to step closer and raise the gun. 'Alyssa?' he shouted. 'If you don't give me back my property I'll shoot the lovely face off this brand-new sister of yours. You've got three seconds. You know I mean what I say.'

'I'm coming. Don't hurt her!'

Frankie turned as Alyssa limped forward. She unwound the strap from her wrist and dropped the carrier bag on the ground.

'Not there, stupid girl. Over here. Pick it up and bring it. Hand it to me.'

Alyssa picked up the bag and limped past. In that second Frankie knew Philip Ward was going to shoot Alyssa. And then her. Alyssa held out the bag.

'I said, hand it to me. Closer!' he snapped.

Frankie dropped to the ground, grabbed one of the chunks of crumbly, dusty stone and flung it. Philip Ward dodged and fired at

366

her, missed. Alyssa dropped the bag and dived sideways. In the distance they heard shouts, people running.

Philip Ward stooped to grab the carrier bag, and Frankie flung another chunk of stone at him. It hit him in the chest. He staggered backwards and fired again wildly, hitting nothing but stonework. There was a rumbling, and a huge, dark object seemed to fall from the sky, hurtling towards them. Frankie realised what it was and gave a cry of terror.

'Alyssa!' she screamed. '*Move*. Get out of the way!'

Alyssa tried to struggle to her feet, but failed. She glanced up, moonlight on her face. Suddenly Frankie could not see her sister any more. The huge block of masonry thudded down, followed by a shower of rocks. The ground shook. Philip Ward crumpled and fell, buried under rock. Armed police rushed forward.

'Frankie!' She felt someone pull her to her feet. 'I couldn't find you; I thought I'd be too late. Are you all right?' She turned to face Tomás.

'I'm fine. But Alyssa ... she was ... oh, *no*.'

He glanced around. 'Where is Alyssa?'

'She was over there. Oh God, don't let her be—'

'Dead male here,' somebody called.

Frankie ran across the nave, averting her eyes from Philip Ward's crushed body.

'Alyssa!' she shouted. 'Alyssa.'

'Here,' a weak voice called.

Two police officers were helping Alyssa to sit up. She looked dazed and terrified, wincing with pain and covered in thick dust, like someone pulled out of a ruined building following an earthquake or explosion. Frankie stooped and put her arms around her, hugged her close and stroked her long, gritty hair. Tomás stood silently watching them.

'Thank God you're all right!' Frankie breathed. Her eyes filled with tears.

'Not God.' Alyssa stared up at her. She managed a faint smile. '*You*.'

Epilogue

'You don't even have to turn up at court. All you have to do, Monique,' her solicitor explained patiently, 'is read those divorce papers and sign them.'

'But it's so final.' Monique took another gulp of Southern Comfort and Coke, her face streaming with tears. She was not supposed to drink, not with the pain medication and the sleeping tablets she took to get herself through each night, but she didn't give a toss. It was not as if she had a life any more. She had blown that. She was just lucky not to have landed herself a terminal jail sentence. Monique did not even care any more that Frankie Sayle had tucked her up good and proper.

She pulled her dressing gown around her, slowly stretched out on the sofa and stared at the television screen, at the DVD of *Gone With the Wind* that Lauren had somehow got it into her head that her mother might like to watch. The movie was approaching its depressing denouement. As if she hadn't had enough of those.

'I'm afraid divorce *is* final, Monique.'

The man was probably laughing himself soft, she thought. 'I don't pay you God knows how many quid an hour to give me patronising crap like that.'

Rhett Butler was asking Scarlett how old she was, because she had thus far managed to keep her advanced age of twenty-seven a secret from him. Monique recalled the first time she had told Conal how old she was. He had grinned, reached across the restaurant table to kiss her hand and told her she would always intoxicate him with her eternal glow, and that he had read that cheesy phrase on a coffee mug.

'I know you're upset, Monique,' the solicitor went on smoothly, 'and I'm sorry. But Conal won't even meet you halfway on this. He's not interested in a reconciliation. You've already sorted out the financial side between the two of you – you were rather more generous there than you should have been, in my opinion – and now he just wants out. I'm afraid where one of the partners is this determined, there's very little–'

'Yeah,' Monique interrupted. 'Thanks for nothing.' She threw down the phone and grabbed her drink, stared at the television screen again. Lauren came in and stood looking at her disapprovingly, hands on her slim hips.

'Mum, you shouldn't be drinking. Why don't I make you a nice cup of tea?'

'A *what*? You're the daughter. Stop trying to be the mother.'

Lauren let that go, now that she seemed to have developed a mature and ironclad patience these past couple of months. She turned and pointed to the window, at the sunny, frosty fields beyond the garden. 'It's nice today. Why don't you get dressed and go for a little walk when the movie's finished?'

'Would you stop using those words? *Nice. Little.* They give me the creeps.'

'I'll come with you. You left hospital weeks ago but you've hardly been out. You know the doctor said you should try and get more exercise. Joanna phoned before, and she says–'

'Yeah, and how long do I have to go on being grateful to her for saving my life? I wish she hadn't bothered. Lauren.' Monique looked at her. 'Just leave me alone, okay? Please. Don't you have a Shakespeare play to study or a spotty boy on whom to practise your seduction techniques? Now that my husband isn't around any more.'

'Shakespeare? Yeah,' Lauren snapped, flushing. 'We're doing *Macbeth*. It's great. Lots of knives and *really* bloody.'

She flounced out and Monique gave a sigh of relief. She got up slowly and painfully to pour herself another drink, then settled on the sofa again. She missed Conal so much it was breaking her heart. There seemed no point to anything any more. She had done everything she could to try to persuade him not to leave her, but her efforts had come to nothing. At times she felt like killing herself. Cowardice and the thought of what Lauren would do if she were left alone stopped her. She felt she owed it to Lauren to stick around, even if mother and daughter were driving each other crazy these days.

Conal had taken a long holiday in the South of France – alone – and on his return had moved into a new apartment somewhere in the city, near the river. Monique was not allowed to know the address, as Conal refused to communicate with her except through his solicitors, and then only about the divorce or the occasional financial detail that needed to be settled. Monique had heard he was looking for a house now. On Guernsey.

She wondered how long it would be before he found another woman. He was young, good-looking, full of charm – and rich. The woman would quite likely be a lot younger than she was. That added to the pain, bitterness and heartbreak.

Heartbreak that was all her own fault. The fact that it was her own fault and she had no excuses tore her apart during every conscious moment. Monique did not think she would get someone else. She could never want or love some other man as much as she loved Conal. Anyway, what man would want her now? She cringed as she imagined bringing someone home, sliding out of her sexy dress and lingerie to reveal the bullet wound and operation scars meandering across her chest, the reddened, raised lines and stitch marks. Not exactly the perfect climax to a romantic evening. No. The only reason a man would want her now was for her money, and she no longer had as much of that. Bay House was up for sale.

Today was a particularly bad day. There was never a good day, just degrees of agony. On less bad days Monique could fantasise about winning Conal back, just as a tearful Scarlett O'Hara was now imagining she could get Rhett back. Conal had loved her so much. Surely that love couldn't just die, even after everything that had happened? He knew she still loved him, and that she was desperately sorry for what she had done, desperate to make amends. There had to be a chance. She wouldn't give up, not yet. She couldn't, because hope was all she had now. Maybe Conal just needed time.

Drunk, dizzy and devastated, Monique stared at the screen as Scarlett launched into her final rant and the music swelled, the camera zooming in on her tear-streaked face.

'Tomorrow,' she whispered along with Scarlett, 'is another day!'

Yeah. *Right.*

'They can shove their precious pardon right back up from whence it came.'

Alyssa poured herself another glass of wine and stared out of the restaurant window at the grey river on which a cold December wind whipped up little waves. 'A pardon implies someone has graciously agreed to forgive you a wrong you did them. It's patronising and insulting. I don't need some bloody civil servant telling me I'm innocent when I – and other people! – knew that all along.'

'No,' Frankie murmured. 'All the civil servants have to do is sort out the compo. Not that money can ever make up for having had ten years of your life snatched away. But at least it's some sort of acknowledgement. It'll be a lot of money. Although quite a while before you get your hands on it.'

'Well, I'm managing at the moment. You've helped me out a lot.'

'Have you made any plans yet?'

'Get myself a therapist.' Alyssa smiled and shook her head. 'No, seriously. I'd like to take up my old profession again, but I don't know if that will be possible. People are looking into it for me. If it isn't possible, I'll have to think of something else. What about your plans?' she asked. 'How are you liking that beautiful new apartment?'

'Very much. All I need to do now is write my novel, get a publishing contract and Robert is your father's brother.'

'You must have plenty of material to draw on.'

Frankie frowned. 'Tell me.'

'Are you getting over ... you know ...?'

She meant shooting Xhani. Frankie sighed. 'I think so,' she whispered. 'It helps to know it was self-defence. I don't feel guilty. It was either him or me.'

'And it wasn't going to be you.' Alyssa sipped her wine. 'Wonder how Lady M's getting on?'

'I read that the police haven't been able to solve the mystery of what happened that night. No leads at all. So they're not planning to arrest anyone for the kidnapping or shooting. I also heard that Monique and her husband are getting divorced. The trauma of their ordeal seems to have driven them apart as opposed to cementing their love.' Frankie paused. 'I wonder if he guessed.'

'Well, whether he did or not, he's obviously decided to just grab his money and run. Wise move. The poor guy's a lot better off without that bitch. Speaking of divorce, is your husband still trying to persuade you to go back to him?'

'Joe phones now and then, but Mum tells him I'm out or that I don't want to talk. He came over once, just turned up, and she told him I'd gone to stay with a friend. He thinks I'm still living with her. I'm keeping my new address a secret; I don't want him to find out about the money. I've told my solicitor – and Joe – that I don't want maintenance. Not that I'd get much. I just want him out of my life. The less I see and hear from him, the less painful it'll be. At least that's the theory.'

Alyssa nodded. She was silent for a minute. 'I didn't want my father to get crushed by that chunk of masonry.' She swilled wine around her glass. 'I wanted him to stand trial and be convicted and sentenced. Go through everything I went through. I wanted him to walk into prison knowing he'd never come out. He hasn't been punished just because he's dead. Everybody dies sooner or later.'

'Yes. Well. Maybe it's better this way. A trial wouldn't have done you any good, having all that stuff resurrected. My God! How could he have taken pictures of himself with his victim while he was doing those terrible things to her?' Frankie shivered. 'I'm glad he's dead. It'd freak me to know a monster like that was still alive, even if he was locked up in a maximum security prison with no hope of release.'

The waiter came to clear their plates. 'Coffee, ladies?'

'Please. And a Cointreau for me.' Frankie glanced at Alyssa. 'Fancy a cognac?'

'Why not? Seems like a good way to round off this lunch.'

The waiter departed and Alyssa was silent once more. She finished her wine. 'I'm so glad Estella wants to see me again,' she whispered. 'You can't imagine what that means.'

'I think I can.' Frankie looked at her. 'There's something else she wants. Something I want too.'

Alyssa glanced up. 'What's that?'

'It's Christmas in a few weeks. We wondered if you'd like to spend it with us. Won't be anything grandiose or exciting. You know – quiet. Just family.'

Alyssa wiped a tear. 'I don't know what to say.'

'How about *yes*?'

'All right. Yes. I'd love that. If you're both sure.'

'Of course we are.'

The coffee, Cointreau and cognac were served, along with a plate of petit fours.

'What about Tomás?' Alyssa smiled. 'I don't mind, you know. Really. I can get my head around it ... you and him. I've given up my stupid fantasies. I can see them now for what they were – a prop to hang on to. I don't need it any more. I'll always love him. But not the way I did.'

Frankie blushed. 'We've met a couple of times. Just to talk.'

'It's okay. You can do more than talk. I give you my permission!'

'Well, thanks. But listen.' Frankie reached across the table and squeezed her hand. 'I won't deny I like him a lot. I really don't think it's a great idea for me to jump into a new relationship though. Not hard on the heels of my marriage breaking up.'

'Since when did it not being a great idea stop anyone?'

'It's stopping me now. You're more important. You're my sister. We're getting to know each other. I don't want anything else upsetting our family tie.' Her eyes glistened. 'Our blood knot.'

Alyssa grinned. 'Do you realise what you're doing?'

'Being sensible?'

'Radical, more like. Eschewing a man because you think our relationship is more important. That's very post-feminist of you. Or is it neo-feminist?'

'Who cares?' Frankie raised her glass. 'Here's to you, dear sister. You've been my friend in stormy weather.'

This was just the beginning. But Frankie had hope now. For herself, her mother. For the future. And for her new sister. Alyssa smiled back at her.

'My life is mine again,' she whispered.

Backlash

Denise Ryan

029480

Shannon Flinder is a criminal lawyer who has been to the edge and back. Now, she's determined to put her past behind her. She also wants to sort out her turbulent relationship with the man she loves but can't trust. But things were never going to be that easy.

New dangers threaten, like the vicious, shocking, apparently motiveless attack on a client. The villain with a sinister past and even more sinister present. Most of all, Shannon is desperate to forget what she had to do to save her life. But how can she? Somebody thinks she's got away with murder - and they're determined to make her pay…

Praise for Denise Ryan:

'A powerful offering' *What's On*

'A cracking debut' *Publishing News*